Spidar Luv

A novel by

Mary Jane Thynne

Happy Reading!

Mary Jane Thynne

copy # 11

1

Dedication

In memory of Gene and Mary,
who helped me stay sane
during my teen years in the 1960s
despite my crazy daydreams.

Spidar Luv, a novel by Mary Jane Thynne
Front cover designed by Ben Hockenberry

ISBN: 978-1-300-63960-2
Copyright 2025 Spirited Muse Press

For reprint permission, to arrange readings, or to order additional
copies, contact the editor at SpiritedMusePress@yahoo.com.

Dear Reader,

The 1960s was a rebellious decade. People rebelled against discrimination, sexual inequity, the Vietnam War, and religions that seemed to say one thing but practice the opposite. Race riots were commonplace. Frustration with corrupt politicians was thought to be at the peak. (Guess we didn't know how bad corruption could get!) Young people protested what their parents and society believed, and many were also into various mind-altering drugs.

There was an increased emphasis on loving everyone else. As teens in the 1960s, we heard about communes, wife-swapping, and adults living together in a large house without marriage between any of them. No one could tell anything about those households, because the people looked like normal citizens during the day.

This story uses songs from the 1960s to create a unique commune of that decade, where all participants shared work and play. This does NOT mean any band ever participated in these actions. This story neither condones nor condemns the lifestyle portrayed. However, it does identify some problems that may arise. As in any home with multiple residents, expect the unexpected.

The 21st century has proven that we use only 10% of our brain power. This story explores what humans might accomplish if we use the other 90%.

Some things have improved in the 21st century. Some have regressed. Only you can decide which is which.

~ Mary Jane Thynne

3

Chapter 1 – October 1965

"That was a bloody workout!" Saul exclaimed.

"Yeah! Yeah! Yeah!" sang Rich, Harry, and Jo-Jo in unison.

The four returned from a two-hour concert performing for 10,000 teens at Shriners' Hall in Rochester, N.Y. The Spidars were a British rock group with Dutch-boy haircuts, drainpipe trousers, and black suede boots with Cuban heels. They were popular all over the world. They were together so much, they were like brothers.

Jo-Jo smirked. "I need a scotch and cola and a bit of a *lovely*." He emphasized the last word.

Harry nodded with a grin. "I'd make do with the cheesecake if we have to choose."

The men stepped off the elevator on their way to the executive suite of the Nolith Hotel. Their manager, Bart, stopped in front of the door as the bodyguard unlocked the door and entered the suite. "Don't start in," he said as he entered the room.

"Remember the kneetremblers with buffs in Deutschland?" Harry asked the others as they followed Bart into the suite.

"I won't do this anymore," Jo-Jo stated, partially turning around again.

"You're giving up sex with buffs?" Harry asked.

"Only in Bart's dreams! I'm packing it in with following his orders. Hundreds of pretty fillies frolic in front of this hotel. I'm going out to ride one." Saul grabbed Jo-Jo's arm. Standing side-by-side, Saul's soft, slightly rounded baby-face with hazel eyes contrasted with Jo-Jo's sharp features and medium brown eyes, similar to the way their songwriting styles

5

differed. Regardless, their collaborations pushed sales figures to soaring heights.

Still holding Jo-Jo's arm, Saul turned to Bart and spoke softly. "We'd all fare better if we relieve some tension."

Harry and Rich nodded as they skipped toward the portable bar. While performing, the two naturally added zest to each song. As the youngest Spidar, Harry's shy smile and expressive dark brown eyes hinted at the true meaning of his gyrations behind the lead guitar. Rich's twenty-five years of life made him the old man in the group and gave him a bolder attitude with his drums, while his blue eyes twinkled with the mischief of a playful pup.

"I had more action in grammar school." Jo-Jo said as he jerked his arm away from Saul. "The rest of us don't get it on with the face-fungus gender. I'm up a spout."

Bart cleared his throat, ignoring Jo-Jo's ridicule of his sexual preferences. "All right," Bart conceded, "but no buffs. The States are strict. Since the buffs here are younger, they can put you behind bars for real."

"We could simply chat," Saul offered.

"After laying on ice, perhaps," Jo-Jo's eyes sparkled.

Bart walked to the phone. "Fix yourselves some drinks. I'll call for a few pros."

"*Front desk, Ralph speaking,*" came a voice from the other end. "*How may I help you?*"

"This is Bart Edelstein in suite 1600. I have four chaps here that have been on tour for a month. Eight more months will pass before they go home. They need some slinky ladies to take care of the lead in their pencils, if you get my drift."

"*I'm terribly sorry, Sir. I can't help with that.*"

"Hmmm, that's not the impression I got from your boss. He said if we needed anything at all, we simply had to call."

"*I can't help you, Sir.*"

"Then let me speak to someone who can, like the boss, himself."

Bart could hear the hesitation in the desk clerk's voice. *"He's... not... here... at the moment, Sir... Oh, wait! There is one girl who would love to come up. She could service all your boys."*

"Doubtful, but better than nothing. Send her up." Bart shrugged his shoulders as he hung up the phone.

"Her, as in ONE?" Rich questioned.

Bart nodded. Rich chuckled at the others. "You blokes can have the arms, legs, and head. I get the body!"

*

Sixteen floors below, Ralph summoned Kathy Voss. He studied her as she walked to the front desk. Kathy's silky brown hair fell in a simple flip, gold specks accented blue eyes, and slim curves puffed the uniform in the right places. Ralph had to admit she was beautiful, especially with that smile of hers, with kindness mixed with a sparkle of excitement. There was something different about her, though. Her blush happened too often. She must be hiding something. Someday, he thought, someday, I'll find out the secret and then...

"Yes, Sir. You called."

"Suite 1600 needs someone right away. Remember they are honored guests. Treat them like royalty. We aim to please." He handed over a set of special keys to the top floor with a smirk on his face.

"Yes, Sir. Anything they want, Sir." Kathy turned and headed toward the service elevator. *As if I can't figure it out from your stupid smirk,* she thought. Ever since she thwarted his advances a few weeks before, Ralph seemed to get a thrill out of giving her the messiest jobs. A guest had probably had a few too many drinks and she would have to clean up the mess. *No matter,* she thought, *someone has to do the job. Besides,* she really needed this job. At $1.50 per hour, well, she couldn't work anywhere else for that kind of money... and she wouldn't even be working here if they knew the truth about her. So, she would smile and take everything in stride as usual.

As Kathy walked along, she reviewed the top floor mentally. There was an executive suite at each end. Each contained a huge living room surrounded by four large bedrooms. The living room was furnished with lush carpeting and overstuffed velvet couches and chairs in browns, pale yellows, and tans. Each bedroom was a different color, either red, yellow, blue, or green. The king-sized beds had silk sheets, down pillows, and taffeta bedspreads that coordinated with the room color. Each bedroom had a bathroom with a shower, hot tub, sauna, Italian marble sink, toilet and bidet. The half-bath off the living room had a toilet and sink.

The designers had planned this floor for efficiency. Besides the two executive suites and six normal-size guest rooms for any entourage, a supply room allowed cleaning to be done quickly, with replacement linens and soaps, as well as a washing machine with gentle agitation, a low-heat dryer, a portable dry-cleaning machine for the furniture and carpeting, a stationary dry-cleaning machine for guests' special clothing, a dishwashing sink for the crystal, an apparatus for pressing and blocking the draperies, and a large cupboard filled with special cleaning solutions needed for the fabrics on this floor.

As Kathy entered the elevator, she studied the keys in her hands. "Keep the keys on your person at all times," the manager had lectured during training. Security was tight on this floor, and keys were needed both to get in and out of the rooms. These suites were only rented to the "cream" of society. The Renoirs and Van Goghs on the walls, ornate lamps, and crystal glassware would tempt the lesser fortunate. Once the keys were given, they were her responsibility until the desk clerk signed the return sheet.

The manager had also stressed that it was important to clean the suites right, or the hotel would have an expensive redecorating project, taken out of her pay, before the rooms could be rented again, and dignitaries would have to use regular rooms.

Kathy stepped off the elevator, feeling shorter with every step. Ignore it, she told herself. I don't need to fear this floor. After I find the mess, I will check the manual in the supply room to get the right instructions and supplies.

Kathy walked lightly to suite 1600 at the end of the hall, even though she knew the walls and floors here had cork underlayment to reduce noises. As she knocked on the door, her sinking feeling changed to alarm. There was something very important she should remember, but she couldn't bring it to the forefront of her mind.

The door opened. Blood flowed to her face as her memory bleeped into action. The Spidars were in this room for the next few days! Standing in front of her was Bart Edelstein, their manager. Light-headed, Kathy took a few moments to find her tongue. "You called for help," she finally said.

Bart stepped back to let her pass through the doorway. Inside the room, her cheeks beet red, Kathy's dizziness increased. In front of her were all four Spidars. THE SPIDARS! They looked at her with raised eyebrows and curious smiles, almost smirks. She adjusted her uniform's mini-skirt and then stood motionless.

Because of the position of his seat, Saul was the first to glimpse the woman who was supposed to take care of all four of them. He admitted she was a fine piece in that sexy outfit that matched her baby blue eyes so well. Saul rose to his feet, set down his glass, and ambled toward her. His chestnut hair bounced above his hazel eyes, which looked brown in this

9

light and decor.

Saul took her hand and squeezed it gently. "Want a drink first?" he asked. As he touched her hand, a spark went straight to his groin and his heart added an extra beat, almost a boom.

Goodness, she thought, he's even more of a dreamboat in person than on television. When he took her hand, she felt a spark through her whole body. Kathy flashed a smile to hide her nervousness as she collected the courage to speak.

Saul repeated the question, and this time she answered in a soft tone. "No, thank you. It's almost quitting time. Just show me where I have to work."

Rich, Harry, and Jo-Jo exchanged glances. Saul smiled and replied, "All ri-i-ight!" Squeezing her hand a little harder, he led her to the first bedroom on the left.

"Surely a simple chat," Jo-Jo grumbled.

Kathy surveyed the room quickly. Unable to find a mess, she hurried to the bathroom. There was the click of a door being locked behind her. She shrugged. Upon examination, the bathroom was shiny clean, other than a few personal items left on the sink. Thinking the dizziness in her head was affecting her vision, Kathy tried to concentrate. No matter how hard she looked, the sink, the toilet, the floor, the tub, she couldn't find anything that would require her services this late at night. She returned to the bedroom.

Saul was standing next to the bed, naked from the waist up and in the process of unzipping his trousers. Kathy's cheeks glowed. She turned her back toward him. "I-I-I can't do anything in there," she stammered, pointing toward the bathroom.

"That's a bit of all right. The action can be in here." Saul put his arms around her from the back, nibbling on the side of her neck and pressing his groin against her soft buttocks.

Kathy's mind raced as she tried to sort out what she knew about this project. The Spidars had called down for help. She had come up. There wasn't any mess to clean. And now this! None of it made any sense.

She tried to protest, but Saul swung her around and kissed her with urgency. Her head spun like a top. Soon, she forgot about trying to decipher anything. She was being kissed by Saul McCarthy of the Spidars!!! Her girlfriends would give up their eye-teeth to experience this.

During the kiss, Kathy didn't feel Saul's hand unzipping the Nehru jacket that was part of her uniform. She didn't feel Saul slowly slide the jacket off her shoulders. She didn't feel his lips follow the sloping curves of her neck and shoulders. She didn't feel his hands rove toward her bra hooks then the mini-skirt of the uniform.

When her skirt fell to the floor, Kathy came out of her daydream. "No!" she said loudly. "I'm not like that!" Her struggle was in earnest now.

"Whatcha going for? More lolly, Sugarboot? With four of us, you'll earn enough tonight."

"Money isn't..."

Saul pressed his lips against hers again and laid her gently on the bed. Lying on the bed with her, he removed her panties and entered her warm cavern. Between his long abstinence and Kathy's tightness, the rest didn't take much time. Saul felt a tingle of excitement then relieved his pressure.

"Yes," he sighed, his arms and legs now limp.

Underneath, Kathy sobbed quietly. This didn't make sense to Saul. He lifted his chest and his whole body suddenly stiffened. She had been tight, very tight. "You were a... a... You never," he whispered. "You were intact, weren't you?"

"I told you I'm not that kind of girl," Kathy said with another sniffle. "I'm the cleaning lady."

11

Saul bolted off the bed. "Then why did that bloody pencil-pusher send you up? He knew what we wanted. I'm dead sure he did."

Kathy swore under her breath. Her sobs stopped. Things began to fit into place. Even Ralph's evil smirk made sense. He was probably having a good laugh right now.

After redressing quickly, Saul left the bedroom. "Bart, we've copped a packet," he said, as he poured himself a straight scotch. He downed it in one gulp.

Jo-Jo looked over the top of his wire-rimmed glasses. "Yes, we heard a bit of a barney. Not very cooperative, is she? Or were you trying to bring off a fast Kyber pass?"

"This is serious," Saul replied. "The lark-about clerk sent up a bloody virgin! This one is a cleaning lady."

"Yeah, sure," Jo-Jo said sarcastically. "And I'm the flippin' queen."

Bart studied Saul's face. When he spoke, his voice contained a hint of worry. "I think Saul's telling it straight on. If so, we have a fine kettle of fish at a boil. We don't need this on top of Jo-Jo's mess about Jesus. We'd better have a think and put the boat in fast."

"You're our PR man," Rich said.

*

Kathy tried to scrub herself clean, but she found it impossible. As she dressed, she scowled at her uniform. If this hotel used normal ones, everyone would know her occupation on sight. But no, they insisted maids be fashionable to attract the businessmen.

Kathy studied herself in the mirror. At least there was solace in her hair. She had won one. When the manager suggested a beehive hairdo, she convinced him that was for teeny-boppers, so she was allowed to keep her silky flip.

12

In a slightly better mood, she freshened her face with the make-up she kept in the pocket of her jacket. When she was satisfied, she walked through the bedroom and opened the door to the shared living room. Kathy moved through the living room to the outer door with her eyes on the floor. She could feel the heat of everyone watching her.

Or was the heat from her own crimson face? Drat the stupid blush anyways! Among her friends, blushing was no big thing, but here... well... hotel maids were supposed to be immune. If Ralph ever found out why she couldn't stop her cheeks from coloring, it would be the absolute end. She would be forced to date the creep to keep his mouth shut. Yuck!

Kathy reached for the knob to open the main door as nonchalantly as possible, but it wouldn't budge. She pulled out her key and inserted it. Still the door wouldn't move. Pulling harder to no avail, she glanced up. A large, burly man, slightly to one side of the door, held it closed. The man looked like a night club bouncer, 6'4" tall with 300 pounds of edge-to-edge muscle. Kathy's slim frame was no match for him, even if his shirt pocket declared him the friendly name of Mo.

"Sorry, Luv," came Saul's compassionate whisper from behind. "We can't let you push off until we decide what to do."

Kathy's eyes blazed with sudden anger. "What do I do in the meantime?"

"Have a drink," Bart suggested.

"I don't drink."

"Have a fag."

"I'm not sup..." Kathy caught herself. Her anger subsided as she realized these men could really be worried about the current events. If they found out the whole truth, they might do something she wouldn't like. *No*, she thought, *this will turn out better if I keep my mouth shut.*

Saul handed her a cigarette along with a drink, despite her

13

negative responses. After a few moments, she accepted both and found a vacant chair turned toward the balcony so she wouldn't have to look at the men, and vice versa.

The next hour passed with Kathy silent at the window. The men spoke in hushed tones, trying to find a graceful way out of the situation. Finally, Bart decided he would think better after a good night's sleep. He ushered Kathy into Saul's bedroom, removed the phone from its jack, and vanished. Mo removed the bedroom doorknob and reversed it, so it would lock from outside the room.

Saul entered the room to retrieve items he would need for a night on the living room sofa. He glanced at Kathy, who stood near the window at the far end of the room. Her pitiful eyes and sad half-smile made her look so vulnerable. Saul felt a knot growing in his stomach. He knew this wasn't right, but he felt powerless to do anything else. He wanted to assure her that everything would be fine in the morning. Instead, he motioned toward the silk pajamas he had thrown on the bed and scurried out.

When Saul left, the door lock clicked. Kathy put a hand in her right pocket and jingled the keys lightly, as if to prove she had some control. Even though one of the keys was designed to work on the side of a locked door that simply has a hole in the middle, the one facing her way now, she knew the special key wouldn't do much good. After Bart left the suite for his single room next door, Mo would sit in front of her door to block any escape attempt. With no way out tonight, Kathy changed into Saul's silk pajamas and slept fitfully.

In the morning, she awoke to the sounds of talking in the living room. She crept to the door and put her ear next to it. Jo-Jo was speaking: "I don't latch on. Anyone wearing a bed-worthy outfit like that can't be maidenly."

"I know a tighty when I feel one," Saul replied.

"You're just trying to keep her for yourself."

"Now, boys," Bart interrupted. "Calm down or you'll spurt. Mixing it won't solve anything."

"Eh-h-h, what do you know," Jo-Jo said, contempt in his tone. "Never mind being an umpire. What we need is to score and you're still sitting on the bench. You never were very good at sports, were you?"

Kathy walked into the bathroom. After pulling her dried bra and panties off the shower rod, she paused in front of the mirror. She had never worn real silk. She slowly slid her hands around the slippery fabric. Her skin tingled. "Someday, I'll have my own," she vowed. Then she glared at her reflection. "What am I saying? How can I enjoy any of this?" She removed the pajamas and dressed. Carefully she applied her makeup. After a final examination in the mirror, she walked into the bedroom. She made the bed and tidied the room, and then she tested the doorknob. It was unlocked.

The air in the living room was filled with the aroma of eggs, home fries, and freshly baked biscuits. "Can I go now?" Kathy asked.

"Not quite yet," Bart apologized, as he poured her a cup of tea. "We still haven't figured out what to do with you."

Kathy smiled demurely. "What's the problem? I'll promise not to tell anyone, if that makes you feel better. Besides, it would be my word against yours, and you outnumber me five to one, six to one if you include Mo."

"It's not that simple," Harry stated before Bart could reply. "Some reporters don't play your odds. They'd love to drag us in the dirt on anyone's say-so."

"Yeah," Rich added, returning Kathy's smile. "They might take us off the top of the charts."

Bart huffed at the flippant attitude. "These boys are on the mat already because something Jo-Jo said was printed out of context. We have to tread on tiptoes for a while."

Kathy nodded. She had read the article. She had thought Jo-Jo was getting a swelled head, saying the Spidars were more popular than Christ. Then again, she could understand what he was trying to say. Compared to Spidar concerts, attendance at churches was poor indeed. And considering there were fans from other religions, she couldn't get mad at someone stating a fact. Sometimes the truth hurts.

Saul interrupted Kathy's thoughts. "Have some brekker, Luv. You must be famished." He motioned for her to sit next to him. Kathy accepted orange juice and a biscuit.

Soon the men left for a press conference to undo the damage of Jo-Jo's statement, and Mo guarded Kathy in the suite. She sat in the living room wondering how long this would go on. People would miss her and call the police. She didn't want to start trouble for the Spidars. This was Ralph's fault, not theirs. Suddenly her eyes lit up. Kathy finally convinced Mo to let her make a phone call. He listened nearby, ready to hang up the receiver if Kathy said anything wrong.

"Hi!" Kathy said into the phone. "The people I work for had a little accident last night. They've asked me to stay until they can work out a few problems... Yes, I'm fine, no trouble... I will. Bye."

Before Kathy stood up, there was a knock on the door. Mo gave her an accusing look. "It wasn't me," she whispered. He grabbed her arm, pushed her into the bedroom, and closed the door after giving her a look that told her to be quiet or else.

In silence, Kathy reopened the bedroom door just enough to watch Mo. A housekeeper was reporting for duty. Mo recognized the uniform, the same as Kathy's. "We have our own chambermaid," he said before the woman could speak.

Kathy chuckled as the woman nodded, relief on her face. The other housekeepers hated this floor. Though Kathy thought of this area as a sign of the manager's trust, most of the others considered it an easy way to get fired if they made the slightest mistake. Hmmm, she thought, Why not? Might as well keep busy. By the time the Spidars returned, the suite gleamed. Mo had allowed Kathy to clean as long as he accompanied her to the supply room each time.

As soon as Saul walked into the suite, he noticed the improvements and smiled at Kathy. He admired people who didn't dwell on life's negatives. When she blushed and returned his smile, the knot in his chest from the previous night dissipated.

After lunch, the men practiced for the evening's performance. Since no one would worry about her, and the men were being gentlemen, Kathy decided to enjoy herself until she could figure a way out. Not every girl had a chance to hear a private Spidar concert. If her friends could see her now!

The time flew after that. Kathy was absorbed in watching the men play. From time to time, she examined Saul carefully. His hands stroked the guitar and glided up and down a keyboard as if the instruments were home to them, as natural as scratching an itch. The curves of his chest rippled through a tight T-shirt. His brown hair was frosting on a baby-face cake. Yes, he was a handsome man. It would be so easy to fall in love with him.

Occasionally, Saul looked her way, which made her spine tingle with excitement. A blush rose in her cheeks and she turned away, pretending to watch one of the other men – Jo-Jo's sharp nose and tough medium-brown eyes, Rich's blue eyes exploding with prank-filled thoughts, and Harry's elongated dimples pointing at his deep brown eyes and wavy hair.

Before long, suppertime arrived. Afterwards, the men had to leave for their concert. As the men departed, Saul stopped and gave Kathy a gentle but firm kiss. Her head began to swim. Dizzy and tingling, she sat down near the television. Her mind reeled. She wondered if she really wanted to escape at all.

*

The men returned exhausted. They accepted the drinks Kathy offered then plopped on the sofas. There wasn't much conversation. They simply wanted to unwind and go to bed. Since Kathy had behaved, Saul convinced Bart not to lock her door when it was time for bed. This time Mo also got a little reprieve. After Bart left, a sofa was moved in front of the main door so Mo could sleep while guarding the suite. Saul used a different one.

The men dropped to dreamland quickly, all except one. When Saul heard the others snoring, he tip-toed toward the blue room. He opened the door without noise. A full moon cast its glow on Kathy's face and accented her sleeping, angelic smile. Saul closed the door, walked to the bed, and slipped between the sheets next to her. The bed was toasty warm. Mm-m-m feels good, he thought. He put one arm around her over the bedding.

*

As Kathy woke Sunday morning, she noticed Saul's fingers stroking her hair lightly. They moved down the side of her face and then her neck, barely touching skin on their travels. She could feel them through the silky fabric as they lightly slid along the shoulders then down the arm lying on her side. From there, they circled her belly button and then up to each breast, circling each one three times in widening circles. She felt a tingling between her legs. Soon Saul caressed her waist, and his voice carried a quiet melody to her ears.

She knew she should jump out of bed, but she didn't. Instead, she rolled over and accepted a gentle, urgent kiss from the man who had occupied her thoughts. Even her dreams were filled with the English rogue. She didn't fight him this time as he filled her with his throbbing love. The tingling between her legs turned into fireworks!

The other men were sitting at a table on the patio when Saul and Kathy joined them. Harry snickered. Rich winked at Saul. Saul smiled and winked back at Rich. Kathy's cheeks turned rosy as she stared at the floor.

"Remember what I said yesterday?" Jo-Jo scowled. "This proves it. Keeping for yerself."

"You don't understand," Saul protested.

"Bunk!" Jo-Jo shot back.

Harry snickered. "Since you two already had a California brekker, you probably don't want pancakes." He pretended to reach for Saul's plate. Saul cuffed his chin.

"What's a California brekker?" Rich asked as if he didn't know.

"A roll in bed with honey." The men laughed. Kathy's cheeks turned redder. Saul pulled her to him and they sat down together. The early morning exercise had made Kathy quite hungry. She devoured her plate of pancakes and sausage and washed everything down with a cup of tea.

After breakfast, Saul strolled over to his guitar and began strumming. Before long, Jo-Jo joined him. Harry had already finished a song of his own, so he donned a beard and hat and went out to mingle. With any luck, his gregarious nature could be satisfied without causing chaos on the streets.

Rich stayed at the table writing on his palm with a fingertip from the other hand. No one would uncover evidence before his next prank was executed. His upturned lips suggested this one might be better than the time he put baking soda in Saul's toothpaste or Silly Putty worms in Jo-Jo's boots. The pranks usually helped relieve tension before shows.

Kathy, on the other hand, was trying to sort out her own emotions. Her heart wanted to take a chance; her mind said she'd be just another notch on Saul's belt. While the men were busy, she went over to the television. In a small case behind the set was a pair of headphones. She took them out, hooked them into the TV, and turned it on. "When your energy is focused," a minister was saying, "you can turn problem mountains into ant hills."

Is that why I can't find a way out of here, Kathy wondered. *Determination landed this job, despite the low chance of success. Can I focus now? How? How can I focus when conflicting things keep crashing in my thoughts? Do I really want out? Or am I hoping some good will come of this?*

"Some day, you'll do great things," another minister had once told her. She believed him and even made that her goal in life – to overcome poverty, earn a good reputation and a good living, and make a difference in this world. Only time would determine how far she could go on that road.

When Harry returned, the television broadcast a different program. *Must have been thinking too long*, Kathy thought. Taking off the earphones, she heard Harry trying to convince the others to take a stroll before their performance today, which was in the afternoon this time. "You can see the city better during the daytime," he said. "After the show, it'll get dark quick."

"You blokes go," Saul offered, lightly stroking Kathy's cheek. Saul's fingers tingled, as did Kathy's cheek. "I'll stay."

The concern on his face and in his voice perplexed Kathy. Her heart wanted to believe he cared, but her mind doubted it.

"There's no need," she replied. "I want to watch TV." Saul hesitated for a moment, then left with the others.

Kathy went to lay on the bed and think. This situation was getting out of hand. Her face tingled when he touched her cheek. *Was this love? With a man who stole her innocence, a man with a jet-set lifestyle, a man in the limelight everywhere he went?*

A while later, the phone rang in the living room. Kathy jerked upright. Mo answered it. "Yes... She's in the bedroom, sulking, I think... Yes... I'll tell her. Ta-ta!"

Mo knocked on the door and opened it. "That was Harry. The boys are running late so they're going directly to the concert hall. They'll be back in a few hours."

Kathy brightened. *There's still time to figure out an escape plan,* she thought, *but first I'd better clean up.* She soaked in the tub as her freshly rinsed clothes hung before the hair dryer.

As minutes turned into an hour and then some, she thought and thought. Every scenario she put together was thwarted by the fact that Mo was the best in his field. Keeping people away from the Spidars meant no distractions allowed. Yet, did he have enough experience keeping people captive? Would a smaller distraction work? There had to be a way, if only she could find it.

She dressed in the silent bedroom of a silent suite. Mo sat near the main door reading a magazine. The phone rang, startling both of them. Mo jumped to answer it, never taking his eyes off the door, Kathy surmised. Moments later, he knocked and walked into Kathy's bedroom. "The show's over," he said. "Saul wants to know if you need anything." She shook her head. Mo exited, relayed the message, and returned the phone to its cradle.

Kathy's heart felt heavy. The time to escape had passed. With a sigh, she walked to the living room to fix drinks for the men. The living room was empty. *Where's Mo?* she wondered. He never left his post while the men were gone. *Stop questioning it,* she told herself. *Get out while you can!* She closed the bedroom door, tiptoed to the hall door and turned the knob. It wouldn't open! Her heart raced; desparation climbed. Then she remembered. Her keys were on the dresser. Anyone needs to have the key on them to get out to prevent leaving without the ability to return.

Kathy scooted back to the bedroom, picked up her keychain, and shut the door again. As she hurried to the hall door, she heard water running in the powder room. So that's where Mo was! Kathy could sense by the sound that he was almost ready to come out. She was careful not to jingle the keys as she looked for the right one. Good! She had it. She unlocked the door and stepped into the hall. Excitement welled up inside her. Freedom was mere moments away.

Mo's footsteps came out of the bathroom as she was closing the suite door. Since he would be suspicious if he heard the knob click, she didn't latch the door completely. Running down the hall, she stopped in front of the service elevator. The other one would waste too many precious seconds to get up to this floor, seconds in which Mo would notice the missing person.

As she shuffled through the keys, she heard the muffled voices of the Spidars in the elevator. Shoot! Saul must have called from downstairs. And of course the men would use the service elevator. The front lobby would be suicide for them. Meanwhile, the keys seemed to glow in her hands. She might have a chance to hide in the supply room if she could find that key fast enough. Listening closer, she guessed the men were passing the fourteenth floor. She only had milliseconds, not

22

enough time to unlock the supply room.

Her eyes darted around for an alternative. An alcove a few steps away beckoned to her. If she positioned herself properly, she would be concealed. Then she would simply wait until the men went into the suite and she would be free!

From the hiding spot, Kathy heard the men step off the elevator. She strained to hear Saul's voice. When she couldn't, she peeked around the wall. He was there, but his gait was slow compared to the bouncy ones of the others.

"You haven't said two words since we walked off stage," Jo-Jo said to him. "What's bugging you, ol' chap?" Saul didn't answer. His eyes held fast to the door of their destination.

"The bloke's frettin' his gizzard about the bird in our room," Harry offered. "He's been holding his jaw ever since I told him she was sulking."

Jo-Jo studied Saul's face. "Is that why you had a head like a sieve during the show? You'd better pull yourself together, mate. She's not worth it. Most likely she deserved what the pencil-pusher did to her. Tarts like to rib a lad until he's half-cracked. Don't let her get to you."

Kathy swallowed hard to squelch an outburst of fury. She hadn't done anything wrong! Well... not much. Not anything that anyone knew about anyway.

Bart pulled out his key to the suite. Suddenly, Kathy felt like she was standing behind a glass wall. The band's manager was sure to get suspicious if the door opened without the key. There was no escape from her hiding place, and it wouldn't take long to find her.

When Mo appeared in the doorway, Kathy smiled and jerked her head back. Yes, the wall was solid again. Bart would assume Mo had unlocked the door and Mo would assume Bart had. The door closed after all the men had entered. Kathy darted to the service elevator and searched for the key. *Hurry! Hurry!*

Inside the suite, Harry, Jo-Jo, and Rich went to the bar to fix themselves a drink. Bart stood near the door talking to Mo. Saul ignored the rest of the men. He walked directly to his bedroom. The knot in his stomach from the first night had grown again and...

The bedroom was empty. He checked the bathroom. She wasn't there either. He rushed back to the living room, shouting at Mo. "Where's Kathy?"

"She was in your room when you jingled. I went to the loo, a tick it took. I figured it was safe, what with you on your way up and all. She couldn't have gone far."

Bart, who still stood near the main door, opened it in time to see a foot disappear into the elevator. He ran to catch her.

*

In the elevator, Kathy pressed the button for the ground floor. She saw Bart running toward her and getting closer and closer. "C'mon door, close NOW, please," she pleaded under her breath... Eternity...

Chapter 2

Kathy let out a sigh. The door had closed a split-second before Bart could grab her. She made it!

She looked at the lights above the elevator door. 16 ... 15 ... 14 ... She was on the way to freedom! 13 ... 12 ... 11 ... 10... Her escape was a mixed blessing. She would miss the warmth of Saul's embrace and the tenderness of his kiss, the tingle of his touch. 9 ... 8 ... 7 ... 6 ... She didn't see the lights below go on. Her eyes were glued to the number 16, a number engraved in her memory forever. 16 twinkled for a moment, if only in her memory.

Suddenly, she was aware of a changed sensation of movement, as if she were now going upward. She glanced at the numbers lighting up: 6 ... 7 ... 8 ... 9... "Oh no!" she muttered as she shook her head. The blink hadn't been in her mind. Bart must know the override procedure!

With an extra quarter turn of the key, a light would come on. If the person held the key in position for three seconds, then turned the key back and removed it, the override would be complete. In vain, Kathy pushed the buttons for the floors between her and Bart. She hoped the elevator would stop, but she knew it was wishful thinking. The override was put in place for emergencies. There could be no interruptions. The elevator would go to whatever floor it had been directed.

10 ... 11 ... 12 ... 13... Tears formed. She had been so close, so very close. Now she'd be at square one again. Or lower. 14 ... 15 ... 16, she made herself appear relaxed as the elevator door opened to reveal Bart's angry face. He grabbed her arm

and pulled her out brusquely. "What do you have to say for yourself?"

Kathy looked him in the eye. "I was going down to get my own cigarettes. Saul's Gitanes are too strong." She knew the excuse was feeble, but it was the only one that came to mind. Trying to move her thoughts from the painful pressure on her arm, her gaze shifted to the right of Bart. Saul stood there. She lowered her head and stared at the floor, cheeks quite rosy.

Having seen a glimpse of Kathy's pained expression, Saul looked at Bart's knuckles. They were white. Saul placed one hand gently on her other arm and took hold of Bart's wrist in a tight grip. Bart released her.

Saul embraced Kathy firmly, the way a parent would hold a child who escaped serious injury. His emotions wavered between anger at her unexpected departure and joy at her return.

"Why?" he asked. As soon as he said it, he knew it sounded as dumb as Kathy's excuse to Bart. He knew why. Despite his hopes, no one in their right mind would want to be in Kathy's situation.

Kathy didn't answer. Saul didn't repeat the question. They stared into each other's eyes in silence. Saul guided Kathy back into the suite and into his bedroom. He ignored the taunts from the others as he shut the door behind him.

Led to the love seat near the window, she tucked her legs under her butt and stared out the window. Stretched-out pink and gray clouds near the horizon signaled another day was almost done. Saul sat down beside her. "Look here, Luv," he began, "I know how you must feel. Sometimes I feel like a monkey in a circus, performing on cue for everybody. Often, I don't have a choice where I want to be or what I want to do..."

"Do you expect sympathy from me?" Kathy asked in a teasing voice, a semi-smile emerging.

Kathy's sudden smile caught him by surprise. His own lips curled. "No, no, no. I mean I know *some* of how you must feel. I know what it's like to be a prisoner of circumstances. I also realize how much harder it is for you. While I'm doing a frog-march, you're a wild bird in a cage, placed near an open window. You can see and smell freedom, but you can't go."

Kathy's gaze returned to the window. "Kathy, look at me," he said quietly. She didn't respond. They sat at the window without talking for ten minutes.

"Look at me, please," he pleaded, his voice showing frustration and turmoil. When she finally turned back to him, he continued, "Kathy, when I found out how poorly you were feeling before our gig today, I had a knot in my stomach as big as my fist. But when I returned and you weren't here, the knot disappeared. It was replaced by something far worse... emptiness, the emptiness of losing a soulmate."

Saul searched her eyes. "I fancy you. You're different from the rest. I can let my hair down with you. I want to get closer, like a matey, not just the other, although being on the nest with you is different too. Your touch energizes me. There is a spark between us. Don't you feel it?"

Kathy's cheeks glowed again. Wordlessly, she nodded and stared at the floor. Saul lifted her chin and kissed her nose. As his lips moved to hers, they both felt a tingling sensation.

"I wish I could do something to show you how I feel. I'd like to..." His eyes brightened. "Follow me," he commanded. He took her hand and led her out to the living room.

The other Spidars were sitting on the sofas, already on their second drinks. Bart was talking to Mo near the hall door. When Bart saw the couple emerge from the bedroom, he crossed over to them, eyes on Kathy. He gave her a large paper sack.

Kathy opened the bag and examined the contents. Bart must have gone downstairs to empty her locker. She glanced at her watch. Yes, Ralph would be on duty by now. He would have cooperated with Bart, and now he'd be having another good laugh at her expense.

"You do realize, girl," Bart said, "that we have to lock you in a room again."

Kathy blushed and lowered her head.

Saul shook his head. "No, Bart. Kathy's not being locked anywhere. She is coming to the concert tomorrow night and…" Kathy's gold specks in her eyes twinkled as if they were fireflies. He kissed her forehead. Inside he felt good again – no knot, no emptiness. "And meanwhile, she's to be treated as my sweetie. She can come and go as she wishes."

"Do you know what you're saying?" Bart asked.

"Yeah," Jo-Jo interrupted, "Have knock-up, will travel."

Saul shot him a disgusted look. Harry laughed out loud. Rich smiled, with a curious eye on Kathy. "Yes, Old chap. I know what I'm doing," Saul said. "She can go anytime she wants. She'll come back. I'm sure of it." Saul looked lovingly at her, but she shook her head. His smile faded. "You won't come back?" he asked. "Why not?"

Kathy touched Saul's lips with one finger. Her whole hand warmed instantly. "I can't." She turned to Bart. "Don't worry. I promise not to tell anyone. There won't be any trouble for your *boys*. You knew this had to happen eventually. You can't keep me here forever."

When she turned back to Saul, she saw the hurt in his eyes. Her voice smoothed to reassure. "Saul, I do feel… I do feel something, but I can't be your girl."

"Why not? Is there…"

"No," she broke in. "There's no one else in my life. I can't explain my reasoning, but I won't lie. Once I'm gone, I'm gone."

28

To stifle a weakening resolve, she glanced around the room. Jo-Jo scowled. Harry's long dimples put his anticipation into parentheses. Rich smiled as if he were simmering a new prank. Kathy used Rich's smile as energy. She inched her way to the hall door. "It's been fantastic meeting all of you. This will make a good story to tell my grandchildren, if I have…"

"You promised not to tell anyone," Bart stated.

Kathy smiled at Bart, then at Rich, with mischief in her own eyes. "I'd ask you all for your autographs, but if Bart is half as smart as he thinks he is, he wouldn't allow it… Evidence, you know."

Rich recognized the cue. He pulled out his wallet and removed a candid picture of himself. Turning it over, he pretended to write on the back. "Nah, he's not all that dragged up. Here, do your worst." He walked over and handed the picture to Kathy.

With clenched teeth, Bart grabbed the picture out of her hand. "You swine!" he said to Rich. Kathy, Rich, and Harry laughed at him. Jo-Jo merely smiled.

Kathy's smile subsided when she saw Saul's sad face. She kissed him tenderly. Her lips tingled. "I'm sorry."

Saul put his arms around her and buried his face in her hair. "I don't want you to go."

"I have to."

Reluctantly, he released her. She moved toward the hall door. In the background, she heard Saul mumble something to Bart. Ahead of her, Mo's lips were turned up at the edges as he opened the door. "That's the first time I've seen you smile since I arrived," she said to him. "You should do it more often. You're downright handsome, you know."

Instead of his smile brightening, the intended purpose for what she said, the lips pursed. He seemed to watch something behind her. She turned to see what it was. Rich, Harry, and Jo-

29

Jo sat on the sofas. Saul shuffled to his room. Bart's hands dropped to his side, as if he had been signaling with them.

When Saul disappeared, Kathy felt Mo's hand on her arm and heard the door close behind her. "What's this?" she asked.

"We can't let you leave. Not yet," Bart explained.

"What?!! Why not? What's the reason this time?"

Bart looked at the men as he replied, more to them than to her. "Saul wants to cancel tomorrow night's show. He says he won't be in any shape to perform. I tend to believe him, after his sloppy performance today." The others nodded.

Kathy shook her head. "You can't keep me captive forever. You're leaving town Tuesday and I certainly won't get on the plane without a fight. IN PUBLIC. I thought you didn't need bad press."

"We don't. We do need you here until after tomorrow night's show, though. The change of scenery in South Carolina should help Saul. The pieces on the beach might make him forget you."

Ouch! The last statement hurt Kathy more than she wanted to admit. She found it difficult to sound nonchalant. "I suppose you have to lock me in the bedroom again."

Mo opened the bedroom door. Kathy entered silently. Saul was slumped on the bedside, elbows on his knees and head buried in his hands. Kathy removed her civilian clothes from the sack.

The crackling made Saul look up. He jumped to his feet and greeted her with a hug. "You changed your mind!" he exclaimed. "That's fab! I knew you'd return. I knew it!"

Kathy was tempted to say something sarcastic, but she couldn't. When Saul held her, she felt like a stick of butter near a warm oven.

"I'm glad you're here," he whispered in her ear.

Kathy summoned her strength and pulled away. She headed for the bathroom to change. She wouldn't look as sexy in her knit sweater and jeans, but she would be a lot more comfortable. And maybe she could think better.

When Kathy came out, Saul was whistling as he hung her extra uniform in the closet and arranged her other things in the drawers. Then he folded the bag and put it in the closet between his suitcases.

Harry knocked on the door and yelled without opening it, "Our oats are here."

"Let's go eat," Saul suggested.

"You go out. I have something to do first."

Saul gingerly kissed the bridge of her nose and left the room. Sparks for both.

Fifteen minutes later, Kathy had not joined Saul at the table. He went to the bedroom to find her staring out the window. "What ya doin', Luv? Aren't you coming out to eat?"

Kathy replied in a cheerful tone, without changing her gaze. "Bart has confined me to my cell. Just pass the bread and water under the door."

Saul was perplexed. Kathy's voice was cheerful, but the words were caustic. "You have to eat some time," he said. "You'll waste away to nothingness." When she didn't move, he went back out to get Bart.

"What's this nonsense?" Bart scolded as he entered. "You are well aware that the lock-up is at night, not when everyone is awake."

She didn't move. Saul's thoughts began to waver between letting her go free, which would bring back the emptiness, or keeping her here and suffering through the knot that grew again in his stomach.

The public knew him as a playboy for good reason. Due to a genetic quirk, one eyelid was lower than the other, and the apparent wink attracted females. He always had plenty of girls to choose from.

Kathy was different, though. He could feel her melt at his touch, yet she had an inner strength he admired. She was submissive, then stubborn. She was mature but young at heart. Saul felt strangely alive with her around. He had never felt this before. He opted for the knot.

Instead of talking further, he reached out his thick hands, took hold of her slender ones, and pulled her to her feet. She didn't resist. She went to the dining table with her head lowered.

The others had finished eating and sipped doctored coffee. Rich watched as Kathy came out. "Good timing," he teased. "You can clear the table."

Kathy smiled weakly. "Chauvinist."

Rich leaned back in his chair. "Quite right. It keeps me away from the dirty work."

Kathy's smile broadened a little. "At least you're honest about it." After nibbling at the food, Kathy sat on a couch with Saul, watching TV. The rest of the Spidars were spread out on the other sofas. Mo stood at the door. He obviously wasn't taking any more chances.

An hour later, Kathy was still silent. She was worried about the amount of alcohol the men had consumed. She knew how some men reacted to it. Her father was an alcoholic. When sober, he was a sweet and gentle man. When he had too much to drink, he turned violent. The family always had to be quiet and not mess anything up when he drank. Once, he had even tried to kill her sister. That's when her mother divorced him. Kathy hoped these men were the type who mellow out with alcohol. Otherwise...

A sense of doom permeated her body and magnified as each minute passed. She didn't like the look Harry gave her.

With alcohol, that look spelled trouble. She wished she could do something to make him stop, but she didn't dare say anything. Her experience with her father taught that it only took one wrong word or tone of voice to start a violent fight. Silence, if possible, was the best response.

At 8:00, Bart left the suite. He said he had to tie up a few loose ends for the next tour stop. He gave Mo instructions before he left. As soon as the door closed behind Bart, Harry walked over to Kathy and grabbed her hand, pulling her abruptly to her feet. "It's time to share your goodies," he said to Saul.

Saul pulled Kathy back to him. Harry pulled harder. She felt like a confection in a taffy-pulling contest. "Hey, stop it!" she yelled.

Saul's pause at her words enabled Harry to jerk her away from him. "She's not a tighty any more," Harry stated. "And I'm collecting on the pact." Saul turned away. *Huh?* Kathy thought. *Well, if he won't fight, I will. I'll scratch Harry to pieces if necessary.* Her free hand rose to strike his face, but Mo caught it in mid-air. His tight grip told her whose side he defended. Kathy knew she was no match for Mo. He was an expert in protecting the Spidars from females, so she reluctantly submitted to the hand leading her to the yellow bedroom. Mo let go of her other hand and followed.

At the doorway, she looked back into the living room. Saul turned away. Rich shrugged. Jo-Jo's face said, "Now you'll get yours!" As Mo closed the door behind Kathy, she was ready to cry. The situation was hopeless. No one would help her. To top things off, one man seemed pleased by this turn of events. Why? What had she done to make Jo-Jo hate her?

Tears welled in Kathy's eyes as Harry roughly undressed her. She wanted to fight now that Mo wasn't in the room, but she knew he was stationed outside the door, listening. He would surely make this a threesome if he heard unwanted noises. She remained silent as Harry threw her on the bed and undressed himself.

Because of the alcohol, he fell on top of her. Harshly, he thrust himself into her, making her yelp in sudden pain. "Ha!" he laughed. "I'm too much man for you!" Kathy merely closed her eyes.

When Harry finished his job – a feat not as easy when alcohol is involved – he traveled off to dreamland. Kathy pushed him off her and slipped from the bed. She soaked in a hot bath for a long, long time.

In the living room, Saul watched Harry's door intently. An hour had passed since Kathy's yelp pierced his chest like a butcher knife. He had trouble concentrating on the television, so he looked over at Jo-Jo, who seemed engrossed in the movie. When he looked at Rich, he was surprised to see him watching back.

"Go in after her," Rich suggested. "You were half-cracked to let Harry do it when he's so sopped. Collect on the pact, I mean. I bet she's quite likable."

Saul nodded slowly. He stood and walked to the third bedroom, opening the door slowly. One body lay under the covers on the bed and a light peeked under the bathroom door. He knocked and gave the door a light shove. He heard the gentle swish of the water in the tub behind the curtain. "Kathy?" he cooed.

She pulled the curtain back enough to expose her head. "What do you want?" she asked harshly.

"To make sure you're okay, Luv."

"As if you care."

Saul entered the room and leaned his butt against the sink. "I do care, Luv. I do... I'm sorry. I couldn't cheese it... I wanted

34

you to know you're supposed to come back to me tonight, not stay here."

"So, I have to go from one drunk to another?" she queried. That might not be the smartest thing to say to someone who had been drinking, but at the moment, she didn't care. "Is that what you're telling me? Next, it'll be Jo-Jo and Rich."

"No one else will touch you tonight, not even me," Saul replied. "I promise." Kathy slammed the curtain back against the wall. Saul's voice rose in frustration. "I said I was sorry. I couldn't stop it!"

"You didn't even try! Just get out!"

"Now wait a tick! I started to, but Harry was right." Saul's voice softened. "Let me explain about the pact."

"I don't want explanations. Just leave me alone!"

"All right. I'll beetle off for now, but remember: Harry was blotto. It wouldn't have happened otherwise. He's really a nice chap."

"I know," Kathy replied, barely above a whisper. "I need to be alone for a while."

Saul left. In the living room, he informed Rich and Jo-Jo that the pact would not be honored for the rest of the night, so they had better behave themselves. Rich smiled at him.

Thirty minutes later, Saul stared at Harry's door. Kathy hadn't come out yet. Jo-Jo's voice startled him. "Take care of your bird before she uses her wings to fly away."

"What's that in aid of?" Saul asked.

Jo-Jo pointed to the phone. One of the lights was lit, signaling an extension was in use. Saul reached the bedroom in time to hear Kathy arguing on the phone.

"Come on, Ralph, you're not funny. Since when do you need the registered guest's permission on a local call? For all you should know, I am a guest. I need an outside line... It doesn't matter that you have only men listed for this suite. I want an outside line now..."

Saul grabbed the phone and spoke gruffly into it. "Never mind, Ralph. She doesn't need to call anyone." He slammed down the receiver. "Who were you calling? The press?" Kathy shook her head. "Who then?"

Kathy remained silent. Her cheeks went from rosy to red as tears streamed down her face. She tilted her head to hide the stream. Saul's anger subsided. He pulled her closer. Tonight wasn't turning out the way he wanted it to at all. He could feel moisture coming to his own eyes.

"Are you two spending the night in Harry's room?" Rich yelled from the living room. Saul took Kathy by the hand, causing the spark again, and led her out to a sofa. He sat in a semi-reclining position with his feet on the coffee table and an arm wrapped around Kathy as they all watched a Jerry Lewis movie. Kathy's silence continued, but Saul was sure he caught a tiny twinkle in her eyes several times during humorous scenes.

As the late news came on, Rich made a hasty exit. Retching sounds came from the bathroom. Kathy looked at Jo-Jo and Saul with concern. Neither of them took any notice. "Well," she said, "Aren't either of you going in to help?"

"Are you daft, Luv?" Saul asked. "Do you want me to unswallow, too?"

"Someone should help him," she declared. "He could suffocate if he breathes at the wrong time."

"There's always a bloke casting the gorge on tour," Jo-Jo jeered. "No one ever croaks from it."

Kathy shot him an indignant look and rose to help Rich herself. "I thought he was your friend," she muttered loud enough for the men to hear her. When she opened the powder room door, Rich's red face hung over the toilet bowl. She knelt beside him, stroked his back, and talked in a soft, soothing

36

voice. "Don't fight it. Relax. Let it out. You'll be okay. Relax."

He raised an arm and pointed to the door. Kathy ignored his suggestion and kept stroking his back and repeating her instructions. She could feel the muscles in his back slowly relax, which meant the rest of his body was relaxing, too. From then on, his stomach emptied rhythmically, allowing him to breathe between the spasms.

While one hand stroked Rich's back, she used her free hand to moisten a washcloth and clean off the stray strands of hair that fell in the stream. She placed the cleaned strands behind his ears so they wouldn't fall again.

Finally, the spasms stopped. He raised his head in relief. Kathy handed him some toilet paper and he wiped his mouth and blew his nose to rid himself of the last few remnants. She wet a fresh washcloth and wiped his face with its coolness.

"Thanks," he said. "I didn't want you in here at first, but I'm glad you stayed."

"Wash your hands," Kathy ordered. She searched the medicine cabinet. "Okay, now stick out your finger."

"Excu-u-use me? Which one?"

Kathy blushed. "Just do it." She applied some toothpaste to his index finger.

After tending to his teeth, he placed a light kiss on her forehead. "Thanks, you're an angel. I feel better now."

Kathy returned to Saul with a smile on her face. She cuddled next to him as the Johnny Carson Show began. When it was time for bed, they fell asleep snuggling in his bed. He made sure that his torso appendage did not touch her.

The next morning, Harry apologized profusely. Saul scowled, but Kathy accepted the apology with grace. She bore him no ill will. She had no bruises, only emotional turmoil, which marked the whole weekend anyway.

After breakfast, Harry left to mingle with Rochesterians. Rich was somewhere out of sight. Jo-Jo and Saul composed a new song together as Kathy watched. She was fascinated by the work that went into each song. She always thought song-writing was easy – all you had to do was sit down and write lyrics and add some music to them. Now she realized that, although it might be easy to write a song for your family or friends, writing for the public meant hours of painstaking perfectionism.

When Harry returned, they all ate lunch and spent the afternoon practicing songs. This was the part Kathy loved. She felt like a queen having a private concert in her palace.

A light dinner was the rule for any night performance, after which everyone dressed. Since this was the final show in Rochester, Kathy could go too. She changed into the extra uniform hanging in Saul's closet.

As the men assembled in the living room, she thought they looked very handsome in their beaded Nehru-style suitcoats with bell-bottomed pants. Kathy's uniform blended nicely. Now she didn't mind the glossy mini-skirt and tunic.

Everyone was ready except Harry. "Put a jerk in it or we'll be late," Bart yelled. Harry came out, the fly on his pants held open by white thread, with another thread preventing the zipper from sliding up and closing.

"Your medal's showing," Rich chuckled, proud of his humor.

"I can't find me bloody clippers."

Kathy smiled as she took an emergency sewing kit out of her purse. It contained a tiny pair of sharp, thin scissors. When she had the scissors close to the zipper, Rich yelled out, "Now's yer chance! Get even for last night!"

Harry threw himself back so fast everyone shouted with laughter. "I won't scratch the jewels," Kathy promised. A few snips later, the pants were as good as new, and she returned to Saul's side for the trip down the service elevator.

At the steel service door in the back of the hotel, the Spidars stopped. "I want me mummy!" Rich quipped.

"Kathy, look lively," Saul warned. "You'll get mauled if you don't run when the doors open." Kathy smiled. Sure, there would be a crowd of people waiting outside the hotel for the chance to see their heroes, but so was half the police force of the city of Rochester. What could happen? "Some fans always bob through," Saul added, as if reading her thoughts.

The Spidars sprinted to the waiting limousine, with Bart, Kathy, and Mo bringing up the rear. As Kathy jumped into the limo, she felt someone brush her leg. She turned to see fifty fans ready to join her. Kathy's eyes opened wide. Mo pushed the fans away and slammed the door. Then he jumped into the front seat. The driver pulled out before the fans could block the escape route.

The Spidars arrived at the hall an hour before the concert was scheduled. Kathy saw the crowd in front of the building from two blocks away. Bart told the driver to take a side road to the back entrance. Kathy assumed that meant they would bypass the crowd.

They didn't. Shoved against the back entrance were people just as eager as the ones out front. This crowd was smaller than the other, but it was at least three times the size of the crowd at the hotel. This time, Kathy braced herself for another run. She put her whole heart into it. They went inside without a hitch. The next hour they munched on pistachios, Nestle Crunch bars, and sour cream potato chips washed down with a few drinks.

When the Spidars went on stage, Kathy stayed in the wings with Bart and Mo. She wiggled her hips to the beat as she watched every move Saul made. She caught every wink he sent her way – real winks, not the ones imagined by the fans. She felt a tingle up her spine every time.

The concert was going well. The fans screamed and jumped to get the attention of their favorite Spidar. Even the stagehands bopped to the beat. Midway through the second half, Kathy grew fidgety. She turned to Bart. "What are your plans for me?" she asked.

"I don't know yet," he replied.

"You'll have to trust me. You can't take me with you."

"Like as not, you're right," he admitted.

"I wish you'd quit worrying. I keep my promises. And tomorrow, I have an eight o'clock appointment. I missed one this morning. If I miss another one, people will get suspicious."

Fans screamed, pulled at their hair, and threw personal items onto the stage. Saul smiled at their antics and went into a discussion with Jo-Jo, who nodded. Saul stepped up to the microphone. "*This next song was written this afternoon,*" Saul said. "*I'd like to dedicate it to a special girl. She knows who she is. Ready, mates? One, two, three, bah!*"

"*...I never realized what a kiss could be...*" [3] Kathy's cheeks glowed. Saul looked over and smiled. Kathy's spine tingled. The rest of the concert flew for Kathy. The Spidars were riding away from the hall before she came down from her cloud.

*

Normally, the Spidars partied on the last night in any city. Tonight, most of them joined Gary Lewis and the Playboys at a dance club, the Parliament Lounge, in a suburb, Henrietta.

Tonight was different for Saul, though. He wanted to spend time with Kathy. After getting comfortable on the love seat in Saul's room, the couple spent hours talking. Kathy seemed to thirst for the knowledge Saul had to offer about his work, and

Saul didn't mind. In fact, he rather enjoyed talking to someone who listened and asked intelligent questions.

When the conversation ebbed, love-making took over. Kathy was both receptive and responsive to all Saul had to offer, sweet, sweet love. When robins began to twitter outside, Saul stroked her neck. Goose bumps grew on his hands.

"Will you come with me on tour then?" he asked.

Kathy didn't reply right away. Her eyes were directed his way, but she looked through him, as if weighing the offer. Saul thought he saw hopefulness on her face. When she focused again, Kathy shook her head. "I can't."

"Why not?"

"I can't explain right now. Sometime soon, I'll write a letter telling you why not. When you know everything, your feelings may change." She looked at her wristwatch. "Goodness! It's six o'clock already! I need to shower and get ready." She jumped up and left the room before he had a chance to rebut.

*

Saul dragged his feet like an injured kitten as he walked Kathy to the elevator in his pajamas and bathrobe. She looked younger to him this morning. She hadn't applied any makeup.

"How can I get in touch with you?" he asked.

Kathy smiled. "Maybe you'll see me in the audience sometime." She kissed him gently and stepped back. The elevator swallowed her. Saul returned to the room and went to the bar. He gulped the first scotch straight.

Bart anticipated Saul's sour feelings, and he'd set his own alarm accordingly. He entered the suite to find Saul already tipsy. He took the glass from Saul's hand. "Go perk yourself with a shower."

Saul was in no mood to argue. All his fight had gone down the elevator. He accepted Bart's advice without comment. As he entered the bathroom to shave and bathe, he spotted an envelope on the sink, his name in Kathy's handwriting. He shook his head. He couldn't read it yet. Maybe after the shower...

*

Bart was pouring a second cup of strong coffee for Saul when the others came out for breakfast. Kathy's letter sat in Saul's pocket. Surrounded by friends, he found the courage to open it. Then his face went white. He handed the note to Bart.

"Oh my God!" Bart exclaimed. "Kathy's appointment this morn was for school!" He looked at Saul. "The manager," Saul said with a nod. They hurried out of the suite, the letter still lying on the table.

Their faces coarse from overnight growth, Harry, Rich and Jo-Jo stared at the letter in silence, not going any closer. Then Harry picked up the note and read it aloud:

Dear Saul,

Thank you for the memorable weekend. Your offer this morning was so tempting. I almost said yes. But alas, it wouldn't work. You see, you're 22, and I'm only 15.

I couldn't tell you before this, because Bart will go off his rocker when he finds out. I couldn't chance it.

I know Jo-Jo doesn't believe I was a virgin the first night. However, at 15, most girls do still have everything in place.

Don't bother trying to find me. As you can probably guess, I've been working here under a false name (and age).

I love you!!!
Kathy

"What a drag!" Jo-Jo exclaimed.

Chapter 3

The office door was open. Bart and Saul entered without knocking. The manager, Foster Chumstable, looked up from his desk and recognized them. He stood to shake hands. "I hope you found your stay satisfactory. You didn't have to come down to settle your bill. I would have brought it up myself."

"Everything was fine," Bart replied. "We want to talk to you about Kathy Voss, one of your maids."

"Oh yes. You just missed her. She said she was late for an appointment. She raced out of here about ten minutes ago."

"Must've been here a while. What did she say?'

"I don't know what you mean."

"It appears there was a mix-up on Friday."

"Employees are not supposed to discuss hotel problems with…"

"She was with us night and day," Saul interrupted. "Some of it was bound to come out."

"Yes, I suppose so." The manager paused for a moment. "As long as you know part of it, I guess you're entitled to the rest. From what Kathy told me this morning, the desk clerk assigned her to being your round-the-clock maid without asking first. The maids must volunteer for that duty at this hotel. I hope her work was satisfactory despite the problem."

"Yes," Saul replied. "She worked above and beyond the call of duty. What are you doing about Ralph?"

"He's been getting complaints from many maids lately. This was the last straw, making my best one quit. I fired him moments ago."

43

"That should have put his kettle on the boil."

"None of it matters to you, I'm sure," the manager added.

"Yes, it does," Saul corrected. "I grew quite fond of her. I need to know how I can contact her. Can you tell me anything else about her?"

"What's to tell? She never complained about the messiest jobs. She's an excellent worker. Many patrons have praised the little extras she does to make their stay enjoyable." He paused again. "Our Lost and Found manager even reported that she turned in a large sum of money she found in the ladies' room off the lobby. Her integrity is impeccable."

"What about a phone number or address so we can contact her?" Saul asked.

The hotel manager clicked his teeth together. This went against hotel policy... But these were the world-renowned Spidars. Chumstable pulled a file out of his drawer. As he read it, he twitched noticeably. "There's no phone listed, and I doubt this address is correct."

"What?" Bart glared. "How could that happen? Don't you check out prospective employees first?"

"Yes, yes usually," the manager said in a defensive tone. "You could say I was up a creek without a paddle the day she applied for a job. I had two conventions booked that weekend, and we were in the middle of a flu epidemic. Four maids had called in sick, so I was desperate. I gave Kathy the lobby and halls. She couldn't get into trouble there and the others could concentrate on the rooms.

"After I received the note from the Lost and Found Manager, she was promoted to rooms. I completely forgot about her secrecy on the job application until now. Did she steal anything of yours? We will pay for whatever it is."

"She stole my heart," Saul replied.

A puff of air escaped from Chumstable's mouth. He pointed to the thickness of her file. "By these reports, Kathy does that to everyone, co-workers and patrons, men and women alike. No complaints in this thick file, just compliments."

He handed Bart the bill. "I added $100 to your bill for the live-in maid service for three and a half days. That's a good deal, should be more. Kathy insisted she be paid only for the time she cleaned. I'm sorry to charge you anything, but that's policy."

Bart brushed it off. "We're not worried about the money. Out of curiosity, does her file mention her age? I mean, she looked young, but she spoke like she's been around a while."

Chumstable studied the papers. "There's no birthdate here, either. As I said, I was desperate. I remember I did ask, but Kathy flashed that brilliant smile of hers and said a lady doesn't reveal her age. I assumed she was over thirty. Women get sensitive about their age around that time in their lives."

He glanced at a framed photograph on his desk. "She did look younger, though, didn't she? It's amazing how some women age so slowly, and other women like my wife, er, never mind that. I could ask the other maids if you'd like."

"No need," Bart said quickly. "Oh, I have some long-distance calls to place. You should wait until we leave to draw up the final bill." Chumstable nodded.

Bart and Saul went upstairs in silence. Inside the suite, Bart called a lawyer in New York City. He talked for half an hour. As each minute passed, more color faded from his face. He was ashen by the time he hung up the phone.

"Well, Mateys," he said to the Spidars, "We have quite a sticky wicket here. Even though Kathy appeared old enough, it doesn't matter. Even if she seduced Saul, he'd be the one in trouble, because, as they say here in the States, she was jailbait. Add the fact she didn't do a tart-act, and we're pickled.

Saul and Harry each could get five-year jail terms. The rest of us get a year as accessories. Then there's holding her against her wishes, kidnapping here in the States, which has its own penalties. There's no way we can give them an eyewash on this one."

"Perfect timing!" Jo-Jo cried out. "There goes our bread and butter."

Saul replied softly. "I beg to differ. Kathy won't put us on the shelf."

"You seem quite sure of yerself," Harry stated. "Do you still think she's so plum?"

"Actually, yes, I do. And rogering her is like a lightning strike nearby."

"Doubtful," Jo-Jo stated. "One twat's the same as another. Right, Harry?"

Harry shrugged. "I was too smashed to feel much."

Saul glared at him. "Kathy's the piece missing from my life's puzzle. She's the frame around the picture. I can't turn off feelings because she's a chick instead of a hen. What's the bloody problem with age anyway? When I'm sixty-four, she'll be fifty-seven. No one would think anything of that."

Bart looked at his watch and rose to his feet. "There's nothing we can do now, so we'd better pack. The Spidar bus departs in fifteen minutes."

"I bundled you two already," Rich offered. "I couldn't skivvy about with the collywobbles." He handed Saul his overcoat for the nippy October weather, a coat he wouldn't need for long. The Spidars were headed south next.

Saul moved slowly as he put on his coat. "We should at least take a look-see for her before we leave." He slid his hands into his pockets. Inside one, he found an envelope. He pulled it out and recognized the handwriting. "From Kathy," he said to the others as he opened it. It read:

46

Dear Saul,

By now you have found out about the money I requested. I'm sure Jo-Jo is saying, "I told you she was a knock-up, and a cheap one at that." You paid only for the time I cleaned. I'm sorry, but if I went home without any extra money, my mother would question it – she thinks I babysit on weekends. Besides, I'll need the extra, since I won't have this job anymore.

Thanks for the concert last night. I could never afford the tickets, certainly not backstage ones. And thanks for letting me see creativity in the making.

Tell Bart not to worry. I'm not as dumb as he thinks. I know the legal problems. My mother won't find out what happened this weekend.

Don't worry about me, either. There are a lot of things I want to do with my life. Someday, I'll make a difference in this crazy world, with my own reputation, not someone else's.

I have memories that will last a lifetime now. Thanks again and again.

Love,

Kathy, a Spidarmaniac

PS: I know this incident wasn't your fault. If I hadn't lied to get the job, this whole episode never would have happened.

A bit teary-eyed, Saul passed the letter to the others. Relief, though doubted, accompanied the group south.

Chapter 4 - June 1, 1966

"We are now arriving in Henrietta, New York," Rich boomed from the front as the Spiders' private bus pulled into Southtown Plaza's parking lot in the Rochester suburb. "The time here is 11:46 a.m. We hope you enjoyed your flight..."

"I fold and you can deal me out," Saul said, picking up his poker chips.

"I still think you're rattled." Jo-Jo stated.

Saul shifted uneasily in his seat. This was the last stop before the Spidars returned to England. This extra show had been added at Saul's request. "I want to make sure she's okay," Saul had said. He didn't vocalize the rest: how he tried to forget her, yet he saw Kathy in the front row of the audience at every concert they played. He knew every time it was only his imagination. After eight months on the road, he hadn't found anyone with the same spark.

The other Spidars had agreed to one more concert because they feared Saul would come here alone, do something he shouldn't, and get arrested. The band could not survive without him or any of its members.

More recently, Saul had hired a private investigator, Bob Pinkerton, to find her. Bob had sent him current yearbooks from the Rochester high schools. Kathy wasn't in any of them. Last night, though, with the yearbooks lying on his bed, he noticed an insignia on one cover – the same marking as on Kathy's ring. He let Pinkerton know which high school she attended. Hope lived!!!

Saul jumped off the bus without using the steps. He waved an arm in the air. A man standing in front of a sign that said

J.C. Penney's walked forward and followed Saul inside the bus. After directing the driver, Bob Pinkerton sat down and asked Saul, "Have you remembered anything else since last night?"

"No. I've gone through the pictures in the Monroe High yearbook with a fine-toothed comb. My Kathy's not in it."

"Don't worry. If you're correct about the insignia, we have a chance. Since Monroe High does have a Kathy Voss, she may be a friend of your girl."

Monroe High School loomed ahead. The brick building was three stories tall and spread a full block. The main entrance had a slanted roof supported by round pillars.

Saul took a deep breath, adjusted his fake glasses and mustache, and joined Bart and Bob outside. They walked together the fifty feet to the door. "Monroe High has 2,000 students enrolled this year," Mr. Pinkerton stated.

Inside, an office secretary escorted them to a counselor's office. Abbey Lane was a 26-year-old brunette wearing a paisley print shirt-waist dress that accented her blue eyes. "How may I help you?" she asked.

"As I explained on the phone," Bob Pinkerton replied, "We're looking for a girl who may be a friend of your student, Kathy Voss. We've gone through your current yearbook and can't find the right person."

Abbey pulled a picture off the wall. "This is Kathy Voss' class – thirty kids who are the most likely to get bored with regular classes. They have main courses together, English, Math, Science, and Social Studies. Do you see the girl here?"

Saul and Bart examined the picture closely. Saul shook his head. "Is anyone missing from this picture?"

Abbey paused as she thought she might recognize Saul's voice. Then she nodded. "Yes, one girl asked to be excluded this year and we completely understood."

"Do you have a picture of that girl somewhere else?"

"Yes, in last year's book." Abbey reached for a book on the shelf. As she searched for the picture, she continued. "I doubt she's the one you're seeking. She's a good friend to Kathy Voss, but she's from a very poor family and needs to earn scholarships for medical school. She's not a trouble-maker."

Saul shook his head. "Our girl isn't a trouble-maker. And she has a smile that warms you all over."

Abbey nodded. "That does sound like Sadie West. When Mr. Pinkerton said on the phone that your girl was absent on October 1st last year, I assumed she was in some kind of trouble that day." Abbey handed an open book to Saul. "Sadie is the third one from the right in the middle row."

Saul's eyes lit up. "That's her!!! Can I see her?"

Abbey nodded. "I can check her schedule." She flipped a Rolodex file. "Sadie should be in American History right now."

After they dismissed Pinkerton, Bart and Saul followed Abbey to the third floor. "This reminds me of my own school days," Bart puffed at the end of the climb.

"You get used to it," Abbey responded. "I watched Sadie bounce up these steps a few weeks ago. If she can do it in her condition, anyone can."

"What condition?" Saul asked. "The last time I saw her, she was quite right. Is she sick?"

Abbey stopped and looked at Saul. "I presume you haven't seen her since October."

"An eternity."

"That explains it. We weren't aware of her problem ourselves until about four months ago. The school board kicked her out on the spot." Abbey laughed. "Then, a thousand students, under Sadie's guidance, threatened to boycott the school. She was reinstated within a week." Abbey's voice lowered. "It's a shame. She will have to buck greater odds than a school board to fulfill her dreams now."

50

Abbey stopped in front of a door and knocked. The woman who opened the door stood straight, a long neck holding her head high. "Miss Weintrout, we're looking for Sadie West."

The teacher responded in a loud and abrasive voice. "The school board allowed teacher discretion. Sadie comes to my class on Fridays to take tests and hand in assignments. She's in the library the rest of the week. I refuse to have my class disturbed all week. Just looking at her turns everyone's stomach."

"That's not what the students say, Miss Weintrout. They respect her determination to stay in school. Many of them have gained appreciation for the educational process now."

A boy came to the door and asked to go to the men's room. Miss Weintrout nodded and returned to her class. The student walked a few steps down the hall and then leaned against the wall as he motioned for Mrs. Lane to join him.

"This is Harvey Swartz, another promising doctor," Abbey said to Bart and Saul. "He is also the class clown." Harvey's blue eyes sparkled and his lips curled impishly at her remark. "Did you want to speak to us, Harvey?" she asked.

"Yes, I heard Weinee's comments about Sadie, and I thought you'd want the truth."

"I think I already know the truth, but go ahead."

"First off, Sadie doesn't disrupt the class. We knew about her problem long before the school did. It's Weinee that bothers us. Her treatment of Sadie is outrageous!"

"What do you mean, Harvey?"

"A few months ago, when Sadie came back to school after her kick-out, Weinee started a new thing: the class would take the normal written quiz on Fridays when Sadie is here in class, and Weinee would give an oral one to make sure no one cheated. The questions were simple until she arrived at Sadie's desk. All of a sudden, a question would come out of left

51

field, something stupid mentioned in class the day before and not found in the textbook. Of course Sadie wouldn't know the answer. Weinee would then rant and rave like a lunatic that Sadie wasn't studying in the library."

Harvey paused as his lips curled again. "Sadie fixed her. By the fourth week of the same routine, when Weinee began yelling, Sadie turned her head and looked out the window. We all thought she was staring at the Nolith Hotel in the distance, not that it matters. Whatever she was doing, she'd turn back with contentment on her face, which blew Weinee's mind.

"That's when the rest of us decided to help in the next mind-blowing session. We took copious notes and gave them to Sadie. The first time she had the right answer, you should have seen Weinee's face! Even now, though, Weinee makes her sit in the back corner as if she's a child being punished."

Abbey smiled. "Thanks Harvey. I wondered why she was the only teacher to complain if Sadie was as bad as Miss Weinee, I mean Miss Weintrout, claimed."

"Yeah, Weinee's just jealous of all the attention Sadie gets." Harvey walked toward his classroom. Before he reached the door, he turned toward Abbey again. "Mrs. Lane, could you do me a favor?"

"What is it, Harvey?"

"Sadie is having a hard time getting from class to class. The trouble started this week. We've tried to get her to take it easier, but she won't listen to us. Maybe she'll listen to you. She respects you."

"I'll try."

Harvey disappeared into the classroom.

Saul's mind whirled. When Abbey suggested he and Bart go to a conference room, Saul didn't argue. He wanted some time to sort things out and clear his mind. Too many horrible things fit the mold of what he was hearing. Inside the conference room, Saul sat down with a thump. "I'll get the others," Bart said.

*

When Sadie came out of the library, Abbey saw Harvey hadn't exaggerated. It was time for Sadie to study at home. "I need to talk to you," Abbey said. Downstairs, Abbey closed her office door. "Sadie, you know what I'm about to say, don't you?"

Sadie sat down. "Yes, Mrs. Lane. I knew this was coming. I just hoped to make it to finals."

"You don't have to worry. Your marks are good enough to pass. You simply won't get Regents credit for this year's courses."

"I need a Regents diploma to get into pre-med!'

"Realistically, you may not even finish high school. Next year will be tough, with babies and a senior load of AP classes. Going to college is almost impossible."

"The impossible just takes a little longer," Sadie replied with a smile. "Mark my words: Someday, I'll be in medical research."

Abbey grinned. "Maybe."

"I will. I may have to take a break for a while, but someday I'm going to make my mother proud of me." Tears rolled down her cheeks.

Abbey leaned over and hugged her. "I'm sure she is already." The counselor handed Sadie a hanky and used one herself. Then she remembered the conference room. "Oh! There are some men here to see you. They say it has to do with last October. They wouldn't tell me..."

"No!" Sadie screamed. "They can't see me like this! No!"

"Alright," Abbey replied, surprised by the sudden outburst from someone who was usually soft-spoken. "You don't have

53

to talk to them. Calm down."

Sadie's voice softened to a whisper as she lowered her head. "Please," was all she said.

"You stay here. I'll send someone to your locker." Abbey patted Sadie's shoulder and walked to the door. "Don't worry. I'll help in any way I can."

In the conference room, Abbey found three extra men with the two she expected to see. "Moral support for Saul, er Tom," Harry offered, scratching his fake beard.

Abbey shrugged and turned to Saul, aka Tom. "Sadie doesn't want to see you," she explained. "I have to respect her wishes. I hope you will too."

"Twaddle!" Saul yelled. "After all I've gone through to find her, I'm going to chat her up before I leave this building!" He stomped out the door and headed toward Abbey's office, where he figured Kathy/Sadie was. The others followed.

Abbey ran past them and blocked Saul's entrance. "It was Sadie's decision, not mine. If she doesn't want to see you, you will NOT see her. She has enough problems at the moment."

Saul softened his tone of voice. "I won't put her in a tight spot. I just want to chat for a few minutes. If she still wants me to leave after that, I will."

Harry grabbed Saul's arm. "Come on, Mate, remember her the way she was. Let her keep some dignity. Be satisfied with the memory of her pretty face and that special smile you've been talking about from pillar to post for the past eight months."

"Oh, her face hasn't changed much," Abbey corrected, "only her muscles. Some of them aren't keeping her as erect as she used to be."

Silence.

"Is there any chance for her?" Bart asked.

54

Abbey began to shake her head, then changed her mind and nodded. "Sadie's like a salmon going upstream against some powerful currents. If there's any chance at all, I believe Sadie will be the one to beat this thing. We're all rooting for her, uh, most of us are."

"Hallelujah!" Saul exclaimed unexpectedly behind her. While Abbey spoke to Bart, Saul had peeked through the small window in Abbey's door. "Mrs. Lane, go tell Kathy, I mean Sadie, that I saw her and I MUST speak with her!"

Anger shot from Abbey's eyes but subsided quickly. "Maybe you can help, too," she mumbled, as she opened the door enough to slide through. Flowered curtains closed across the window, preventing further invasion.

"Sadie's okay!" Saul beamed. "She merely makes Buddha look like Mister Universe." The others shrugged, not understanding his reference.

Abbey returned. "Saul, Sadie says she'll talk to you – only you." He walked inside with confidence.

Ten minutes later, Saul left Abbey's office, carrying a pile of books and grinning from ear to ear. Behind him came Sadie. She wore a tent dress with a geometric pattern, which accented her gravid belly more than she would like and made her look like an A-frame house on stilts.

"What've you got in there?" Rich asked. "A watermelon patch?"

Her face rosy, Sadie smiled. "My mother always told me that whenever I do anything, I should do it right. One baby seemed too ordinary."

Saul smiled proudly. "We need to go someplace to chat," he said to the men. "Sadie doesn't want to go to the hotel. Yet."

"For some odd reason," Rich added.

"She has some family friends she trusts bag and baggage. You can drop us off there." The other Spidars nodded and went out to their bus.

Saul walked slowly beside Sadie. As they emerged through the front door, her face turned ashen. Saul tightened his hold on her arm to prevent a fall. Moments later, her color and smile returned.

"Are you over the weather now?" Saul asked. She nodded and waddled the rest of the way to the bus.

Though the outside of the bus appeared like a Greyhound, the interior had been overhauled to provide the comforts of a mobile home, including a refrigerator, sink, hot plate, and electrical outlets for small lamps and electric instruments. Sadie sat between Harry and Saul on a side couch.

"I hear Weinee's been giving you a hard tick," Saul said as they rode along.

"Nothing I can't handle," Sadie giggled. "You've been talking to Harvey, haven't you? He's the only one who can get away with calling her that." She leaned her head against Saul's shoulder and closed her eyes.

"You look flaked out," Harry observed.

"I am. Today's been one of those days when everything went wrong."

"Including me finding you?" Saul asked.

Her eyes remained shut. "Well, you must admit, I've gained a few pounds since you last saw me."

Saul patted her belly. "A fine few pounds."

"At least I don't have to worry about a table in the school cafeteria. I carry mine with me."

At that moment, a bump appeared on the side of her mound. Saul and Harry watched in fascination as the bump moved toward Saul's hand, stopped underneath it, then disappeared. Saul beamed!

"How old is she now that she's in the pod?" Bart mumbled from the front seat.

"I promised not to make trouble, and I didn't," Sadie replied. "No one knows the father's name."

Saul shot Bart a look that said *I told you so*.

A short pause later, Sadie continued, "Usually my mother understands things, but she's changed lately. After the babies are born, I hope she'll go back to normal again."

Saul smiled. "I'll find out how nice she is when we meet."

"What?!!" Sadie exclaimed, her eyes popping open. "You're crazy!"

"Why? I came back, didn't I?"

Sadie shook her head. "If I gauged Bart correctly when all this started, he checked out the consequences of statutory rape." Sadie rested her hand on her belly. "With this new development, my mother could put you in jail for five years and get fifty percent of your net worth. Don't be stupid now."

Bart sighed, as if a burden lifted.

"I take care of my responsibilities," Saul replied. "I told you in Mrs. Lane's office why I returned. I haven't changed my mind. I'm as determined as ever to make an honest woman out of you. After all, you have my tots inside."

Sadie smiled at Rich. "Don't you just hate know-it-alls?" With a serious expression, she looked at Saul. "You don't need to brag to me. I knew about them a while ago." She laid her head back and closed her eyes again, a hint of playfulness on her lips.

The bus pulled up beside a white Cape Cod with blue trim. The short driveway went to the side of the house, where a man in his late twenties was weeding a flower garden. He had a muscular build, dark hair, and bushy eyebrows.

Saul stepped off the bus and the man walked toward him. A woman about the same age came from the house. She had a slender, pretty face framed by medium-length brown hair.

"Can we help?" Harry asked as Sadie labored to the edge of her seat.

"Yes, you can close your eyes. It's hard to be lady-like with a sixty pound weight glued to one's mid-section." She managed to get to her feet and step out.

Bart was already standing outside with Saul. "Are you afraid I'm going to kidnap Saul this time?" Sadie asked Bart.

"I wouldn't be surprised," Rich responded from an open bus window. "You're already a thief."

Saul shot Rich a disgusted look. "What's that in aid of? She never nicked anything from us."

"She most certainly did." Rich winked at Sadie. "She filched your heart."

Sadie smirked. "I don't get mad. I get even. He stole something of mine first." The bus pulled out of the driveway with its occupants laughing. The bus would return after Rich, Jo-Jo, and Harry were safe at the hotel.

"This is Gene and Mary," Sadie told Saul.

"Enchanted," Saul replied, taking Mary's hand and kissing the back of it.

Mary's eyes lit up as she recognized the voice despite the mustache and glasses. "Come inside for tea?" she asked. The others followed her through the side door into a brightly decorated kitchen and out to the enclosed back porch that ran the full width of the house. The upper half of the porch had windows all around it with screens letting a breeze offset the blazing sun.

Sitting down, Sadie searched Bart's face. He shook his head No. Saul caught the silent conversation. "It's okay, Luv," Saul countered. "If you trust 'em, so do I."

58

After Mary poured tea and sliced a coffee cake from Gene's bakery, Sadie outlined some details of that long-ago weekend. She left out the fact that she wasn't allowed to leave. At the end, she admitted Saul was the father of her babies.

Gene had to clear his throat before he could speak. "This is a shock." He looked at Saul. "I should explain something to you. Sadie's mother has been hounding her for the name of the father, but Sadie's been adamant to protect your identity. Mary and I never expected… I've been praying for a miracle, but I never expected anything like this."

"Sometimes we get more than we expect," Mary whispered, knowing Gene still didn't realize who Saul was.

"Sadie, how could you get a job?" Gene asked. "And how did you keep it for so long?"

Sadie blushed. "I experimented with make-up until I looked older without being cheap. Then I figured hotels wouldn't ask too many questions from a part-timer eager to work weekends and weekend overnights. I tried several places during that bad flu epidemic, and at the fourth hotel, I found a harried manager who accepted my evasive replies.

"I was grateful for the $1.50 an hour, which was three times what I make babysitting, so I worked hard. You know, I was averaging forty or fifty dollars each weekend including tips. I couldn't make that kind of money anyplace else at my age."

She paused, then continued. "I tried to justify the lie by making sure I tithed my income, but I guess God doesn't work that way. In any case, you can see why I couldn't make trouble for the Spidars. This wasn't their fault. They shouldn't have to sacrifice their careers for my mis…."

Saul interrupted. "To be on the square, Sir, Sadie has left out a lot of things." He hugged her tighter as she lowered her head. "The most important thing was that before I left town, I

59

asked her to tour with me."

"A fifteen-year-old can't run off in this state!" Gene scolded.

Sadie looked up. "He didn't know I was fifteen until after I left. By then, he had no way to find me. In fact, I don't know how he did."

"It wasn't easy." Saul kissed her forehead. The familiar tingle in his lips and the resulting effect in his groin made Saul sigh. He had missed that tingle the rest of the tour. "Marriage would do nicely."

Mary had watched the way Saul and Sadie looked at each other. She saw tenderness and admiration in their eyes. "What will you do now? At sixteen, Sadie still needs her mother's permission to marry, and Lucille may not give it."

Saul squeezed Sadie's hand, with the expectant tingle afterwards. "She hasn't said yes yet. Once she does, we'll find a way."

Sadie's face-color deepened. "Gene, do you remember the conversation with my mother a month ago... the one where she called me a whore? That hurt, even though she may not have meant it. Her comment sliced deep. Well, the way I see this, if I were to marry Saul just because I'm having his babies and without knowing if I really love him, then she'd be right. I would be a whore. Plain and simple, I'd be selling my body and soul for security. That's not right."

She turned to Saul. "I need to get to know the real you better, not the 'you' in the movies or onstage or in the magazines. I need time. Can you understand?"

He kissed her hand. "Yes, my sweets. You'll have to let me stick around this summer, though. Deal?" Before she could reply, she turned ashen. "Are you all right?" he asked.

Mary's mouth opened to speak, but Sadie interrupted, "I think it's time to go. Saul's taking me to the show tonight and

I'm awfully tired. I'd like to rest a bit first."

"Do you think it's wise to go to a concert?" Mary asked. "Won't you get too *tired* there?" Her emphasis on "tired" showed that she knew what was really going on now.

"I'll be fine," Sadie replied. "I just need to rest a bit."

"Are you sure? Maybe you should have some help while Saul is on stage" Mary looked at Gene, who was slowly moving his head between the others, then his eyes lit up as he realized who Saul was.

Sadie smiled. "Are you offering your services, Mary?"

"N-n-no," Mary stuttered. "I don't mean to interfere."

Saul questioned Sadie with his eyes. She nodded. "I guess I would feel better with Mary there."

"That settles it then," Saul stated.

The bus was back in the driveway. Saul, Bart, and Sadie left the house together. Mary kissed Gene good-bye and whispered to him, "I hope she tells Lucille soon. It would ease her mind."

He nodded. "But we can't do it. She trusts us."

"I know," Mary said then hurried to board the bus.

Along the way, the bus stopped at a maternity shop. Saul wanted to buy something for Sadie to wear to the show. The two of them were inside the building a while. When they came out, he carried a garment bag over one arm and held onto her with the other one.

"Sorry we took so long," Sadie apologized to Bart and Mary in the bus. "I had to try on so many outfits, I lost count. Most of them were made for women expecting one child. They were so tight on the belly, I felt vacuum-packed. Other ones, big enough for my belly, fell off my shoulders."

"Obviously you found something," Bart stated.

"Wait until you see it!" Sadie replied with glittering eyes.

Saul gently stroked her hair. "It looks quite fine on you."

At the hotel, Sadie's heart beat fast as she wobbled onto the elevator. Memories surfaced, some bad, the majority good. The elevator stopped on the sixteenth floor. Bart led the way, Saul helped Sadie down the hall, and Mary followed.

Taking a deep breath, Sadie watched as Bart unlocked the door and opened it. Everything was the same as that weekend long ago – same furniture, same pictures on the wall, even the men sitting around with drinks in their hands – Déjà vu. This time, the living room's earth-tone colors warmed Sadie's eyes.

"We must stop meeting like this," she said to the men.

Harry rose and greeted her with a kiss on her forehead. "Welcome home, Pet."

"This is Mary, a friend of mine," Sadie said. "I'm really pooped. I can't stay and chat. Saul and Mary will have to explain. Blue room?"

Harry bowed to Mary, replying, "Yeah, same room." Sadie smiled. Of course, Saul would take the blue room, Jo-Jo would take the green, Rich would take the red, and Harry would take the yellow one. She wobbled into Saul's room and fell onto the bed without pulling down the bedspread.

In the living room, the Spidars greeted the room service man with a delivery cart and told Saul to check on Sadie. She wasn't hungry, just pooped, so the men didn't wait. They helped themselves to the food the man tried to arrange neatly but finally gave up and left. Mary then sat down to eat a little something herself.

After dinner, the men practiced for the night's show. Saul found extra energy in two songs: "...a girl in a million... I lost someone..." [6] and "...you sent my girl... now she is mine...." [7] Mary checked on Sadie and then watched from the sofa.

As show time drew near, the men separated to dress. Saul found Sadie applying make-up in the bathroom. "I couldn't sleep, so I took a bath and got dressed," she explained. Her hand brushed along the bright blue satin pantsuit, the gathered empire waist, and Oriental collar. The upper half of the sleeves were puffy, with the snug zippered lower-arm half bordered in the same white beaded lace as the bodice. The slacks were made with ample material, and white lace on the seams and hem coordinated the outfit.

"This thing's gorgeous!" she squealed.

Saul smiled and thought, *She's still angelic, just like eight months ago.*

Sadie finished and turned to him. "Okay?"

"Loverly," he whispered, adding a gentle kiss to her forehead.

As Saul prepared to shower, Sadie went to the living room, where Mary offered her a turkey sandwich. "No thanks."

"How are you feeling?" Mary whispered.

"I couldn't sleep. The pain is twenty minutes apart now."

Mary opened her mouth to speak, but Sadie cut her off, "We don't have to worry until the pains are five minutes apart for a first pregnancy. I want to go to the show tonight. Don't spoil it. Please."

The men emerged from their rooms in bright blue tuxedos with fluorescent yellow shirts. "Whew! I need my shades," Sadie teased.

"You look pretty dapper yerself," Rich offered.

She twirled to show all sides. "Thanks. We match a bit."

To prevent knowledge about their modified bus from leaking out to the fans, they rode to the Shriner's Hall in a rented stretch limousine. On the way, Rich listed the pranks he had pulled in the last few months. He was especially proud of the time the group was skinny-dipping in the Gulf of Mexico. Rich was the first one out and he couldn't resist leaving the rest stranded without their clothes.

"Yeah," Harry chimed in, "We had to wait until some lovers loaned us some flippin' towels."

Sadie would have laughed at the old prank, but another whiteout exploded inside. She concentrated on her breathing to get through it without attracting attention. When the pain passed, she let out a sigh of relief. She looked up and saw Jo-Jo staring at her. She could tell he knew what was happening – he had gone through it once with his own wife. Hopefully, he could also guess why she didn't want Saul to know. She smiled at Jo-Jo. He scowled back. Well, some things don't change.

*

During the break backstage in the middle of the show, Jo-Jo grimaced whenever he looked at Sadie. When Saul left her side to speak with Bart, she whispered to Harry, "I wish there was some way to change Jo-Jo's mind about me. He still thinks I'm a tramp. Don't deny it. I can see it on his face."

"Things aren't always as they seem," Harry replied with a smile. "Listen to the next song we play. Jo-Jo added a couple lines directed at Saul."

The group was called back to the stage.

Sadie listened intently as the second half began. "...don't be afraid... go out and get her..." [8] Did Jo-Jo really write those lines? She smiled at him, but he wasn't looking her way. Halfway through the song, another whiteout came with searing pain. Sadie's smile faded. Her head throbbed. Her palms sweated. She closed her eyes and concentrated on her breathing. Her fingers stroked her belly in a circular motion.

When the attack finally passed, she opened her eyes and noticed all the Spidars watching Saul and then her, as he beckoned her to the stage.

"What's happening?" Sadie asked Bart.

"Saul wants to dedicate a song to you. A might dotty, but go ahead."

"I don't think so..." she began, but Bart pushed her past the curtain's edge. She'd look silly if she backed away now, so she wobbled out and stood next to Saul.

"...look her over...ain't she sweet..."[9] Sadie's cheeks were beet red by the end of the song. When Saul put his arm around her and tapped her belly with pride, the fans screeched. Several girls in the audience fainted and had to be removed for their own safety.

Sadie felt close to fainting herself. "These lights are too hot for me," she said to Saul.

He accompanied her to the wing. As they were about to pass Jo-Jo, Sadie's hand went up to stroke his face. Jo-Jo jerked away and strummed his guitar. She smiled and wobbled off the stage. With her safely in the wing, Saul returned to his place and the Spidars began another song.

This time, a whiteout struck like a bolt of lightning. "That's a good one, isn't it?" Mary asked. Sadie didn't reply. "How far apart are they now?" Sadie still didn't answer.

"Oh, no!" Bart exclaimed. "I thought you were closing your eyes to listen. How witless!"

Sadie finally responded as the pain eased. "About six minutes." Another attack came piggyback, making her double over this time. "I think it's time to leave."

Bart shook his head. "Baby or no baby, Saul can't leave in the middle of a gig."

"He doesn't need to. If he wonders where I am, just say I went to lie down. That's true. I hope to lie down in the hospital. After the show, tell him what these attacks really are and where I am. Okay?"

"Sure," Bart responded in relief.

"Can I borrow the limo?"

Bart hesitated. "Shouldn't you take the meat-wagon that's outside for emergencies?"

Sadie shook her head. "No, if I arrive at the hospital in an ambulance, the hospital can release any information they wish. If I go in a private vehicle, they have to keep everything confidential."

"That's all very well, but be sure to send the limo back."

Sadie nodded.

Chapter 5 – 1966

"Why didn't you tell me?!" Saul said, fists raised towards Bart when the show was over. "I would've gone with her!"

Bart stepped backwards quickly. "Precisely why you weren't told."

Saul ran outside and instructed the limo driver, "To the hospital where you took the two women. And step on it. You can come back for the others."

Fifteen minutes later, he arrived at a tall, white building. He squared his fake glasses and floppy hat. An antiseptic odor greeted him inside. He walked to the reception desk. "My girl's having a babe. Where do I go?"

"Maternity is on the second floor, sir. You need to sign papers in Admitting before you go up. That's around the corner to your right."

"Thanks." Saul ran to catch an elevator. Behind him the receptionist called, "You need to check with Admitting, sir!"

"No time," he replied.

Upstairs, he opened each door until he found the right one. Mary was wiping Sadie's forehead. "Is everything all right?" he asked.

"I'm fully dilated and effaced," Sadie said, exhausted. "The doctor is getting the delivery room ready now." She motioned for Mary to leave.

Before Saul could think clearly, Sadie was wheeled into the delivery room and doctors presented him with a son, Carl, and a daughter, Roxanne. Saul held a baby in each arm. He recognized his own round face, hazel eyes, and long eyelashes on both of them.

"Here comes another one," Sadie said, breathless. He looked up in shock.

He tried to kiss her forehead, but she pushed him away. "I was only..." Another baby's scream interrupted him. This was a boy Sadie named Jason. Jason had an oval face, dark brown eyes, and a nose slightly pushed in at the tip.

*

In her private room, Sadie puffed a cigarette as the doctor entered. She had the bed pulled to the center of the room so the smoke would go to the exhaust fan in the middle of the ceiling.

"I thought I told you to give those things up," the doctor scolded.

She ignored him. "The nurse said all three babies weigh over six pounds. From what I've read, even twins are usually around five pounds at birth. No wonder I felt so huge!" Saul kissed the top of her head. "And, by the way, California hospitals keep the babies in the mothers' rooms. According to reports, the children seem happier."

The doctor scowled. "This isn't California, and that is against hospital policy."

"Well, perhaps I should take my babies home tonight."

"They can't go home this soon. You never know what will happen."

"Then let the babies stay in my room. And you can note on my chart that since I have a private room, the hospital rules can be ignored."

"The rules were made for your benefit, Missy."

"Exactly! Therefore, any that don't make sense can be waived by the doctor on the case – namely you."

"I'll make decisions one by one."

"Good enough," she replied. "I can live with that."

An hour later, the other Spidars snuck up for a visit. When they entered Sadie's room, they saw three babies near the door.

"Good show!" Jo-Jo said, his sharp features smoothing.

Saul sat on the bed, talking on the phone with his accountant. "...That's right, a check for four thousand pounds made out to Sadie West. To get an apartment and set up a nursery..."

Bart thumped Saul's shoulder. "Triplets! Man, what a story this will make!"

"Can you wait a few days?" Sadie asked. "I know reporters are chomping at the bit since the concert, but I don't want them, or Spidar fans, to invade my privacy all the time. If you wait a while, they won't know where I had the babies. You can get your publicity without interfering with my life. Okay?"

Bart thought for a few moments and then nodded. "Quite right! You sound like a seasoned professional, I dare say."

"I don't need lessons in public relations for this. My eyes and ears function. These guys can't even take a walk in private unless they're in disguise. I'd like to give my kids buggy rides."

When Saul hung up the phone, Rich and Harry stood over the babies.

"Sadie, what blood type are you," Rich asked.

"O-positive, same as Saul. Why?"

Rich looked at her. "We may have a ticklish card to play, then," he said in an exaggerated British accent.

"Yes, I noticed," Sadie admitted.

Saul looked at Sadie and then at Rich. He started to rise from the bed, but Sadie grabbed his arm. "Saul, wait... please. Sit down and let me explain something to you." He complied, with caution on his face. "I don't know how to begin. Um, Saul, you know Carl and Roxanne are yours. They have your

69

features already. But Jason ... how can I put it? Well, plain and simple, Jason's not your son."

Saul's eyes widened. "What?"

Sadie continued in a whisper. "You would have found out eventually." Minutes passed in silence. "Saul, say something."

"What am I supposed to say? I searched for you for months, my insides empty. When I finally found you, I was happy about the babes, but now you say one isn't mine." Saul's voice rose with every word he spoke. "You had some blue-eyed stud waiting for your return – like that Harvey fellow. Maybe you should let him keep you bloody safe."

Sadie kept her voice low. "Harvey and I are friends, just friends. Besides, if you remember your high school genetics, it is impossible for a blue-eyed father and a blue-eyed mother to produce a brown-eyed child. Harvey is not the father."

"So after that weekend, you became a trollop," Jo-Jo said with a scowl. Rich raised an eyebrow at Sadie quizzically. Harry didn't hear the conversation. He just stared at Jason.

Sadie looked into Saul's hazel eyes. "I never made love voluntarily with anyone but you."

"Who's the bloody father, then?" Saul asked.

"It shouldn't matter."

"That's all fine and good. Maybe it doesn't matter that I'm pushing off, either."

"Do you want to cancel your check?" she asked.

"No," Saul snorted. "Make it last. You won't get any more. Let Jason's father pay some support!"

Silence fell over the room again as Saul waited for Sadie to respond. She didn't. She stared at her hands resting on her lap. Saul took hold of Sadie's chin, his fingers pressing into the hollow of her cheeks. "I can't believe I fell for your act twice? I must be brain-dead."

Sadie raised one hand and stroked the skin on the back of his hand. "You're hurting me."

"Not as much as you've hurt me. I've been through hell the last eight months, wondering if I'd ever see you again, and now this!" Saul's arm flew into the air, releasing her cheek. "I was a pudden-head. At least I found out when I did. Now I won't stand around like a square peg over a round hole the whole flippin' summer with you!"

He stomped toward the door, where Rich grabbed his arm. "Don't leave now, mate. She'll tell you who the father is." Rich turned toward Sadie. "Won't you?"

Saul waited without turning back around.

Sadie continued to study her hands. "It shouldn't matter."

"That's right," Saul shot back. "No matter who he is, he can have you." Saul pulled his arm away from Rich and left. Bart was right behind.

"Sauly, c'mon." Bart begged, "Think! You had her on stage. She'd be a dead winner in a paternity suit. We don't need trouble again."

Saul shot Sadie a nasty look through the doorway. "She won't do anything. If she did, she'd be the clever clogs getting the bad press, anyway. The whole world would find out her true occupation. She's a slut!" Jo-Jo scowled at her and joined Saul, with Harry coming slowly behind.

Rich shook his head and ran after the rest of the group, catching up to them as they stepped into the elevator. "You're getting the wrong end of the stick, Matey," Rich said to Saul. The elevator doors closed and it began to move.

"No," Jo-Jo corrected, patting Saul on the back. "I told you she wasn't worth going up the spout about. She played you for a schmuck to get your lolly."

Bart turned to Jo-Jo. "If that were true, why didn't she contact us when she found out she was gravid?"

71

Jo-Jo's hand rested on Saul's shoulder. "Most likely, she didn't know who sired the tots. Once the birthing took place and she saw who belonged to whom, it would be a different matter. She would've sued by the time we landed in England."

"And now she can start a paternity suit against TWO Spidars," Rich stated. He stopped the elevator between floors.

"What?" Bart asked.

"Yes. What? What question did I ask Sadie before she told Saul he wasn't Jason's father?" Without letting them answer, Rich continued, "What's Jason's blood type on his crib card?"

They all shrugged. Rich smiled. "Jason is A-positive. What does that tell you stone-heads?"

"Are you sure?" Harry asked, his eyebrows raised. "I'm A-positive."

"Quite positive, no pun intended," Rich quipped. Harry looked at Saul. Saul looked at Jo-Jo. They all looked at Bart, who wasn't in the room that fateful night long ago, but he knew what happened by the next day.

"I was a bit of a twerp, then," Saul muttered. He pressed the elevator button to return to the second floor.

Rich stood in front of the door to block the exit. "Expect to get your butt kicked out of her room. You said some right nasty things to her." Saul lowered his head.

Harry beamed as the group emerged from the elevator. He ignored Saul's request for everyone to stay in the hall. As Saul tip-toed into Sadie's room, Harry followed. The room was darker than before, with music playing on the television. The curtain had been pulled to block light from the hallway. The men heard the bed squeak and then a clicking noise, as Sadie dialed a phone.

Next to the two men stood the three bassinets, but one was empty. Saul and Harry slipped through the curtain behind the raised head of the bed. Sadie sat in a semi-reclined position, her knees bent to support Jason on her thighs. The phone had been pulled onto the bed and its base sat next to her so the cord would reach her head. The men silently watched her stroke the baby's face as she spoke on the phone.

"Hi, Mary. It's me... Yes, two boys and a girl, 6-9, 6-13, and 6-10... Right after you left, an hour ago now... Carl, Roxanne, and Jason... Yes, they're all gorgeous... No, I'll call Mom in the morning... I don't know yet, probably just enough to stop her from worrying... Yeah... Thanks... Love you too. Bye."

With the phone back on its base, she bent forward and kissed Jason's cheek. "That was Mary. You'll like her. She's helped me a lot these last few months." Sadie played with Jason's tiny fingers. "Don't you worry. We'll make it. And don't you listen to anyone who says you're different from the other two. To me, you're just as special as the others. Your father is a talented, hard-working man too. Someday, when you're grown, I'll explain things." Jason's eyes twinkled. He had Sadie's gold specks mixed with the dark brown.

"I may not be able to give you all the fancy toys your father could, but I promise you'll get all the love you need. We'll make it. With love, we can do the impossible, see the invisible, dream the unimaginable."

Tears ran down Sadie's cheeks. "Although... maybe if I did have money, I could..." She took a deep breath and stopped her tears. "NO! Money can't buy love. As long as you have the necessities, you can survive. And at least your Uncle Saul has helped us get through the first year, so I can get my high school diploma and a good job."

Saul reached out to smooth Sadie's hair, but Harry grabbed his arm and shook his head. Sadie continued, "I'd prefer to stay home with you guys, but I can find a good babysitter, Mary maybe, and we can enjoy the weekends together." She hugged Jason tenderly. "Whatever happens,

73

don't forget that I loved you the first time I felt your kick."

Jason hiccupped and she giggled. "So you're the one with that problem. Now I know!" She giggled again. "Considering how you were conceived, it's not a surprise." Saul and Harry both smirked. She continued in a more serious tone. "You'd better watch out when you grow up. Remember, although a little alcohol can help relieve stress, too much can make you do things you wouldn't otherwise."

Jason's eyelids drooped, as if weighted. "You're tired, aren't you, Sweetheart? Well, I'll let you sleep. We have the rest of our lives to talk. Sleep in peace. God will take care of us. We'll make it together."

She rose and gently laid him in his bassinet. "You resemble your father already." Tears gathered again. Voices in the hall caught Sadie's attention. She looked up from Jason's crib as a nurse entered, followed by Bart, Rich, and Jo-Jo. The nurse walked to the bassinets and reswaddled the babies.

"Now what do you want?" Sadie asked the men as they entered. "If you came back to convince me not to sue, you needn't bother. My original promise still stands. I won't make trouble. Just leave me alone. I don't need any of you. Go back to your *beautiful people*, as you call them, and stop bothering the commoners."

Saul and Harry moved out from behind the bed. When Sadie turned to go back to bed, she bumped into Saul, which made her jump. Retrieving her tongue, she asked, "How long have you been here?"

"Long enough," he replied. He put his arms around her and held her tight, planting a soft kiss on top of her head. Moments later, he lifted her chin to look in her eyes and wiped tears from her glowing cheeks. "Can you possibly forgive a man with foot-in-mouth disease? I..."

"Gentlemen!" a nurse interrupted. "Visiting hours are over. It is time for you to leave. The new mother needs to rest."

Sadie nodded. "Yes, in two more hours, it will be feeding time at the zoo. In any case, goodbye. May your careers soar to new heights."

"I hope that doesn't mean what I think it does," Saul whispered in her ear. "Please give me another chance. I jumped ship too quick. It wasn't sinking. I'm sorry, Luv." He kissed the top of her head again.

Sadie pushed him away and climbed into bed. "It won't work. And I'm too tired to argue."

"But, Luv..." Saul began. Bart guided the men from the room. "C'mon, Saul. You two can tiff later."

As the Spidars waited for the elevator, Harry smiled at the others. "She's a bit spunky, isn't she?"

"So is Saul, when he wants to be," Bart replied. "My money's on him." Saul smiled mischievously, a good imitation of Rich's smirk.

*

The next morning, Sadie spent a few tense moments with her mother, Lucille, who had come to the hospital.

"Well, young lady, what do you have to say for yourself now? You could have called last night to say you were in labor. When you weren't home for supper, I worried. You may be a mother now, but as long as you're under my roof, you answer to me."

"I'm sorry," Sadie said sweetly. "The babies' fathers came to see me last night and wanted to talk..."

Lucille's eyes flared. "If you had just talked eight months ago, you wouldn't be here right now. Who is the bum?" clearly not noticing the plural.

"It doesn't matter," Sadie replied with a determined expression on her face. "I received a check for the first year's support. I'll be moving to an apartment."

"The man belongs in jail."

"Mom, the whole thing was an accident. Besides, if a father is in jail, how can he support the babies? Aren't they gorgeous, Mom?!"

*

After her release from the hospital, Sadie set up her home in an apartment complex called Clayton Arms. The complex included five three-story buildings housing twenty apartments on each floor, a total of sixty per building and three hundred in the complex.

Sadie's first-floor, two-bedroom was small and easy to keep clean. The working kitchen had ample cupboards. The L-shaped living/dining area had a bay window in the dining room and sliding glass doors off the living room, with a tiny patio outside. Closets lined the hallway that led from the living room to the bedrooms and bathroom at the end. Low-pile, variegated brown carpet softened the floors except in the kitchen and bath. White walls surrounded all the rooms.

$200 a month rent seemed extravagant to Sadie, but the quiet location outside the city meant one less worry during her studies when summer ended.

Besides caring for the babies, she kept busy furnishing the apartment with cheap, functional second-hand pieces. The Women's Association at the East Baptist Church gathered old dishes, pots and pans, glasses, and most utensils she needed in the kitchen.

In the living room, Sadie arranged a mint green sofa-bed, pine lamp stands, a playpen near the sliding glass doors, and a two-tiered table with a 19-inch television on top and a record player on the bottom. Flowered curtains with shades of blue, green, and brown on a white background brightened the room. In the dining room, a plastic chandelier hung above a blue Formica table with four matching chairs. Extra folding chairs and a leaf for the table hid in the hall closet.

Sadie had more fun with the nursery. She painted the walls pastel yellow. On the window hung brightly colored curtains full of little bears, lions, rabbits, and giraffes. Three wooden cribs were donated by church women who had already completed their families. She painted the cribs blue, yellow, and pink, so she didn't get confused as to which child goes where. She also made brightly colored mobiles from yarn and construction paper to hang over each crib.

The nursery size presented the biggest problem. With a changing table in front of the window, a rocking chair next to it, and the cribs, no room remained for dressers. Sadie made a few calls until she found a secondhand shop with shallow dressers that fit in the closet.

The master bedroom could wait a while. For a week, Sadie permitted Saul's daytime attentions and sent him to a hotel at night. When she finally let him sleep overnight, he slept on the sofa bed, while she used a sleeping bag behind the locked door of the master bedroom. A sheet served as the window curtain in that room.

Two days later, Saul's mother, Ruth, flew from England to meet her grandchildren. Saul had explained the situation, but Ruth refused to accept Sadie's sleeping bag arrangements. "If my son can't afford to treat you right, then he should leave." Sadie blushed and dropped the subject.

Ruth insisted that Saul accompany her to a furniture store. Before she went home to England, the master bedroom contained a king-sized brass bed, solid oak dressers and night stands, and crystal lamps. The sheet on the window was replaced with purple velvet drapes to match the bedspread. Pale pink paint on the walls accented the whole arrangement.

The first night after the furniture arrived. Sadie closed and locked the bedroom door, pulled the sleeping bag out of the closet, and laid it on the floor.

*

On a bright July morning two weeks later, Sadie stood in front of her full-length mirror in the bedroom with a wide smile on her face. Between the breastfeeding and special exercises, she was now able to sque-e-eze into her pre-maternity clothes. Another couple of weeks like this, she thought, and I'll have my figure back.

Saul was getting himself a second cup of tea in the kitchen when the phone rang. He answered it and Sadie could hear him as he spoke: "Hello... Oh, hi, Rich!... They're great... No, not yet... On the flippin' couch right now... Yeah, that's dead straight... Sounds fab! Four are ready on this end. This place would be tight, rather like a bedsit... No, she won't mind. Let's have a crack, then... I don't know about that one. Wait a tick. It might work out better for me... See the rest of you next month then. Ta-ta!"

Sadie took one last look at her reflection and walked to the kitchen. "What was that about?" she asked, pouring a glass of milk and joining Saul at the dining table.

"My mates want to come here next month. We need to practice the new songs for the upcoming record and small tour. I told them to come ahead, if it's set with you, then?"

Sadie looked around the small living room. "Where would you practice in here? Won't it be cramped? Won't the babies bother everyone?"

Saul put his arms around her. "I told them this place is small – we'll use the acoustic stuff. When the tinies bug us, we can slag off at the pool. If that doesn't aid us, I could go to their hotel room, but I'd prefer it here with you. What do you say?"

Sadie smiled. "I'd love it!" He was getting to her again, and she knew it. The past month he had been a perfect gentleman. He helped feed the bottled baby and changed a few diapers.

"Luv, there's one more thing," Saul said. "Harry wants to come early to get acquainted with his son." Sadie's eyes widened. He looked into them and said earnestly, "Those were his words, not mine. You know I haven't favored any."

Saul was right. He treated them all the same. "When does Harry want to come?" she asked.

"He'll be here at three tomorrow. He could have the couch while I join you in the other room."

"I don't know…" Sadie began to say. Saul interrupted with a passionate kiss. It worked. Sparks began to fly and Sadie melted.

*

During the day, Sadie kept busy with the babies while Harry and Saul talked, wrote songs, and swam. In the evening, after the triplets were put to bed, Saul and Sadie cuddled on one end of the couch and Harry sat on the other end. They watched TV until bedtime.

Another ritual developed, too. Each evening, Saul asked the same question: "Do you love me yet? Will you marry me?"

"I'm not sure," Sadie usually responded. "And to me, marriage is for life."

After almost a month of the same response, Saul assumed he would get the same, but two nights before Jo-Jo and Rich were due to arrive, Sadie kept her eyes on the television as she replied calmly, "Yes to both questions."

Saul automatically turned back to the television. When he realized what Sadie said, he jerked his head toward her again. She grinned at him, a flicker of tease in her eyes.

"Do you mean it?" he asked.

"Yes."

His arms circled her shoulders and he gave her a strong, urgent kiss.

"Can I have one of those," Harry asked with a smirk. "I need practice kissing the bride." Saul consented and went to the phone in the kitchen.

Sadie turned toward Harry, expecting a peck. What she received was a repeat of Saul's kiss, sparks and all. Shocked, she tried to pull away but couldn't. Harry held her too tightly.

In the background, Saul spoke to Rich. "...You'd better bring your tuxedos. She said yes... I don't know. Soon I hope... Thanks. Me too..."

*

"I know this is what I want to do, but I'm scared anyways," Sadie said as she waited in the bedroom. The babies had been fed, changed, and put into the playpen, for ease of transportation when they fall asleep later.

"All brides are nervous," Mary replied. "Don't worry. As long as you love him and he loves you, you'll be fine."

"But he lives in a different world. Will I fit?"

Mary smiled. "No matter who you marry, life changes. Don't lose faith. It will carry you through the rough times."

"My faith is what finally convinced me to marry him. Somehow – I don't know why – I think we were meant to be together."

Sadie walked down the hall wearing a magenta colonial-style gown. She had made up her cheeks to match the color of the gown. Her sister, Carol, stood as maid of honor in hot pink.

80

Harry was best man. He and Saul wore bright blue tuxedos. Rich and Jo-Jo sat on the couch wearing their white ones.

Sadie's mother had signed the papers for Sadie to get married, but she refused to come to the wedding. Gene and Mary gave Sadie away, and Reverend Bee officiated.

After changing clothes, everyone walked to the club house of the complex, closed to other residents during this reserved time. Harry and Saul carried the playpen with the triplets sound asleep inside. Pretzels, veggies, chips, and various dips lay on a long table as appetizers. Pizza with the works would be the main course. Gene, a baker by trade, provided a traditional wedding cake for dessert.

The receiving line stood in the shallow end of the pool in swim suits. Everyone congratulated the bride and groom with a handshake or peck on the cheek, with one exception: Harry gave Sadie a long, lingering kiss. Her cheeks turned rosier.

"It's a good thing this isn't the deep end," Rich snickered. "They'd drown."

"Hey, Harry, come up for air!" Saul exclaimed.

"Just having a giggle," Harry chuckled as he released Sadie. Luckily, the water came up to his waist.

*

The Spidars quickly settled into a routine. During the day, the men practiced new songs as the triplets listened in the playpen for hours at a time. In the early evenings, the men went for a swim. Supper was ready when they returned. Afterwards, Rich and Jo-Jo went to their hotel room. Harry continued to sleep on the sofa-bed.

One night at the end of the summer, Rich and Jo-Jo stayed later than usual. The day had been very hot. Sadie wore her checkered hot-pants and midriff top. Harry helped her put the triplets to bed. Finished with Jason, he stood at the doorway, watching her sing to the children.

"Rock-a-bye baby, on the tree top,
When the wind blows, the cradle will rock.
When the bow breaks, the cradles may fall,
And Mommy will catch them, babies and all."

She repeated the verse to each baby individually. As she sang, she stroked the baby's back until eyelids dropped. When they had all fallen asleep, she tip-toed out of the room and shut the door behind her.

In the hallway, Harry kissed her gently on the lips. "I need to speak to you, Pet," he whispered as he guided her into the master bedroom. Sadie's heart beat faster.

"Has Saul explained the pact we made when we formed the Spidars?"

"Yes," Sadie replied. "He told me you guys share supplies because someone always forgets something."

"Did he tell you we share everything?"

"Like replying to journalists and such? Yes."

"Did he mention about women? When someone feels like a stud without a filly, the rest share theirs."

"What?" Sadie screeched.

Harry put his hand over her mouth. "Sh-h-h, you'll wake the tots. Relax. I'm not sopped this time. If it makes you feel better, we also share responsibility. If anything ever happens to Saul, you'll be well-tended..."

Sadie didn't hear any more. She was in shock. By the time her senses returned, it was too late. She lay naked on the bed, with Harry on top of her. His fervent kiss made sparks fly as his body gyrated to the beat in her heart. A few minutes later, it was over and Sadie wept softly.

"I've taken a shine to you, too," Harry said as he dressed and left to join the men.

"Collecting on the pact, huh!" Rich quipped. "How was it?"

Harry smiled broadly. "Fab! She is a bit brassed off now, though." He glanced at Saul. "Sorry."

"Thanks a long chalk," Saul growled.

"Goodnight, Vienna," Jo-Jo said. He rose and left the apartment. Rich joined him.

*

Saul and Harry woke the next morning to the babies' screams. This was not normal. Sadie never let them get past the whimpering stage. Both men vaulted to see what was wrong. When they couldn't find Sadie, their worry intensified. With babies in their arms, they searched the halls. They searched the lobby of the building. They searched the basement laundry room. Still no Sadie. They returned to the apartment shrugging their shoulders.

While Saul prepared bottles for the infants, Harry amused them in the playpen. When he glanced upwards, Harry noticed the lock on the patio door turned sideways. The door was unlocked. He walked to the door, then called Saul over.

Sadie lay on a lounge chair over to the side, eyes closed. A broad smile covered her face.

"Must be a good dream," Harry remarked.

"Not necessarily," Saul countered. "She always kips with a smile." He shook his head. "What would she be doing out here? How did she get out without us hearing her? Why?" He wondered if her unannounced departure had something to do with Harry's actions yesterday. Maybe Saul's later cuddles hadn't soothed her as much as he had thought.

Chapter 6 - March 1967

"Do you know where you've been?
Do you know where you're going?
Are you going forward or backward?"

The words from last Sunday's sermon stuck in Sadie's mind. In less than a year, her path had curved sharply – from student to mother and wife. She didn't know where her life would lead. After the triplets were weaned, Saul convinced her to join him on tour at least one weekend each month. This was her third trip. Sadie's mind wandered. Each time, Harry had been his usual ardent self—she was accustomed to him now. However, during the last visit, Rich and Jo-Jo had collected on the pact, too.

Sadie's upbringing told her this situation was wrong, but something inside said to be patient. Everything would work out. After all, she thought, the men share a special closeness, closer than brothers, like a common mission in life. Maybe the men need to be as close to the Spidar women, too. Or was she merely making excuses for it? Only time would tell.

She watched out the plane window as they approached the Las Vegas airport and the plane began its descent. She smiled. Saul wasn't expecting her this month. She had told him she couldn't get a sitter. Both Mary and Sadie's sister, Carol, were busy.

Last night, though, during a phone conversation with Saul's mother, Sadie had mentioned her canceled trip. Ruth arrived at the apartment first thing this morning. *Ruth's a sweetheart,* Sadie thought as she walked down the ramp. She looked at her watch and smiled again. She had plenty of time to stop at the beauty salon a neighbor had recommended.

This trip would be fun. Sadie liked the way Saul's eyes lit up when she surprised him with little things, like the homemade apple pie she had taken with her last month. Hopefully, he would be pleased this time too. And this time, although they have a show tonight, they have the whole day off tomorrow.

By the time Sadie emerged from the salon, the sun had set but the air was warm. Las Vegas was lit up like a giant Christmas tree. She decided to walk to the Hotel Sahara. She would see more of the city this way.

Stopping in front of a haberdashery, she stared at one display in particular. A clasp of velvet doves held a short net in front of a mannequin's face. She moved until her reflection was in line with the mannequin, and she studied the reflection. Her hair was layered, with bangs falling to her eyebrows and the top feathered to increase height. The netting covered her eyes completely. The beautician had also applied a waterproof make-up and taught Sadie how to add color in the right places and amounts.

This might be better than I planned, she thought. Saul won't recognize me, especially since the veil covers my eyes. The clasp will fit right at the base of the feathering.

*

"...*You're gonna say you love me, too-o-o...* "[3] As Saul adjusted his guitar for the next song, he noticed movement in the wings. A lady approached Bart. She wore jeans and a tight turtleneck sweater that accented shapely assets.

"Who's that?" Saul whispered to Jo-Jo, with a jerk in the lady's direction.

Jo-Jo glanced over. "Don't know. Most likely one of the

pieces for tonight's bash."

"Oh." Saul turned back to the audience and spoke into the microphone. "This next song is about a very special girl."

"*...in love for the first time...*" [12] In the wings, Bart spoke to Sadie. "Saul said you weren't coming."

"I wasn't. I couldn't find a sitter until this morning."

Bart fumbled with his suitcoat buttons. "I, uh, arranged for some ladies at the party later. Saul's been down-in-the-dumps since your call. I thought they, uh, could jolly him up. The party is for the roadies, too, but the women for the Spidars will be dressed a little differently to avoid mix-ups."

"That's fine," Sadie said with a smirk. "Those women can take care of the other three. Don't let on who I am. I want to do it my own way." Bart nodded his agreement.

"*...She done me good...*" [12] As the last phrase of the song sank in, a blush rose on Sadie's cheeks, a smile on her lips. When she looked toward the stage Rich winked at her. Oops. He knew who she was. She wiped the smile off her face, put her finger to her mouth, and pointed toward Saul. Rich winked again and nodded to show he understood.

"*...Good night,*" Jo-Jo said to the audience an hour later. "*We hope you enjoyed the show.*" As the curtains closed on the second encore and the stage lights dimmed, the men skipped off stage.

Sadie could hear the fans yelling for more, but she knew by Jo-Jo's headshake that there would be no more live music tonight. Two encores were enough. Rich was the first to reach the wings. He put his arm around Sadie. "Glad you could make it," he whispered in her ear.

She pushed him away with a discreet smile on her lips, then turned toward Saul and put an arm in his. She had to quicken her pace to keep up with him. "I hear you're feeling down," she said in a husky voice he wouldn't recognize. "I'm here to help you feel better."

"No thanks."

"Why not? A headache?" Sadie replied, a twinkle in her eyes. Saul didn't notice through the veil nor respond in any way. "I can get you in the mood," she offered.

"No, thanks."

"Bart told me you miss your wife. When he ordered the girls and told me how you felt, I came to take care of you personally."

"No one can make me forget my wife," he muttered.

Sadie could hear Rich's chuckle behind them. She almost laughed herself, but she remembered how fast Rich had recognized her smile earlier. She put one hand over her mouth until she regained a serious expression. "I don't want you to forget your wife, believe me." Rich chuckled again. "I just want to make you feel better tonight."

At the door of the limousine, Sadie stepped aside and waited until all the Spidars had jumped inside. Then she climbed in and sat on Saul's lap. "Pick on someone else," Saul grumbled.

"I'll volunteer!" Rich exclaimed.

Sadie controlled her smile but couldn't control her blush. "Yours is waiting at the party," she told Rich.

Saul noticed the sudden color of her cheeks. "Oh, a blushing knock-up! That's a whore of a different color."

"Yes, I'm different and proud of it. I'm the best. I will take you on a trip out of this world."

"You couldn't come close to my wife."

Sadie put her hands on Saul's forehead. "You mean the way your wife strokes your forehead with her fingertips when you're tired or the way she brushes your hair to the sides?"

Her hands moved along the path she described. "Then her

fingertips gently glide down the side of your face, making you tingle with excitement as they meet at your chin and trace your lips ... before wandering ... uh, lower."

Sadie's hands stopped at the neck. She could feel his response under her butt. She could hear Rich whisper to Harry and Jo-Jo. All three chuckled when Saul's face changed from anger to desire. "And when your wife kisses you, you say sparks fly." She gave him a peck on the cheek, but before he had a chance to respond, she slid onto the seat beside him. "Do Englishmen ever offer a cigarette to a lady?" she asked in an innocent tone.

Flustered, Saul took a moment to catch up to the conversation. "A lady, yes. As for you, I don't know." Saul reached into his shirt pocket and pulled out his pack. Sadie's voice lost its huskiness. "Oh, never mind. Those English ones are too strong. I'll smoke my own." She reached into her purse, brought out a Winston, and smiled openly.

"Why, you little...! Why didn't you tell me you were coming?" Without giving her a chance to reply, he pulled her back onto his lap and kissed her. The other men laughed at him. As she broke away, she pressed her fingertip on Saul's lips. "Later." She returned to her seat and lit her cigarette.

"So, why didn't you tell me of the change in plans?" Saul repeated.

"Wasn't this way a little more fun?"

Saul licked his lips. "Mm-m-m," was all he said.

A rambling log home housed the after-show party. At the main entrance, a hallway to the left led to four bedrooms. On the right, one large room contained a living room in the near half and the kitchen and dining room in the far half. An island with a butcher block surface separated the kitchen and dining room. The mahogany dining table pushed against the side wall was laden with foods and beverages. A semi-circle of captains' chairs faced the living room. Burgundy carpeting cushioned the three rooms. On the other wall of the living room stood a floor-to-ceiling entertainment center, including a 30-inch color television, a stereo with state-of-the-art components, and rack after rack of records and tapes.

While the others went to the dining table to fix a drink, Saul and Sadie made a left turn at the hallway. An hour later, Saul emerged, grinning and holding up three fingers. Sadie appeared flushed.

James Brown music filled the air. Rich and Jo-Jo were dancing with two pretty women in the middle of the floor. Contented looks on both men's faces revealed that they had made trips to the left side of the house themselves.

Harry sat on a contemporary couch along the front wall of the living room. A cute, blonde woman talked to him, but he stared into space.

"What's wrong with Harry?" Saul asked Bart.

"I don't know," Bart replied. "That's the second bird he's given a miss to. We only have three more not spoken for."

"Must be sick."

"He was fine in the limo."

"I'll go over and chat with him," Sadie offered. "Maybe I can get him to open up." She walked over and sat on an overstuffed chair perpendicular to Harry's couch.

"Would an Englishman offer a cigarette to a lady?" Sadie asked. The blonde woman rose and walked away.

Harry started to reach into his pocket but pulled his hand away as a grin spread across his face. "Only the strong English gaspers, I'm afeard."

Sadie smiled. "That's okay. I have my own." She removed one from her purse, lit it, and took a long drag. As she blew out the smoke, she looked around the room. A few couples danced to a slow Elvis tune. The other Spidars gathered near Bart, who gestured toward some women standing in the kitchen.

Turning back to Harry, Sadie smiled again. "Bart tells me you're acting strange. Are you feeling all right?"

Harry's grin faded. "He can toss himself off."

"He cares about you. We all do. Something's wrong. You're normally the first one to pick out a sex-kitten and make your exit. Care to talk about it?" She smiled brightly.

Harry didn't reply right away. He gazed into Sadie's eyes. "I feel like... I'm missing something. This scene gives me the nadgers. Seeing you with Saul in the car made me wish I had a bird of my own, full of surprises, yet easy to chat up. I'm dead tired of the dolly-bird groupies who throw themselves at me... or the ones we pay for. I want one like... you." The last word came out in a murmur.

Sadie laughed.

"Thanks a lot, Pet!" Harry pouted. "I pour out my soul and you have a bit of a giggle about it all."

"Sorry," she replied, trying to stop. "I'm not laughing at you. I was just thinking how different a star's real life is... compared to how fans visualize it. A lot of men envy you for the thousands of women who are easy marks. You should take that as a compliment. If fans treat you like a brother, you put on a good show; if they treat you like a lover, you're the best in town." Sadie couldn't resist adding, "at the moment."

"So what do you suggest? Should I accept their gracious offers for the rest of my life?"

"Could you handle all of them? ... Still, look around you. There are good women everywhere, even here."

Harry laughed. "Here!? These are clean knock-ups Bart hired. They relieve our frustrations without worry about consequences."

"Wait a cotton-pickin' minute, Harry. You're judging these women before you know them. They have lives too."

He scanned the room. Bart was talking to three women in the kitchen. The other Spidars stood in the dining room, smiling devilishly as they watched Bart.

One of the women walked over to Harry and sat next to him. "I hear you need a pick-me-up." Harry ignored her.

Sadie waved her index finger at Saul in playful scolding. He winked at her. The next woman sat on Harry's lap with her arms around his neck. "So, you're a little upset," she cooed. "I can fix that. I'll take you into clouds of pleasure…"

"Go chase yourself," Harry growled as he pushed her off. Sadie giggled, her hands over her mouth. She thought about moving but decided eavesdropping was more fun.

The third woman wore skin-tight pants and a halter top. Draping her oval face, her chestnut hair reached for her shoulders but didn't quite touch them as it curled under and came forward to her chin. The woman said nothing. She knelt on the floor in front of Harry. Her determined blue eyes met Harry's dark brown ones and held his attention as she deftly unsnapped his pants and worked on the zipper. As her warm probing fingers found their target, Harry broke from her spell.

"Keep your mitts to yourself!" he yelled. "You… you… you tart!"

The woman jumped up. "You have some nerve!" she yelled back. "You think you're better than me, but you're not!" Sadie's giggle made the woman turn to her. "What are you laughing about? I suppose you think you're better, too, because you're married to one of these guys!" Tears formed in the woman's eyes.

Sadie rose and took the woman's hand in hers. "I'm not laughing at you, Peggy," she chuckled. "Just at the actions and reactions of both of you. Think about it."

Silence followed. The woman turned back to Harry, her facial muscles relaxed. "I guess I overreacted. I wanted that bonus so badly, I was mad when I lost it."

"What bonus?" Harry asked.

The woman glanced at Bart. "Oops! I shouldn't have mentioned it."

"What bonus?" Harry repeated, sternly this time. The woman shrugged and admitted, "Bart offered a five hundred dollar bonus to the girl who could put a smile on your face tonight."

"That bugger! My knuckles will sandwich his bum-fodder face." He stood quickly and stormed toward Bart.

"How did you know my real name?" the woman asked Sadie after Harry left. "I use the name Ingrid in this job."

"You look like a Peggy," Sadie shrugged.

Peggy and Sadie talked for over an hour. Peggy had lost her parents in a fire when she was ten. There were no other family members. Because of a glitch in the state law, she spent eight years going from foster home to foster home, forming no lasting relationships with anyone. When Peggy was legal age, she rented an apartment and worked as a bank teller. For three years, she tried to save enough money to get a degree in accounting.

About a month ago, she realized she would never be able to save enough on a teller's salary, so she changed jobs. Although she had to split her fee with her house-mother at this job, she could keep all bonuses or tips for herself. In the last four weeks, her savings account doubled. "Soon, I'll be able to get out and never stoop this low again," she told Sadie.

The conversation lightened as they discussed children, politics, and music. Later, they went to the powder room together, where Peggy tested Sadie's new make-up. As the two women returned to the sofa, most of the men in the room noticed the change. Harry noticed too, and he sauntered back to the sofa for a longer chat.

A new stack of records rotated on the turntable. The unmistakable beat of a Spidars' tune set Sadie's feet twitching. Without a word, she glided toward Saul, raised an eyebrow, set her glass on the table behind him, slid her hand into his, and nodded toward the dance floor.

"...*Dress it up and they call it pretty*..." [13] Saul and Sadie moved like a team, bodies swaying, hips swinging, and feet moving. On fast tunes, Sadie's eyes remained on Saul's as she matched his every move. The exception was during twirls, but her eyes quickly reconnected afterward. On slow tunes, her head was on his shoulder, but her feet still mirrored every move he made.

"I didn't know she could get her knickers down like that," Rich said.

"Neither did I," Bart replied. "They look like a modern-day Astaire and Rogers."

"Like as not practiced all summer," Jo-Jo piped in.

"Doubtful," Rich retorted, pointing toward the sofa. Harry sat holding Peggy's hand and staring at Saul and Sadie on the dance floor. "Harry looks as surprised as we are. Maybe..." He took a sip out of Sadie's glass. "Nope. Just ginger ale."

Saul and Sadie stayed on the dance floor until it was time to go. They were exhausted, but contented smiles engraved their faces. "You took the biscuit out there," Harry told Sadie. "What are you on?"

Sadie winked at him. "I'm high on love." She intertwined her fingers around the back of Saul's neck and gave him a long kiss. The Spidars, plus Sadie and Peggy, walked leisurely to the waiting limo, which dropped Peggy off at her apartment and returned the others to the hotel.

The next morning, Sadie rose before the men. She dressed

and left without waking anyone. Peggy was already sitting at a table in the coffee shop downstairs.

"Hi," Sadie said cheerily. "Sleep well?"

"Not a wink," Peggy replied. "I couldn't get Harry out of my head. He's not as bad as I imagined. In fact..." She paused.

"In fact, what?"

"He's... kind... of... special," Peggy hesitated. "Isn't he?"

"They all are. So are you. Each one of us is special in our own way." The girls chatted for an hour before heading up to the room.

Upon entering the Spidar suite, Peggy walked into the powder room, carrying the bag of make-up Sadie loaned her. Sadie stood still and listened to the suite noises. She could hear showers running in most of the rooms, but at Harry's door she heard nothing. She opened it and found Harry still in bed, facing away from her. She walked around and sat on the edge of the bed.

First, she shook his shoulders gently. When that didn't work, she tickled his feet. She thought about putting his hands in warm water, but that would make him pee the bed. How about splashing cold water? No, that wouldn't be nice.

There was only one way... the same way she woke Saul many mornings... with a slight revision, of course. She stroked his face with her fingertips and whispered, "I love you."

Harry's eyes shot open with excitement and expectation. Sadie laughed out loud. "Works every time," she giggled. "Peggy awaits out there." She pointed to the door. "Do you want help getting ready?"

Harry bolted out of bed. "Yeah, sure." He ran into the bathroom and jumped in the shower. Sadie followed. She prepared his electric shaver, put paste on his toothbrush, and handed him the towel to wrap along his beltline, his soldier protruding.

94

As Sadie turned toward the door, his arms circled her waist and pulled her closer. "Can you take care of a little problem before you leave," he whispered in her ear.

"No way!"

"Please, Pet. You started it. I can't walk out there like this. It won't take long. You could use your marvelous fingers."

She wet a washcloth with ice cold water and gave it to him. "Here, hang this on it." Sadie giggled and broke his hold on her. She went to the bedroom to lay out his clothes, humming as she worked. Last summer paid off now. She knew which outfits allowed Harry to be comfortable yet sexy. To be prepared for any eventuality, she added his brown bikini undies and sprinkled some of his favorite cologne on his socks and on the collar of his sweater. Then she left.

Saul and Jo-Jo were pouring their second cup of tea at the dining cart when Sadie emerged from Harry's bedroom with a broad smile. She walked over to Saul and gave him a kiss. "Good morning, Hon."

"What were you doing in there?" Saul asked, pushing her away. "When I surfaced this morn, you were gone."

"Did you miss me?"

"You know I did. And you didn't answer my question."

"I had to wake Harry up and then I laid out..."

Jo-Jo broke in angrily. "You left your husband's bed to join Harry – of your own accord!!! I was right about you. You're nothing but a money-hungry she-dragon. You're a slag, to boot. You're...."

With her eyes wide, Sadie listened to Jo-Jo's outburst. Her face turned red with anger, not blushing. By the time Jo-Jo finished, she could control herself no longer. "I didn't do anything wrong!" she screeched at Jo-Jo. "You're the ones who have that stupid pact, the pact that prevents YOUR wife from joining you on tour. You have some nerve, the absolute nerve, to call ME a whore!" Jo-Jo tried to say something, but her screams drowned him out. "I'm tired of your cruel remarks. I'm tired of your evil looks. I'm tired of your garbage music. I'm t..."

Saul slapped her arm. For a moment, she stared at him. Then she ran to the bedroom. He followed her. "I lost my head, Luv." She slammed the door in his face. Rubbing his nose, he turned back to the others.

Harry rushed out of his room, carrying his socks and shoes. He looked at Rich in the bedroom doorway across the way. "What's Sadie on about?" Harry asked.

"I'm in a tizzy, too," Rich said with a shrug, coming into the living room.

Turning to Jo-Jo, Harry repeated, "What's she on about?"

"She wasn't right in the head, so Saul smacked her," Jo-Jo replied with a smirk.

"What set her off?'

"How should I know? All I did was ask why she went to your bed without Saul's permission."

Harry shook his head. "She did nothing." His dimples lifted. "I'll admit I did try to give her the bull." His voice lowered when he saw Peggy walk out of the powder room. "She gave me a pass."

Saul noticed Peggy at the same time. Then he remembered Sadie was meeting her early and walking her up to the suite. He turned and tried the knob on his bedroom door. It wasn't locked, so he opened the door and entered, closing it behind him. He lay on the bed next to Sadie. His arms girdled her. A red handprint emerged on her arm.

"I'm sorry, Luv, but you seemed to have lost your head. And you were saying some dotty things to Jo-Jo."

"He said nasty things to me first." Sadie knew she sounded childish. Oh well, spoken words could not be retrieved.

96

"Come now, Luv." Saul's fingers combed her hair. "You're keen. You know chiding is Jo-Jo's way. You also know he's sensitive about his music. Besides, he and I had been chatting quite a few ticks before we saw you leave Harry's room. Even I had thoughts."

"I didn't..."

Saul nodded as he pressed his finger gently on her mouth. "I remember. You planned to have tea with Peggy this morn. Sorry." He lifted her face and gently kissed her. "Still and all, you should go out and apologize to Jo-Jo."

"Me apologize?" She stared into Saul's eyes. In them she saw the same warmth and compassion that first attracted her to him. She calmed as she realized he was only trying to keep peace between the Spidars.

Without another word, Sadie went into the bathroom. The red mark will fade quickly, she thought. She reached for her make-up case, but remembered she loaned it to Peggy. It didn't matter anyway. Not even tears could smudge this new make-up. When she went to the living room, Harry and Peggy were sharing a love seat. She smiled at them and went to Saul near the dining table.

*

The Spidars spent the rest of the day sightseeing. Because Sadie was underage for gambling, the men would save that for another day. There were enough sites to see anyway. Many casinos had landscaped their exteriors. Sadie especially loved the beautiful garden in front of the Tropicana Hotel. It had a pineapple spurting water in the air in the middle of a round pool surrounded by well-trimmed bushes. Sadie thought the effect was gorgeous.

The many fountains at Caesars Palace also impressed her. The underlying pool had sculpted edges around all three fountains, and a 15-foot tall arborvitae surrounded it, looking as if they guarded the place.

At the Sands Hotel/Casino complex, the group walked around back and between buildings to see a nicely decorated pool with slot machines on one side and table games like craps and cards on the other, guests staying cool in the pool as they played.

Sadie liked Circus Circus Casino best, though, because it was more family-oriented. The second floor was filled with carnival games for children. Looking over the railing on the balcony, she saw the action in the casino below: a pygmy elephant going from table game to roulette wheel to slot machine, jugglers and clowns walking around, and high-wire acts performing throughout the room. Sadie giggled and pointed to the gamblers directly below the tight-rope walkers and other acts. "Those people like to live dangerously." Peggy agreed with a laugh.

The fun-filled day ended with smiles on every face.

*

The next morning, Sadie took the hotel's van to the airport. Before she left, she said good-bye to the men and turned to Peggy. "It's been really nice meeting you. I hope to see you again sometime."

Peggy smiled. "You will. Harry asked me to join him on tour, and I agreed it would be fun."

"Great!" Sadie hugged her. Being cupid is fun, Sadie thought as she left the suite.

Chapter 7 – June Vacation 1967
Part A – Henrietta Apartment

Buzz-z-z-z-z.

"Yes?" Sadie said into the apartment microphone.

"It's us," came Mary's voice.

"Come on in." Sadie pressed the buzzer to open the main entrance door.

Sadie opened the apartment door and waited for Mary and Gene. Fragrances of freshly-baked bread and simmering spaghetti sauce drifted into the hallway. Her blue eyes shone brightly, matching the June sky outside.

"We came for instructions while you can still think clearly," Mary said.

"What do you mean by that?" asked Sadie. She motioned for them to sit on the couch.

Mary smirked. "Once Saul arrives, your head will be in the clouds, like it was at Christmas."

Sadie blushed. It was true. Today Saul would begin three months of vacation from touring and recording, and she felt like a new bride, with the same anticipation and excitement that precedes the wedding night.

"Their plane should have landed ten minutes ago. They'll be here in half an hour." She handed Mary a notebook. "I wrote down most of the instructions. I feel a little guilty, leaving the kids for a month, but Saul wants this to be the honeymoon we never had."

"Young lady," Gene replied. "The only times you've been away from your children were your few visits to Saul and when you went to take the tests for your diploma. How you were able to learn everything in a home study program, I cannot fathom, not with three infants in the house."

"So, where are you going?" Mary asked.

Sadie smiled. "I'll see Saul's home country, England, for two weeks and then we ski in Switzerland for two weeks. The phone numbers are written..."

A ring of the phone interrupted Sadie. "West's Nursery," she said into the phone. "We plant seeds of love. Oh, hi, Rich! Where are you?... Darn it! Can I speak with Saul?... Why not?... Well, tell him I'll be thinking about him tonight... Yeah, I'm sorry, too. See you tomorrow."

Her eyes dulled as she turned back to Mary and Gene. "They missed their flight," she explained. "Do you want to stay for supper? Without the others, I made way too much."

"Did you make your famous homemade noodles?" Gene asked.

"Of course. Nothing but the best for my men."

"Men? Are they all coming?" Mary asked.

"Yes, the others will be with us the whole month." Sadie turned to Gene. "The men are close. I think the closeness helps them cope with the time they spend away from home."

A few minutes later, light knocking came from the apartment entrance door. "Who could that be?" Sadie wondered.

When she opened the door, her eyes brightened and the smile returned to her face. "Why you rat-fink! You got me good this time!" She threw her arms around Rich's neck. Rich guffawed and gave her a soulful kiss.

"Mm-m-m-m, something smells great," Harry said as he entered.

Jo-Jo smirked. "Yeah, it's good we didn't miss our flight."

Peggy smiled as she came in the door. "Honestly, Sadie, the rest of us didn't know Rich's plans until it was too late. On the way here, we stopped so he could pick up some ciggies. He told us about the phone call when he returned to the van. And then he insisted on being the first one you saw."

"Peg, there's no need to explain Rich to me." Sadie looked past her to Saul. He entered and embraced her. There were no words as he and Sadie walked slowly to the bedroom. Yet, the communication was evident to all. Finally, the couple was out of sight with the bedroom door closed.

Thirty minutes later, they returned. Saul smiled from ear to ear and held up three fingers. Sadie glowed. "Where's Gene and Mary?" she asked. "I invited them to stay for supper."

"They went out as we came in," Peggy said with a chuckle. "I heard Gene say something about clouds and they will be back here just before we leave in two days." Sadie blushed.

After supper, everyone relaxed in the living room. Sadie brought out an old iron pot and spoon, handing them to one-year-old Roxanne. All three children screeched with delight. The two boys, Carl and Jason, scrambled to the nursery and returned with two plastic guitars.

"Wuv, wuv me do..." the toddlers sang, as they swayed their hips and bopped their heads up and down. "...I aways be too..." Nobody cared that the guitars sounded tinny. Everyone was too busy laughing. "...So pe-e-e-ese, wuv me do."

After two more songs – "...see wuvs you, ya, ya, ya..." and "...I sood be sweepin' wike a wog..." – the children were worn out but happy. Sadie helped them put away their instruments and get into pajamas. Then they made the rounds saying good night.

Holding Jason in his arms, Harry smiled proudly. "How did you teach them to play, Pet? They're just tinies."

"It's probably in their genes."

Later, after watching television for a while and talking, Sadie rose and moved the television stand and transformed the sofa into a queen-sized bed. The bed stretched from one wall of the small living room to the other when fully extended. Anyone wishing to go from the dining room to the bathroom would have to either walk through the kitchen first or climb over the bed.

"I still can't figure out how four of you will sleep on this thing," Sadie said to the group now sitting at the dining room table.

Rich smiled. "There are six adults here. We're splitting between the two beds."

Sadie tilted her head and a crease formed between her eyebrows. "There are four men and two women, not half and half. That still means two women on one bed and four men on the other."

"Not quite," Harry chuckled. "We discussed this on the way in. We are splitting it down the middle, two men and one woman on each bed. Tonight, you'll lay in here with Jo-Jo and meself. Tomorrow, you and Peg switch. The next day we tootle off."

"You're crazy! Saul just came home!" She looked at Saul with a pleading expression. He shrugged.

With a sly smile, Jo-Jo replied, "You already had your ticks with him. Now it's our turn."

"Besides," Harry added. "We think Saul's yapping about three in-and-outs in one short session is a physical impossibility. We want you to do to us what you do to him."

Sadie scowled at Saul. Saul kissed her on the forehead. "I simply mentioned there's no wait between. That's all."

Harry pulled her away from Saul. "Enough chin-wagging. It's time for some fun."

Forty minutes later, freshly showered, Harry and Jo-Jo reclined on the sofa bed.

"Saul's right," Harry said. "She is quite magical when pressed. Those hands can get a man to fullness just by touching the face."

Jo-Jo nodded. "A nice bit of crumpet. Wonder what she's up to now?"

Harry butted his cigarette out. "I'll have a look-see." He walked down the hallway and found Sadie in the bathroom doorway, staring at the master bedroom door, tears running down her cheeks.

"What's the matter, Pet?" Harry whispered.

Sadie wiped her face. "I miss him so much when he's gone. Now, it's worse. He's in the next room and I miss him more than ever."

He pulled her close to him and she sobbed quietly into his shoulder. He raised her head and looked into her blue eyes. "Go on in, then. And tell Peg to come out to me. They're done. Peg can get one per man done quickly. I heard them all clean up while you were working on Jo-Jo. Go on in."

She lowered her head and looked at the floor. "No. I don't want to be a wife who clings."

"Suit yerself. You can't lurk out here all night, though. C'mon to bed. Jo-Jo and I will keep you plenty warm." With one arm around her shoulders, Harry led her back to the living room. Jo-Jo noticed her red eyes but didn't say anything. She fell asleep in the middle of the two men, with her head resting on Harry's chest. When she went into a deep sleep, the smile returned to her face.

"So what's up?" Jo-Jo whispered to Harry.

"She misses her hubby."

"What a drag."

"Not so. You'd like someone to pine for you that way, too. Every bloke feels better when a bird loves him this much."

"Maybe."

The men woke to the smell of blueberry muffins, bacon sizzling in the pan, and pecan pancakes on the griddle. Sadie whistled as she glided between the kitchen and the dining room, setting the table, flipping the pancakes, and pouring the juice, coffee, and milk.

Harry walked into the kitchen and pecked her cheek. "Feeling chipper, I see."

"Don't tell Saul about last night. Please."

"If you say so, Pet."

Sadie smiled. "Thanks. You men will have to serve yourselves. I hear the kids stirring."

She glanced at Jo-Jo on her way through the edge of the living room. "Get it while it's hot, sleepy-head." At the beginning of the hallway, she turned around. "Can you two please make that thing back into a sofa, please?"

She knocked loudly as she passed the master bedroom. "Rise and shine! Don't waste a beautiful day in bed."

Rich yelled back, "That's not what you say when you're in here with Saul."

Vacation Part B – England

"We are now landing in Liverpool," the flight attendant said over the loudspeaker. *"Please remain seated until the plane comes to a full stop. On behalf of the Queen, we hope you enjoy your visit. The time here is 14:04. You will need to adjust your timepieces…"*

Relieved from the hectic tour and recording schedule, the Spidar men relaxed. They had filled the seven hour trip across five time zones with laughter and song. Both Peggy and Sadie were excited yet nervous. This would be their first encounter with the entire McCarthy and George clans. They couldn't lean on each other for the introductions, either. The first night, each Spidar would visit his own family and then meet up the next night to travel the rest of the trip together.

"Oh well," Sadie sighed. "Day by day, we will survive. As my mom always said, a positive attitude can knock down the thickest wall."

"Yes," Peggy agreed, "Keep a stiff upper lip and all that."

Sadie smiled at the British saying. "Tomorrow will be better," she added.

Saul shook his head. "We're not going to be in Transylvania, girls."

Sadie blushed. She thought they were talking low enough so the men couldn't hear.

Saul's parents, Ruth and Keith McCarthy, lived on the outskirts of town, on a street of well-kept homes. The cab pulled into the driveway of a baby-blue, colonial-style house with yellow shutters. Strips of flower beds lined the driveway. Yews spread at the four corners of the house and at the entryways. The house was smaller than Sadie imagined but large enough for company.

The house quickly filled with aunts, uncles, cousins, and close friends. The evening passed with pleasant conversation. Later, Sadie plopped onto Saul's childhood bed. "You were right, Hon. Tonight wasn't all that bad."

"Hmm-m-m," Saul replied, as he slowly removed the nightgown she had donned.

"Your mother said she wants to meet Harry's girl, so I invited her to go shopping with Peg and me tomorrow. In fact, your Mom talks about Harry and the others as if they're all her boys. Wh..."

"Hush," Saul whispered as his hands roamed the inside of her thighs.

"Oh."

*

Normally, when Sadie shopped at home, she liked to browse. She rarely bought anything other than the item she needed, but she enjoyed a game in which she found nonsense uses for essentials and practical uses for unusual items. This shopping trip, she saw gag gifts in a display window. She convinced Ruth and Peggy to go inside. Soon, all three women played the game.

Ruth stopped in front of a bikini made of red licorice, labeled Candy Pants. "Wouldn't the men have a jolly good time watching a girl swim in these at Blackpool!" Ruth said. "The salt water would crumble them to dust. Then the poor lass would come out in the all-together." Sadie and Peggy smiled at each other.

When the women returned to the McCarthy home, Peggy and Sadie carried bulging bags. Keith met them at the door. Sadie put a smaller bag down near the entrance door. That one would go with Sadie and Saul when they left with the other Spidars.

Ruth smiled at Keith like a school girl, her hair now a bluish hue. "Sadie insisted," Ruth explained to Keith, "What with it being our anniversary and all." Keith held Ruth's hand and escorted her to the den. Sadie sent Harry and Saul to chaperone.

She and Peggy scampered into the kitchen with their loads. No one else was allowed to enter the kitchen for a while, not when Jo-Jo arrived with his wife, nor when Rich brought a foxy redhead he met at a garden party the first night. The redhead would accompany him one more night and then had to go back to her work. The four went into the den with Saul, Harry, and Saul's parents.

Soon, the aromas of steak, potatoes, corn, and freshly-baked cherry pie wafted to the den. "What are they doing in there?" Keith asked.

Ruth rose to check. "Why, bless your little cotton socks!" Ruth exclaimed at the kitchen door. The others joined her.

The table had been moved to the bay window. A lace cloth covered the table, as did fine China, silverware, and Ruth's best crystal. An ice bucket chilled a bottle of wine.

"Chow's ready," Sadie said, scooping the last of the beef gravy into a silver bowl and placing it on the kitchen table with all the other food on the end of the table farthest from the window. Two servings of each course were together with its accompaniments, so the couple could serve themselves without getting up from the table. They were lined up in the order that they would be eaten, and protected from heat loss with pot lids.

"It's time for us to be off," Sadie said. "But before we go, this is for you two." She hugged Ruth and Keith and handed them a brightly-wrapped package. "Happy anniversary! The gift is from all of us," Sadie giggled. "Peg and I picked it up while Mom was at the hairdresser. Have fun tonight, but don't do anything we wouldn't do."

"That leaves the range wide open," Keith replied with a smile.

"By the looks of the kitchen, you did a lot of shopping for tonight," Ruth said, as she opened the package with care. Her eyes opened wider and a blush rose on her cheeks, but she didn't touch the item inside. "Whatever will I do with these?!"

Keith smiled. "I may be able to find a use for them." He pulled out a pair of Candy Pants.

Saul scowled at Sadie as the rest of the group said their goodbyes to Saul's parents. "That's me Mum," Saul scolded quietly.

"Older people can have fun too," Sadie whispered back. "Did you see the twinkle in your dad's eyes?"

*

The Spidars ate at a quaint café with outdoor tables near their hotel. The evening was clear and warm. A salty ocean breeze perfumed the air. Sadie wasn't surprised everything tasted so good. In this atmosphere, anything would.

Afterward, they rode a few miles in their mini-bus and stopped at a row of buildings. Sadie's eyes stuck on a sign near the basement entrance: "Spidar Night! Audience Participation Welcome!" A line of people pretending to be Spidars waited for entrance. She giggled. A quick exit from here should not be necessary. People would think the men were disguised to look like Spidars. They could enjoy themselves without crowds.

Inside, heavy smoke and a faint hint of mold greeted their nostrils. Sadie squinted to see in the dim lighting. A bar claimed one end of the room, a small stage at the opposite end. Forty tables and a small rectangular dance floor filled the middle. A waiter moved three tables together for the Spidars group. The regular band played until ten o'clock. Their renditions of Spidars music sounded like the real thing, but Sadie thought they missed the special aura of the songs.

The band leader stepped to the microphone, saying, "Now it's your turn. Would anyone like to sing or play a Spidars tune?"

Several men took turns singing along with the band. Sadie listened with interest. Some passed. Others sang either off-key, out of tempo, or with words that didn't belong. One man tried to play the guitar while singing along. His playing was good by itself and his voice was good by itself, but together, his timing made the song horrendous.

The audience laughed and joked at each person's attempt. The Spidars laughed along with them. Harry especially enjoyed the man who succeeded in copying his hip gyrations. Too bad his voice was flat.

Sadie looked over at Peggy and winked. "Should we try? We can't be any worse than some of these guys."

Peggy shook her head. "I can't sing."

"Yes you can. I've heard you in the shower. You have a nice voice. Certainly you must know the words by now too." Peggy nodded, still with reservation on her face.

When the two walked up to the stage, the band leader shook his head. "And here we have two females who will try to imitate men." Ignoring his ridicule, Sadie gave the audience her sexiest smile and the girls began, "..*If there's anything I can do*...."[15] Peggy sang soprano, Sadie alto, in good harmony. The two women knew the right moves: the winks, the hip swing, even the head tilt. The audience sat spell-bound. "...*Keep you satisfied*..."[15]

When they finished, the audience stood to clap. "More, More!" Rich yelled. Others took up the chant.

Sadie giggled into the microphone. "Thanks, buster. Now see what you've done!" Rich replied with a belly-laugh, as Sadie conferred with Peggy. This time, they changed the lyrics slightly. "*...You'd love him, too...*"[16]

"They're full of surprises, aren't they?" Harry asked Saul proudly.

Saul answered without taking his eyes off Sadie. "Yes, I never knew."

"*...He gives me everything...*"[16]

Saul continued, "If we do to our audiences what Sadie is doing to me at the moment,..."

Jo-Jo interrupted, "Don't go getting ideas."

When the song ended, silence filled the air. The band leader stepped up to the microphone. "Not bad for women."

"It's easy for a woman," Sadie offered at her microphone.

"How do you mean?

"Well, I just pretend I'm singing to one of the Spidars."

"Yes," Peggy added, "and I'm singing to the other three." The audience laughed, rising as they clapped. When no one else wanted to participate, the band began again and Peggy and Sadie walked to their seats. Some couples in the audience went to the dance floor. Others sat back down and talked.

Saul remained standing to greet Sadie at the table. Wordlessly, his fingertips stroked her face. Sadie's cheeks colored. The tingling between her legs told her what was on his mind. "We'll return in a short," Saul told the others. Jo-Jo just shook his head.

*

In the morning, Saul, Harry, and Jo-Jo sat at the table in the Spidars' suite, drinking coffee and chewing on licorice strings from Candy Pants. Sadie sat between Rich and Saul. Rich pouted. "You do realize, don't you, Sugar, that I'm the only one who didn't get panties. When do I get mine?"

"Yours are saved for a special time."

Rich didn't argue. Everyone knew the redhead wasn't a permanent fixture, even for this part of the trip. After breakfast, they drove the narrow roads of Yorkshire, where rural policemen rode bicycles and carried nightsticks. The group took the causeway to Lindisfarne, an island at high tide and a peninsula when the water was low.

The next day, they stopped at a Middleborough café, where the men introduced Peggy and Sadie to chip-butty sandwiches. Skirting the coastal town of Seaham, the roofs of the houses looked like giant stairs on the sloping coast. The group enjoyed cornets in Scarborough and attended a play at the local theater. Rich's redhead left the next morning.

On the way to Wells to see the cathedral and eat the famed cockles, they passed the flat green spinach fields of Lincolnshire. In Stratford, they went to Shakespeare Memorial Theater and later had fish-and-finger pie. In Jaywick Sands, a shanty town, the homes were as small as Sadie's patio. In Canterbury, the houses were larger and picturesque.

They watched sports car racing in Goodward and polo in Coudray Park. Sadie enjoyed the Asian flavor of the Royal Pavilion in Brighton and the old-world thatched houses in Godshill on the Isle of Wight. She and Peggy tried steak and kidney pie at a London pub. They all witnessed the changing of the guard in the forecourt of Buckingham Palace and admired the classical architecture of St Paul's Cathedral that crowned Ludgate Hill.

Though the days were filled with plenty of pleasure for the women, the men controlled the evenings. After supper, the men brought out a top hat and three cardboard circles. #1 circle would get the first pick between Peggy and Sadie, #2 would get the second woman, and #3 would go without anyone. (Jo-Jo's wife refused to participate, so Jo-Jo always went to his room with her.) When finished with the game, each woman would return to her own man to sleep.

The men seemed happy with this arrangement, unless they happened to be #3, so Peggy and Sadie didn't complain. By the end of the second week, though, Sadie could sense that Saul was quite upset that he was #3 this time. "Care to talk about it," she cooed as she slipped into his bed after the game.

"What's to chat about?" he replied grumpily. "I'm not tickled by this set-up."

"Well, say something to the others then. This certainly wasn't my idea. In fact, as I understand the pact, you guys were only supposed to share women if someone was alone. Jo-Jo has his wife, Harry has Peg, you have me, and Rich, well, he may have a girl tomorrow night to take along to Switzerland. I think this sharing thing has gotten out of hand."

"That's dead straight." He stared at the ceiling. "They've all had a taste of your sweets. If you didn't get them in such a high feather with your magic hands, this wouldn't happen."

"So this is all my fault, now?"

Saul nodded, pulled Sadie to him, and fell asleep with her body nestled in his arms.

Vacation Part C – Switzerland

"We are now landing in Davos, Switzerland. We hope you enjoyed your flight. Thank you for flying Balair. Please remain in your seats until the plane comes to a complete stop."

The Spidars hopped onto a bus that would take them to St. Moritz, a southern town with a population of six thousand, where they could enjoy high elevation summer snow-skiing on Piz Corvatsch. Once there, they checked into the Palace Hotel, five minutes from the action. They relaxed the first evening, but the next day...

"What gives?" Rich asked Sadie after breakfast in the hotel's restaurant. She had no ski equipment nearby, yet she made no move to gather any either.

"I have a phobia about getting hurt," Sadie said with a smile. "There's no way you'll get me on those high slopes."

"Why didn't you say something while we were planning this holiday, then?" Jo-Jo asked with obvious annoyance.

"It doesn't matter. You guys want to ski, so you ski. No big deal."

Harry tilted his head toward the mountain. "What will you do while we're up there?"

"I'll be good, don't worry." Her smile broadened. "Actually, there's a lot to do here beside ski. The desk clerk told me that a wing of this hotel houses a branch of the Laboratory of Scientific Research. They do experimental surgery, and this branch works on broken bones. I'll spend the day watching them. You enjoy vacation your way. I'll enjoy it my way."

"Yuck!"

After the others left, Sadie walked over to a young man in a

113

white lab coat. He put the last bite of toast in his mouth. "Parlez-vous anglais?" she asked in the only foreign language she knew.

The man replied in a familiar accent. "Yes, I speak English, but my French isn't too hot."

"You're American!" she exclaimed.

The man was equally surprised. "So are you! I thought I saw you with that British group."

"You did. I'm Sadie, Saul McCarthy's wife. I'm from upstate New York. Your accent sounds like you may be too."

"Yes. I'm Ivan Gothic, the Third. Fancy, isn't it?" He snickered. "I grew up in Canandaigua, where my father is an obstetrician. What part of New York are you from, Mrs. McCarthy?"

"Call me Sadie. I'm from Rochester. When I was young, my mother took us to Roseland Park in Canandaigua once or twice. It's a pretty town." A long pause in the conversation helped Sadie gather her courage. "Are you connected with the experimental surgery?"

"Yes. I'm a doctor, like my father. I chose a different specialty. Why do you ask?"

"Medicine has always intrigued me. At one time, a while back, I planned to become a doctor. Something came up. I... kind of... hope you might let me watch you at work, or even help, if I could."

"I don't think so, insurance and all."

Sadie flashed a sweet smile. "What will it hurt? I won't break a leg, will I? And, I promise not to leak any deep, dark secrets to the world."

Ivan laughed. "We don't keep secrets here. On second thought, maybe you could help with the English-speaking patients. Since all our nurses are Swiss, you'll have the advantage of native tongue. Come with me, if you promise not to faint when you see blood."

"I promise."

Sadie followed Ivan out of the restaurant and across the lobby. They walked past a blazing, circular fireplace where the past week's injured had gathered to recount their injuries. Sadie giggled as she heard some of their conversations.

"They show off the casts like trophies," Ivan murmured. He stopped at a door with a sign that said: "No admittance – employees only." He inserted a plastic card into an electronic box on the wall and the door opened.

As they walked down a long, white corridor, Ivan wore a more professional demeanor. His voice deepened as he explained, "Each physician has his own office, but the bulk of the work is done in the labs at the end. Since we're usually slow first thing in the morning, I'll show you around the equipment now. In an hour, the first casualty should be admitted. From then until the end of my shift, we'll have a steady stream of patients."

Sadie began her tour at the portable machine the doctors used for two x-rays, one when the patient enters and one after the bone is reset. The machine was much larger than a camera, but it worked the same way. Someone lined up the injury in the eyepiece and snapped a button, and within seconds, a negative of the underlying bones slid out the side of the machines. The secret was in the beds, where the radiation rose at the click of the camera.

Sadie also learned the current procedure. There was no need for general anesthesia or to prep for major surgery, just a xylocaine local, along with sterilization of the area involved. The broken bone was reset in minutes. From start to finish, this new procedure took ten minutes for a compound fracture, five to seven minutes for a simple one, with a few more minutes for the cast. By the time a patient in a normal hospital was wheeled into the operating room, the doctors here put the last touches on the cast.

"Of course," Ivan explained, "everything depends on the patient's mood. He or she must relax. Settling them down can add thirty or forty minutes to the time. If too many excited patients come in at once, the labs back up for the day. That's where we can use you the most: to prevent the backlog at the start. In other words, your job will be to calm the patients. Any questions?"

"Just one," she replied. "What if someone comes in with something more serious than broken bones?"

"You won't see that here. Extensive injuries are flown directly to Davos by helicopter. Davos has the equipment to handle other problems. We only take care of broken bones."

Ivan's timetable proved correct. At the end of the hour, patients began to arrive. The other doctors and nurses appreciated Sadie's help. Her soothing voice while holding a patient's hand calmed everyone's nerves. The nurses could prepare patients faster. The doctors could operate faster. The hall remained free of any backlog. Once in a while, she could even watch a surgery.

At noon, Ivan walked out to the hall. Sadie was trying to calm a novice skier who had tried Dead Man's Run. When she finished and the man was wheeled into the lab, Ivan tapped her shoulder. "Ready for lunch?" he asked. "My treat."

Sadie smiled. "Sure, but first you have to answer a question."

"What?"

"Why would a novice do something so stupid – go on a route that's dangerous even for experienced skiers? He's lucky to be alive at all!"

"Ah-ha! Good question. One I can't answer, I'm afraid. If we could stop the foolishness on the slopes, we would prevent more than half the injuries we treat." They walked to the other end of the hall and entered the hotel section.

At the hotel's restaurant, Sadie couldn't decide what to order. "What's good here?" she asked Ivan.

"That depends. Do you want to eat American or Swiss?"

"Swiss, of course. I can eat American at home."

Ivan ordered Chucheoles (an egg dish eaten with sweet mustard), Berner Rosti (sliced potatoes lightly browned with bacon cubes), and Sales au Fromage (cheesecake) for dessert. As they sipped coffee afterward, a nurse from the lab scurried into the restaurant and over to them.

"Sorry to bother you, Doctor," the nurse said in a heavy Swiss accent. "We have an Englishman who won't settle. Dr. Guattery wants a consult with the two of you."

"What's the primary diagnosis?"

"A compound fracture of the tibia with minor bleeding. Dr. Guattery noticed how your lady-friend pacified patients this morning and he would like you two to help on this one. We're already backed up because of him. We can't take the first x-ray – he refuses to lie still. We're almost desperate enough to use a general anesthesia."

Ivan looked at Sadie. "Would you mind? You have a magic touch."

She smiled. "Flattery will get you everywhere, Doctor." She turned to the nurse as they left the restaurant. "You said an Englishman. Do you remember the man's name?"

"George, Harry George, I think. Why?"

Sadie's pace quickened. Her smile faded. As soon as the electronic doors opened, she heard Harry's screams from the other end of the long hallway. If the other patients lining the hallway listened too long, they would become jittery too.

117

Entering Dr. Guattery's lab, she saw a blood-soaked pant leg shaking sideways on the table. Harry's face was ghostly-white. His glazed eyes focused on a bone protruding midway between his knee and his ankle.

"Harry," Sadie said smoothly, moving his head to get his eyes off the injury. "Harry, it's me, Sadie." His eyes remained cloudy. She turned to Ivan. "He doesn't recognize me. There's only one way I can do this, but it's a bit unorthodox."

"Whatever works, do it," Ivan replied. "We specialize in new methods." Dr. Guattery prepared the portable x-ray machine to get a quick shot as soon as the leg idled.

Sadie bent down and gave Harry a passionate kiss. The fuzzy look left his eyes immediately. "Harry, do you know me?" she asked.

"What kind of question is that?" Harry replied, pulling her down for an encore. The nurse behind Sadie chuckled.

Moments later, she pushed away and turned to the doctors. They had taken the picture, given the local, and were placing the bone in position. Satisfied, she turned back to Harry.

"You'll be okay," she said. "I've watched these men work. They're good." Fear returned to Harry's eyes. Sadie didn't want him to go hysterical again, so she kissed him lightly.

"Some therapy," Ivan said in a teasing voice. "I thought you were Saul's wife."

Sadie blushed without taking her eyes off Harry. "Haven't you heard that love heals all wounds?"

"I can see that. Your lips work better than any pain killer we know. He didn't even flinch when we adjusted the bone. I need another picture and then we can apply the cast."

She turned to Harry with a sexy curve to her lips. "Smile for the camera, Harry. Good publicity, you know." He laughed.

As the doctors examined the last x-ray, Harry told Sadie how the injury occurred: "I was minding my own business when a flippin' tree reached out and grabbed my ski!"

"Did you see a double yellow line?" Sadie asked.

"Are you kidding? I saw stars, not a bloody line!"

"Well, I thought you may have passed the tree in a no-passing zone." Sadie giggled and glanced at her watch. Ten minutes had passed since the last x-ray. Why were the doctors taking so long on the easy part? All they had to do was look at the second x-ray and apply the cast.

"Harry, lie still a few minutes. I want to speak to the doctors. I'll be right back." Harry kissed her hand and waved her away. She walked toward the illuminator. X-rays usually hung in the order they were taken. Yes, Sadie thought. There's the first one with the protruding bone and the second one after the doctors reset it. Huh? The second one after... She bent forward to get a better look.

"I don't see any place that has been reconnected. Did you x-ray the correct leg?"

Ivan went back to Harry, took another picture, returned and hung it on the illuminator. "Here's the one that's bloody."

"This is impossible," Dr. Guattery mumbled. "In all my years in medicine, I've never seen bones heal that fast."

"Maybe it was Sadie's magic kisses," Ivan joked. "The first one stopped the pain fast. Maybe the last one..." As he continued, his voice changed from playful teasing to serious, "Maybe it... No, this can't be."

"Are we dreaming all of this?" Dr. Guattery asked.

Ivan turned to Sadie, his voice soft, but professional. "Have you noticed anyone feeling better after contact with you?"

Sadie laughed. "Not to my knowledge, unless you count..."

"Count what?"

"Oh nothing."

119

"Please tell us," Ivan requested.

"Well, sometimes when the men bicker amongst themselves, I'll make the rounds, giving them individual attention." She winked and continued. "They seem to perk up and get back to work or whatever."

"Has anyone else, other than the men, ever been affected by you?"

"A-ffected, or IN-fected?" Sadie asked with a laugh. Then her face turned serious. "Well, I guess our pediatrician hasn't become rich from my kids."

Ivan didn't smile. Instead, he turned to Dr Guattery. "What do you think? Her first contact subdued the patient better than any painkiller we know. And she gave him another kiss as we placed the bone before we took the second picture. Is it possible?"

Dr. Guattery shrugged. "I can't think of any other reason. This was a compound fracture, not a simple slit."

"Sure, sure," Sadie said. She returned to Harry, who began to fidget. The nurse washed the blood off the leg. No broken skin remained in the area where the bone had protruded.

"All right, Harry," Sadie said with a grin. "You can get up now. You're all better."

"Are you off your rocker? I can't walk on this thing without a cast. The bone'll break again."

"Harry, I don't know how you managed it, but you can tell Rich the joke worked." She raised her voice a little. "And the doctors were very good, too... I'll go out with you, so Rich can have his laugh."

Harry shrugged. "If you say so." He slid off the table and walked gingerly at first. When the pain didn't return, his normal gait did. He and Sadie left, leaving the doctors puzzling over the x-rays.

The Spidars sat in a circle near the fireplace when Harry and Sadie emerged. Peggy jumped up and ran to Harry.

Sadie laughed at Rich. "You got me good!"

"Huh?" Rich asked soberly. "Where's Harry's cast?"

"The doctors say I have magical lips – one kiss and his leg healed."

Jo-Jo shook his head. "Don't be a saucebox. Harry, what happened when they ran the tape over you?"

"Not a glimmer. All I know is I can walk n..."

"Admit it," Sadie interrupted. "You guys were annoyed I didn't ski with you, so Rich cooked up this scheme to get even."

"Don't soft-soap yerself, my dear," Jo-Jo said. "We were having a jolly-good time before this happened. I, for one, didn't think about you at all."

"If you say so," Sadie mimicked Harry's earlier expression.

For the rest of the vacation, Harry kept an eye peeled for grabby trees and no more Spidar injuries occurred. Sadie continued to help Ivan during the day. In exchange, Ivan showed the group around town in the evenings. Included in the tour were museums, the Via Serias Dance Hall, and many beautiful gardens.

Before long, the two weeks ended. Ivan accompanied the Spidars to the bus stop and handed Sadie a large box of assorted chocolates. "I'll miss you in the labs," he said.

She smiled warmly. "Thanks for making these two weeks so interesting. I learned a lot. I hope you didn't get into any trouble on my account."

"Not to worry," Ivan replied. "Dr. Guattery is the boss. He enjoyed your help as much as I did. I wish you could stay longer."

"Sure you do. You don't have to pay me." Sadie's soft laugh lingered as she climbed aboard the bus that would take the

Spidars to Davos to catch their plane. She waved goodbye to Ivan and moved to the back of the bus, where she curled her body on the seat beside Saul. "Can't waste the little time we have left of your summer vacation," she whispered to him. He combed his fingers through her hair.

By the time the bus was close to Davos, Saul stood. "Listen up, mates. Sadie and I have an announcement. She is going off the pill. This gestation won't be an accident. With a spot of luck on the timing, a new tike will be born when the triplets are two years old."

"So why are you telling us already?" Harry asked.

"Because, Harry, while we're working on a tot, the pact is disengaged. We want to make sure this one is mine. No hanky-panky with Sadie until bread's baking, old chaps."

Amidst the grumbling that followed, Harry stood. "This would be a good time to give my own news, then. I had hoped to surprise you, but I can't compete with Sadie or Rich for that. Peggy and I will be married this summer."

Sadie's eyes lit up. "Great!"

Rich snorted. "Harry, you can't surprise us with facts we already guessed."

Sadie and Saul boarded a plane to New York. The others flew to England.

Chapter 8 – April 1968

Help! Help! Can anyone hear me?

Sadie woke with a start. A pitch-black window told the approximate time of night. Must have been a bad dream, she thought as she slowly rolled over in bed. She had to do everything slower now. Her belly had grown large again. She was six months pregnant and her doctor had confirmed another multiple birth. With an early delivery expected, her birthing should occur around the same time as Peggy's. Sadie wiggled until she found a comfortable position then tried to go back to sleep.

Help! Help! Can anyone hear me? a child's voice repeated.

Sadie bolted upright. This wasn't a dream. Someone was in trouble. Who? She rolled out of bed to check the triplets. They all slept peacefully. What other child could it be? In the kitchen, she dialed the number for the Tokyo Nolith Hotel and asked for extension 396. The phone rang twice.

"Hello?" Jo-Jo said. Sadie lost her train of thought. Why did Jo-Jo answer the phone? Peggy always did that so the men could relax after a show. "Hello?" Jo-Jo said louder.

Sadie smirked. She pinched her nose between her thumb and index finger and spoke in a high-pitched voice. "This is the operator. I have a person-to-person call for a Peggy George from her fiancé in Nevada."

"What?!"

"Is there a Peggy George at this number?"

"Yes, a married one."

"Please put her on and I'll connect her fiancé." Sadie could hear the excitement in the background as Jo-Jo repeated what she had said.

"Hello," Peggy answered with hesitation in her voice. "I think you have the wrong number."

Sadie removed her fingers from her nose and her voice returned to normal. "No, I don't. Is everyone perked now?"

"Sadie, you creep!" Peggy replied. The men laughed in the background. "What's up?"

"I was thinking about you and decided to call. How are you feeling?"

"A bit tired, carrying this extra weight. What about you?"

"I'm fine. I thought I might join you for a day or so. I could be in Tokyo by morning your time. Are you sure you're all right?"

"Yes, I'm sure. An hour ago, I felt a sharp pain in my side, but it went away. I'm fine now except for exhaustion."

"You probably need some sleep. You'll feel better in the morning." Sadie's hand pressed against her chest. She felt like she was lying, but how could she explain the voice in her head – the babyish voice that spoke in clear English – and the gut feeling of where the voice originated?

"I hope so," Peggy replied. "Do you want to talk to Saul?"

"No, just tell him I'm on my way. I'll see him in the morning. You go to bed. Okay?"

"Happy to oblige, Dr. McCarthy."

Sadie called the airport next. A charter flight to California would leave in one hour and it had room for one more passenger. Another plane could take her across the ocean. She made arrangements for her sister, Carol, to watch the triplets. Then she showered, dressed, and threw a fresh pair of undies in her purse. When Carol arrived, Sadie grabbed reading material for the trip and hurried out the door.

124

The plane zoomed toward the purple sky ahead. A reddish-yellow horizon pushed from behind. *Help! Help! Can anyone hear me?* The voice seemed crisper yet weaker in intensity. Have I done the right thing, Sadie wondered? If Peggy is in trouble, she should get to a hospital right away.

The sun followed at the same distance all the way to California, as if the plane towed it with chains. *Help! Help! Can anyone hear me?* Yes, the voice spoke much clearer now. Sadie's next flight was already boarding. She hobble-ran through the terminal, breathing in short gasps going up the incline to the plane. By the time she reached her seat, she fell into it and closed her eyes.

She tried to rest, but that small voice kept nagging: *Help! Help! Can anyone hear me?* The voice was clearer, yet it seemed more panicky. And it didn't stop. Exasperated, she concentrated on the thought, *I'm coming as fast as I can, for goodness sake. Keep your pants on!*

The voice calmed instantly. *Thanks. My food goes away.*

Sadie jolted. The message changed! Had she communicated? She tried another message, *Can you tell me what your mother is doing? Is she sleeping?*

No, came the reply. *I kicked her awake a while ago and now I'm losing my food even faster. She's crying and Daddy woke up. They're talking about me. Hurry. Please!*

I am, Sadie thought back. She covered her face with her hands. *What is going on*? she wondered? *Am I losing my mind*?

She thought hard again. *I'd rather call you by a name. Are you a boy or a girl?*

What's that?

Well, do you have a tiny leg that can't kick between two long legs that CAN kick?

125

No.

Then you're a girl. Okay. May I call you Amanda?

Yes.

Okay, Amanda. Do you know what happened to cause your problem?

I think so. Where I get my food, what do you call it?

Your placenta.

Is the placenta attached to Mommy too?

Yes.

The placenta is what's wrong. Last night, Mommy took me to Daddy's show. I couldn't hear much, so I kicked to move. Part of the placenta burst. Ever since, some of my food goes through a hole. I tried to kick out, but it makes it worse. Will you be here soon?

My plane is about to land. I'll call your mommy from the airport. Try to stay still. Your kicking pushes blood out faster.

Hurry, please!

I will.

When Sadie walked into the terminal, she hurried to a row of phones. She went to the one marked "English" and gave the operator her instructions. Sadie listened as the main operator spoke Japanese to the hotel switchboard.

"Hello?" came an anxious voice.

"Harry, this is Sadie. How's Peg?'

"Oh, Sadie!" he replied with a crackle in his voice. "She feels bloated. The baby stopped kicking too. We think he's dead."

"Relax, Harry. Peggy must be scared enough for both of you. She needs you cool-headed. She had a weak spot in her uterus. A kick from the baby popped a hole through it. That's why Peg feels bloated – she's bleeding internally. The baby stopped kicking now to slow the blood loss. Tell Peg that so far Amanda is alive."

Harry paused. "Who's Amanda? And how do you know so much?"

"Amanda is your daughter. It's a long story. I'll explain later. For now, call an ambulance and get Peggy to Tokyo General. I'll meet you there. In case I get there a few minutes after you, tell them she needs something to get her to relax. Don't let them give her a transfusion, though. Do you understand?"

"Yeah."

"Good. Trust me. See you there."

For a moment, Sadie stood in front of the phone. Why had she said no transfusions? Common sense dictated extra blood for internal bleeding. Why did a gut feeling warn of trouble if Peggy received any blood? *Is this woman's intuition*, she wondered, *Or am I totally nutso*? She rushed to take a taxi to the hospital.

Saul waited in the hospital lobby. When Sadie arrived, he led her to Peggy's room. Instead of antiseptic white walls like those in the States, the walls of patients' rooms in this hospital were covered with pastel-print vinyl wallpaper.

A doctor spoke to Peggy in Japanese. A woman stood nearby, interpreting what he said into English. "That's Miki Uno, Jo-Jo's girl," Saul whispered to Sadie. "She joined us on tour a couple days after your last visit. She came to the hospital because she speaks fluent Japanese as it's her native tongue."

Sadie didn't know what to say. She had spoken with Jo-Jo's wife, Prudence, and knew there were problems. But this?

Peggy's tired voice broke through Sadie's thought. "Look at you, Sadie. Here I am feeling exhausted with the extra weight and you make me look like I'm a fashion model. You must really fag out now."

Sadie laughed. "Well, sometimes I feel like an elephant

with ostrich legs, but most of the time, I'm okay. Once we fix your leak, you'll feel better, too."

"Harry told me what you said on the phone. How'd you come to all those conclusions?"

"You look awfully pale, a possible sign of internal bleeding."

"You couldn't see me on the phone, Sadie."

"Well... I can't explain how I thought of anything. Believe it or not, I have another idea too. I'd like to try something before the doctor does his job."

Harry shook his head slowly. "They're type-matching Peg's blood right now. They say if she doesn't get some blood soon, she and the baby might... they might... I can't ..."

Sadie gently stroked his face. "She'll be okay. I know it."

A nurse brought in a bag of blood and started to hook it up. Sadie placed her hand firmly on the nurse's arm and looked between Peggy and Harry. "I'm getting a bad feeling about this transfusion. Please let me try something first."

Miki interpreted Sadie's words into Japanese for the doctor. The doctor waved his arms around. His voice rose in anger. Miki spoke again, this time in English. "The doctor says Peggy needs the transfusion or she'll die. He says you Americans expect miracles. You bring in a very sick woman for treatment and then you won't let the doctor do his job. Are you a doctor?"

"No."

Miki continued translating. "A nurse?"

"No."

"A medical technician even?"

"No."

"So you have no medical background at all. Yet, you try to stop the treatment that will save this woman's life."

Sadie's hold on the nurse's arm loosened. The doctor could be right. "I only need ten minutes. Then you can do whatever you want." She waited while Miki spoke to the doctor. This time when the doctor spoke, Sadie didn't need Miki to interpret. A voice inside Sadie's head translated. *No, Ten minutes could mean death. She's lost too much blood already. Let the nurse do her job!* Sadie stared into the doctor's eyes. Slowly she released her grip.

The nurse finished connecting the tubes. As she turned the valve that allowed the blood to flow, another nurse entered, screaming in Japanese. The doctor lunged forward and ripped the needle out of Peggy's arm. Nothing from the tubes had reached Peggy's arm yet.

Sadie's eyes moved rapidly from one person to another, but the doctor and the two nurses spoke too fast for her. She looked at Miki, hoping for an explanation.

Miki stared at Sadie in awe. "How did you know Peggy shouldn't get that blood?"

"I had a gut feeling is all. Why? What happened?"

"It seems the blood passed initial tests. Since the doctor had requested a code, meaning he needed it an hour ago, the lab sent the blood up as they finished the rest of the tests."

"But Peggy wasn't here an hour ago."

"That's just an expression. The lab finished the minor tests while you argued with the doctor. That's when the reaction occurred. It seems there's something obscure in Peggy's system that makes some blood deadly to her. The reaction doesn't show for a while, but once it comes, it's like an explosion. There would have been no time to perform any emergency procedures. You just saved her life."

Harry bent down and kissed Peggy tenderly. Saul gave Sadie a squeeze.

Miki continued. "The doctor says the lab will need another fifteen minutes to..."

"To thoroughly test a new batch of blood," Sadie interrupted. "He says I can have that time to do my thing, since he will be in the lab overseeing the testing himself."

"How..."

Sadie interrupted again. "A person doesn't need to know Japanese to figure out what the doctor said this time. It's just common sense. Tell him I say thanks."

Sadie didn't know exactly what she would do, but she did know that standing next to Saul would accomplish diddly-squat. She stepped closer to Peggy.

After the doctor and nurses left, Sadie put her hands on Peggy's belly. Sadie's eyes glazed and her mouth moved, but no sounds came out. Her hands moved too. In one spot they stopped. Peggy's belly jiggled, then the hands moved to another spot to repeat the procedure. Another jiggle and the hands moved again. By the fourth time, Peggy's eyes sparkled.

Sadie's eyes cleared. "Peggy, please relax," she scolded. "When you're excited, your blood pumps faster, which means you lose it faster." Peggy opened her mouth to speak, but Sadie placed her index finger on Peg's mouth and continued, "Think of a deserted beach on a sunny day. Amanda and I will fix you up." She didn't wait for a response. Her eyes glazed into the trance again and she mumbled aloud, "with a lot of help from above."

"Sadie, the baby's alive!" Peggy exclaimed. "I felt her kick!"

Harry took Peg's hand. "Do what she says for now. Calm yourself. We can talk later."

Sadie moved her hands in large circles. Her fingertips barely touched the belly. The circles slowly shrank until one hand stopped completely. No kick this time. Instead, a pulse of energy flowed from her fingertips to Peg's abdomen. Then the hand circled again. Six more times, one hand stopped and energy flowed. Finally, she mouthed something and her eyes lost their glaze.

The doctor returned. He fastened a fresh bag of blood to the post and a nurse was about to put a needle in Peggy's arm. Sadie grabbed the nurse's hand and held it firmly as she looked back to the doctor. "That won't be necessary, Doc. Peggy is okay now. The leak is plugged and other weak spots have been fixed. This won't happen again." Miki translated.

The doctor responded with a shake of his head. He spoke faster than Sadie could understand, so Miki had to translate again. "The doctor doesn't believe you. He says this blood will help until he can do surgery."

"Tell him to take Peg's blood pressure. That should be sufficient proof." As an afterthought, she added, "Miki, can you please ask the nurses to bring in two glasses of orange juice? One for Peg and the other for me. I'm whipped!"

Peggy's mind worked faster than her mouth. "How?... What?... Is?..." Sadie put a finger on Peggy's lips. "The baby is fine. All her limbs work. That was the reason for the four 'kicks' you felt in the beginning. I was making sure. You'll both be fine as long as you don't deliver a fifteen pound baby."

"I certainly hope not!"

When Sadie turned to the doctor, he nodded. "Peggy's pressure is up to ninety over sixty now," Miki stated. "He says she should take it easy for the rest of the pregnancy." Sadie nodded. She had understood that without translation.

The doctor left the room. Miki followed. She would inform Jo-Jo, Rich, and Bart about Peg's condition while Saul, Sadie, and Harry waited for the discharge papers.

"I owe you one," Harry said to Sadie, his eyes on Peg. "No, I take that back. I owe you two. You saved the two loves of my life." He patted Peggy's belly.

131

"I didn't do it," Sadie stated, pointing upward. Out the window, the sun shone brightly in a clear blue sky. Birds sang.

*

When Sadie entered the hotel room, Rich came up behind her, picked her up, and raised her into the air, extra weight and all. "It's good to have our angel with us again!"

Sadie recoiled, gray as an old sheet.

"Are you under the weather?" he asked, as he quickly put her down.

"I'll be fine." Her blush resumed. "I just have a phobia about heights, remember?" The expression on Rich's face said he didn't recall at all.

"You must remember that I wouldn't go skiing. At the time I could see myself passing out on the lift. I'm trying to overcome the phobia, but it's getting worse instead of better. If my feet aren't firmly planted, I feel like I'll fall and hurt myself. It's horrendous on planes."

Rich chuckled and patted her basketball belly. "This could be the culprit. It must change your center of gravity a bit."

"Maybe… Oh, speaking of the babies…" she turned to Saul, her eyes sparkling. "I found a gorgeous house that will be perfect for a large family! Do you remember Ivan in Switzerland? Well, he wrote to tell me his grandfather wanted to move to Florida."

Sadie's voice rose with excitement, "Ivan told me I should go look at the house and I did! It's beautiful! It has eight bedrooms upstairs – the kids can have their own rooms when they're teens – and a huge kitchen and living room and den and dining room and a pool and it's on the lake with its own private beach and a dock and a security fence and a two-bedroom apartment for a housekeeper and her family." Sadie paused to take a breath. "And a cottage for the security

132

personnel and ten acres of land, and the people of Canandaigua are so friendly, and we can have it for a song, and..."

"Not a song of mine, I hope," Rich broke in.

Sadie laughed when she realized how fast she had been talking. "I sat down with Ivan's grandfather. If we give him a cash offer – without making him fix anything and before he lists with a realtor – we can have the whole kit-and-caboodle for a hundred grand. That price even includes all the furniture."

"What kind of work does it need?" Saul asked.

"A good cleaning and some fresh paint is all I can see. Well, maybe some new furniture, but most of that is in good shape. In fact, some of the pieces look like antiques, which could be valuable by themselves. I know I'm talking about a lot of money, but you should see the house. It's fantastic! It even has an intercom system in every room. No matter what room I'm in, I'll be able to hear the kids wherever they are."

Sadie's voice lowered. "Why are you smiling so funny? You think it's too extravagant, don't you. Yes, you must."

Saul kissed her. "No, I smile because you're so full of beans when you talk about this house of yours. If you have that much of a yen for it, ring the accountant and have him transfer the amount into your household account."

"I couldn't do that until you see the place."

"Why not?"

Sadie looked at Jo-Jo. "I wouldn't want anyone to accuse me of marrying you for your money."

Harry laughed. He could still remember Sadie's words: "I don't get mad. I get even."

"That was a long tick ago," Jo-Jo stated. "Sounds like the best house green stamps could buy and when we come for a cuppa char, we won't be sardines in a can."

Sadie smiled at Saul.

After lunch, Harry asked Miki for suggestions on entertainment. Miki began to list the many attractions she though everyone would like.

"Sorry, fellas," Sadie interrupted, "Count me out. I have to head home. I only made emergency plans." She turned to Peggy. "I think you should come home with me. Traveling is hard on people in good health and your doctor told you to take it easy."

Peggy looked at Harry. "Would you mind? I know I'll be worried the whole time we're on the road."

Harry kissed his wife. "Take good care of her, won't you, Sadie?"

"You bet I will!" Sadie replied.

Chapter 9 – May 1968

"What could they be doing in there?" Harry asked, his long dimples deepening. "It's been a bloody hour. It's time they were up and about." The Spidar family group sat in the living room of the Henrietta apartment, with Saul and Sadie greeting each other in the master bedroom.

After a month in London making a movie, Harry and Saul insisted on a four-day weekend so they could see their wives in the States. Curious about Sadie themselves, Rich and Jo-Jo came too. Rich's blue eyes rotated in a circle. "In Sadie's condition, they can't have normal how's tricks."

"There are other ways to get satisfaction," Jo-Jo snickered. "She's good with many."

"Yes, she comes with unlimited mileage and guaranteed satisfaction," Harry said. All three Spidars chuckled.

Peggy frowned. "You guys talk as if she's a car or a toy. She's very sweet and she thinks the world of you all."

Harry scrunched his face. "Just having some jollies, Pet. We think she's a bit of all right, too."

Rich drummed on the table. "No one can do what she does. It's a positive gift, Sugar. Hasn't Harry explained?"

"Yes, he told me about her abilities. And I learned more this last month living here with her. You men don't fully realize the extent of her gift. Don't you always feel better when you're with Sadie?'

Jo-Jo snickered again. "That's because we usually have it away with her."

Peggy shook her head. "No, it's not because of the sex. You feel better because of her hands."

135

"Yup, her hands work wonders... all over the body."

"No, I mean she has power in her hands that you don't realize. Two days after I came here from Tokyo, Sadie met with Gene and Reverend Bee. The Reverend is a nice man, a retired school teacher, I think he said. Anyway, I was resting on Sadie's bed during the meeting, but my door was open so I heard some of the conversation. Sadie told Gene and Reverend Bee about Harry's leg last year and how she saved my baby and me in Japan. She's frightened about her healing powers. This past month, she's tested her powers. Rev. Bee called her to the hospital three times." Peggy took a sip of her tea.

"So what's all this got to do with us?" Jo-Jo asked. "Are you saying we've been dying and she cured us?"

"No, you were never that sick – that I know of – but Jo-Jo, do you remember the time, a few months back, when we thought we'd have to cancel a show because you couldn't stay out of the bathroom for more than ten minutes at a time?"

"Yeah, I recollect," Jo-Jo replied. "Sadie massaged my forehead and cracked some funnies until the Kaopectate worked on the squitters."

"Maybe neither the jokes nor the medicine made you feel better. Maybe Sadie's hands..." Peggy stopped short when she heard the bedroom door open and Saul and Sadie appeared.

"How was it?" Rich asked with a chuckle.

"Wouldn't you like to know?" Sadie shot back, a blush rising.

Saul's smile widened. "Fine, real fine. She done me good... again." He pulled her close and kissed her.

"Enough of the soppy bunk," Jo-Jo said. "What took you so long?"

Harry laughed. "They're getting haggard. Everything takes longer with age."

Rich put his hands on his hips. "Humph! Some hosts you are, leaving us here for an hour to muck about."

Peggy shot the men a disgusted look.

"Don't worry, Peg," Sadie said with a laugh. "I'm not easily offended. My first priority is to my own man. The rest can cool their heels – and anything else that's hot." Then she turned to the men. "Actually, Peg was your hostess while I was busy… And Saul and I aren't getting old. When we finished our own calisthenics, the babies did theirs. We lost track of time while the babies showed their father how strong they are. They're hams, just like the triplets. They auditioned their whole act."

"It was dead queerical," Saul added. "I thought a head would pop through the belly button any tick."

Harry smiled. "Right-oh. The first time I saw that happen to Peg, I thought her skin would break open. It can only stretch so far! Now that I look back, though, Peg's corporation was only half as fubsy as it is now and she hasn't popped yet."

Saul laughed out loud. "Don't worry about Peggy. She has a bloody long chalk to go before she's as rotund as Sadie. How will the belly look a month from now?"

"I don't care to think about it," Sadie said with a grimace. "It's hard enough getting around with this waddle now. In a month, I'll have to roll along sideways like a blimp with twigs for legs and arms, a marble for a head."

A sly grin spread across Jo-Jo's face. "Not to change the subject, but didn't either of you females make supper?'

Rich picked up the cue. "You know the old saying: two cooks spoil the porridge. We should take Peg back with us."

Jo-Jo nodded. "Yeah. Then the next time we come, we'll have some home-cooking again."

Sadie pointed to the kitchen. "We thought you guys could make dinner for us for a change. You weren't *beautiful* people from birth. I'm sure you learned how to cook something."

"How about bubbles and squeak?" Rich offered.

Peggy shuddered at the thought of beer and fried mice for supper. Harry pulled her closer, thinking she caught a chill.

Sadie laughed. "Sorry, we had the leftover cabbage yesterday."

"I can make cheese-butties, then," Harry offered.

Sadie smiled at him. "That's not necessary. Peg and I prepared food ahead of time and froze it. All we have to do is heat it up and mix some things together. You'll still get your homemade meals. You just won't get the aroma."

"That's the best part!" Jo-Jo exclaimed.

"Well, if that's all you want, we can buy an air freshener and eat Harry's cheese sandwiches, with tall bread for dessert." Sadie walked down the hall toward the nursery, where the triplets were waking from a nap.

*

That evening, the Spidars enjoyed lasagna, Italian bread with melted garlic butter, a fruit Jell-O, tossed salad, and banana cream pie topped with whipped cream and juicy red strawberries. Sadie ate like a sparrow, but she made sure everyone else polished off the food.

After dinner, the men leaned back in their chairs. Their bellies extended more than usual. No one moved from their spot, except Sadie. She hummed as she cleared the table.

"Can't that wait until we're a bit more mobile?" Saul asked. "Then we can give a leg up."

She kissed him on the cheek, looked at the others, and laughed. "Now you men know how bloated Peg and I feel. You have an advantage, though."

"What's that, Luv?"

"Within a few hours, you'll return to normal. Peg and I have longer to wait."

138

The men held their stomachs as they rose to their feet to help. Sadie laughed harder and waved her arms. "Relax. I'm uncomfortable even when I sit, so I'll clean up... if you do me a favor later."

"What's the favor, Sugar?" Rich asked with a mischievous smile. "Do you need more than Saul can provide?" Harry and Jo-Jo snickered.

"I can give her all she needs," Saul replied. "I'm ready, willing, and able to serve." He patted his own belly. "As long as it isn't at the present moment."

Sadie winked at Rich. "Saul's right, you know. He's all I need. Besides, sex is like money. It's nice to have, but you can live comfortably without much of it." Rich groaned, and she continued, "Actually, I'd like all of you to go to the new house tomorrow and give me your ideas on colors and such. I'm closing on it next week, and I need to have the place ready before I deliver." They all nodded agreement.

The next morning, Sadie rose early. She drank tea at the table as she studied a map by candlelight so the dining room light didn't wake anyone. Peggy and Harry slept on the living room couch, and Rich and Jo-Jo lay on cots where the playpen used to be. The cots blocked the patio door, so she couldn't go outside either.

Sadie had gone to the house in Canandaigua twice. Each time she went, she traveled around the countryside to get a feel for the area. Now, she visualized the best route for the men to see Ontario County's beauty. With a red pencil, she traced a path on the map and made notes on a separate piece of paper. When she was satisfied, she sighed and put everything in her purse... Time to fix breakfast. She would make the meal light so the men could enjoy the trip.

*

"I'll tell them," Peggy said as she hung up the phone and turned toward the men at the kitchen table. "That was Bart. He says a camera broke and you have a couple extra days before you have to go back."

"That's strange," Sadie replied, pouring milk on the triplets' cereal. "Don't they have more than one camera?"

"Why ask?" Rich teased. "You want us to mog off sooner?"

"No, I'd prefer it if you never..." She stopped short.

"Never what?"

"Never mind." She left the room. "I have to get dressed."

Before she returned, the phone rang again. Peggy rose without giving it a thought. "Hello... She's indisposed at the moment. Can I take a message?... Yes, I'll tell her." Peggy shrugged at the men and headed for the bedroom. She found Sadie in front of the mirror, brushing her hair. "That was Reverend Bee on the phone. He's at the hospital. He wants you to turn on the radio."

Oh no, Sadie thought. Not today! She wobbled to the night stand and turned on the radio.

"... To repeat: An explosion woke the residents of Alexander Street this morning. A faulty line on a gas stove is thought to be the cause. By the time firefighters arrived on scene, the home was engulfed in flames. The fire trapped a two-year-old girl on the second floor. A new member of the rescue squad, Theodore White, found the girl hiding under her bed. He ripped off his jacket and wrapped the girl before he carried her out.

"Paramedics say the child is doing fine. The jacket protected her from burns. However, Mr. White has second and third degree burns over eighty percent of his body. He is on his way to Strong Hospital. The fire chief doesn't expect the man to survive the day. We will report more details as they are revealed, so stay tuned to this station. The high temperature today will be..."

"I, I..." Peggy said in shock.

Sadie dialed the hospital. "Please page Reverend Bee." During the pause, she spoke to Peggy. "Did he say anything else besides listen to the radio?"

"Yes, something about him performing pastoral duties and hoping you can ease the man's pain. He said Gene will pick you up in ten minutes." Peggy looked at her watch. "Five now. I should have let him talk to you directly."

"Don't worry about it," Sadie said quietly. "Can you watch the kids for a few hours?"

"Sure."

"Thanks."

Peggy left the room. Turning back to the phone, Sadie raised her voice. "Reverend Bee, this is Sadie. I'll be there as soon as I can. Meanwhile, tell the doctors not to give any pain-killers... Oh? Boy, they work fast. Well, tell them to disconnect that tube and put on a fresh bag. I'll also need the chemical formula for the drug he's already received. The important thing in this case will be to have him as drug-free as possible when I get there... Yeah. Bye."

Sadie hung up and waddled to the kitchen, where she poured a large glass of orange juice and chugged it. "I know you guys thought I was a bad hostess yesterday, but today I'll be even worse."

"I'm going with you," Saul stated from the kitchen doorway. "You're in no condition for this scurrying about."

"I know, Hon, but this man can't wait. I should explain all of this to you, but I don't have time right now."

"Peg told me some things while you were on the blower. Everyone else knew yesterday, while we were occupied in the other room. It seems I'm the last to know. I'm coming along. I'll find out for myself what's going on."

"You're very welcome to come. I'd love to have you with me. But, this won't be a pretty sight. Even small burns are ugly. This guy's covered with them. Are you sure you can stomach that sort of thing?"

"If you can take it, Luv, so can I."

"Okay." Sadie hurried out the door to answer Gene's beep outside. Saul ran to catch up.

In the emergency department, a nurse led Sadie, Saul, and Gene to an isolated room, where the odor of molten flesh and scorched hair putrefied the air. Saul's breakfast churned in his stomach.

On the bed was a long lump of red-brown-black flesh, with small specks of white dotting the long lump. Facial hair was gone. The eyelids were mere blobs. Along the far side of the bed, Theodore's family – father, mother, wife, and teenage son – sobbed. The doctor leaned over the disheveled body with his back to the door. Reverend Bee's head was bowed in prayer.

Saul was immobile, wondering how anyone could stay inside a room with such a foul odor. Gene stood near the door, waiting for instructions. Sadie didn't hesitate, though. Without missing a step, she wobbled to the bed. "He's in shock," she mumbled. Her open palm traveled in the air an inch above Ted's forehead. "His temp is 105 degrees and rising. Do you have the chemical formula I requested?"

"Yes, on this paper," the doctor replied. "It won't do any good. Nothing can be done now, except make his last moments as comfortable as possible."

"You never can tell, can you?" Sadie replied. She looked at the patient and spoke softly. "Ted, I know it hurts real badly, but don't block everything out. You'll be okay if you don't lose hope. I'm here to help. If you can hear me, blink."

The doctor snorted. "He can't blink, as you can see."

Sadie shrugged. "A little humor never hurt anybody."

"Leave him alone!" Ted's father yelled. "He's suffered enough. Let him die in peace!"

"I can't do that. I believe your son will not only survive but return to his handsome, witty self, and I need your help."

"Wh-what could I possibly do?"

"Mr. White, you believe in God, don't you?" When Ted's father nodded, Sadie continued. "Then I need you and your family to go to the cafeteria. Have something to eat and a cup of coffee or tea. As soon as you leave this room, start praying. Pray as if there were no tomorrow. Reverend Bee will go with you to help. And don't come back here until we send for you."

Doubt showed on Mr. White's face.

"I won't hurt your son. It may sound like it, though. He'll start screaming as soon as I get his attention. That scream will pierce right through you. Don't turn back. Put your faith in God. Trust him to heal your son."

Mr. White didn't move. "I've never heard a doctor talk like this before. What's your name?"

"My name isn't important and I'm not a doctor. Reverend Bee called me."

"I don't know..."

"Listen, Mr. White. I'm sorry to be gruff, but every moment we waste, the closer your son comes to death. The doctors have given up. A moment ago, you sounded like you had too. So, you have nothing to lose and everything to gain by letting me try. The doc and I will work together on your son."

Sadie turned to Gene before Mr. White could reply. "Gene, will you please help Ted's wife? And on your way back, bring a pitcher of orange juice. I have a feeling I'm gonna need it. Just put it on my tab."

As Gene assisted Ted's wife, Sadie turned back to the patient. "Okay, Ted, are you ready to help now? I need your mind back inside your body if I'm going to do anything today. The pain will be gone soon, I promise you. Come on, Ted. Acknowledge your body."

Nothing…

"You should hear what people are saying, Ted. Everyone's proud of what you did for that little girl. Come on back."

Ted scrunched his face and let out a horrifying screech, as the door closed behind his family. The terror in his voice startled Saul.

"That's it, Ted," Sadie said softly. "Now I can work…" Her voice trailed off. Her eyes glazed. Her mouth moved, but no sound came out. She placed her hands a quarter inch above the skin on Ted's forehead and glided them down the length of his body.

Saul watched Sadie's hands intently, so intently that he jumped when Sadie reached Ted's feet and she spoke. "This is going to be worse than I expected." She pulled a packet of sugar out of her pocket. "All I did that time was counteract the drug he received and already I'm tired."

Gene returned, bringing the orange juice, as well as a wheelchair, which he parked near the door. Sadie drank half the orange juice.

Slowly, Ted's screams increased in volume. Thirty seconds later, the noise was so intense that Saul and the doctor held their hands over their ears. Sadie didn't seem to pay any attention to it at all. The doctor shook his head. "He'll black out soon from the pain. We need to restart…"

"Not yet," Sadie interrupted, still swirling the sugar around in her mouth. It takes a minute for the body to get rid of the drugs." After she swallowed, she continued. "While I work, you can't touch either me or the patient, unless you need to alert me to something urgent. Understand?"

"E-E-E-E-E-I-I-I!" Ted screeched.

"Okay, Ted. Now concentrate on that pain." She went back into the trance. Her hands returned to his forehead, again not quite touching, but oh so close. Her hands moved at an agonizingly slow pace. Saul watched them crawl down Ted's forehead, nose, and mouth. She worked her way down Ted's chest, but Saul didn't notice. He didn't notice that Ted stopped screaming either. Not until he heard Gene yell, "Don't!" That's when Saul looked up from Sadie's moving hands.

Gene grabbed the doctor's hand, which was near Sadie's shoulder. "Only touch her in an emergency!" The doctor hesitated but recalled Rev. Bee's reputation, so he complied.

"Mr. White is going into a coma. I think that's slightly important," the doctor said as he jerked Gene's hand away.

Gene looked at Ted. "Wait a minute. She usually checks bodily functions every few seconds. She'll notice soon."

As if on cue, Sadie's hands quickly moved to Ted's temples. The screaming resumed and her hands returned to work on his chest, crawling along again.

While Sadie worked, Gene informed Saul and the doctor of upcoming events. "When she gets to the feet, we'll have to turn him on his stomach." He noticed the doctor's questioning eyes. "That's right. If you touch her, it will break her concentration. If you touch the patient, it will change the readings she gets on bodily functions. Then she could misinterpret them and change her treatment unnecessarily. However, in this case, she'll expect it. We have to be quick and gentle. If we take too long, she'll waste energy going in and out of the trances. She doesn't have extra energy to work with. The babies are getting bigger and all..."

Gene clarified the specifics, making sure Saul and the doctor fully understood their duties on the roll-over. When the time came, the three men worked in unison.

As Gene explained the next task, reversing the procedure to get Ted on his back again, Saul noticed the sharpness of Ted's screams ebb away. "...The hardest part is yet to come. Saul, after we turn him back over, get behind the wheelchair I

145

brought in. If I know Sadie, she'll work until the last possible moment. When she comes out of this trance, she'll drop to the floor. Since I'm used to watching for signs, I'll catch her, while you slip the chair under her."

"Why would..."

Gene interrupted, "She'll put all her remaining energy into coming out quickly."

"What do you mean?" Saul asked. "Won't she come out naturally?"

"We don't know for sure," Gene replied. "Sadie thinks she may pass into the next world, instead."

Saul's heart skipped a beat. He almost missed his cue to flip Ted over again. The screams stopped and Ted was fully alert. Saul watched Sadie's hands go to Ted's face and continue working. "Why is she repeating what she's already done?" he asked, seeing Gene's worried expression. "What's wrong?"

Gene replied without taking his eyes off Sadie. "She's draining too much. Doctor, grab that pitcher of juice. We'll give her five seconds to snap out of it before we do it for her. Touching her won't work anymore. Saul, get ready with the wheelchair. One, two, thr... Good, here she comes!"

Sadie began to fall and Gene grabbed her. Saul quickly slid the wheelchair into position. Sadie's face was void of expression.

"You waited too long," Gene scolded as he tipped the pitcher of orange juice into her mouth.

She swallowed before answering. "I know. I wanted to start the healing process on the face." She sipped more juice, noticing Saul kneeling beside her, stroking her hair. She reached over to touch his face. "Don't worry. I'm okay."

"I thought you worked on the whole body," the doctor said. "That's why we turned him over. Or did you time your act so you would catch him when the morphine really kicked in?"

146

"No," she replied weakly. "I don't have enough reserves to do everything at once. I temporarily deadened all the nerve endings so Ted can't feel pain. I replaced your drug with Ted's endorphins."

Sadie paused to sip more juice. "And he'll see again soon. While I recuperate in another room, there are some things for you to do. Put wet, sterile gauze on his eyes for a while." She turned and looked at the bed. "Ted, the doctor has to cover your eyes, so the lids have a chance to come back. You won't be able to see well for the next 24 hours, but hopefully by this time tomorrow, you will be able to blink and see again."

"Some reality, please," the doctor said. "Aren't you rushing things a bit?"

Sadie reached for the nurse-call button. "Ted, the nurse will take you to another room where you'll be immersed in cool water. That should stop the burn from going any deeper into your skin. Even though you can't feel it, the burn is still there."

When she raised her head again, she looked at the doctor. "Please stay with him. The water should be kept lower than 97.5 degrees. If it gets up to 98, it's too hot. And he needs a plain glucose solution. When I'm ready for the next phase, I'll send a nurse to let you know."

Gene turned the wheelchair to face the incoming nurse. "This patient needs to go to the water tub," Sadie said to her. "Also, I need a private room for a couple hours. Can you arrange everything?"

"Yes, Ma'am. There's a vacant room down the hall on the right. I'll take you there if you wish."

"No, thanks. I have plenty of help. You tend to the doctor and Mr. White."

Sadie turned to the doctor. "Do you have any questions?"

"What?" he snapped. "I am the doctor. This is my patient. I give the orders here. You don't..."

Ted interrupted, his voice hoarse and crackling, "I'd like you to do as she says."

The doctor huffed. Without another word, he applied wet gauze to Ted's eyes.

*

"How are you doing, Ted?" Sadie asked, wobbling into his room two hours later. Saul and Gene followed.

"Fine," he replied. "How about you? The last time I heard your voice, you sounded exhausted."

Sadie smiled. "I have rested. Thanks for asking. Would you like me to remove the bandages?"

"Please!"

She worked swiftly. As the gauze was removed, both Saul and the doctor stood with open mouths. Ted's eyelids lacked lashes, but they were fully formed, pink as a newborn baby's skin, and functional. His eyes seemed to have regained a tiny bit of sparkle. The other facial skin was raised with thousands of tiny bubbles.

"Ted," Sadie said, "although you can't feel pain, be careful not to touch your face. The burnt top layer of skin acts as a barrier against germs while the healing takes place underneath. By tomorrow, your face will be good as new."

"Don't get his hopes up too high," the doctor warned, with a touch of hesitation in his voice. "There should be a great deal of scarring."

She scowled at the doctor. "You still don't believe God is healing Ted, do you? Even after you've seen the miracle with the retinal burns and eyelids, you're hesitant."

The doctor snorted. "So, you're claiming to be another Christ, I suppose."

148

"I said no such thing. I'm a human who lets God work through me. There were many people who had this healing power in biblical days."

Turning back to Ted, her smile returned. "For now, I have a job to do, so let's get on with it. Ted, this won't hurt a bit," she chuckled as she went into her trance.

"That's what they all say just before they jab you with a needle," Ted replied. Sadie didn't hear him. Her hands had begun their arduous journey from his neck to his feet, then repeating the process on his flip side.

An hour later, she held his hands in hers and smiled weakly. Ted's family had returned, as did Reverend Bee. "Ted, my part's done. Now it's up to you and your family. Pray. The pain will return as the nerves regain their function, but it won't be as bad as this morning. A dull, throbbing ache will change to an incessant itch. Don't scratch anywhere nor take any medication. Both will affect the healing process. I had a lot more area to cover on your body than on your face, so the itching may last a few days. Try to bear it."

She sipped the orange juice Gene offered again. "And try to drink as much water as possible. You'll be on glucose bags for 24 hours, but any extra fluids you can drink will help." She let go of his hands. "Ted, before I go, I want to say I'm proud of what you did for that child. I hope if there's ever a fire at my place, someone like you will make sure my kids are safe." She kissed her fingertips and gently placed them on his eyelids.

"I don't know," he replied, "I don't think I can ever go back to firefighting."

"Do what your conscience dictates. Remember, though, the fire department needs men like you. Again, thank you." She motioned to Gene, who wheeled her out of the room and out of the hospital. Saul followed in silence. Silence ruled the ride.

In the apartment, Saul sat on the couch watching a blank

television while Gene carried Sadie to her bed. "How did she do?" Peg asked Saul. He didn't answer, so Peggy waited for Gene and repeated her question.

Gene answered with a broad smile. "Great! You should have seen her work!"

Rich gawked down the hallway to the bedrooms. "Peg warned us that Sadie would be tired enough to sleep on a clothesline. Still and all, I expected her to leg it on her own trotters. Will she be okay?"

"She'll be tired the rest of the day. Peggy knows the routine. Sadie won't be able to resume her full duties until tomorrow, but after a nap, she'll walk around again."

Harry chuckled. "You mean dodder around, don't you?"

Light laughter filled the room. Peggy motioned to Saul while looking at Gene. "What's wrong with him?"

Gene shrugged. "You know Saul better than I do."

*

During dinner that evening, Saul stared at his plate. Several times, Sadie tried to coax him into conversation, but he answered with a simple yes or no. Afterward, as Peggy cleaned up the kids and cleared the table, Sadie tried to sit on Saul's lap.

He pushed her away. "Are you trying to break my legs?"

She knelt in front of him. "Is something wrong?"

"Yes, you're sticking Peg with all the work. If you have the energy to frolic, you should be able to help a little." He turned his head to look out the window. Sadie remained motionless for a moment. Then she rose and went to the kitchen.

Peggy followed with another load of dishes. She put her hand on top of Sadie's in the sink. "You're tired. Go sit on the sofa. Saul didn't mean what he said."

Sadie's reply came in a whisper. "You're wrong on that one, Peg. He did mean it and he's right. I'm tired, but it doesn't take any more energy to do the dishes than it does to monkey around. If you finish the table, I'll wash the dishes." She ran hot water into the basin. "Oh, by the way, thank you for watching the kids. I appreciate it."

"Twas nothing. The men took care of the children. All I did was make lunch and clean up. Feel like talking about the fireman?"

"Not really."

When Sadie finished the dishes, she surveyed the living room. The toddlers were building a house out of Lincoln Logs, Saul stared into space, and the others watched television. She wiggled out to the patio, closing the door behind her. Resting her belly on the railing, she lit a cigarette.

Buzz-z-z-z.

"Yes?" Peggy asked at the intercom on the wall.

"Reverend Bee."

"Come in." Buzz-z-z-z. She opened the door and waited for him to walk down the center hall. When the minister stepped into the apartment, Peg said, "I'll get Sadie."

"No no. Don't bother her. I simply want to drop off these before-and-after Polaroids. I know how she worries until the final results are in. This last one was taken a little while ago, before I left the family. The burnt skin already fell off Ted's face. Sadie should be pleased."

Peggy glanced and then actually stared at the pictures. "Wow! Look at the difference! He looks as good as that old photo they showed on the news tonight!" She passed the pictures to the others as Reverend Bee departed.

"No wonder she's fagged!" Rich gasped. When the pictures were passed to him, Saul stared at them for a long moment.

Looking toward the sliding glass doors, he rose and walked outside.

On the patio, Sadie heard the door open and close behind her. She looked around. "Are you ready to talk?" she asked.

"Why didn't you tell me about this power of yours? First, I have to find out from Peggy that you have some healing dynamisms. Then, when I watch, I find out the whole flippin' story. That's not right."

Her hands went up to caress his face. "Honey, I thought you knew I had some powers after I took care of Peg and her baby a month ago."

"That was different," he muttered.

"How?" When he didn't answer, she continued. "It was different because you couldn't see the healing process. Today you could. Today, you could hear with your own ears how the pain went from unbearable to nothing in fifteen minutes. You could see with your own optic nerve how his eyelids regenerated." Sadie smiled. "I'm a magician. My hands are quicker than your mind."

"Don't be a smart ass," he yelled, then stomped back into the apartment. Sadie lowered her bulk into a chair and lit another cigarette.

Sadie was still outside an hour later when the children had changed into their pajamas. They made their rounds with goodnight kisses. "Why is Mommy outside?" Roxanne asked. "Was she a bad girl?"

Saul hugged her. "Yes she was."

"Is that why you yelled at her?"

"What makes you think I yelled?"

Roxanne slipped off his lap. "I heard you. Was she really, really, really bad?"

Before Saul could answer, Peggy spoke. "No, she wasn't bad. Your father just has a bad temper sometimes."

152

Harry pulled Peggy toward him. "Don't talk like that to the tikes," he whispered.

"Why shouldn't I be honest? Sadie's pregnant... and exhausted to boot. His temper is inex..."

Harry covered her mouth with his fingers. "I know how you feel... but Sadie wouldn't want you talking to the tikes that way. Cool down."

Ignoring Peggy's outburst, Saul answered Roxanne's question. "No, she was giving cheek. She thought it was funny to keep a secret from me. You would never keep a secret from Daddy, would you?"

Carl jumped into Saul's lap. "I have a secret!" he squealed. "I love you!" Jason repeated the secret to Harry. Both men chuckled as they gave each boy a hug.

Roxanne didn't jump on Rich's lap. Instead, she tugged at the sliding door. "What are you doing, little moppet?" Rich asked her. Tears flowed down her cheeks. "I want to tell Mummy I love her, too. Maybe she'll feel better."

Rich grimaced at Saul. "Did you hear that?"

"How could I not hear?" Saul rose from the sofa. "Roxy, you sit here and keep my seat warm. I'll go make Mummy feel better."

When Saul walked out, Sadie smiled at him. He sat next to her. "I'm sorry I lost my head. You're right. I did know you had some peculiar powers."

"But...."

"No, don't interrupt," he said quietly. "I'm sorry. I was a bit green about the gills seeing the Ted thing. Can you find it in your heart to forgive me and come inside? Please!"

Sadie giggled like a school girl. "I can't. I'm stuck in this chair!"

Chapter 10 – The Next Day

The delayed trip to Canandaigua was as beautiful as Sadie had hoped. The sunshine was bright and puffy clouds dotted the skies. With the children being tended by Mary, Sadie was relaxed... well, as relaxed as she could be in the excitement of showing the house to the family.

The Spidars went southwest from Henrietta, through Mendon Ponds Park with its picnic areas, walking trails, and an abundance of wild flowers and birds. They passed rolling pastures with cows and horses, yellow wheat fields, and deep green alfalfa fields. They saw farms with red barns and colonial-style houses.

Farmers' wives weeded vegetable gardens or hung laundry. Children played ball or swung on tires hanging from tree branches. Dogs chased butterflies and shadows, and cats sat at the edges of fields, ears perked for any sounds of mice.

Some farms had chickens pecking at pebbles in the driveways. Others had geese swimming in natural ponds. At one farm, Saul had to stop the van for a duck family strolling across the road.

A few miles past East Bloomfield, in the hamlet of Centerfield, Sadie directed Saul down a winding road. A windmill towered over a distant hill and powered the dairy farm below. Corn fields waved welcome and hay fields undulated in the breeze. Further on, a farmer plowed brownish-red soil as sea gulls circled, swooping to grab newly exposed bugs.

"The Seneca named this Ganundagwa," Sadie explained. "It means Chosen Spot."

At the top of knolls, the Spidars saw the blue waters of Canandaigua Lake, broken only by a few colorful sailboats. As they neared their destination, they heard birds sing sweet melodies and smelled the dew of a new day's dawn.

One road ended near the lake. Saul turned onto West Lake Road, running parallel to the lake. Here, the scenery changed. The land was no longer fields, but manicured lawns of the well-to-do. Gardens became more elaborate and house designs changed to contemporary or rambling ranches with large windows overlooking the lake.

"That's gorgeous!" Peggy gasped as they passed a newly-built house on its own peninsula of land. Fingers of tennis courts and sculptured gardens extended toward the road.

Sadie smiled. "That's the Wegman home. Mr. Wegman owns a chain of grocery stores here in New York. I met him on my last tour of the house. You should've come with me, Peg. He's our nearest neigh..." Sadie interrupted herself. "Ah! Here we are."

Stopping at the gate, Saul pressed a buzzer. A brick wall surrounded the estate on three sides, with the fourth side being the lake. Large maple trees lined both sides of the curved driveway beyond the gate, so their view was limited to a small cottage near the entrance. The cottage had lavender trim on a white background, with stenciled flowers on the shutters. A small overgrown garden crowded the front door.

Rich chuckled. "I thought you said a B-I-G house. This one's the size of a bedsit. Where do we kip? Under the trees?"

"Nope, this is Saul's dog house," Sadie quipped. The gate opened electronically. "Actually, it's for security personnel. Inside, special televisions show the secluded spots on the property and... We might as well start the tour here."

Inside the cottage, a refrigerator and numerous cupboards covered the right wall near the entrance. In the middle of the floor was an island with a sink, stove, table-top, and two bar stools. To the left of the island, furniture in the living room faced the left wall, with a large security console, two phones, six closed-circuit televisions, a regular television for entertainment, and a panel of buttons. A set of double doors on the far wall led into the bedroom.

"When this house was designed," Sadie explained, "Mr. Gothic wanted the security people happy." She ran a finger along the counter and showed a thick layer of dust. "As you see, no one has lived here since Mrs. Gothic died a year ago. Mr. Gothic says he had the security here to protect his wife, whom he loved dearly. When she died, he couldn't see sense in the extra expense, so he modified the gate system to work from the house. His wife's death is also why he's now selling the house. It's much too big for just him and the housekeeper."

As the Spidars left the cottage, they saw the lemon-yellow main house in the distance. Trees blocked the view from the gate but not from the cottage. The Spidar family walked down the driveway.

Halfway down, Sadie led them to a pathway to the right, leading to a red, four-foot-high wooden, privacy fence. A wide ledge ran along the top edge of the fence. "Perfect for flower pots," Sadie suggested. She stopped at a white, Oriental-style gate and pointed to a small building next to it. "This is where people can use the porcelain conveniences or change without running in and out of the house."

"Change to what?" Rich asked. "Supermen?"

"He couldn't piddle in a phone booth in that outfit," Harry said.

Sadie smiled. "You two are incorrigible!"

"That's right! You can encourage us any time you want."

Sadie shook her head. "At the other end of this fence is a building with the water heater, filter, and other pool supplies, along with the parts to a plastic, insulated dome for winter use."

"The changing rooms may come in handy then," Rich quipped.

"Yes," Harry agreed. "Then our family jewels won't freeze."

Sadie laughed. "I thought you might appreciate this whole thing." She opened the gate to reveal a 16' x 80' pool, surrounded by a ten foot deck on each side. A 12-foot strip of grassy area ran along the length of the west fence, parallel to the road. This fence contained a second gate to a forest area. "Perfect for a kids' play area," Sadie said.

She led the group out a third gate at the opposite end. A five-acre tree grove ran from the lake to the road. "This is another part of our forest. We have maple, pine, beech, ash, walnut, cherry, peach and apple trees in here, as well as blueberry bushes. We shouldn't have to buy fruit. We only need to pick 'em and can or freeze 'em."

They continued along the edge of the forest past the house to the deep backyard. Jo-Jo's eyes lit up when he spotted a lime-green, twenty-man sailboat at the end of a long dock. Sadie smiled at him. "Yes, Jo-Jo, the boat comes with the property. It has an outboard engine for windless days."

While the men walked down the dock to investigate, Peggy went to the large oak midway between the house and the water on the north end. Sadie joined her, sitting in its shadow. They sat in peaceful silence, listening to the men chatter in the distance. Birds sang worries away.

"It's so quiet here," Peggy commented.

"That'll change with the kids," Sadie said with a smile.

"I can see why you wanted us to see the place first without the triplets."

"Peg, Mr. Gothic is older. He may have had eight children of his own, but now he's used to a sedate home. I wouldn't dream of imposing with a mob. I'm glad Mary offered to watch them at the apartment. She is such a gem."

Minutes later, Sadie glanced at the house and saw a familiar face in the window. "Ivan!" she squealed and jumped up to scurry like a penguin to hug her friend as he stepped from the house. "Ivan, what on earth are you doing here?"

Ivan returned the hug and smiled. "Aren't you supposed to say hello before you start an interrogation?"

"Hello. I thought you... I didn't know... I..."

"Grandpa wrote to tell me that if I wanted to see this place one last time, I'd better come quickly. So, I took an early vacation. Enough about me. Look at you! My, you blossomed! What are you carrying in there? A merry-go-round?"

Sadie giggled and patted her belly. "When I do something, I do it right." Saul came up behind her and kissed her neck. The other Spidars were behind him.

"Have you picked a doctor here yet?" Ivan asked. "Or do you plan to go to Rochester with that load."

"No, most of these roads have weight restrictions. I thought I'd deliver them myself... Actually, I remember that first labor all too well. The car ride was way too long and painful. I thought I'd talk with your father sometime next week and see if he has room for another patient. Do you know if your father goes strictly by the book? Or is he willing to bend policy to suit the mother, like a woman having quads?"

"Quads!? Has that been confirmed?"

"Yes according to old wives' tales, I've broken four things during this pregnancy... well, one was able to be repaired, so the fourth is iffy."

"That's proof enough for me. What if you break four more?"

Sadie's eyes opened wide in mock horror. "Don't even hint at that! It might come true!" Rich chuckled behind her. "Does your dad give quantity discounts?"

"He probably will. It's not every doctor who gets to handle a case like this. I can call to find out." He went into the house ahead of the group.

Sadie led the Spidar family through the doorway into the kitchen. "It's a bit larger than my present kitchen, isn't it?"

"A bit!" Peg exclaimed. "This kitchen is bigger than your whole apartment!"

Sadie pointed to the twelve-foot-long, maple trestle table before them. "This is just the breakfast nook. The dining room is beyond that far door on the left. I admit it sounds redundant. I plan to use the dining room for storage and my office desk."

She paused as the group digested the room. The nook took up half the room, separated from the other half by a long arm of base cupboards and a hand that extended upwards at the end of the arm, not quite touching the ceiling. The arm served as a pass-through, since it had no upper cupboards. The hand consisted of a glass-front hutch on the nook side, with a stove with a double-oven above on the kitchen side.

Perpendicular to the arm on the kitchen side along the outside wall were upper and lower cupboards, a built-in dishwasher, a double sink with a small window above it, and a large side-by-side refrigerator/freezer amongst upper and lower cabinets on the other side of the arm. Light yellow marble lay on the floor, and Bach flowed softly through an intercom speaker near the light switch.

When she thought the group had looked long enough, Sadie walked to the back door they had entered from the backyard. "As you can see," she began with a twinkle in her eyes. "There are seven doors leading from here to other parts

159

of the house and the outside. Which one would you like to open first? Door number one, two, three, four, five, or six, since we came into the room through door number seven?"

"Only a room this big could support seven doors," Peggy commented.

"Let's give number three go," Rich suggested. "It's double wide, for when we eat too much."

"Good choice. However, trick question, we should probably go in reverse order. Door number six leads to the side yard and extra parking lot." She opened the inside doors as she went along and they all looked briefly through the doors. "The fifth leads to the garage. Door four leads to a bathroom, which is nice, but when you've seen one, you've seen them all. We'll skip number three and go to the second one, which leads to the front hallway. And as I said, the first goes to the formal dining room that has a full bathroom off it as well."

"Now, the third ..." Sadie opened the double pocket doors into the walls and stepped aside to let the others through the doorway. Two brown brocade couches with matching love seats were arranged in a semi-circle, centered on a large television above a brick fireplace on the right. Purple satin drapes hung on the two large front windows. Dark gray plush carpet covered the floor. The left wall was papered with small, fluffy blue flowers and pale green stems and leaves on a light tan background. The textured ceiling seemed to move in circles. Both the ceiling and the three remaining walls were eggshell white.

"We could all LIVE in this huge room!" Peggy exclaimed.

"That's why it's called a living room, I guess," Sadie dead-panned. "Really, though, Peg, when you get eight kids in here, plus any company we might have, it won't seem so large. I plan to make the far half of the room into a kids' play area. They'll be near yet not on top of us."

"This place is nice," Saul whispered into her ear.

Sadie's smile broadened. "You ain't seen nuttin' yet." She led them out a doorway on the left of the living room into the hallway. She held the carved banister as she wobbled up two steps of the wooden staircase. On the other side of the staircase was another double door.

"What's in here?" Rich asked, still at the bottom with his hand on the knob of the double door.

She turned. "Never mind. I want to save the best for last. You'll see soon enough."

Rich turned the knob without opening the door, but Sadie missed the tease. Ivan had returned from the kitchen phone. "My father says he can fit you in today if you'd like. I warned him you can't sit in the waiting room for long. He said he'll tell his receptionist to get you right in. Why don't you go now and let me show the rest of the house? You shouldn't go up these stairs."

"Nonsense! I'm pregnant, not sick. I can't drive myself anyway. The driver's seat doesn't go back far enough for my belly. When it does, my legs won't reach the pedals."

"Alright," Ivan said. "You lead the way. I'll bring up the rear in case anyone has questions."

"Where's your grandfather?" Saul asked.

"He's resting in the formal dining room, which we turned into his bedroom. He thought he'd be out of the way there."

Sadie resumed her penguin climb with difficulty. Peggy fared better, but both women breathed heavily at the top. Bedrooms, four on each side of the stairs, had plush carpeting and king-sized beds with matching bureaus and vanities. Velour bedspreads matched the color scheme of each room. The four corner bedrooms each had private baths; the four middle rooms shared two baths, one on each side of the stairs.

Ivan turned to Saul. "Your lady has driven a hard bargain with my grandfather. She wanted all the furnishings."

Sadie blushed. "That's not completely true, Ivan. Your grandfather said he didn't want to transport much and he wasn't about to store the household stuff he wouldn't use any more. That's why I typed 'all the furnishings' on the purchase offer. When your grandfather called me and said he wanted to give something to each grandchild, I changed the offer to include the things he didn't want."

Ivan smiled. "In any case, we each picked an item we wanted. Some picked furniture, some picked heirlooms. I took the engraved silver tea set given to my great, great grandparents on their 25th anniversary. In all, you'll probably have to refurnish two of the bedrooms. "

Sadie giggled. "That'll be fine. The kids can't use the beds in the rooms anyways."

The group moved to the small housekeeper's apartment directly in front of the stairs. Inside, the furniture was simple: a couch, recliner, and television in the living room, a full-sized bed and dresser in each of two bedrooms, and two closets. The apartment had a small kitchenette and a bathroom. A door from the living room was an exit to the back of the house so the housekeeper could come and go in privacy, and stairs also went down to the basement.

Peggy noticed something was missing in this room. From the moment the Spidars entered the house, they had been serenaded by the intercoms in each room. "Where's the music?" she asked.

"Since this is the hired help's private quarters, the music isn't wired into here," Ivan explained. "To contact someone here, you use a button on the phone."

Finished with the second floor, the group walked toward the stairs. Sadie stopped at the top. "Ivan, those songs you've been playing aren't in the order of any record. They seem to go from one album to another and then back. I haven't heard any disc jockey, so it can't be the radio. Did you make your own tapes?"

Ivan shook his head. "No, I put them in this order to show you the possibilities with Grandpa's electronic system. If I know him, he probably only showed you how the second record player turns on when the first one is done. However, you can also adjust them to individual songs. When one song is done, the first player turns off and the second or third one comes on. Then you can go back to where you left off on the first one. You can even skip a song you don't like on an album. In that case, the speakers to that turntable turn off, but the turntable keeps going until it reaches the end of the song. Then it stops, ready for another cue to begin. Meanwhile, a record on another turntable plays to fill in the gap. It's all in the timers. I can show you how they work if you'd like."

"I think you'll have to," Sadie replied. "It sounds complicated."

"Not really. All you need is the timing for each song. That's usually listed on the record."

"I presume the instructions are in a booklet of some sort in case I forget."

"No, regretfully, grandfather didn't have any use for that feature and threw away the booklet. I can drop by again before I return to Switzerland to make sure you understand everything. Will you be here next weekend?"

"Yes, I have a lot of things I want to do before we move in, so I'll be here every day after closing. You should plan to make a quick exit after reviewing the system with me, though."

"Why?" He glanced at Saul who was getting a bit edgy.

Sadie giggled. "I will put every able body to work."

"I'd be glad to help. On one condition."

"What's that?" Saul asked, not wanting to be ignored.

Ivan looked at Saul and then back to Sadie. He chose his words carefully. No joking right now. "On the condition that when I feel homesick for this old place, I'll be welcome."

Sadie reached out and held his hands. "Friends are welcome any time."

"Thanks." Ivan kissed her cheek. "I think I can help next week anyway. A doctor should be here to make sure you don't do too much in your con..."

"Get your mitts off our bird," Jo-Jo growled.

Sadie glanced at Jo-Jo then at Saul's red face. She quickly changed the subject: "And now for the room you've been wondering about." She hobbled down the stairs and opened the door to the room Rich had wanted to explore. "The room you guys will enjoy the most, what we will call the music room!" She stepped aside and let the men see it for themselves.

In this room, variegated, textured, brown carpeting offset bright yellow walls. A mahogany desk held a phone shaped like a ship's communication wireless. Adjacent, a Steinway grand piano ruled on graceful legs of carved angels. Rows of records and tapes stocked the compartments along one wall. At waist level, a waxed shelf held three turntables, a cassette player, an eight-track player/recorder, speakers, and a machine with many buttons and small clocks.

Shimmering ship rudders hung on another wall, flanked by a wooden wheel, a large compass, and a picture of the first U.S. submarine with its crew posed on the foredeck in their clean white and blue uniforms. The captain, standing in the center, bore a striking resemblance to the youngest Ivan Gothic; obviously the genes had passed to the grandchild. In the middle of the ceiling, a periscope chandelier could be pulled down and turned 360 degrees to light the eighteenth century day beds arranged around the room. Each one had eight legs and two long arms. All the wood in the room had been meticulously hand-carved in intricate patterns.

Harry surveyed the room slowly. "Wow!" he exclaimed. "I feel like I'm in a yellow submarine."

"Or else an octopus' garden," Rich added.

*

On Wednesday, as the men packed their clothes to return to England, Sadie prepared for the house closing, tucking a certified check in her purse. Mary would drive the men to the airport and return to take Sadie to Canandaigua, and Peggy would watch the children.

Jo-Jo and Rich said their good-byes and went out to the van to wait. Both Harry and Saul were hesitant to leave their wives now that delivery was so close. "Are you sure you can hold down the fort?" Saul asked as they stood in the hallway.

"I'm sure," Sadie replied with a smile.

"Don't be long," Peggy said to Harry in a whisper.

Harry hugged her tight. "We have one more scene to shoot and then editing on a few and we're done. We'll be home as soon as a plane can get us back here."

"Speaking of planes," Saul added, "Bart thinks it would be good publicity to show off you girls. He wants to schedule a live show in London. You girls need to fly over in two weeks."

"That's not such a good idea," Sadie said.

"What do you mean?"

"Well..."

"Well, what?" Saul disliked Sadie's habit of keeping him guessing for a while then blurting out something so logical he couldn't argue with her. "Is it because of Ivan?" he asked with a straight face. He knew that would speed her explanation.

165

"That's it, isn't it? You want to have more bloody time with Ivan." Outwardly, he scowled at her.

"Ivan is only a friend. No. It's... it's just... I don't think a long plane trip is right for women in our condition. The car ride to Canandaigua was long. A plane trip to London, seven hours if the winds are with us ... Is there any way you could perform the show in Rochester and then send the tape to England real fast? Wouldn't that be almost as good as a live performance?"

"Maybe," he replied in a frustrated tone. She had done it again – made perfect sense. "You know, if you lived in England, we wouldn't have these problems."

"We've already discussed that. I love you. Please hurry back." She kissed him and he didn't argue further.

*

During the following week, Sadie scrubbed and painted the interior of the new house. Then she called an appraiser to look at the antiques. After a cursory glance, he gave her a cash offer to buy the furniture for twice what she had paid for the house itself. She knew the furniture had to be worth much more. She paid him the appraisal fee and sent him on his way.

She didn't tell Saul about the appraisal, but she and Peggy shopped with smiles on their faces in celebration. No longer feeling guilty about spending Saul's money, she bought one crib and three juvenile beds. Peg bought a crib too. As for the apartment furnishings, well, everything except the three cribs, children's dressers, and master bedroom suite would go to the church women's group for reassignment.

More good news came. The Spidars had finished a week early and they'd do a live concert at the Shriner's Hall for a Rochester television station with national affiliations. The broadcast would go to England via satellite. They would come home tonight. And Miki would be with them this time.

*

WELCOME HOME, LUVS
You, too, Rich

This was the sign hanging on the front gate, illuminated by the rental vans' headlights. The men thought a rental van was more appropriate than a limo ride, since they might need a second vehicle for separate deliveries, unless the women went into labor at the same time. Rich smirked as Saul pressed the buzzer on the pole.

A man came out of the cottage and stood a few feet from the gate on the other side. "May I help you?"

Surprised, Saul sat in silence. Jo-Jo spoke from the back window. "Yes, this here's the master of the house. Open the gate."

Jo-Jo's gruff voice didn't ruffle the man. "I will let the ladies know you are here. It should only take a moment." The man turned and looked toward the house.

"Just open the bloody gate!" Saul snorted. "You don't need permission. I own these digs."

"Get in gear, gov'nor," Harry added. "We're tired and hungry." The man didn't move. He merely watched the house.

Rich watched the house too. At night, the lights from the house cast the trees in faint silhouette along the driveway. The silhouettes faded.

The guard muttered something and opened the gate with a hand-held remote. "What did you say?" Rich yelled out the window.

"I said I can let you in now. By the way, my name is Jerry."

"Funny old stick," Harry mused.

"Yup," Rich replied. "Sadie's up to something. That guy was told to stooge around while the girls darkened the house."

"Oh?" Harry said. Then a smirk grew on his face. "O-o-o-oh!"

The rented van moved up the driveway and they verified Rich's theory. The only light lit was on the front porch. "I guess Sadie wants us to use the front door," Saul said.

"Let's go to the side instead," Rich snickered. They walked silently to the kitchen/garage side door. Rich turned the knob.

As the door opened, a delicious aroma greeted them. Inside, two eight-tiered candelabras graced the ends of the table, with mounds of food in the middle.

"She didn't pass me by," Rich chuckled. He heard a muffled laugh next to him. "You didn't let me down either," Sadie replied, kissing him lightly on the cheek.

"What's that in aid of?" Rich asked.

"I knew you'd be suspicious when you saw the sign. Then when Jerry didn't let you in right away and only the front light was on, I figured you would come in this door."

"We would've come this way anyway," Jo-Jo said.

"Yes, but you wouldn't have had the same fun and anticipation."

Rich pulled her back to him and reciprocated her kiss on the lips this time. "You nutter! You think you have me pegged," Rich said with a broad smile.

"No," she giggled, "Harry is Pegged." Rich shook his head at her mediocre pun.

Saul retrieved Sadie from Rich's arms. His hot kiss enveloped her soul. After a few moments, the loud growling of Saul's stomach reminded him of the waiting food. Which should he have first? Food or Sadie…

"Remember," Sadie said to the group with a twinkle in her eyes. "Whatever doesn't get eaten up tonight will be tomorrow's supper."

With an arm around Peggy and serving himself from the nearest serving bowl with the other hand, Harry asked: "Is that a threat or a promise?"

"That depends on if you like the food."

Despite the girls' humor, Saul thought they both looked tired. "Hard day, Luv?" he asked as he and Sadie sat down.

"Not really," she replied. "Peg and I have been spoiled by early bedtimes lately. We go to bed when the kids do, which is where they are right now. Anyways, I can't have hard days anymore."

Saul knew she referred to her hiring her sister, Carol, to help with housekeeping and as an occasional babysitter. She had also hired Joshua, her sister's husband, as the gardener. The couple lived in the apartment at the top of the stairs.

*

A hush fell over the crowded Shriner's Hall as Sadie and Peggy were introduced to the fans. The hush didn't last long, though. As the two women wobbled onto the stage, a man in the audience yelled, "Didn't we see Sadie like this a few years ago?"

Sadie took the mic from Saul's hand and winked at the audience as she lifted one foot in the air. *"Yes, but I have shoes on!"* A moment of silence was followed by laughter as people realized she meant pregnant but not barefooted, opposite the 1950's expression.

The heat on the stage seared through the pregnant women quickly. After the audience quieted, Sadie patted her belly and spoke into the microphone. *"Let's get on with the show. These kids are gentler when there's music playing."* The women wobbled to the wings, waving goodnight to the crowd as the band began their concert.

The Shriner's Hall manager spoke to Bart in the wings. Motioning for the man to wait a moment, Bart turned to the women and explained that members of the press had assembled in the meeting room. They wanted to interview all the Spidar women, including Miki Uno, Jo-Jo's girl.

"Is that wise?" asked Sadie.

"You did fine on stage," Bart replied. "You whetted their appetites. You'll do fine again. Just don't let them back you into a corner, if you know what I mean."

Miki faced the stage. "I'm not going," she stated.

Once in the meeting room, Peggy and Sadie stood behind the podium, which hid their bulging mid-sections. Questions came like bullets from an enemy plane. Both women stood with their mouths half-open.

"Ladies and Gentlemen of the press," Bart interrupted. "These two women are not used to being bombarded. Let's have decorum so they can answer questions properly." As hands rose, Bart gave each person permission to speak.

"The American people, especially young women, would like to know what it's like being married to a Spidar, with their exceptional popularity. And what are they like in private?"

Peggy smiled as she answered, "You can see by our present conditions that we're quite happy with our private lives. As for the men's popularity, it causes inconveniences. Sometimes, it's hard to even get groceries without drawing a crowd of people wanting to know what we feed them. To tell the truth, Sadie is better at getting in and out of stores without recognition."

"Sadie, in your condition, how can you possibly not be recognized?"

Sadie smirked as she moved to the mic. *This is fun*, she thought. Aloud, she said, "If I told you, people would know what to look for. Next Question."

"We have heard that you two live in New York. Does that cause any problems, with the men in England for much of their work and traveling the world at other times?"

Peggy whispered to Sadie and sat down. Sadie would answer the rest of the questions. "Yes, it causes problems, but I knew when I married Saul that he would be gone a lot."

"Why don't you move to England to make it easier?"

Sadie collected her thoughts for a minute. "When a woman raises small children, she needs help from her support group of friends and family. It helps to talk out problems and find that your own mother used to get frustrated, too, and that hard times will pass. A new mother also needs someone she can trust to watch the kids occasionally. That's not easy when you move to a strange place."

An English reporter didn't raise his hand. *"Are you saying England is strange?"*

"No. Life would be more difficult in Pennsylvania, too. I wouldn't know anyone. As I've said, living in New York State causes some problems. We are coping with them."

She looked at Bart, who nodded proudly at the way she handled herself. He pointed to another reporter.

"Why isn't Miki here with you? Is she ashamed of her present position?"

Sadie could tell by the accent that this was another Englishman. "I can't answer for Miki. However, from what I've read recently, she probably feels this would be more like a lynching than a news conference."

"Do you condone her affair with Jo-Jo?"

"I don't think the relationship between Miki and Jo-Jo is any of my business. Nor yours either. You know, it seems like the British press gets very upset whenever one of the Spidars marries someone who isn't British. I know. I've read some nasty articles about me, articles written by reporters I've never met. The stories range from my parents being filthy rich all the way to me blackmailing Saul into marriage, neither of which is true." Her face paled.

"Are you saying you did not get pregnant just to get Saul to marry you?"

"What?" Sadie had been so careful to keep her private life private. People should assume that she and Saul were married before her first appearance at a concert. Her cheeks flushed as she turned to Bart and Peggy.

"One of the boys let it slip at a press conference in London," Bart whispered. "I thought you knew. It was in the papers."

Peggy cleared her throat. "It's my fault, Sadie. I should've told you. Remember the week you let me do the shopping? News of the premarital pregnancy was in all the tabloids that week. I knew you'd be hurt, so I kept it to myself. I should've known they wouldn't let it drop. Sorry."

"In the past, you have said that your parents aren't rich, either. If Saul had disclaimed your pregnancy, would you have sued him to pay rent and feed the kids?"

"I gave my kids over to God. I knew He wouldn't let..."

"Are you saying God approved of your pre-marital sex?"

"No, I ..."

"When will you tell your kids they're bastards?"

The room quieted. "They're not..." Sadie stopped herself. In a strong voice, she continued. "This interview is over. The show is in the auditorium, not here." She wobbled to the door and Bart helped Peggy rise from her seat.

"Wait, Please!" came a young woman's voice. *"Mothers everywhere wonder how you are holding up under the prospect of another multiple pregnancy. Can you comment on that?"*

Sadie turned. "You're Pam Hope from U.P.I., right?"

"Yes."

"I've read your articles. I like the way you write. Come with us and I'll answer your question."

"That's not fair!" others yelled in unison.

Sadie looked around. "What's not fair? This reporter doesn't victimize the person she's interviewing. Even famous people make mistakes. They should also have basic human rights, like the right to privacy. I don't like my faults being blown out of proportion to sell more papers." She waddled from the room with her head held high.

In the dressing room, Sadie broke down and wept.

"It's over," Peggy soothed. "You can relax now."

"Yeah, until the articles come out and Saul gets furious. If the reporters can blow up innocent remarks, they'll have a field day with the juicy tidbits today."

Bart shook his head. "No one'll get miffed. The men know how the press can badger. Now YOU know how the slip about the triplets happened."

Sadie nodded and dabbed her eyes with a tissue. As she looked up, she noticed Pam in the doorway. "Sorry. I forgot you were here too."

Pam smiled meekly. "I'm the one who should apologize. For the rudeness of my colleagues. Should I come back later?"

"No, let's get this done," Sadie said, her face losing color. Pam set her tape recorder in front of Sadie and stood quietly as Sadie recomposed herself. Her color returned.

"To answer the question you posed earlier, I am excited and apprehensive at the same time. Most women feel like that when they're pregnant. I always dreamed of getting married and having lots of children, but I didn't plan to do it this way.

"Feeling the babies kick and move around inside me is nothing short of a miracle. It brings out maternal instincts. I want them to have the best of everything. Luckily at the moment, I can afford to indulge them somewhat, but I remind myself that the best of something isn't always the most expensive. Loving attention is the absolutely, positively, most important thing any mother can give her child.

"That's where my apprehensions surface. I have three children, and I think I may be having four more. It's hard to imagine being able to treat them each as individuals. It's not the work. I know I can do that. The thing that worries me is the ease of treating them in assembly-line fashion, forgetting to show them the individual love they need."

"Is this pregnancy any easier than the first one?"

"Yes. The first time, I worried about the work and my financial situation. After praying about it, my worries subsided a little, but not completely. The women at my church helped a lot too. By not condemning me for my mistakes, they showed me what Christianity really means."

"Why were you worried about money? Did Saul leave when you told him you were pregnant?... You don't have to answer that one if you don't want."

"Saul didn't know about the pregnancy." Sadie began to fidget in her seat. "It's a long story and much too personal. Suffice it to say, I was keeping a promise I had made." She smiled weakly at Bart, who returned it with a genuine one.

"One more question. I know you're tired. Do you plan to have any more children after this?"

Sadie laughed. "I think this is the wrong time to ask. Even Peggy would say no at the present time. And this is her first. The last few months have been very uncomfortable for both of us. Now that Peggy's in the first stage of labor, she..."

"What?!!" Harry exclaimed as he entered the room. The mid-concert break had arrived. The other Spidars slapped his back in congratulations. He put his arms around Peggy. "Why didn't you tell me before this gig?"

"The contractions didn't get hard until we went into the press conference," she said. "If Sadie can stick it out, so can I."

Sadie's face lost color again.

"Are you planning to wait until the last minute again?" Saul asked in a scolding tone.

Sadie's smile was strong and true as her color returned. "No, we'll have a longer ride tonight. Dr. Gothic said to come in when the contractions are ten minutes apart. They aren't even regular yet. So this could even be false labor. Don't get excited." She turned to Harry. "Don't you worry, either. Peggy's contractions are twelve minutes apart. She has plenty of time to enjoy your show."

Harry looked baffled. "Can't they get down to ten minutes in a spit-spot?"

Peggy laughed. "Yes, they can, but I don't go to the hospital until they're five minutes apart since this is my first pregnancy. It's only future ones that'll be quicker."

The tension in the room was getting too high and would affect the second half of the show if not eased. Rich crossed over to Sadie and Peggy and gave them each a kiss.

"Good timing. If we hadn't finished up in London early, we would've missed this," he chuckled.

"What's so funny?" Bart asked.

"I don't think it's a bit droll," Saul added.

Rich smirked. "I wasn't laughing at that. I remembered what Sadie said about the tinies' actions when music's playing. In my mind's eye, I imagined little moppets, unable to talk or roll over, but when Sadie handed them guitars the size of a tablespoon, their fingers and arms knew right where to go to

175

play her favorite: 'Got to be rock and roll music, if you want to dance with me.'"[21] The Spidars smiled. Pam didn't fully understand, but she smiled too.

Sadie turned to Pam. "May I read your article before you send it in?"

"Of course!" Pam replied. "Maybe you'll be able to add something. It'll be done tomorrow. Give me your number and I'll call when it's finished."

"No, I'll call you. What hotel are you staying at?"

Pam's voice lowered. "I'm cheap. I'm staying at the Quality Court on West Henrietta Road."

"Don't apologize for thriftiness. I respect that. When I call you tomorrow, I should be able to give you the exclusive on the births, too."

Pam's smile widened. She left the room, but instead of going back to the reporters' room, she went out to watch the show with an air of confidence.

Peggy and Sadie sat in the wings during the last half of the show. That is, they sat most of the time. At one point, when Rich noticed Sadie dancing in the wings with Bart, his eyes glimmered with mischief. All the men knew she concentrated on her partner completely when she danced, which was probably why her waddle disappeared. Rich used this concentration to plan his strategy. Between songs, he spoke with Bart.

Ten minutes later, Sadie found herself in the middle of the stage at the end of a song. When she saw the nearby audience, her mouth opened in a large O. She spun around in time to see Bart laugh along with the fiendish, conniving drummer.

"You clowns!" she yelled, waddling off the stage. She sat down with Peggy. There was no way they'd trick her again! She simply wouldn't dance any more tonight. Period. The men on stage were still chuckling as they began their next song.

After the concert, the group went home to pick up suitcases and inform Carol of her duties for the next few days. Sadie also went into the triplets' bedroom and gave each of them a kiss goodbye.

Dr. Gothic met them at the hospital. Due to Sadie's telephone request earlier in the evening, he had a double room ready for them. They planned to avoid the labor and delivery rooms and make this as much like a home delivery as possible, within the safety of the hospital. If something went wrong, they would be seconds from the delivery room equipment and only a minute from the operating room.

As soon as Peggy lay on her back, she moaned.

"I warned you that position increases pain," Sadie stated.

When the contraction ebbed, Peggy tried to sit up. "Oh, no!" she shrieked. "Here comes another one! Sadie, do something for the pain! Fast!"

Standing next to the bed, Sadie shook her head. "It won't be long. When the pains come piggy-back, you're almost done."

"Quit lecturing and give me something for the pain! My toes are curling!"

"I can't do anything for the pain of labor. I told you that last week. If I were to kill the pain, it would affect the contractions and possibly even the baby. Try to grin and bear it, Peg."

Dr. Gothic examined Peggy. "You're nine centimeters dilated and fully effaced. A couple more like that one and you'll be ready." He turned to Sadie. "You should lie down and let me look at you, too."

"Not necessary doc," Sadie replied. "I know where I am in the labor process." Her face turned white.

"You need to lie down NOW. Have you felt dizzy during contractions?"

"No, this is just how I react to pain. I'm okay." Her whisper was barely audible. "I warned you this wouldn't be a run-of-the-mill delivery. You promised to let me do it my way." When her contraction was over, her face regained its pinkish glow. She placed a hand on Peggy's belly and concentrated. "Doc, Peg is ready to start pushing," she stated calmly, turning white again.

"How do you know?" Dr. Gothic asked. He looked at Peggy, who nodded agreement. He checked for full dilation of the cervix. "Go ahead." He moved away to allow Harry to get into position.

"Sadie," Saul said as she went white again, "How far apart are your pains?"

"Two minutes," Rich answered from near the other bed. "I've been timing 'em."

"I suppose you know how long they last, too, with that new watch of yours," Sadie said.

Rich didn't have a new watch, but he understood the hint.

"I see the head!" Sadie said suddenly. "Come on, Amanda. Daddy's waiting for you with open arms!" She dimmed the lights. "Peg, stop pushing." Harry grimaced, with the baby's slimy head in one hand. The doctor nodded.

"I can't," Peggy replied.

"You must," Sadie said sternly. "The head is out and the shoulders need to move slowly. Pant and think about the relief that comes after the shoulders finish. The rest will slip out fast, like Jell-O."

As the shoulders inched their way out of the hole ever so slowly, Sadie guided Harry's free hand under the baby's upper torso, preparing for the climax. The others watched attentively as the baby slid out with a 'pop!' Dr. Gothic suctioned the mouth.

Amanda cooed contentedly in Harry's arms as the doctor cut the umbilical cord. While Peggy pushed again and the doctor caught the placenta, the others fawned over the pretty new addition to the Spidar family, with her deep brown eyes, pin-curl hair, and long lashes.

Sadie walked to her bed and climbed onto it, her face staying white now.

When the doctor finished the placenta, he told Harry to give the baby to Peggy. "She should suckle on a breast to get the colostrum flowing. Colostrum contains the ingredients to prevent..."

"Say, Doc," Jo-Jo interrupted, "Sadie's about to go off!"

The others turned to her, but Sadie was oblivious to their attention. She was concentrating on her breathing and on the circular movements of her hands. Suddenly, she looked up. "Doc, I need you. NOW!"

She began to push and a baby's head emerged, followed slowly by the shoulders. The room quieted as Dr. Gothic guided Saul's hands into position. He also summoned two nurses and a pediatrician, just in case. Saul caught the first one and moved over so Rich could take his place at home plate. Jo-Jo took a turn on the third one, and Dr. Gothic caught the fourth one, handing it to Sadie, to be suckled while he finished his work. A nurse attached wrist bands quickly to make sure each baby received the correct tag.

As each baby had its turn at Sadie's breast, its eyes were glued on her face. She stroked its forehead and made a circle around its head. By the time the babies returned to the men's arms and the pediatrician examined each of them, they gurgled happily.

Sadie's eyes gleamed as she looked at Saul with a proud smile. "They're all healthy!" she whispered.

"Was there ever any doubt?" he replied, his own eyes gleaming proudly.

Dr. Gothic patted Sadie's shoulder. "You did a good job, young lady. Now get some rest. When you take this litter home, you won't get any more chances."

Sadie smiled. "I know, Doc. I learned that lesson two years ago."

*

The next morning, Sadie called Pam at the motel. "Hi! It's Sadie McCarthy... Yes, I'm fine. Do you have your writing done yet? ... Please do." Sadie wrote notes as Pam read the article to her. "That's good, but I do have a few suggestions. The second paragraph might be misunderstood. Could you change it a little?... Yes, that's better. Also, in the last paragraph, the first sentence, while true, it's very personal. Do you have to include it or will your editor be satisfied without it? ... Great! Thank you.

"Now for the new news. Amanda George was the first born. Then came Vera, Chuck, Dave, and Rita McCarthy, in that order. All five are healthy and gorgeous like their fathers. And they were all born with full heads of hair, mop-tops you could say.... Yes, Peggy and I are doing fine."

That evening, the *Democrat and Chronicle* paper carried the United Press International story: "FIVE NEW SPIDARS ADDED TO THE WEB!" by Pam Hope...

Chapter 11 – June 1968

As Peggy brought a tray of tea and cookies into the music room, the phone rang. "I'll get it," Rich offered. "Rich's mortuary. You stab 'em, we slab 'em." Jo-Jo snickered and Saul smiled.

Rich took the phone away from his ear and looked at it quizzically. Deciding it wasn't defective, he put it back to his ear and spoke. "Harry, slow down, mate. You're as clear as mud."

"Why would Harry call?" Peggy whispered to Saul. "He and Sadie only left thirty minutes ago." Saul shrugged.

"I still cannot understand," Rich said into the phone. "Put Sadie on. She's cool-headed … Sadie? Is that you? Speak up, little lady." He motioned for quiet in the room. Saul closed the windows to block out lake noises. "Where are you? … What! What happened? … We'll be there in a short."

He slammed down the phone and ran to the hall door. "They're at hozzy! Sadie's…"

Saul interrupted. "On another mission of mercy, I suspect. Don't get so bloody strokey."

"No. They were in quite a prang. By the sounds of it, Sadie's been hurt … bad." Peggy jumped to the phone and pressed a button. "Carol, we have to leave ASAP. You're in charge of the kids when they get up from their naps."

On the way out, Jo-Jo grabbed Miki from the living room, where she had been reading. Three men and three women climbed into the disguised Spidar van.

*

The morning had begun innocently enough. Sadie had gone through her normal routine of feeding the toddlers, putting records on the stereo, and then exercising in the kitchen while the triplets played in the living room. She left the double doors open between the two rooms, but all the hallway doors were closed, so the music wouldn't bother anyone upstairs as long as their intercoms were off.

Sadie was still exercising when Peggy entered the kitchen. "I wish I had that much energy," Peggy said wistfully. "I don't know how you do it. Aren't you tired from getting up during the night?"

Sadie smiled and continued her improvisations. She didn't do exercises that could be found in any books. They were more like exaggerated dance steps. They had reshaped her hourglass figure quickly. On the other hand, Peggy's belly was still large and limp, making her feel ugly and undesirable. She knew it would tighten up eventually, but impatience reigned along with a bit of jealousy. Sadie was back to normal after only two weeks. And the men had begun their flirtations again. Envy was hard to suppress.

When the song ended, Sadie poured two cups of coffee and sat down. "Peg, I wish you'd stop comparing yourself to me. You're on schedule, and Harry loves you the way you are."

"I know," Peggy blushed. How did Sadie always guess what she was thinking? "But, I've been hoping you could do something to speed up my progress."

"I can't. If I mess around with your body, it will affect your milk. And I don't use my powers for cosmetic reasons."

"Yes you do. What about the fireman?"

It was Sadie's turn to blush. "Okay, you're right. I did more than necessary to save his life. That was different. Ted would have been terribly scarred. You, on the other hand, will be fine in a few months." She rose to prepare breakfast for the adults before the infants needed her.

*

Later in the day, while the children were napping, Sadie interrupted the men in the music room. "Could someone take me to the store, please? Doc wants me to wait a while before driving. He says my mind will be gone for a few weeks." The men smiled. She didn't give them time to add their own remarks. "Actually, he said I won't be as alert as normal, and my longer reaction time might cause a problem."

"Why don't you have Miki drive?" Jo-Jo offered.

Sadie shook her head. "She would be recognized too easily in this town. I need someone who is experienced in the art of incognito travel."

The men turned to Harry. He was the one who enjoyed going out in public. Harry laughed. "Sure! I love driving pretty girls around. It's good for my image." Sadie put her hands on her waist and wiggled her hips.

"Act proper-like," Rich warned Harry.

Harry raised his eyebrows. "No promises given mean none broken." He headed upstairs to change.

Sadie waited outside next to Harry's canary yellow Impala. Sunlight bounced off the clear blue water of the lake, spreading like an eagle's wings and shining on everything in its path. A gentle breeze fluffed her baggy shirt and farmer's coveralls.

Harry came out dressed in black tie and tails. His long hair was pushed under a short gray wig, a top hat over it all.

Sadie giggled. "You're supposed to avoid attention, you know. In that get-up, everyone's gonna stare."

"They won't know who I am."

"And the bag lady, me, now has a chauffeur." They both laughed as the car roared down West Lake Road.

Drawing closer to their destination, Harry stopped at a red light. "...*Something in the way she moves*...."[24] came over the radio as Harry waited for the light to turn green. He glanced at Sadie. She was putting a floppy felt hat on her head to complete her ensemble.

Harry lifted his right hand, which had been resting on the back of Sadie's seat, and brushed her cheek lightly. A familiar excitement rose in his groin. "I can see through the excess fabric," he commented. She turned to him and smiled.

H-O-N-K! came a blare from the car behind them. Harry rolled the car away from its stop. With confidence, he peeked back at Sadie, who now looked at their destination.

Too late, he looked beyond her out the passenger window. Too late, he saw the beat-up maroon car speeding toward them. Too late, he saw a police unit, with red lights flashing, chasing that car. Too late, he noticed the maroon car not slow down. Too late, both hands clutched the steering wheel as he floored the gas pedal to try to outrun it.

The maroon car hit them on the front passenger side at eighty miles an hour. Metal on metal, the noise pierced the ears like a thousand fingernails on the same blackboard at the same time. Sadie's body thumped against his. The Impala traveled sideways, like a crab, in a northward direction, the opposite of where they desired to go. After interminable moments, the Impala finally came to rest with the front tires on a grassy median 160 yards from the intersection.

Harry stared ahead of him, at the oncoming traffic, inches away from his front hood. His right side felt the pressure of Sadie's body.

A policeman looked into the car. "I'll call an ambulance," he said as he rushed away.

Harry turned to Sadie. The passenger seat curled over her, the door scrunched into it. Her face looked white despite the bronze make-up she wore.

"You'll be okay," he lied. "Hold on." His movements felt fuzzy.

"Have them call Dr. Gothic," Sadie whispered.

He shook his head slowly. "He's an obstetrician!" Harry exclaimed. "He can't help you now."

Her reply was slow. "Dr. Gothic is from the old school, back when they trained doctors to handle everything. I don't want a stranger."

*

"Listen, Harry," Dr. Gothic was saying when the others arrived at Sadie's hospital room, "You're not doing her any good like this. If you don't calm down, I'll have to medicate you." Peggy rushed over and put her arms around Harry.

Saul walked to the bed and reached for Sadie's hand. The doctor grabbed his arm. "Watch where you touch. She has internal bleeding over most of her right side." Sadie smiled weakly.

He kissed her forehead gently and turned to the doctor. "Why aren't you giving her bagged blood or something?"

"She says no transfusions," the doctor replied. "I checked and she's right. Her body won't even tolerate plain plasma. She won't let me operate, either. Maybe you can change her mind, but you'd better hurry. We don't have much time."

"Why do you need her permission to save her life? Just do it!"

"Under normal circumstances I would, but this must be done without anesthesia. She thinks she's allergic to that too. With her full cooperation, we would have less than a 50-50 chance of saving her, due to the blood situation. Without it,

185

our chances diminish considerably. There's no sense if she doesn't want me to operate."

Saul turned to Sadie. "Why won't you let him carve?"

"My body will reject the stitches," Sadie whispered.

"What can be done, then?" Rich asked from behind Saul. "We can't stooge around and let you bleed all inside yourself!"

Sadie closed her eyes without replying. Except for Harry's mumbling, jerky movements, and pacing, silence filled the room. Heavy breathing could be heard as the doctor placed ice packs along her right side to slow the circulatory system as much as possible.

Finally, Peggy spoke: "There IS something we can do. Sadie knows what it is, but she won't accept help for herself. It has always been for others. Isn't that true, Sadie?"

Sadie didn't open her eyes. "Yes, there is something you can do. You can promise to help Saul with the kids for the first few years."

"Stop talking as if you're going to die!" Peggy yelled.

"Harry would take Jason on a moment's notice," Jo-Jo stated.

Sadie's eyes shot open. "No! It's all or nothing. I don't want my kids split up!" She looked around the room at the men. "Remember your pact. You promised to accept the responsibilities if you share the benefits. Well, I've done my bit. In fact, I've done my very best. Now you do the rest. It's my turn to collect. Promise ..." Her voice trailed off like a radio with a weak battery.

"Maybe it's time we go our separate ways," Jo-Jo replied.

Peggy shot him a disgusted look. "Sadie, don't listen to him. He will help. You know he will." Harry's mumbling intensified. "As for Harry, I don't know if he can." Harry's arms flailed the air, his mumble now a scream. "She'sgonnadie! Ik-k-killedher! Ikilledher!"

186

Peggy held him as tightly as she could. "If you won't let us help you, at least tell us how to help Harry, please!"

Sadie put her hand out to Harry. When he came closer, she motioned for him to bend down. Though hysterical, he complied. Sadie caressed his face with her hand. His fast, jerky movements vanished and his face turned placid.

"I'm sorry," he said to her. Sadie's lips tilted at the edges in a Mona Lisa smile, her cheeks gaining a slight pinkish glow.

Rich recognized his cue to lighten the mood. "I guess new fathers shouldn't drive for a few weeks either."

Sadie's new glow gave Peggy an idea. "Sadie," she said, "To calm Harry, you removed his excess energy, right? Couldn't you use energy like that to doctor yourself?"

Sadie closed her eyes again.

"I'm getting miffed, Lady. There must be a way to get through to you." Peggy thought for a moment and then smiled. "You always say we need each other, that no one is any better than anyone else. Yet now you try to act so perfect. Stop the pretense and let us help you."

Sadie's eyes opened. She glanced around the room, stopping at Miki and staring. Miki stared back. For a few moments, the two women seemed oblivious to the others in the room.

Then Sadie's eyes closed again. "Sadie says to stop using her own words against her," Miki said.

"How would you know that?" Peggy retorted.

"She told me telepathically. She says you're right, Peg. There is a way she can take energy from other people, but if she takes the minimum amount necessary in this case, it would kill the donor. She won't do that just to save herself."

"Why would she tell YOU all of this, and not one of us?" Turning back, Peggy snarled, "Thanks a lot, Sadie. After all we've been through together, you prefer to speak to an outsider. I thought you and I were closer than that." With that, she stomped out of the room.

Sadie's eyes opened again and this time she stared at Harry. Her color ebbed. The lids fell. Quietly, Harry went out and brought Peggy back into the room.

"Fine, I'm here," Peggy said. "What's the message Sadie just gave you, Harry?"

Harry looked at the others in the room. "Sadie said to tell Peg in your presence." He squeezed Peg's shoulders. "Peg, we're all a bit slow on the uptake about what Sadie does, but I know why she chose Miki a few minutes ago."

"Why?"

"Do you see how pale she is now?" he asked. Peggy nodded. "Well, she didn't lose color when she talked to Miki's mind. She lost it when she spoke to me. She had to use extra energy to get through to my mind. She doesn't need extra with Miki, because Miki has trained her mind to stay open."

Harry paused, trying to remember everything. "Peg, Sadie says you have the same ability, but your brain was blocked by the anger that Sadie was refusing help."

Peggy blushed in embarrassment. "Sorry, Sadie. Here you are sicker than a dog and I get offended by who you talk to. I really am sorry." No response from Sadie.

"Oh, she said one more thing," Harry continued, "It seems even talking through my thick skull uses up less energy than it takes to speak out loud. She can't answer you anymore. She doesn't have enough sparks left."

Silence again filled the room. A few minutes later, Peggy smiled at the family. "Sadie's afraid she might drain one of us too much, right?" They nodded. "Well, how about all of us? Miki, see what she thinks about us holding hands in a circle. Ask her if she can do it that way."

Sadie's lips curled. Miki snickered. "She says she's not deaf, just dumb, and Rich, she's not talking about her intelligence. We can talk to her directly and she will answer through me."

Rich laughed aloud this time. "Right-oh, so how about the idea, Sugar?"

"Quite under the weather," Saul stated, smoothing her hair absent-mindedly.

Miki looked up. "Peggy, your idea's good, but she says you can't be in the circle. You don't have any spare energy with the nursing and all."

As Peggy began to protest, Miki waved her remarks away and continued. "Dr. Gothic can verify it if you wish. She also says we'll need someone to drive us home afterwards, because we'll be tired and our reflexes will suffer. She wants Harry to stay out of the circle too. She only took out his excess energy. He still has his normal stuff."

"Put our lives in his hands?!!!" Rich teased.

Harry shook his head. "You're off your rocker. I'm packing it in. I won't drive again for a long chalk."

"She says that's exactly why you have to be the one to drive us home," Miki stated. "If you don't try now, you'll end up with a phobia the rest of your life."

"No way! Someone else can spin the wheel."

Sadie's face went limp. Miki's face turned sour. "She says this is the only way she'll consider our help."

"C'mon, Harry," Saul begged, "You know Sadie can be headstrong at times. You'd better do as she says. If you try to wait her out, she may be stubborn enough to croak on us." Reluctantly, Harry moved behind the night stand.

"She needs the head of the bed propped," Miki said. As Dr. Gothic obeyed, Miki continued, "Rich, then Jo-Jo, stand on the right side of the bed, Saul on the left, then me."

"Why so picky?" Jo-Jo asked.

Miki responded in a matter-of-fact tone, "Sadie's afraid she may drain someone a little too much, so she'll keep track of Saul and Rich through their hands. Your vital functions and mine will transmit through my brain. How? I don't know. I'm just repeating what she says."

Sadie's eyes stayed closed as Saul and Rich each took hold of one of her hands. The circle was complete. Within moments, her eyes opened. She pulled her hands from the circle and hid them under the sheet covering her body. As her hands moved, she stared at the ceiling. Normal color slowly returned to her face. With a sigh, she brought her hands out.

Saul and Rich grabbed her hands again to reform the circle. "That's not necessary," Sadie giggled, "unless you just like holding hands."

"You didn't have the ticks to take much from us," Saul stated.

Sadie smiled devilishly. "How much time does it take?" Then she turned serious. "I took all the energy that was safe. You'll have a delayed reaction. By the time you get to the van, you'll feel drained. Besides, I already fixed my worst problem, the leaking artery. By tomorrow, I'll be able to fix the little spurts with my own steam. Thanks to you all."

Her eyes fixed on Harry. "Stop blaming yourself. If that drunk hadn't been on the road in the middle of the day, running from the cops to boot, it wouldn't have happened."

"If I hadn't had my mind on ..." He paused. "You would've been safer driving yourself."

She reached over to the nightstand, grabbed Harry's top hat and put it on his head. "Not necessarily ... And the ride wouldn't have been as regal." She glanced at the others. "I need to rest now, and so do you. Thanks again."

Dr. Gothic ushered the family from the room, but Saul hesitated. "I'd rather stay."

"No," Sadie replied. "Go home and give the kids a hug for

190

me. I love you."

*

That evening, after the toddlers were in bed and before the nine o'clock feeding for the infants, the adults gathered in the living room. Everyone who had participated in the circle admitted to fatigue, but Saul was the only quiet one. Peggy tried to improve his mood with a blueberry cobbler Sadie had made before the accident. He refused his piece.

"Matey," Jo-Jo said to Saul between bites. "She'll be fit as a fiddle soon."

"Yeah," Rich added, "she'll be home in a tick. You know how quickly she springs to life after her energies have been drained."

"That's not the point," Saul blurted out. "Harry hasn't told us how it all happened. What's with the drunk and the cops? And most of all, what were you thinking about?"

Full of regret, Harry explained as much as he could recall, in honest detail. When he finished, Saul's face was fiery red. "This is all because your headspace was in her hole!" Saul shouted.

"I wish I could begin the day again," Harry admitted. "What more do you want? If I could trade places with Sadie right now, I would."

Miki whispered something to Peggy, who nodded. "Saul, maybe you should go to bed," Peg suggested. "You'll feel better in the morning."

"Doubtful," Saul mumbled as he headed upstairs.

When he was out of earshot, Peggy flicked the transmitter on the wall to the Off position. "Okay, he can't hear us," she said. "What's wrong with him, other than the obvious?"

Rich snickered. "Most likely riled that he won't get any tonight." Peggy shot him a sour look.

191

"No," Harry said absently. "He's dead right getting a mood on. I'd go off me head, too, if someone almost killed my wife because..."

Miki interrupted him. "You're both wrong." She saw scowls directed her way from around the room. "I didn't mean that the way it sounded." She turned to Peggy. "It wasn't my idea he go to bed. It was Sadie's. She's worried about him."

"C'mon, Sweets," Jo-Jo said. "The lady is at least three miles away. Don't fob us off."

"Believe what you will. Sadie told me she knows what's bothering him, but she won't tell me what it is. She said she tried to communicate with him directly, but his mind is blocked by guilt."

"Why would he feel delinquent?" Harry asked. "I did the driving."

Jo-Jo shook his head. "Why wouldn't she give a ring? He can't block out the blower."

"I don't know," Miki replied. "Let me ask." She closed her eyes to concentrate. A minute passed, then another and another. Suddenly, she laughed and opened her eyes.

"What's so waggish?" Rich asked.

"I had a tough time getting through. She put me on hold! It seems she's having trouble with a night nurse and she was in the middle of an argument with her when I tried."

Rich replied with a chuckle, turning to Harry. "That sounds like Sadie. Remember Saul's flap about how she argued the toss with the doctor after that first delivery?" The other men smiled too.

"In any case," Miki continued, "She couldn't use the phone. A while ago, the nurse removed the phone from the wall jack, saying Sadie wouldn't get any rest if she was on the phone all night. She had been speaking with Gene and Reverend Bee. Just now, the nurse argued about the television, but this time,

Sadie won. The television is too heavy for the nurse to remove and has the on/off switch in the same box as the emergency nurse-call-button. She says the nurse left in quite a huff."

"That's our Sadie!" Jo-Jo quipped.

Rich laughed. "Yeah, she'll likely leave the telly on all night just to put years on the nurse." He rose from his seat. "I'm going for a spin."

*

Sadie giggled when Rich walked into her hospital room. "You know it's past visiting hours, don't you?"

He winked. "Yeah, the lady at the front desk told me. I said my wife was having a baby, so she let me up."

A mischievous smile rose on Sadie's face. "Their first line of defense is easy. The fun part will be to convince my nurse about the baby. She already dislikes me... for some stra-a-a-nge reason."

Rich smiled, glad he decided to come. All evening he had wondered if Sadie merely pretended to feel better. She had done it before to prevent worry. Yet her giggle couldn't be forced, and neither could the prankish attitude. "You're in good spirits," he said. "Did you get enough rest?"

"Maybe." She thought for a moment. "I felt a lot better after I got the nurse's goat about the television. It was good medicine for me. Now that you know I'm okay, are you going to stay out of trouble by leaving?"

"Only if you really want me to go."

"Good. I hoped you'd stay."

"I could get your blower back from the old grumble-guts."

Sadie giggled again. "You'll be pleasantly surprised. The nurse is not an old woman. She's in her mid-twenties, a cute blonde with a bit of a stubborn streak. And, you can forget about the phone. I already figured out what I'll do."

Rich waited quietly for a few seconds. "Well?"

"Well, what?" Sadie asked, feigning ignorance.

"Are you going to explain your trump?"

"It's simple, really. Tomorrow, I'll walk down the hall to the pay phone when I'm sure she will see me. I'll falter a bit here and there on the way."

Rich frowned. "You might get hurt. I'll stay with you all night, and if you want to call someone, I'll see to it pronto."

"You're no fun!"

Rich climbed on the bed and lay with his arm around her. Sadie put her head on his shoulder to watch *Dr. Kildaire* on the television. She was asleep before the first commercial ended.

When the nurse did her next rounds, she took one look at Rich and scolded quite loudly, "You should not be in here!"

"Sh-h-h-h!" Rich warned. "She's asleep."

The nurse lowered her volume. "Visiting hours are over. You may have brainwashed the doctor into canceling many rules, but you can't break all of them. You must leave. NOW!"

"Why?" Rich asked with a smirk. Sadie was right. The nurse was cute, with strawberry blonde hair, a turned-up nose, and round dimples.

"Because the patient needs her rest. That's why."

Rich shook his head. "When I arrived, your patient was a bundle of nerves. At present, she's sleeping like a baby. You must admit my presence is restful."

"Perhaps..." she faltered. "NO! I'll admit no such thing. It's against hospital policy. You must leave."

Rich's face turned serious. "Call Dr. Gothic. If he says I should tootle off, I will. If it's all the same to you then."

The nurse stood silent, remembering the instructions written on Sadie's chart: *Allow patient to bend minor rules. Call me only if her ideas are dangerous.* Dr. Gothic had a reputation for being bearish when disturbed at home. She didn't dare call him with this sort of thing. She turned abruptly to leave. As she grabbed the door handle, someone pushed it from the other side. She stepped back quickly.

Saul entered. "How's she doing?" he asked Rich in a whisper.

"Right fine. She settled once I folded her to my heart. I suppose you'll take over now."

"No. Don't wake her. I'll watch telly with you from the chair."

"This has gone too far!" the nurse exclaimed. "There's absolutely no way we can allow both of you to stay in here! How will the patient get any sleep?"

Sadie's eyes flickered, then opened. As she rubbed them, Rich spoke harshly, "You're more of a rotter to her than we are."

"Be off!" Saul added. "Another nurse can take over here."

Rich chuckled. "That won't be needed, Mate. Sadie knows her onions." He smirked at the nurse. "Looky here, Honey Pie. Our luvin' angel doesn't get mad, she gets even." Sadie giggled.

"I'm not afraid of her!" the nurse shot back, pointing a finger at her own chest. "I follow rules."

"Whoa!" Rich exclaimed. "Sadie was right. You are quite spunky."

"I am not!" she yelled.

"Control yourself or you'll spurt," Saul said with a laugh. "From Sadie, that's a compliment."

"Oh," she said softly. A moment passed as the nurse regained her composure. When she did, her voice was calm and professional. "I still must ask at least one of you to leave."

Rich kissed Sadie tenderly and slid off the bed. "Quite right. Now that Saul is standing guard, I can kip myself." He started to tag the nurse out of the room. In the doorway, he winked at Sadie and patted the nurse on the rump. "Stay alert!" he warned. "Sadie will get you yet."

"Not like that she won't!" The nurse slapped his face and continued her rounds.

"Ho-ho!" Rich said as he rubbed his face and followed her, his hips wiggling in imitation.

*

The next morning, Saul came home to help tend to the children. When he walked into the kitchen, the household was eating breakfast. He glanced at Rich and snickered.

"Did she do it?" Rich asked.

"Yup, before Martha's shift ended this morning."

"M-m-m, Martha, pretty name. She wouldn't tell me last night." Rich smiled. "I warned her to watch out for Sadie. You heard me."

"That you did," Saul replied. "You should've been there. Sadie had ME convinced she couldn't walk right on her own."

"What the heck are you two gabbing about?" Harry asked. Saul explained the scheme to the family. As the others had a morning chuckle, Peggy shook her head. "Something doesn't make sense. Why was the same nurse still on duty this morning?"

"Someone called in sick last night and Martha worked a double. Sadie thinks that's why she was a bit grumpy, knowing she still had a lot of time to go. Anyways, you should've seen her face when Sadie stumbled down the hall this morn. Needless to say, the jingler returned immediately. Sadie was chatting up the nurse up as I left."

*

"Why do you hate me so?" Sadie asked the nurse at her bedside.

196

Martha replied with venom. "I don't hate you. I hate what you stand for."

"What do you mean?"

Martha glared into Sadie's eyes. "The costumes don't fool me. I know who your guests are, who you are. You don't have to live by the rules. You have the money to change any rules to suit your whims. That's not fair. Everyone, rich or poor, should live by the same rules."

Sadie smiled. "I agree life isn't fair, but it can be enjoyed nevertheless. Also, I believe rules are made as guidelines for proper conduct. None of them are absolute. If we were robots, there could be one set of rules for everybody. Since we're not, we can adjust them to suit individual needs as long as we don't jeopardize other people's rights."

"You wouldn't get away with that philosophy if you weren't rich and famous."

Sadie shook her head and giggled. "Believe it or not, I bent some rules long before I had any money. I know what it's like to be dirt poor. My family barely stayed afloat when I was growing up. We went without many things other kids took for granted." Martha lowered her head in embarrassment.

"Oh, don't get me wrong," Sadie continued, "I don't look for pity. Never did. I had fun as a child, a lot of fun. We didn't have store-bought things, but we made our own toys and used our imagination. Behind our house, there was a gully that was wet most of the time. We loved to play there. We would use cattails as swords, the ditch as a moat around our castle.

"We missed having our mother home with us, though. Most of the other mothers on our street stayed home, but my mother had to work so we could eat. Oh, well, I do tend to ramble. The point I'm trying to make is that we, the Spidar family, are just ordinary people who..."

Martha interrupted. "Ordinary? Your husband and his

group are kings of the world. Do you call that ordinary?"

"Yes, ordinary. The men have normal male needs and desires. They also worked very, very hard to develop their talents. They made personal sacrifices to achieve group goals. In the process, a special bond grew between them, a bond cemented with love."

"Are you saying they are queer?"

"Certainly not!"

"You said…"

Sadie nodded. "Unusual but not queer in the sexual sense. They have a strong brotherly love. You know, none of them had it easy growing up either. None of them was born with money, especially Rich. His family had less money than mine did."

Martha looked at her with suspicion. "Why are you telling me all this?"

"Because I get the feeling you like Rich a bit."

Martha cleared her throat. "What makes you think that?"

Sadie raised one side of her mouth. "It is true, right?"

"Maybe a little."

"Would you like to see if anything can develop?"

Martha tilted her head. "Why would you help me after I've been so nasty?"

Sadie pursed her lips as a mother would do. "Many people wear a tough exterior to prevent others from seeing inside. You're sensitive to the underdog. I think you may be the other person we need to make our group soar to new heights. Are you willing to try?"

"I guess so."

Sadie smiled. "Good! Then here's my plan…"

Chapter 12 - Homecoming

A full day passed. After breakfast the following morning, Martha drove Sadie home. The yellow sun glowed in a sea of blue. Arriving at the gate to the McCarthy estate, Martha parked over to the side so the brick wall would hide her car if anyone from the house happened to walk down the driveway.

Jerry opened the pedestrian door at the left of the gate and talked with the girls for a few minutes. He confirmed that the men were in the pool area and then warned that Peggy, Miki, and the triplets had returned to the house a while ago and the pool gate was open facing the driveway.

Sadie looked at her watch and altered her plans a little. She and Martha walked briskly along the inside of the brick wall until they reached the trees. They walked the length of the orchard, passing the pool from the closed sides as quietly as they could so the men wouldn't hear them above the music coming from the music room. Once past it, Sadie picked up speed. By the time the two women reached the back of the house, Martha huffed and puffed.

Sadie opened the back kitchen door quietly. Miss Rita's voice filtered in from the television in the next room. Sadie tip-toed into the living room, making sure the intercom was off as she passed it. Peggy sat on one couch, breast-feeding two babies, and Carol and Miki juggled the bottles for the other three.

Roxanne was the first to notice Sadie. "Mummy!" she squealed with delight.

"Hi, Sweetheart! Did you miss me?" The noise level rose, drowning out Roxanne's reply. All three toddlers squealed and

199

danced around their mother. The other women in the room smiled too. They knew Sadie must be up to something, showing up unannounced like this.

When the triplets settled back to their television program, Sadie took two of the babies and put them to her breasts. Then she looked closer at the one Miki still held in her arms. "Peggy! Why is Amanda being bottle-fed, while you breastfeed Vera and Chuck?"

"They're taking turns. I didn't think it was fair for Amanda to get the good stuff all the time, while your kids had to settle for bottles." Peg's smile broadened. "You would have done the same thing if I were injured. In fact, I'm paying you back for the times you fed Amanda in the middle of the night so I could sleep. You could have given her bottles, but you gave her the real thing some of the time."

"How did you find out about that?"

"One night during that first week, I got up to use the privy. Since it was almost time for a feeding, I went to the infants' room. There you were breast-feeding Amanda and singing softly to her like you do with your own. I was tired, so I went back to bed. From then on, I didn't worry if I slept through a feeding. I knew you'd take good care of her." Peggy shrugged. "It was selfish, sleeping while you took care of all five. Sorry."

Sadie smiled at the two babies at Peg's mammaries. "You have nothing to be sorry about. I think we're even now. Thank you. I appreciate it."

She turned to Miki and Carol. "And thank you too. I know everyone's had more than the normal workload lately. These kids can wear a person out fast."

"You're right," Miki admitted. "Even with the men helping, we're exhausted by the end of the day. How do you do it?"

"It's magic," Sadie teased. "I twitch my nose and the work is done. Then I can play with my family."

As Sadie laid Dave and Rita in the playpen, she glanced up at Martha, standing in the doorway. "Oh, where did I leave my manners? Girls, this is Martha McGuire, my favorite nurse at the hospital. Martha, this is Peggy George, Miki Uno, and my sister, Carol VanMark. C'mon in and make yourself at home."

Martha didn't move. She didn't speak.

"Martha," Sadie said louder, "Are you okay?"

"Huh, what? Oh, yes, I'm fine. I was just marveling at the teamwork in this house. I can feel the warmth you women share, the kind one hears about but rarely sees in action."

"I think it's special, too." Sadie's face turned serious. "But, I want to warn you. I put you on the payroll for a reason. You will see some things that are unacceptable under normal circumstances. I want you to remember that if things don't work out the way we hope, you are – above all – a nurse. You can't talk to anyone, ANYONE, about a patient or her family life. Agreed?"

Martha nodded. "I understand."

Sadie's smile returned. "If things go as planned, you will become a part of this loving family."

"You devil," Peggy snickered. "Are you being cupid again?"

"Ma-ay-be," she replied coyly. "Rich needs someone to call his own. I'm sure he's getting tired of us by now."

Miki shook her head. "Maybe he's tired of Peg and me, due to her condition and the fact that I'm only human, but according to Jo-Jo, all the men are anxious to resume relations with you. Have you explained our lifestyle to Martha yet?"

"No, she'll see for herself." Sadie turned to Martha. "Keep your mind open and try not to judge until you fully understand."

Martha tilted her head. "If you're talking about Peggy breast-feeding your babies, there's nothing wrong with that. It's not run-of-the-mill, but it's perfectly acceptable."

201

"We share more than the work," Sadie replied with a twinkle in her eyes. "You'll see." She turned to her sister. "Carol, I know you've been overworked the last few days, but I have one more favor to ask. Can you watch the kids while I make a grand entrance at the pool? You can call Josh in from his duties and say it's my request." After explaining her plan, Sadie took Martha upstairs to change. Peggy went outside.

Martha came down wearing a one-piece, pale-blue suit with a flowered skirt. Sadie wore a pop-lilac bikini. White gossamer dresses covered both suits. Sadie slipped into the music room and emerged later with a devilish grin.

"All set?" she asked when Peggy returned.

"Yes, the adapter's on and both hoses have nozzles."

"Great!" She flipped the switch back on for the intercom in the living room as the women left the house together. Peggy and Miki walked along the driveway, while Sadie and Martha slunk along the front of the house. Sadie grabbed the ends of the hoses and pulled them toward the pool, stopping behind a maple tree to ensure the men hadn't heard the swishing noise as the hoses snuck along the grass. Then she continued the trek.

When Sadie and Martha were in position, Miki and Peggy went into the pool area, shutting the gate behind them. They stopped in front of Saul and Rich, since the men were all in a row of lounge chairs along the fence.

"Where are the triplets?" Saul asked.

"Carol's watching them for a while," Peg replied. "Their favorite program's on TV."

Rich smiled. "Hm-m-m, more telly than Sadie allows?"

"No, I'm sure Sadie wouldn't mind today."

Behind the fence, guided by the voices, Sadie had her hose in position. She silently directed Martha's. Then she held up three fingers and started to count down. At zero, they each squirted, dropped the hoses, and hid under the ledge of the fence.

Saul and Rich jumped up with a loud "Hey!" They looked over the fence and saw the hoses but couldn't see who had done the deed. "I think the moppets are out," Saul said to Peggy. "You'd better check on 'em"

Peggy pushed the button on a panel to speak to Carol in the living room. "No, the kids are watching Miss Rita," Carol's voice came back.

"Perhaps they escaped when Carol wasn't looking," Peg offered the men, "and they returned before she noticed. They're getting a lot like their mother, aren't they?"

Behind the fence, Sadie waited until she heard the men sit back down. Then she motioned for Martha to crouch down and tip-toe to the opposite side of the pool. When enough time passed, she grabbed both hoses. This time, after squirting and throwing down the hoses, she ran to Martha. Her feet hardly touched the ground on the way.

Jo-Jo and Harry laughed fit to bust, but Rich and Saul ignored them. Realizing the culprits could hide under the ledge, Rich went out the pool gate on the end and Saul went out the gate on the side. As they stood at their respective corners on the outside, their eyes met in the middle.

"Man, the tots run faster than I thought," Rich said, staring at the dead hoses.

"Yeah," came Saul's reply, "Still and all, they'd better put the mockers on if they don't want their buns warmed."

The two walked back to their chairs and sat down. Saul waited a few minutes and then stood up and turned around quickly, hoping to catch the children in the act. He sighed when he didn't see anything.

"Are you getting paranoid now?" Jo-Jo asked with a laugh.

"You would, too, if you were drenched with ice water." He

sat down again.

Sadie returned to her position under the ledge without Martha. When she thought all the men had relaxed, she squirted. This time, she sprayed Harry and Jo-Jo.

"E-E-E-E-I-I-I-I!" they yelled.

"See what I mean?" Saul asked.

"They're gonna get it!" Harry exclaimed. He jumped onto a casual table Rich had made from a VW hood. He would have cleared the fence easily, but a squeak of the far gate interrupted him. Sadie ran in and hopped onto the diving board.

"Hel-l-l-o-o-o, boys!" she said with a wiggle of her hips. Removing her dress, she dove into the water and swam around the large ear painted on the bottom of the pool. Then she climbed the steps and the diving board again. Her body showed no bruises from the accident or stretch marks from the pregnancy. Suddenly the music over the intercom speakers changed. "... *purpose of a man is to love a woman*..."[25]

"Don't I get a welcome home kiss?" Sadie asked with another wiggle of her hips.

"C'mon over," Rich said. "I'll tend to you."

"... *purpose of a woman is to love her man*...."[25]

"Nope, you have to catch me if you can!" she replied.

"That sounds like a dare," Saul laughed. The men removed their shirts and jumped in.

Sadie did a swan dive and landed in the middle of them. As they closed in, she went underwater and swam away like a mermaid, fast and graceful. She avoided them for five minutes. Then she climbed onto the diving board again.

"Hey!" Jo-Jo said breathlessly. "You're supposed to be recuperating. Where are you getting all the bally pep?"

She giggled. "I rested all day yesterday." Peggy and Miki smiled. Martha stood next to them on the deck, eyes open wide.

"You were quite fagged last night," Harry argued. "That's why we kept our visit short."

"My dramatics are good, aren't they?" Sadie laughed. "I had a bit of energy."

Saul scowled. "Fobbin' us off, huh?"

"Nope. I didn't lie. I never told you I was tired, but you never asked how I felt. You assumed I'd be tired, so I played the part. Now I have an overabundance of energy built up. None of it should matter, though. There are four of you brawny men against one li'l ol' me. So catch me already."

The men huddled for a moment discussing strategy and then spread out. Sadie came off the diving board in a triple-twist cannonball, swimming with all her might once she hit the water. She swished in and out between the men, tickling lightly here or brushing her hair against bare skin there.

Tired and frustrated after a few more minutes, Rich floated on his back to relax. Sadie couldn't resist. She wiggled underneath, tickled his feet, and swam away. Caught by surprise, Rich went under the water and came up choking.

"Are you okay?" Sadie asked, swimming closer.

Rich grabbed her arm. "Gotcha (cough, cough). I knew (cough, cough) this would do it! (cough, cough)"

She didn't fight him. Instead she waited patiently until he stopped choking and then accepted his passionate kiss, returning it with sparks.

"Hey!" he yelled. "Are you trying to electrocute me?"

Sadie giggled. "The kind of sparks I send can't be transmitted by water, only by humans." She kissed his lips tenderly, as a mother would kiss a bruised elbow. "Did it hurt?"

Rich pouted. "A little, but..." He winked at her and smiled. "It was ecstasy!"

"Okay then, let me go so I can avoid the others."

Jo-Jo came up behind her and grabbed her other arm. "Too late," he said in a low voice. "I've got you already, Duckie." When his kiss finished, he turned her over to Saul.

"That's simply not fair," she protested.

"What's the matter, Luv?" Saul asked, feigning hurt feelings. "You don't want to say hello to your husband?"

"Of course I do, but you guys aren't playing by the rules."

"Perhaps you need to explain them better," Rich offered.

After taking care of Saul's greeting, Sadie looked around, expecting to find Harry nearby. Instead, he stood in the shallow end, staring into the water as he paced the width of the pool. She swam over to him.

"What's the problem? You don't like my shocking personality or something?"

Harry walked past her in silence. "Don't you feel well?" No answer. She glided in front of him, blocking his way. Then she bent down so her face was in line with his gaze. "Earth to Harry. Come in, Harry." She gently pushed his hair out of his face. "Talk to me, Harry. Something's bothering you. What is it? What did I do wrong?"

He shook his head. "You did nothing. It's... Oh never mind."

"Maybe I can help. If you don't tell me, I'll think I did something terrible."

Harry put his hands on her shoulders. "It's not you. It's me. I know if I collect your lips, I'll begin to get those thoughts again, the same ones that put you in the hozzy. I don't want to hurt you again."

Sadie looked around and kissed his wrist. "I don't see any oncoming vehicles here. And the accident was not your fault."

She felt someone's fingers on her back. She turned to see Rich swimming away, holding her bikini top high in the air. "You bugger!" she squealed, covering her chest with her arms.

206

"If you want it, come and get it!" Rich yelled back.

"Okay, buster!" Sadie swam at the bottom of the pool until she caught up to Rich in the deep end. Coming up halfway, she tugged hard at his shorts, bringing them down to his ankles.

That's when Rich noticed Martha, who stood with her mouth open. He dropped the top and pulled up his shorts.

Meanwhile Sadie whisked her property away and went to the bottom of the pool to put it back on. When she came up, Rich grabbed her by the waist. "You owe me one for that!" he warned.

"By my book, we're even."

"I won't argue the toss." Rich's voice dropped to a whisper, as he remembered Martha again. "It's been almost a year since we've been allowed the real thing with you." He put a hand on her buttocks and pulled her to him so she could feel his growing appendage. "Those hand jobs are good, but not as good as the real thing." He looked into her eyes and pouted. "I'm hurting, Sadie, hurting bad."

She shrugged. "Not in the pool. You know I hate an audience."

Rich winked at Saul. "I'm borrowing your bird for a mo." Saul nodded.

"What?!" Jo-Jo exclaimed. "What gives you special privileges?"

Rich pointed to his temple. "I caught her first, if I recall rightly. And I'm the only one on me tod for the last year."

Jo-Jo shook his head. "Come off it. All the girls have looked after you."

"Not often. This won't take long." He led Sadie out the gate to the woods.

The others tried to converse with Martha, but she replied with one and two words, no explanations, no comments. From the orchard, Rich let out an ear-piercing scream.

Saul laughed. "She was too much for him after so long."

"Nay," Harry said. "Most likely got stung by a bee – with his bare arse sticking in the air and all … Ha!"

Jo-Jo laughed, too. "Swollen marbles coming his way!"

Martha scowled. "You men are terrible. Maybe he's really hurt." She rose and walked to the gate, her nursing instincts overcoming any other feelings.

"I wouldn't go out there unless you want a peeperful," Saul warned. Martha's eyes shot arrows at him from the gate.

"Hi!" Sadie greeted as she and Rich slid into the pool area past her. Rich smiled contentedly but Sadie wore a worried expression. Martha ran past the two of them in tears.

Sadie turned and followed her, catching up to her near a peach tree filled with many tiny fruits. "You knew our lifestyle was different."

"I thought Rich was hurt," Martha said between light sobs. She was silent for a while. "I'll never be able to do that."

"Listen, Martha. We have something special here. You said that yourself in the living room. You could feel warmth filling the room. I agree that sex without love allows us to become like animals, or less. Yet, with love, sex can be very beautiful."

"You, you…." Marth faltered.

"Yes, I know. It seems we go against the grain, breaking all society's rules. Well, to paraphrase a philosopher named Pire: In today's world, it's not what you believe or don't believe, but whether you care."

"This may be a mistake," Martha responded. "I shouldn't have come here. I'm not … I can't … Communal sex is beyond my limitations."

Sadie chirped, "Rich won't touch you until you're ready. As for the other men, you don't have to worry until you and Rich get serious. And he will protect you for a while afterward. By then, you'll see it's not just casual sex. It's sharing and caring.

It's pushing a person to their greatest potential, sometimes when they don't have the gumption to push themselves. We know what makes each other tick. Why, Jo-Jo even tried to use my maternal instincts – that my kids would be separated – to energize me when I had given up hope at the hospital.

"Remember, I promised that if you're not comfortable by the end of one week, you can leave with no hard feelings. And you'll have our gratitude for trying. Okay?"

Martha hesitated. "I guess."

"There is no one compares with you."[26]

Chapter 13 – July 1968

A warm breeze blew, pushing colorful sailboats across the crystal clear, blue lake. This weather was much too nice to last long. Vacationing people dotted the shoreline before a predicted storm threatened the tranquility.

The Spidar household was no exception. They sailed, played croquet in the back yard with the triplets, and had a picnic lunch under the oak tree. Later, the women fed the infants while the men entertained the triplets with a sing-along of nursery rhymes.

Then, storm clouds rushed overhead and stole the sunshine. Everyone ran to the house with the first downpour. As the women put the children in bed for their naps, the men set up card tables and chairs in the living room for a game of Clue on one and Flip Your Wig on the other.

When the women returned, Sadie smiled devilishly and sat at the Clue table. The cards had already been dealt. Three cards hid in the "secret" pocket. No one had picked up a hand.

"Not bloody likely!" Jo-Jo quipped. "You and Miki sit at the other table.

"Why?" Sadie asked in mock innocence.

"We don't trust you," Harry replied. "We all think you cheat, using your telepathy to find out which cards we hold."

"I resent that remark." Sadie tried hard to look hurt, but the harder she tried, the more she giggled. "I don't deny it. I just resent it. Oh, by the way, you'd better redeal."

"Why?" Harry asked. "We haven't begun."

"Because Professor Plum did it with the knife in the ballroom."

Rich pulled the three cards out of the pocket and looked up, nodding his head. Sadie giggled again. "It's not telepathy that helps me win. It's extrasensory perception."

Harry glanced at Peggy then at the other men. Peggy had been known to sense things, too. "I think we should change things a bit. Let the women play at one table and we can play at the other. At least we men don't cheat."

"Speak for yourself, mate," Rich stated. "I have some powers of me own." He closed his eyes, laid his palms flat on the table, and his expression turned serious. "My senses tell me Sadie wants to play a different game – with me."

Not likely, buster, Saul thought. For the last month, Rich had been preoccupied with getting Sadie into bed. He seemed to want Sadie badly, yet each time the couple returned from their fun, Sadie's eyes were always sad, as if Rich hurt her or something. She always denied it, but who knows?

"Really, Rich?" came Sadie's reply. "Shouldn't you save some for your old age? I'd rather stay here."

Rich's eyes lost their luster. Martha whispered to Sadie and both women walked to the kitchen. Sadie closed the doors behind her and turned around. Silently, she waited for Martha to speak, but all she did was pace the floor. Back and forth Martha walked, from one end of the room to the other, back and forth, her eyes on the floor.

After a few minutes, Sadie put her hand on Martha's shoulder. "You're trying to find the right words to say. You forget I can read your mind. I know."

Martha sat down at the table. "I know something's wrong, but even as a nurse, I can't figure out what it is. The past two weeks, Rich's sex drive hasn't been right. You have already checked him for high testosterone and said that wasn't it. What could cause this?"

"One problem is identified," Sadie whispered.

211

"Tell me."

Sadie's expression changed from sympathy to concern. "Right now, it wouldn't help you or anyone else to know. I'm researching to find a cause. As soon as I get a letter I'm expecting, I should be able to remedy him. I just wish the letter would get here …" Her voice trailed off.

Martha blushed. "Can you…? Will you…? If you don't go with him now, he'll want me. I can't. I'm getting worn out." She stared at the ceiling. "Imagine this! A month ago, if anyone suggest I'd ask someone else to bed my boyfriend, I'd have dialed the number for a good psychiatrist."

Sadie tried to reply, but Martha stopped her. "I know you took care of him completely those first days while I got comfortable... and even after I gave in. Yet, I still must ask. Three or four times a day wears a person down... Please."

Sadie gave her a hug. "Of course I will. Relax. Soon, he'll be back to his norm. As he used to say: 'Once a day keeps the doctor away.'" Sadie giggled and walked to the hallway.

In the living room, Rich stood at the fireplace, mumbling in a low voice no one could hear. "I can swim twenty laps. I go as strong on the last song of a concert as I do on the first. This can't be physical. Am I going mad? With only Sadie, it'd be okay – she makes sex like going to heaven alive – but it's the same with Martha. Ah, Martha, loving, gentle Martha. If only I could be as gentle with her as she is with me. How can I explain it to her? What used to be an urge is now a demand for fast relief. Even some of the fun is gone."

Rich silenced as he turned and stared at the others. Would they understand? Or tease him for being oversexed. Movement in the hall doorway made him look beyond the group at the tables. Sadie smiled and motioned upstairs. He followed, relieved he didn't have to discuss anything yet.

"This takes the biscuit!" Saul said loudly in the chair facing the hall. "He gets my flippin' wife whenever he wants, yet we don't get to taste Martha's honey!"

Neither Harry nor Jo-Jo replied. They stared past him. Saul turned his head to see Martha in the kitchen doorway, her face crimson. She ran out of sight, slamming the kitchen doors. They could hear the sounds of the storm louder and then another door slammed shut, muffling the sounds again.

"Good show, Saul!" Peggy exclaimed. "Now someone has to go outside and find her before she catches pneumonia."

"She'll be back," Saul replied. "It's raining stair-rods out there. Besides, I'm telling it near the knuckle. Harry would go bonkers, too, if someone messed with you without trading."

"You'll get your turn. Give her a break. The rest of us had time to get used to your pact."

"Not Sadie," Jo-Jo stated. "Your hubby invoked the pact two nights after she and Saul got it on. They hardly knew each other yet." Peggy shuddered and walked to the kitchen.

"That's not a fair crack of the whip, mate!" Harry recoiled. "I was out of my mind, dead sopped. And none of us, except Saul and Bart, believed her tale about being a 'tighty.'"

Peggy opened then closed the envelope doors behind her. Martha was sitting at the kitchen table. "Are you okay?" Peggy asked quietly, joining her at the table.

"I guess so," Martha's said, her eyes red. Her cheeks glistened with freshly wiped tears. "I made a fool of myself, running out like that, didn't I?"

"No. We understand. We thought you ran outside."

A half-smile emerged on Martha's face. "That would take a total fool. I tried, but you can't see two feet in front of you out there ... Peg, I'm simply not ready."

"Don't worry. As long as Sadie's here, she can ward the men off you. Eventually, you'll grow to love them all as we do.

By then, it won't seem like such a big deal. In fact, you may enjoy the extra attention. Each of them uses a different technique for…. exploring."

Silence fell as Martha stared at the floor. Peggy busied herself making tea. When she set two cups down, Martha looked up again. "I overheard the men's conversation about Sadie. What on Earth were they talking about?"

"Oh right. You never heard how they first met Sadie." Peggy walked to the counter, picked up a plate of cookies, and set them on the table, too. Then she began a short version of Sadie's story. Martha sat spellbound as Peggy wove the colorful tale.

"… So you see. It hasn't always been peaches and cream for her," Peggy said. "If it happened to me, I would've sued the pants off them. Not Sadie. She was somehow convinced she was being punished for lying, so she didn't even try to contact Saul to tell him about the pregnancy."

Martha looked puzzled. "Would she have called him after the birth?"

"I doubt it. If there's one thing I've learned about Sadie, she keeps her promises."

"Aha! Talking about me again!" Sadie said as she whisked through the kitchen. "I hope it wasn't all bad."

Peggy scanned Sadie's droopy eyes and forced smile. "What's wrong?"

"I have to get the mail," Sadie replied as she slid her arms through the sleeves of her raincoat.

"You can't go out in this storm!" Martha stated. "You'll land in the hospital again. You won't see the front of the car, let alone the road."

"Best time to go. No one will be out in this weather."

"You shouldn't either," Martha tried to argue. Sadie was already out the door.

Peggy smiled. "She's stubborn."

"I still can't figure out why she doesn't have the mail delivered here."

They walked toward the living room as Peggy replied, "To keep our home life as normal as possible. If fans or the press ever found out where we live, we wouldn't get any privacy."

Spidar mail was addressed to a post office box in Rochester. Instead of a normal box, though, the number belonged to a large mail bag. When full, the bag would be sealed, tagged, and forwarded to Canandaigua. The tag contained only a number. The Canandaigua post office allocated a corner of their room for these bags as well as a small open bag for local mail like electric bills and such, usually addressed to Sadie West. Once a week, Sadie drove up to the mail truck area and a mail carrier loaded her car. She signed for the bags and returned the empties on her next trip.

The postmasters of Rochester and Canandaigua had agreed to this arrangement without a fuss. Because Canandaigua mail went through Rochester first anyway, this system meant each letter would be handled one less time. Only the two postmasters knew Sadie's identity.

Thirty minutes later, Peggy walked into the kitchen to make tea for the men. She found Sadie at the table surrounded by seven mail bags, six already empty, and several brown grocery bags on the table were almost full. Sadie was busy sorting the seventh mail bag. "I didn't know you were back already," Peg said. "With this storm, I thought the trip would take at least an hour to creep along."

"No one was on the roads," Sadie replied. "Anything happening in there?'

"We're playing Yahtzee. The men think it's a game of pure luck so they have a better chance of winning." Peggy began to laugh. "I've won two games and Miki and Martha have each

215

won one. Now the men are going to work in the music room."

Sadie joined the laugh. "Weren't they going to put you at a separate table?"

"They thought this game would be safe enough. Anything good in the mail?"

"A few belated birthday cards and presents for Rich, then the usual." *Not the one I need*, Sadie thought. She finished sorting and put each couple's mail in front of their normal seats around the table. Then she glanced at the clock. There was still another hour before the toddlers woke. She walked into the living room. "Play time is over. The mail is ready for your inspection."

"Oh no-o-o-o!" the men groaned in unison.

"Come on. You know you enjoy the letters. And you wouldn't want to make Bart mad, would you?"

"No, Mumsie," Jo-Jo replied with a snicker. "We wouldn't think of putting Bart in a wax." He smiled at the others. "Perhaps we should tell him we burned the whole lot by accident."

"Then we'd see a real fire!" Harry exclaimed. "Flames from the dragon's mouth."

Saul studied Sadie in the doorway. She did not look happy. "Let's get it over with, chappies," he said, "so Sadie will stop giving us the evil eye."

"I was doing no such thing," she protested. "I was just deep in thought."

Rich turned on the light near him so Sadie could turn out the bright overhead light. He, too, had noticed the lack of luster in her eyes. Hope I didn't do it this time, he mused.

"Thinking about what, Sugar Boot?" he asked aloud.

"Oh, about how good-looking you guys are in this dim light."

"What about in good lighting?"

216

Some of her sparkle returned. "Wel-l-l." She flitted back to the kitchen for her own letters and to write checks for the bills. The men followed.

*

A week later, the Spidar family was sun-bathing in the pool during the children's afternoon nap. Rich returned from the orchard with a smile on his face.

"Where's Sadie?" Saul asked.

Rich dove into the pool. "She went to get the mail. We'd better enjoy a good swim before she returns. After that, you know what we'll have to do." He chuckled. "Sometimes, she can be as demanding as Bart."

Saul stood up and peered over the fence. As Sadie drove by on the way out, she smiled and waved at him, but he could see that her eyes drooped again. He looked back at Rich. "I'm gonna have to limit your encounters with Sadie, mate. You have your own bird now. Hang around her for a while." Martha blushed.

"You know quite well that it's not the same bloody rogering!" Rich exclaimed. "You're trying to keep her to yourself is all." He climbed onto the diving board and jumped off again.

The others nodded to each other. Rich was right on all three counts: 1) having sex with Sadie was as different as different could be, 2) Sadie commanded the mail, and 3) if they wanted to swim this afternoon, they'd have to do it now.

Whenever Bart insisted letters be answered, the men gave him a hard time, but they couldn't fight Sadie. She had developed a system that made the mail easier on them. Each letter warranting a reply would be assigned a number. The Spidar would record his answer on a tape recorder. At the end of the session, Sadie would collect the recorders, any extra tapes the men had used, and the original letters.

After the children went to bed that evening and the adults were watching television, Sadie set up a card table in the corner. On it, she placed a typewriter, the tapes, a tape player with earphones, paper, envelopes, signed wallet-sized pictures of the group, and paper clips. She spent the evening typing replies and addressing envelopes. Many mail nights, she slipped out of bed after Saul fell asleep and finished in the wee hours.

The next morning, a pile of mail would greet each Spidar at the breakfast table, awaiting his signature. No one received any food until the letters were done. On that morning each week, the other women cleaned up the breakfast dishes while Sadie stuffed and sealed the envelopes and returned the original letters to the men for disposal or saving. Then the outgoing letters were rubber-banded according to destination.

Today, the Spidars were swimming in the pool when Sadie's car reappeared in the driveway. She beeped as she passed – the sign for them to dry off and come inside. After dressing, they walked into the kitchen and sat down. Individual grocery-sized bags were set around the table. Without looking up, Sadie continued sorting into piles. When a pile grew too large, she dumped it into the proper bag. Her hands moved quickly. Before long, she broke the seal on the last bag – the one for her. She raised a large manila envelope from the bag and her eyes lit up.

Miki and the men were busy with their own mail, and Peggy was refilling coffee cups. No one except Martha saw Sadie cross to the kitchen cupboards and place the manila envelope into the receipt drawer. She returned to the table and sorted the last bag in no time. Most was garbage mail. She wrote checks for the bills.

Sadie hadn't looked at the family as she worked on the six bags. When she finally looked up, she saw Martha smiling a question at her. Sadie smiled back and nodded. Silently, Sadie retrieved the manila envelope from the drawer and disappeared into the den to read. When she returned, she hummed softly. Her smile sent a shiver of excitement through Martha. Yes, the smile said, our troubles are over!

That evening, as the women bathed the children and put them to bed, the men set up Sadie's card table for typing. This time, though, when she came downstairs, she did not begin work. Instead, she walked over to Rich, sat on his lap, and began to massage his temples and forehead.

"What the hell are you doing, woman?" Saul yelled.

"Leave her be, ol' chap," Rich retorted. He put his arms around her waist and pulled her closer for a heavy kiss. "She wants some fun before work. Don't you, Sugar Boot?"

Sadie slipped off his lap and giggled. "Just teasing!" She walked over to her table and began the first letter.

"You swine!" Rich exclaimed. He rose from the couch. "You can't leave me high and dry!" He walked over to her and pulled the chair away from the table. Bending over, he put his hands on her waist and lifted her into the air. Then he carried her to the hallway door and set her down, with one arm around her shoulder to prevent an escape. She shrugged with a smile on her face.

"Serves you right, woman," Saul scolded. "You can't toy with a billy goat's affections and expect to go about your business before the follow-through."

Sadie giggled as Rich led her upstairs.

*

When the pair returned to the living room, both Sadie and Rich smiled. Saul looked at his wife quizzically. He had

219

expected the droopy eyes again, but she seemed happy this time. *Why?* he wondered. *What is she up to? Why did she purposely get Rich horny? Is she trying to make me jealous? Well, it won't work!*

Chapter 14 – Beginning of August

"Get out of my house!" Saul yelled at Sadie. "And take your flippin' kids with ya!"

*

This morning, the men worked in the music room. The open windows grabbed fresh, aromatic air from the orchard but left enough for the women and children playing in the shade outside.

After lunch, the children napped while the adults gathered at the pool to play their favorite adult game: the first man to catch and hold Sadie was the winner. He would get her for the second part, which included additional exercise in the orchard. The losers chose between the other women.

The simple rules worked fine most of the time, but there was one catch: Martha wasn't ready for the partner exchange. When Rich lost, he couldn't have a choice of women. This made him try harder. Yet, when he did win, someone was annoyed at being stuck with nothing.

While Miki and Peggy rooted the men on, Martha sat in silence. She knew her modesty would again cause problems at the end. *At least this isn't a daily event*, she thought. Only once or twice a week when everyone was so inclined.

As Peggy and Miki cheered, Rich caught Sadie and left the pool with his prize. Saul was the "nothing" man this time. He shook his head, grumbled, and climbed out of the pool. With a fresh drink in hand, he sat on a lounge chair and closed his eyes.

"Might as well kip," he said loudly. His foul mood festered the rest of the afternoon. His spirits improved slightly with good cooking at supper, though he remained unusually quiet.

While the adults ate dessert, Sadie put a load in the dishwasher. Then she went into the living room to play with the children, her alone time with them.

"What's your notion, Sauly?" Rich asked, sipping his tea. The men were discussing the recent demonstrations at American colleges. Saul sat in silence, watching the women. Rich shrugged and the men continued their conversation.

Miki cleaned the table and counters, Peggy washed the few remaining dishes by hand, and Martha dried and put the dishes away. Because the women worked in harmony, the kitchen was clean by the time Saul finished his second cup of tea. Saul stood and walked toward Martha as she put the last serving bowl away in the top shelf above the sink. "What's that?" he asked, pointing to a black spiral notebook in the far corner of the shelf.

"I don't know," Martha replied. "Sadie writes in it once in a while." She closed the cupboard door and went to the table, sitting beside Rich.

Saul reopened the cupboard and reached for the notebook. Peggy put her hand on his arm. "She told us it was a diary of sorts. I don't think she wants anyone to read it, not even you."

"Bilge!" he exclaimed. "I'm her hubby." He pulled the book down and went back to the table. As he flipped the pages, his nose flared. "Listen to this drivel, mates!" He began to read aloud, pausing between many phrases.

"This is from last year: 'If only the men knew. I can sexually arouse them by transferring some of my energy... I sent a letter to Ivan... The answer's in the testosterone level... I'm going to test my powers.... It should be interesting research....'" Saul looked up toward the men. "She's using us as

222

guinea pigs, chaps!"

"Saul, you're not supposed to ..." Peggy repeated.

"Hush, woman," Harry interrupted, "We're entitled to know what she's doing to us."

"Yeah!" Jo-Jo and Rich said in unison.

Saul returned to the book, flipping a few more pages. "Let's see. Here she's talking about Peg in May of this year: 'If only she would trust herself... She's learning to use her influence to get things done in the family.'" Saul turned to Peggy. "So Sadie's teaching you to manipulate us, too, huh?"

"Not exactly. We..."

Saul ignored her and continued, "Another entry about using people, still in May: 'I met a nice reporter tonight... I'll send stories her way to build rapport.' And another one in June: 'I have to figure out some way to help them accept Miki into the family,' and later, 'I found it!'"

Saul flipped a page. "Ha! Here's a bloody good one: 'This week I found a partner for Rich... Hopefully, she and Rich will hit it off...'" He turned another page. "What the heck! Listen to this! It's still June – two months ago. I can't believe she kept something this important under the covers!"

"So read it already!" Jo-Jo commanded.

"Phew! Here goes: 'I wrote to Ivan today... While making love to Rich, I noticed he has prostate cancer.'"

"What!" Rich exclaimed. "No way! I'd know if something was cockeyed..." His voice trailed off as he remembered the problems that surfaced for a while.

"So that's why she wouldn't explain your problem," Martha mumbled.

Harry stared at Martha. "You knew Rich had a problem and you kept the mockers on, too? Is Sadie training all you dowagers?"

Martha sat straight up in her chair. "You men knew something was wrong, too. Don't blame me! I didn't realize how serious it was either. Sadie said it wouldn't do any good to know." Her voice softened. "She was right. The only cure for prostate cancer in a younger man is surgery. That would make Rich..."

"Make me what?" Rich yelled. Martha refused to answer.

"Speak," Harry commanded. "Spit out the truth."

Martha rose to leave the room. Rich grabbed her arm and pulled her back. "Sing it, woman."

"Never mind the clam," Saul said. "It's written here. Sadie says: 'After surgery, the patient will most likely be impotent.'"

"Ouch! Me aching cobblers!" Rich exclaimed.

Saul continued, "A little further down, she wrote: 'If he doesn't have surgery, the cancer could spread.'"

"So I'm damned if I do and damned if I don't. What a bloody choice! Still and all, it should be my choice, not hers."

Saul looked up. "Need I go further?"

"Yeah," Jo-Jo replied, "Let's have a look-see in other news."

Saul flipped another page. "Ah! Listen to this one! 'I love the evenings... I lie in bed letting my mind go from room to room, examining everyone's thoughts... I know the family would get mad if they ever found out, but... it's fun!'"

"What the hell!" Jo-jo exclaimed. "What bloody right does she have? Even in Hitler's Germany, thoughts were private!"

"That's not the worst," Saul said, more to himself than to the others. "In this next entry, she threatens to leave me." He turned another page. "Maybe I'd be better off! Maybe we all would."

Peggy shook her head. "She wouldn't say all those things. That's not the Sadie I know. The way you're turning the pages so quickly, are you reading all of it?"

"I'm reading enough. Here's another entry about Rich. In the end she asks, 'Did I cause the cancer with my research on Rich's hormones?"

Saul read the next two entries to himself.

"All of it, Saul," Peggy implored. "You pick and choose what you want to read aloud. You're not being fair. On that last page I caught a glimpse of some words in large print about Rich being fine now. Did she cure him?'

"Yeah, he can live a long, sexually-active life now."

Rich sighed. "That's a relief."

"Now she's researching the rest of us to find a way to take away our drugs."

"She can sod off!" Jo-Jo snorted. "She's not our mummy. We can do what we damn well please..." Sadie opened the doors from the living room and bounced into the kitchen. "And don't you forget it!" Jo-Jo yelled at her.

Sadie took a step backwards. "What did I do now?" she asked, as she scanned the angry faces around the table. Then she noticed the book. "Oh that." She moved over to Saul and sat on his lap, stroking his face. "I should explain a few things."

"Frig off, you whore!" Saul exploded. "Who the hell do you think you are?" She stood up quickly.

"Who gave you permission to twerp with our hormones?" Rich asked.

Jo-Jo shook his head. "You could've killed him with your experiments!"

"I didn't do..."

"No excuses, girl," Harry yelled. "You messed with our bodies, you messed with our minds, you messed with our women. You're not the angel I thought. Now I see why Saul treats you the way he does. You're a positive deuce!"

That last sentence stung. "No, I'm not," Sadie whispered.

"Get out of my house!" Saul yelled. "And take your flippin' kids with ya!"

Sadie ran from the kitchen.

Ten minutes later, she returned wearing a smile. "I have the children and a few of our things in the van. I'll send for the rest later. Have fun!" She went to leave by the front door. Peggy followed. When Peggy returned to the kitchen, her eyes were moist, but she glared at each of the men. "I don't believe you did that!"

"What's your quandary?" Jo-Jo asked. "She was tickled to leave. I heard a chuckle when she told us to have fun."

Peggy's eyes lit with fire. Before Peg could speak, Martha replied softly. "That was a crackle, Jo-Jo, not a chuckle. She was holding back tears."

"How would you know? You're the new bug." Martha silenced.

"She's right," Peggy blurted out. "Sadie broke down at the front door. She's not happy to leave. She's quite upset, in fact. I can't believe you guys threw her out of this house, a woman who loves you the way she does. She would never hurt any of you. You are the deuces, the evil ones!"

"Don't go off in a snit, Pet," Harry soothed. "We fancy her, too. Still and all, she can't toy with us whenever the mood strikes. Her games could have killed Rich."

"I don't believe that, either." Peggy grabbed the journal from Saul. "The only thing Sadie said at the door was: 'Take good care of the family, Peg. Please.' That doesn't sound like a woman who toys with people for the heck of it. There has to be a reason for what she did."

Peggy opened the book upside down by mistake, thus noticing an entry with no date. She read it aloud:

Dear Reader,

I'm writing this letter, because I know you will be annoyed with some things in this book. I would prefer to explain in person. However, in case I'm not present, here goes nothing.

I think the main things that will upset you are the invasion of privacy and me fooling with your body chemicals. Maybe I would feel the same way if I were in your shoes. I don't know.

The invasion of privacy is covered quite well in the body of my notes – refer to the tenth entry under June 1968. If you are still upset, please remember that you have invaded my privacy, too, by reading this diary. I have a reason for my actions. What's yours?

As for my experiments on your bodies, all I can say is I need to practice on someone. There's a lot to learn before I can be good at what I do. Working on a bunch of strangers would mean being away from home a lot more than I care to be. With progress, I may be able to telepathically have people's own brains make chemical adjustments. For now, I can do a better job on you. I know what makes each of you tick.

With Love,
Sadie

PS: Saul, once I discovered how I turned the men on, I figured out how to control my powers. After that, I never initiated any interchanges, except when medically necessary. I know this question still bothers you, doesn't it? I'll repeat: I did not initiate any sexual adventures. However, I admit, I did use my powers for multiple orgasms in each session. I'm not perfect, I guess. I enjoy making you all happy.

Peggy looked up at the group with tears in her eyes. "Now that sounds more like the Sadie I know." She turned back to the beginning of the book. "I think we should reread the whole doggone thing. Saul had a bug up his butt before he even found this journal."

She read the entries softly as Sadie would:

December 1967 – If only the men knew! They've told me my love-making is different than any other girl they've had. They say I have an electric personality. How right they are!

I realized today that I can somehow sexually arouse them by transferring some of my energy to their bodies. I don't know how I do it or how to stop, but I do know that is the reason they can have several orgasms in a short time. I sent a letter to Ivan to see if I can find out what's happening.

January 1968 – I received a letter from Ivan. The answer's in the testosterone level. He says only greatly elevated levels would enable a man to have multiple orgasms. I'm going to test my powers and see if I can raise and lower this hormone and others. It should be interesting research.

March 1968 – I'm worried about the men. Their bloodstreams carry some strange chemicals. I clear up the condition every time I 'see' them. They act healthier right away, but the problem comes back quickly. I can't tell them. They think I'm just being friendly when I greet them by gliding my fingertips along their foreheads.

May 1968 – Peggy is working out well. She is developing her financial instincts. Soon, she should be able to multiply Harry's riches the way I do with Saul's. She has a keen mind for abstract principals. She also shows signs of what a lot of men laughingly refer to as women's intuition. She can usually spot a good buy in the stock market or in real estate. If only she would trust herself and run with the ball. I've tried to explain that she has to lose

228

sometimes, but she turns despondent if she picks a loser. The ensuing fear of failure prevents her from losing too much, but it also prevents her from realizing her full potential.

"All right, Peg," Saul said in an irritated tone, "So tell me what that's about."

Peggy smiled, but it was Harry who replied. "Peg asked to borrow $10,000 for a game she and Sadie were playing." He gave Peg a hug. "My bird quadrupled the money in less than six months. If this keeps up, I won't have to work the rest of my life."

"You already have enough to live quite comfortably," Peggy scolded. "But Sadie's right. I am cautious."

"So?" Saul said. "She faults you, but I haven't seen any of her flipping lolly. Can't she pick any masters?"

Peggy laughed and went into the dining room. When she returned, she carried a large, fire-proof, metal box. "See for yourself what she's been doing."

Silence followed as Saul examined the savings account book. "So why would she say you're too conservative?" he asked Peg. "According to this book, she borrowed $10,000 from me and she only doubled her money. She paid my accountant back and has another ten grand in here."

Peggy smiled again. "She hasn't contacted your Spidar accountant for household expenses since we began to play the game. I've seen some of the bills. The electricity alone is over a thousand a month, yet she won't let any of us contribute, even towards the groceries. She said the two of you have more money than you could spend in ten lifetimes.

"That particular account is just her ready-cash fund. She said it's always a good idea to keep part of the funds liquid for emergencies. Look at the deeds to real estate and her monthly statement from Merrill Lynch. A few weeks ago, she was very proud of the fact that she was now worth a million dollars herself."

Saul examined the large pile of deeds. "So why aren't there any rent deposits from all these places?"

"The rental income's in a separate book – somewhere in that box – but you won't find much of a balance there, either. Do you know why?"

Saul shook his head.

"I'll tell you why. Because our family angel..." Peggy let the word sink in, "uses the real estate for tax purposes, not for income. She's working with the Salvation Army to provide shelter for people who are down on their luck. The little rent money she receives goes toward fixing up the properties." Peggy laughed. "She said she feels like Robin Hood, taking money from people who can afford to play the market and using it toward shelters for the homeless."

Saul examined more documents.

Peggy went back to the notebook and continued reading aloud, still in May:

Peggy is learning to use her influence to get things done in the family. I have a few other things to teach her. One day, she'll be needed to hold the family together. In this family, each individual's talents compliment the others. That makes them very special. I think God has a mission for them. He will use the love they've developed for each other in that mission. I still don't know why I have my powers, or even if they are different from any other people. I read somewhere that everyone emits enough electricity to light a 120-watt light bulb. Maybe everyone has these healing powers.

I met a nice reporter a few nights ago. I have a feeling we're going to need her for something special in the future. I'll send stories her way to build rapport with the press. I've read her work. She knows how to turn a phrase positively.

230

June 1968 – The family still doesn't accept Miki. She puts up a good front, but I can tell she's upset about it. I have to figure out a way to help them admit her into the group. I have a feeling we're going to need her telepathic abilities in the future.

I found it! This week I was badly hurt in an auto accident. I used Miki's telepathy. She told me later that the rest of the family has finally welcomed her. If only the public would. I guess that will take time.

This week I also found a partner for Rich. Maybe he'll be happy now. Martha senses people's true feelings. We can use that. Hopefully, she and Rich will hit it off. I'll keep my fingers crossed.

I wrote to Ivan today. While making love to Rich in the orchard, I noticed something that scared me. Later, I went to the old medical books Ivan gave me. I found out Rich has prostate cancer! The only known cure, according to the book, is surgery to remove the prostate, but after such surgery, the patient will be impotent. How can I tell Rich? I'm tempted to ignore the whole thing. He's too young for this fate. How would his ego handle a trip like this?

On the other hand, according to the book, if he doesn't have surgery, the cancer could metastasize to the bones. I can't let it go. I need to do more research. Hopefully, Ivan will know someone currently working in the field.

"Does sound a bit different," Rich said. "Explains her teary eyes when we finished. I couldn't imagine hurting her enough to make her blubber."

Martha tilted her head. "You were kinda rough."

"I'm aware. Sorry."

"Enough of that," Harry proclaimed. "Read on, Peg. You were at the end of June..."

231

Ha! Today I decided I'd better write about my practice reading minds. I love the evenings we spend watching TV. I get a chance to go from person to person and see what they think. Their thoughts are delightful, especially when a sexy movie is on!

Also, after Saul and I have finished our nightly exercise and before sleep overtakes us, I lie in bed, letting my mind go from room to room. During the mind examination, I've learned about human nature. For instance, even though our thoughts are completely private (usually, ha!), humans tend to guard those thoughts when they are in a group. Only when they're alone do they allow their mind free reign.

I know the family would get mad if they find out about this invasion of their privacy, but someday I may need to communicate long distance. What if Miki isn't with them at the time? Will I talk to them as a group or as individuals? Do I need to memorize their particular brainwaves?

I wonder if individual brain waves are like fingerprints, each a little different. Maybe it's not true, but so far in my research, no two people have been exactly the same. And everyone has the ability to change the waves for short periods.

This research is fun most of the time. Other times, it's a pain. I "hear" things they would never say to my face. I have to convince myself the next morning that their negative thoughts don't mean anything.

"See! Peggy exclaimed, looking up at the group. "It's not all fun and games for her either."

Except for Saul, the men regretted their remarks. They said nothing as Peggy continued, still in June:

Saul and I are headed for problems. I can see it in his thoughts. He wonders what his life would be like if he had never met me. He used to be a playboy, and now he's stuck with me and the kids. He loves the kids, but I cramp his style. Maybe I need to give him more freedom. Haven't I given him enough? Maybe the kids and I should go away for a while. Maybe that's what he needs, a break from us when he's home, not just when he's working.

Separation would be hell for me. When he's not here, I feel ... it's like loneliness, only stronger. I wish I could tell him, but I'm afraid of ending up like Prudence with Jo-Jo. So, when he has to leave for a tour or a movie, I smile on the outside. Inside, my heart breaks. I wonder if he'll come back or find someone else. He has such mixed thoughts in his head. I never know for sure.

Peggy looked at Saul, who had lowered his head. "She isn't threatening to leave you. She's afraid you'll leave her! How could you misread that entry?"

Saul hesitated. Then he changed the subject slightly. "Why does she write to Ivan about our personal problems? He must think we're a big rag!"

Martha replied with sympathy. "Perhaps she'll explain in a later entry. Let's continue, Peg. We've gone this far. We might as well finish."

July 1968 – It's been two weeks and still no answer from Ivan. I went to the University of Rochester yesterday to see if anyone is researching prostate cancer. No, but they offered a ray of hope. Switzerland has a team working on the problem. Maybe Ivan will get an answer. Maybe that's why he's taking so long to answer my letter. He's talking to researchers themselves.

Meanwhile, I checked some up-to-date medical books, which said frequent sex can decrease the chance of getting this cancer.

Could the testosterone level affect the outcome? Did I cause Rich's cancer with my research on his hormones? Did I forget to lower his level when he was done with me, way back, before they left for London? Was his level too high for seven months?

"See!" Saul said half-heartedly. "I didn't misinterpret that."
"Sshhh!" Rich said. "Go on, Sweets."

It's been three weeks. When will Ivan's letter come? I feel a little better, though. Today I realized I couldn't have caused the cancer. I would have noticed the extreme hormones at my next session with him. However, he's always had a higher natural level than the other men. When Ivan's letter comes, I'll have to lower the level. Maybe that will prevent the cancer from returning. But how will I get rid of the present glob? If Ivan's letter doesn't come within a week, I'll have to tell Rich. I can't take the chance of the cancer spreading to the bones. I just wish this hadn't happened until I was more experienced.

IT CAME! Yesterday, Ivan sent a copy of the research team's original notes. Digesting everything took a bit of time, but I think I found the answer. I was right about the testosterone level as a major factor. (His drainpipe trousers during puberty didn't help either.) I lowered the testosterone and increased his estrogen and zinc absorption slightly. As for removing the existing cancer without surgery, the Swiss doctors think a substance in the body called interferon can inhibit the growth of cancer cells. It took me a while to find the interferon in Rich from the chemical equation Ivan sent. Once I did, it was easy to increase. (The family thought I was getting horny in the process. Ha!)
There's also a substance they suspect may help rid cancer. They don't have a name for it yet, but by the description of its

actions, I'll call it "Tumor Necrosis Factor," that seems to be a protein that eats abnormal cell growths. Not enough studies have been done to determine its effectiveness. I found it in each person's body but in minute quantities. I questioned whether I should use something so toxic, so I increased Rich's level of TNF at the prostate, not in the blood stream. I don't want the junk eating good cells too. I checked Rich later and the cancer had already decreased in size. I will put the TNF back to normal levels when the tumor is gone. HE'S GOING TO BE OKAY!!!!

I checked the rest of the family for the interferon substance. The men were all low. Harry's was highest. Maybe that's why he seems the healthiest, whereas Jo-Jo's level was almost non-existent. I corrected the level for everyone, including the women.

I also increased the surfactant in Jo-Jo's lungs as well as his peptide level. Hopefully, his cough will disappear. It's not bad enough for him to notice yet, but he tires easier in the pool because of it.

This interferon business makes me wonder: how do drugs affect the men's immune system? I also wonder about all the strange chemicals in their blood streams. Could opium cause the brain to stop producing its own opiates? Does marijuana or cocaine decrease endorphins? Should I tell the men? Probably not. They'll think I'm a busybody.

"That's it," Peggy said, turning a few more pages. "The rest are blank." Her voice gained sharpness. "Do you have any more questions about Sadie's integrity?"

Silence.

The men fidgeted in their seats, thinking about their sharp words to Sadie. Finally, Jo-Jo spoke. "We were a bit slow on the uptake, but I do have one question. Why does Sadie work only with you, improving your ability with money? Why not with Miki's telepathy and on Martha's, uh, whatever?"

Miki put her hand on Jo-Jo's arm. "She does work with me. My mind needs to relax more so I can receive messages without the other person sending them. I didn't want to tell you until I succeed. It's like learning to play the piano. You don't want people to know until you can at least demonstrate a simple song."

"She's working with me, too," Martha added. "Sometimes, while you men work in the den and the children are in for naps, she checks with the Salvation Army to see if they have anyone who needs temporary housing assistance – they usually have a long list. I go with her to interview the people. After talking for a short period, she and I go to another room, and I give my opinion."

Martha beamed at Rich. "I've been right 95% of the time. There was only one man I misjudged. I said he was okay, but Sadie disagreed. A week later, the man made the papers as an escaped convict in jail for murder. I felt terrible, but Sadie said there was no way for me to know. He believed his own lies."

"So how did Sadie know?" Rich asked. Martha shrugged.

"I can answer that one," Peggy said with a smile. "She combined all her powers, including a glimpse into his subconscious past. Later, after the newspaper report, she mentioned to me that he would be a good subject for another research project of hers. She wouldn't tell me any more about it, other than that she would wait until his new trial finished. "

Silence consumed the kitchen once again. Tick, tick, tick. The minutes seemed like hours. Occasionally, Amanda cooed and kicked her feet – alone in the living room, without the other four infants in the over-sized playpen and without the three toddlers on the floor.

Saul stood and went to the hall. He returned with a sweater.

"Where you off to, mate?" Harry asked.

"I need to find her. She won't come home if I don't."

"She was upset," Martha stated.

Peggy shook her head. "Sadie knows this area better than you do, Saul. If she doesn't want to be found, she won't be."

"I can't sit on my arse all night!"

Peggy stood in front of Saul. Her anger dissipated when she looked into his wistful eyes. Then she combed his hair with her fingers. "Don't stay out too long. While you're gone, I'll make some phone calls to a few of Sadie's friends. Maybe one of them can help. Hmmm, one works for the NY State Police. What was his name?" She moved to the bill drawer, opened Sadie's address book, and skimmed the pages. Saul hurried outside.

An hour later, the family was watching television in the living room. The outside kitchen door slammed. Peggy went to the kitchen and found a bottle of scotch in Saul's hand. His head hung low and his shoulders hunched. He was falling apart inside.

Peggy took a bottle of cola out of the refrigerator, opening it as she walked toward Saul. She reached around him and tipped the bottle over the glass on the counter, but had to pull it back quickly. The glass was already full... of scotch. She set the cola down.

"Don't," she said as she took away the glass. "Sadie will be back. I got through to her State Police friend, Ted. Remember the fireman she healed. He's now a cop. He couldn't put out an APB on her, but he promised to spread the word to watch for the van."

Saul replied in a monotone, "Why would the constabulary get sweaty? A lot of mates have bust-ups. Bobbies don't have the ticks to put their oars in, even if they're the friendly sort like Ted. Besides, she won't come back after what I said." He grabbed the glass from Peggy and downed half of it before taking another breath. Then he walked to the table and sat down. "First time I've warmed tonight, that's a fact," he mumbled.

Peggy shook her head. "I told the cop her husband had heart problems after she left. He said he'd do his best to spread the word... Saul, are you listening? She'll be back. She's always forgiven you before. "

Silence.

Quietly, the others joined Saul at the table. Peggy poured each of them a scotch and cola and prepared a snack. She had a smile on her face when she brought two plates of cherry pie to the table. Harry noticed her sudden cheerfulness. As she went back to the counter to get the next two plates, he followed. "What's jollied you up, Pet?"

"I was thinking about Sadie's sexy technique for getting Saul's mind off his troubles."

Harry thought for a moment. Slowly, his lips turned up at the ends, with long dimples putting his smile in parenthesis. "She does the same for all of us. No man can stay in a stew when Sexy Sadie's on the job."

As time passed, drawn faces spread to Harry and Peg again. Pie was eaten in silence. For the second time, the Spidar family minus eight heard the ticking of the clock on the wall. They heard the hum of the refrigerator. They heard the creaks and groans of the house.

His own pie untouched in front of him, Saul finished the glass of scotch and rose to pour another. Peggy watched him at the counter, ignoring the cola. As his glass filled with straight scotch again, Peggy joined him, laying her hands on top of his.

"Don't," she begged, "Sadie wouldn't want this."

238

Saul brushed her aside and went back to his seat. He set the glass on the table and stared at it. Abruptly, he pushed it away. His head fell into his folded arms on the table.

Martha rose from her seat and placed her hands on Saul's arms. Even his bulky sweater couldn't hide the tension in his muscles. Skillfully, she massaged his back and neck. When his muscles still wouldn't relax, she shrugged and searched the faces around the table.

Miki suddenly lifted her head. Her eyes opened wide, staring at Saul.

Martha shrieked, "The police found Sadie! She's checking on Saul!"

By the time the others looked over, Miki's eyes returned to normal. As she opened her mouth to speak, the phone rang. Peggy ran to it. "Peg's Ship Builders. We sail on oceans of love."

"*What are you trying to do to me?*" Sadie's voice boomed. "*Ted's here and he said Saul had a heart attack!*"

Peggy chortled. "That was the only way to get the police to help. I didn't say heart attack. I said Saul was having a heart problem. He is, Sadie. His heart is broken."

Saul crossed the kitchen to Peggy, who handed him the phone. "No, you talk," he whispered. "I've been drinking. Tell her to come home. Tell her I love her. Tell her..." He threw his hands into the air. "Oh, what's the sense?" He went back to his seat at the table.

Peggy put the phone back to her mouth. "We're staring at each other here. The men are sorry. Saul's sorry. Everyone's sorry. Come home ... Why not? ... I see. Could Harry and I come watch the kids and you return home? ... Sadie, Saul needs you, before he ... I know. What can I do? ... Fine. Are you sure about the other?" Peggy's voice lost its sparkle. "All right then. We'll see you in the morning." She hung up the phone, went to the table, grabbed Saul's glass, took it to the sink, and dumped it down the drain. Saul's head was resting on his folded arms on the table again.

"What's happening?" Rich asked.

"Sadie's worried about alcohol poisoning."

Harry scowled. "That's not what Rich asked. Why won't she come home 'til tomorrow?"

"The kids are in bed and she's an hour away. She'll stay with them and return in the morning."

Peggy knelt beside Saul and raised her hand to his face. "She says she didn't mean to hurt you. She believed you really wanted her out. That's why she went. You should go to bed now. She'll be home by the time you wake."

Saul put his arms around Peggy. In his mind, he hugged Sadie.

*

The next morning, biscuits baked and bacon sizzled in the pan. Saul didn't bother to dress. He ran down the stairs two at a time. Through the living room door, he could see the toddlers romping around the room and the babies in the playpen. He didn't stop. He rushed into the kitchen, over to Sadie, turned her around, and lifted her into the air before holding her tight.

As the bacon sizzled, Saul and Sadie climbed the stairs, hand-in-hand. Neither acknowledged the smirking adults going the other way.

Chapter 15 – Mid-August – Party Time

About to pass Rich and Martha on a single lounge chair in the back yard, Saul grabbed Martha's arm. "Let's go for a sail," he said.

"You're drunk," Martha proclaimed, as she held Rich tighter.

"Nope, but I dare say I'm a bit of all right."

"I'd rather stay here."

Rich pushed her slowly and gently away, his actions showing evidence of the joint he just smoked. "Go. Have some joviality, Sugar."

*

Jo-Jo and Miki had flown to Paris after a Justice-of-the-Peace wedding. Pushy reporters demanded attention at every venture out of the hotel. The couple returned to Canandaigua quickly. "With the house in Sadie's maidenly name," Jo-Jo reasoned aloud to Saul, "only our mateys know we're here."

So Sadie planned a lake-front party as a wedding reception, delayed though it was. Jo-Jo's closest friends were invited, as were Miki's. The whole group spent the afternoon sun-bathing, swimming in the lake, and sailing.

Later, Sadie brought out big bowls of shrimp and macaroni salad, fruit salad, Jell-O, a relish dish, and plates of grilled hamburgers and sausages, with watermelon slices for dessert.

After supper, several guests brought out bags of marijuana, pills, and vials of cocaine to share. Sadie took one look at the bags, pills, and vials and quickly gathered the children together. She and Peggy took them to Carol's apartment on the second floor of the house. "Keep your doors locked," Sadie told her sister. "Call Jerry if anyone tries to break in." Her sister laughed but agreed to comply.

An hour later, Sadie, Martha, and Peggy were the only ones who hadn't dipped into the drugs. Martha sat with Rich near the docks. Sadie and Peggy had walked back to the house to prepare trays of snacks. Neither saw Saul take Martha onto the boat. With the stereo noise, they didn't hear the engine purr to life when the sails refused to go taut.

The sun was beginning to set and its light dimmed. Saul guided Martha to the cockpit, sitting down and pulling her onto the seat next to him. Another couple climbed aboard and went to the bottom deck. As Martha began to inch away from him, Saul put an arm around her shoulders. "I won't bite," he said with a smirk. He put the boat in gear and drove around slowly.

"Do you feel it, Luv?" Saul asked. Moans of lovers in heat floated up from the lower deck.

"Feel what?" Martha replied absently.

"The breeze. The way it flows along your skin, raising hairs straight up, like soldiers at attention, making little hills and valleys, like the earth must look from high in the sky... And the breeze sounds like a seashell as it blows gently into your ears."

Martha wasn't really listening. The groans from the lower deck had intensified. She began to turn her head. Saul gently guided her head back to him again. "It's not polite to watch," he said.

She shivered, uneasy without Rich or Sadie around. Thinking her shiver was coldness, Saul slowed the boat. "There. Is that a bit warmer?"

"A little," she replied. "Maybe we should go home so I can change."

Saul shook his head as the noise on the lower deck stopped. "I think not." Saul idled the motor and embraced her with both arms. She pushed away and jumped down to the deck. Saul rose from his seat and walked leisurely down the steps.

"Looks kinda eager," the other man said with a laugh. The woman with him tittered and followed the man up to the cockpit.

Martha ignored them and ransacked the surroundings with her eyes and mind. The boat sat in the middle of the lake. The shoreline lay in the distance – too far to swim. The only other boats in the water were traveling along the shoreline heading home. In the daytime, anyone would be hard-pressed to see her waving at this distance. With the present dim light, the feat would be darned near impossible.

As Saul came up behind her, she could feel his hot breath on her neck. She stiffened her body and whirled around, her arms poised to strike. At the same moment, the engine roared. She was thrown off balance and wound up on the floor. "Sorry, mate," the man yelled from the cockpit.

"Quite alright," Saul howled as he purposely fell on top of her. "Don't fight, Luv. This is your time."

Martha screamed. He quickly covered her mouth with his own lips. His hands unzipped the flowered shift that covered her two-piece. Slowly, he eased his lips away from hers to see if she'd scream again. She didn't. "Cooperation makes things easier, Luv."

As he gently tugged at the waistband of the suit, Martha swore under her breath. She used to wear a one-piece suit, but this two-piece one was easy to remove – the main reason Rich had given it to her a week ago. "I want to see more skin, Sugar, more skin," Rich had said to her.

After the bottoms eased past Martha's hips, Saul moved to one side of her, one arm still loosely around her waist. One hand gently glided the panties down her thighs then her knees. As they whisked past her calves to her ankles, she tensed. This might be her last chance. When her feet were free, she bolted, rising and rushing to the other side of the boat. She stood stiff, holding her shift closed.

Saul didn't come after her. Instead, he stood, laughed, and backed away, holding her panties in the air, letting them wave in the breeze with the boat's movement. "If you want this little thing back, you'd better come closer. Or I might happen to drop it in the lake."

"You wouldn't dare!"

"Oh? Wouldn't I? Uh-oh, the wind's picking up. I won't be able to hold on much longer." He removed one finger at a time, until he held a very small piece of it with only his thumb. Then he began to lower his hand over the side of the boat.

Martha ran to him, leaned over the edge, and tried to grab her property as it fell. Quickly, Saul circled her waist with an arm. "Oops!" Saul said with a laugh. As Martha watched, the bottom of her suit floated out of view, her heart sinking faster than the material.

Saul pulled her down onto the deck. This time, she tried to claw like a tigress, but Saul grabbed her wrists and won the battle. When he was on top of her again, he chuckled. "This reminds me of the first time with Sadie. She fought hard, too. In the end, it was worth it."

He pressed his groin into hers. "Mm-m-m, feels fine already." Methodically, his lips gently walked through the fleshy pages of her kitteny soft bosoms. Not for long, though. Her squirming prevented any long-term enjoyment of her salty flavor. With his lips wandering back to meet hers again, he removed his swimming trunks with one hand and tried to slip his assets into her warm, inviting vault. Every time he was close, she squirmed and he had to begin all over. Finally he gave up the gentleness. "Okay, Luv," he stated, "You asked for it." He roughly threw open the doors and thrust into her.

Martha's moist pipeline encircled him firmly, priming his pump. A gentle breeze climbed over him. He grunted in ecstasy as his oil gushed from the well. Relieved, he sat up and lit a cigarette. With a victorious smile, he offered one to her. She declined in silence. She zipped up her shift, her face devoid of expression.

On Saul's instructions, the boat headed for home, pulling up to the dock slowly upon arrival. Before the engine sputtered off, Martha jumped to the dock and ran to Rich, still on the lounge chair.

Saul's victorious smirk remained as he strolled toward land. Harry glanced at him from the backyard, did a double-take, then motioned for Jo-Jo to look. Unmistakable! Jo-Jo waved his arm for Harry to meet him near the dock. They reached it at the same time Saul stepped onto land.

"How did it go, mate?" Harry asked.

Saul edged his way toward Martha, who cuddled closer to Rich. He responded loud enough for her to hear too, but soft enough not to be overheard by other guests. "Quite quenching," he said with a sparkle in his eyes. "There was only one nut to crack... She did so much toing and froing, for such a long tick, that I unloaded myself before she could get rubbed up, if you know what I mean." He winked at Martha.

She shot darts with her eyes and cuddled closer to Rich. "That's fine, Mate," Rich stated, "I can take it from here."

Saul kept his eyes on Martha as he snickered. "That's not exactly what I had in mind." Her darts kept coming. He turned to Harry and Jo-Jo. "I thought you two might like to see if you could tickle her fancy."

"Superb idea, ol' chap," Jo-Jo said.

Harry held his hand out to her. "I'd be glad to oblige."

"NO WAY!" she yelled.

"Oh goody, a feisty one," Jo-Jo said with a chuckle.

"Rich, say something!" Martha said. "Tell them to stay away from me, like before!"

Rich took another puff of the joint and moved with much deliberation. He stood up and helped her off the chair, then stood next to her, gently stroking her hair and the soft curves of her face. He gave her hand a gentle squeeze and raised it to his lips. As he brought her hand down in front of him, he laid it in Harry's hand.

"What are you doing?" Martha screamed.

"You know our style, Sugar," Rich explained in a tranquil voice. "You knew this would happen eventually. The first time's the worst. You've done that with Saul. The rest is cakes and ale." He kissed her again and returned to his lounge chair.

Martha cried softly. "Not now, please."

"Too late sugarplum," Harry replied, encircling her with his arms. His swimming trunks bulged. "I'm set for some amorosity."

"Not tonight," came a quiet but firm voice from behind.

*

Peggy didn't hear Martha's scream. She had gone to Carol's apartment to check on the children. Sadie heard as she brought out trays of snacks, including a fresh bowl of unadulterated popcorn to replace the one sprinkled with cocaine by some smart ass. For Sadie, one look at the familiar victory smile on Saul's face and she knew what happened. She set down the trays and walked around to the back of the Spidar men. She stood with her hands folded in front of her.

Harry recognized the voice and turned quickly. "What do

246

you mean, not tonight?" he asked. "She's been primed."

"I can see that," Sadie replied.

Saul snickered. "Take a peek under frock, mateys."

Harry raised an eyebrow at Saul and used one hand to lift Martha's dress slowly. Martha squirmed, which did no good. His other arm held her tight. As soon as the dress rose enough, both Harry and Jo-Jo exclaimed in unison, "Alright! Nothing will stop the fun now."

Sadie shook her head and cleared her throat. Looking at Saul, she murmured, "I can't believe you did that, Saul." He shrugged, but the victorious smile didn't leave his face. Then she looked back at Harry and spoke clearly, "Think, Harry. Martha's first encounter with you should be when you are in top form, not when you're high as a kite on coke or weed or other drugs."

Harry nodded but adopted a bit of a sly grin. "Are you saying you will volunteer your services right now?"

Sadie glanced at Martha's trembling body. "I guess that would be better, though not what I meant." She closed her eyes for a second and when they opened again, she smiled and wiggled her hips slowly. "It should be interesting. You say I make fireworks under normal circumstances." She cocked her head. Her hands roved around his dimples and high cheekbones. "What will it feel like with the drugs' influence? A rocket launch, maybe. I wonder..."

Harry released Martha and pressed his groin into Sadie. "We'll see," he said. Martha ran toward the house without speaking to anyone.

Sadie pulled away as Harry began to nudge her bathing suit bottoms down her legs. "Not here. Too many voyeurs."

Harry pointed to the far end of the dock. In that dim light people shouldn't be able to see much of anything. Harry, Jo-Jo,

Saul, and Sadie walked toward that spot in the moonless night. Rich remained in his chair.

All three men "helped" Sadie undress. She lay on the end of the dock and they surrounded her, nibbling here and there as they explored and took care of their needs. Sadie kept looking at the house to make sure Martha made it up to Carol's apartment safely. All she could think about was the amount of time it was taking.

Ten minutes later, the men were almost finished and she finally saw someone looking out Carol's back window. She sent a zap throughout her body and the men released her, but they were too busy with their super-orgasms to notice they lay to one side of her.

Sadie quickly stood up and dressed, then walked toward the house, letting her mind drift. Didn't the men say they could write better music when they could feel each drop of rain? Or see each ray of sunshine? Or hear each note in a bird's song? If cocaine heightened the senses, why had the men been so rough? Why had they bitten so hard? Why had they slammed their bodies against hers? Was this cocaine/marijuana/drug thing an illusion?

At the kitchen door, Sadie met Peggy, who carried more trays of chips and pretzels. No more popcorn tonight, which usually only lasted five minutes before someone sprinkled cocaine on it.

"Where were you?" Peggy asked. "I was beginning to worry."

"On the dock with the men," Sadie replied, forcing a smile onto her face. "Right now, I need you upstairs."

*

When Peggy and Sadie emerged at the top of the stairs again, Martha and Carol had joined them, along with the eight children. Chuck was strapped to Sadie's back and she carried Vera and a diaper bag. Peggy carried Amanda and another diaper bag. Martha had Dave on her back. Carol carried Rita, and the three toddlers walked by themselves.

The triplets waited at the top of the stairs with Martha, as the other women walked down. With four more steps to go, Sadie glanced through the open doors into the living room.

"Darn it," she whispered to Peggy, "The party moved indoors." The furniture was being moved for dancing, but no one was dancing yet. Everyone just sat around the floor like the finish line at a marathon.

"They might not notice us," Peggy whispered back.

No such luck. "Where you going, Sweets?" Jo-Jo asked from the love seat in front of the bookshelves. Miki had flopped next to him.

Sadie handed Vera to Peggy and stood at the bottom of the stairs, catching the triplets as they rode down the banister. "I'm taking the kids to visit my mother. They haven't seen her in a while."

"Have a bully hen-party," Harry called from his fireplace seat.

Roxanne rode down last. She gleamed as Sadie set her on the floor and turned to retrieve Vera from Peggy's overloaded arms. Martha walked down the stairs with Dave on her back.

"What a pretty baby doll!" came a voice from the living room. It was Steve, one of Jo-Jo's childhood friends. Sadie could tell by the way he walked that he had just smoked a *Jim Jones* – marijuana laced with cocaine and dipped in PCP. His movements had become fast and jerky already. The other partiers appeared to let the alcohol take over.

Steve walked to Roxanne and picked her up by the waist, his hands under her pajama top. "You look happy, pretty girl," he said.

"I am," she replied with an innocent smile. "I like to ride the uh, the uh, oh that thing over there." She pointed to the banister.

"Ah-h-h, you like to ride, huh? I could give you a ride..."

"PUT HER DOWN!" Sadie screamed. "GET YOUR FILTHY HANDS OFF MY DAUGHTER!"

With Roxanne on his hip, Steve ignored Sadie and began to unbuckle his belt. "Would you like to horsey on my lap, pretty girl?" One hand worked on his snap and then his zipper. Laughter came from the room behind him.

"I can't believe you men can just sit there!" Peggy yelled.

"What's the knot, Pet?" Harry asked, looking from behind Steve. "Steve won't hurt anyone."

Sadie handed Vera back to Peggy and waved her and Martha toward the front door. "Get the kids out of here."

The women complied as Sadie grabbed for Roxanne with one arm and her other hand went to Steve's temple. His arms relaxed immediately. Roxanne slid onto Sadie's hip as Steve's knees buckled. His head fell forward and sideways in a jerky motion. Then his body fell to the ground. Sadie touched his temple again and people in the living room stood quickly and rushed to the hall.

"What the hell did you do, Sadie?" Saul asked.

"She killed my oldest mate!" Jo-Jo said. "That's what she did."

Sadie scowled at both men. "He's not dead, though he deserves to be... He's just sleeping. "She inched backwards from the crowd. "You can put him in the guest room. He'll sleep for a long, long, long time."

Rich lumbered around the crowd near Steve. "He's a diabetic, Sadie. He takes insulin."

Sadie shook her head. "A diabetic should not do drugs," she mumbled. She took another step back. Her conscience would not accept her excuse, though. She knew she should go back to Steve, but the others stood around him, glaring at her.

Sadie set Roxanne down near the door and sent her scurrying out to the van. "I can't help him like this," she said to Rich when he reached her. "If I go near him, one of those guys will kill me."

Rich laughed lazily. "You're exaggerating a bit, Sugar. They're not teddies."

"They have murder on their minds presently."

Rich could see by their faces that she could be right, so he didn't argue. "Is there something I can do?"

"Yes. Get everyone away. I can help him if they don't interfere." She disappeared out the door as Rich herded the guests and other Spidars back to the living room. When Sadie returned, she no longer had Chuck on her back. She cautiously walked to Steve and bent down, placing her fingertips on his temple.

A few men rose in their seats. Rich blocked their path. Within seconds, Sadie stood up. "Steve will be okay, but you'll still have to carry him to the guest room for a while." With that, she turned and left the house.

*

The next morning, Sadie called Gene and Mary to her mother's house. Over a cup of tea, Sadie explained what happened with Steve. Peggy and Martha stayed outside with the children. Carol had returned to her husband in the apartment above the McCarthy home, using the private entrance in the back of the house.

"I told you Saul was no good, the rapist!" Lucille chided.

"Mom, that was a long time ago. Haven't you forgiven Saul yet?"

"I'll never forgive him!" Lucille paused and her features

251

softened. "I'm sorry. Steve was the villain this time. Yes, I have forgiven Saul for what he did to you. Since then, I've seen how much you love each other. But things like this drive me crazy!"

Sadie kissed her mother on the cheek. "I understand. You're trying to protect me the way I protect my own kids. I'm grown up now, Mom. I came here for advice, not lectures. Please. I don't want to do anything rash."

*

When Gene, Sadie, and Peggy returned to the Spidar estate mid-afternoon and entered by way of the side kitchen entrance, the Spidar men were sipping coffee around the kitchen table.

"Morning, Luv," Saul greeted his wife, standing to receive a kiss. "Where were you?"

Sadie walked past him without stopping. "It's afternoon and I came to talk about last night."

"Good picnic," Jo-Jo stated. "The last thing I recall is when the goodies came out." He licked his lips.

"There was something," Harry said. Sadie watched him try to concentrate. A few minutes later, he shrugged.

"You men really don't know what happened?" Sadie looked from one man to the other.

When she looked at Rich, he replied with sadness in his voice. "My memory's fine. I didn't do the snow or other drugs, just a few Mary Janes. You don't have to look so nasty-like. I stayed on the sidelines."

Voices wafted from the living room, making Sadie wince. She glared at Jo-Jo. "Are your friends – and I use the term loosely – still here?" she snapped. "I'd strongly advise you to show them the front door – immediately, if not sooner. If I see any one of them, I may lose it. Then I won't accomplish what I came here to do."

252

Jo-Jo opened his mouth to yell back, but her expression made him think twice. This was not the time for an argument. He and Harry went to the living room. Guests grumbled and shuffled around collecting their personal belongings.

"I can't find Steve," Jo-Jo said when he and Harry returned to the kitchen.

Sadie looked at Rich, who nodded. "He's in the guest room," she said. "I guess he'll have to stay there for a couple of days. Last night, I chemically altered the drugs in his body, so he'll sleep until there's no trace of them left in his blood."

"He'll die without his insulin!" Jo-Jo exclaimed.

"Luckily, Rich had enough sense left last night to tell me that. Steve's problem was in his adrenal glands. I fixed those. He no longer needs insulin."

"You cured him?" Peggy asked with incredulity. "That man was going to rape your two-year-old daughter and you cured him?" Sadie nodded slowly.

"So that's why his medal was showing when he was lying on the floor," Rich mumbled. The other men stared at Peggy.

"If I'd known, I would've chipped in," Saul offered.

"You did do something! You laughed. You thought it was very funny indeed."

Silence filled the room as Sadie calmed herself. "The reason I came here today was to tell you I'm moving out. I cannot endanger my children with any more of your stupid drug parties. I was going to send a truck to pick up my things, but Gene convinced me to come in person and talk it over with you first."

Saul glanced around the room for help. None came. "I thought you didn't believe in divorce," he said meekly.

Sadie recognized the psychology. She kept her voice under control by speaking slowly. "I said I'm moving out, not divorcing you. I love you, but I need time to forgive you all for

253

last night."

Silence.

"Granted, we shouldn't have guffawed, but we were behind the action," Jo-Jo finally stated. "Seems to me, you're being a bit two-faced. You cured a life-long illness in the bloke who tried to hurt Roxie, yet you can't forgive us for laughing, even though we didn't know the scope of the intrusion. Isn't that niggling a bit?"

Peggy's silence terminated with a roar. She flailed her arms and stomped her feet. The men could only understand bits and pieces of what she said. "... not all ... on the dock ... bruises ... body ..." The rest was incoherent.

Sadie pressed her fingertips lightly on Peggy's forehead. Peggy quieted. Her facial muscles relaxed. Sadie sent her to the living room to lie on a couch.

"What was that about?" Harry asked.

Rich began to answer: "The problem with Roxanne wasn't the only one last night. On the dock..."

Sadie interrupted. "The dock incident doesn't matter. I know it was the drugs. I'm okay. Jo-Jo, to answer your question, it is much easier to forgive someone you don't know. When friends let you down, the disappointment is much greater. From you all, I expected more."

Silence again.

Until now, Gene had simply observed, finding out what Sadie had neglected to say at Lucille's house, but now he spoke. "Sadie, is that the only reason you want to leave?" He hesitated. "Perhaps you and I should talk privately for a moment."

Sadie led Gene into the unused den and closed the door.

*

254

An hour later, Gene and Sadie emerged from the den. "I'm going for a walk," Gene said. Sadie nodded at him then smiled at the men gathered at the kitchen table.

The Spidar men lowered their eyes. Rich had told them what he knew about last night, including what they did to Sadie on the dock and how bruised she was as she walked past him.

Saul's voice crackled as he embraced her. "I'm so sorry."

"I know." Sadie's voice had regained its sparkle and vitality. "Gene helped me realize that I'm madder at myself than at you guys. I don't want to admit, even to myself, that I totally lost control last night. I was so furious at Steve that I killed him. Yes, for a second or so, he was dead. Luckily, I came to my senses fast enough. He was alive again by the time he hit the floor."

She paused for a moment and continued, "It's a scary thing, this power. I have learned to kill. I don't want that. That's why I cured Steve's diabetes, to try to erase my overreaction. Sadly, life doesn't work that way for most people. I need to remember the Steve incident so I never lose control again." She bowed her head in shame.

"So what's with Peg?" Harry asked. "She subdued so quickly."

Sadie's lips turned into a half-smile. "She couldn't handle thoughts about last night, so I erased all of them from her memory and lowered her adrenalin. I should go back to Mom's and do the same thing for Martha. I wasn't thinking straight this morning."

She walked to the side door. Saul arrived there first and leaned against it. "Will you return?"

She tousled his hair. "Yes, I'll come back. However, when you have parties in the future, I will take the kids elsewhere."

255

Saul silently questioned the men at the table. Together they all let out a sigh of relief and nodded.

"Steve will get the boot as soon as his peepers open," Jo-Jo offered. "And never come here again."

"We've nailed the flea in our ear," Harry agreed.

Chapter 16 – September 1968

It was mid-morning, yet the day remained dark and dreary. Black clouds hung low in the sky. The Spidar children had been fed. The infants watched from the playpen as the toddlers played with toys nearby. The adults sat around the kitchen table finishing their coffee.

"So what are you going to do now?" Peggy asked Saul, her eyes puffy from lack of sleep.

"The last time, her bobby mate found her," he replied. "Perhaps he can do it again."

Peggy shook her head. "Saul, the last time, the police had to spot a van and a woman with a brood of children. A person traveling alone in an unknown vehicle will be next to impossible to find." Tears flowed down her cheeks.

Martha put her hands on Peggy's shoulders. "We'll find her. Don't worry."

"How? We've called Ted and all her friends. What else can we do?"

Silence.

Peggy scowled. "You caused this, Saul. If only you would stop treating Sadie so nasty."

"Come on," Saul protested, "You and Harry argue the toss too. It is perfectly normal not to get on occasionally. She's the one who walked out on her family." He lowered his voice. "I don't even remember what started the tiff."

"She only left after you said you wished she was dead!"

"Calm, Pet," Harry said. "If you remember rightly, Sadie was the one who said Saul would be happier if she were dead."

257

"But he didn't argue. He could have denied it instead of standing there with that smirk on his face!" Peggy lowered her head and covered her face with her hands, sobbing quietly. "I can't take much more of this. Saul has to help more with the kids. I can't handle everything!" Harry put an arm around her shoulder.

"You yap as if you do all the flippin' chores yourself," Saul replied sharply. "You don't. Carol's here. Maybe we need her and Josh to take on more of the chores. And Martha and Miki help while we work, and then we do what we can."

Peggy glanced at the other two Spidar women. "Yes, Saul, you're right. They all do help. Just look at them. They are as exhausted as I am. Carol's up in bed herself. Sadie's only been gone three days now and we're all done in. Caring for eight children as young as they are is no picnic. I don't know how Sadie did it and still kept her smile all the time."

Peggy's voice changed to a mumble, as if to herself. "She's always the first out of bed. She feeds the kids. She plans the meals for the day. She cooks a fantastic breakfast. She even exercises. She does all that before the rest of us are even out of bed. On top of that, she's the one who gets up in the middle of the night with the infants. I don't hear them because she shuts off their intercom before they get loud enough to wake me..." Her volume diminished to nothingness.

"I may be the newest member of the family," Martha said quietly, "So correct me if I'm wrong. Doesn't this seem unusual for Sadie? I mean, she's left before, but doesn't she usually get over her anger quickly? Three days is much too long. She should have been back a while ago."

"Precisely why it's getting on our wick, Sugar," Rich replied. "Something's happened. She would never leave her kids for this long, no matter how riled she is."

"She would've called by now," Jo-Jo added. "That means she can't get to a phone. Or worse."

"She acted strangely those last few days," Martha said.

"Ah! Someone else noticed!" Saul exclaimed. "It wasn't all in my mind."

"Yes, I noticed. She seemed edgy."

Harry raised his eyebrows, as if surprised. "Sadie? Are we talking about Sadie? She never yelled or anything, not until her ding-dong with Saul at the pool."

Peggy stroked his hair with her hand. "You might not notice. When she's upset, she busies herself with household tasks. She avoids contact with us whenever possible, so we won't be exposed to her sharp tongue."

"Sharp isn't the word for it," Saul said. "A carving knife is sharp. When she's in a mood, her tongue could slice a diamond like a tomato."

Rich laughed. "Then we're lucky she isn't a cranky sort, or we'd be in bits."

Peggy didn't smile. "Saul, normally you can get her out of bad moods. She told me all you have to do is cuddle and her problems melt away. So, why do you insist on fighting?"

"Hey!" Saul protested again. "Why is it always my fault? I'm not her wet-nurse. I've been in a tight spot lately myself. Ask the other chaps. They went through the same thing. We're still a bit nadgered from going cold turkey. With her powers, Sadie could have helped, but she chose not to. Don't give me a telling-off for being the hard nut to crack."

Peggy glared into Saul's eyes. "I can see her point. She's been ridding your bodies of drugs every week for a long time, yet you kept doing them. Now that you've had to suffer through withdrawal, you may be more apt to stay away from them ... Martha, why are you shaking your head?"

259

"You're all trying to fix the blame," Martha replied. "I think we should forget about that and concentrate on finding her. Peg, Saul's actions may not agree with us sometimes, but I don't think her problem had anything to do with him – or us."

"So what's her problem then? Maybe we could figure out her whereabouts if we know what was bugging her."

Martha's gaze lowered to her tea mug. "I don't know."

"Oh goody!" Saul said with mock excitement. "So we're back to where we began. We have no idea where Sadie is and no idea what's the matter, so we have no idea where to look and no idea what shape she's in. In other words, we don't know a whole hell of a lot."

Peggy rose from the table and went to the sink. She washed the dishes by hand, not bothering with the dishwasher, as tired as she was.

The room fell silent again. The clock ticked the passing time. Squeals came from the living room as eight children played, yet the kitchen was quiet. Even the swishing water in the sink and the clinking of the dishes were subdued.

A loud knock on the side door startled them. Maybe, just maybe, Saul thought as he hurried to the door. "Oh... it's you, Jerry."

"Hello, Mr. McCarthy," the security man replied. "I, uh, need to talk to you. I know I'm not supposed to bother you unless it is an emergency, but I think this is."

"You look strung out," Saul said, "Come in and have a cuppa char."

"No thanks." Jerry sat at the head of the table. He spoke as if a ton of molten lava poured off his chest. "She said she'd fire me if I told you or any of her friends, but I can't keep it in any longer. The nights get cold now. I tried to cover her with a blanket after she fell asleep, but last night she woke up and yelled at me. She said she wants to die like the old Indians,

260

alone and never more a burden to those she loves. She refuses food and drinks, too. She's dwindling to nothing."

"Who's the 'she'?" Saul asked. "Are you talking about Sadie? Do you know where she is?"

"Yes. She was always thin. Now she's skin and bones. I've never seen anyone lose weight so fast."

The noise level rose as facial wrinkles disappeared and headaches dissipated. The whole room's mood elevated.

"Sadie's metabolism is different, Jerry," Martha explained. "She burns energy faster than the rest of us. That's how she stays so skinny despite all she eats."

Rich prodded Martha's ribs. "She doesn't eat all that much. Her plate's loaded the same as you lambs who always seem to be dieting."

Martha exchanged an amused glance with Peggy. "Haven't you ever wondered why she always cooks for the family?" she asked Rich.

Harry's eyes went to the ceiling, thinking of the delicious meals he had eaten. "Why would we give a rap why? She's strong on it."

"You're right. She is good. However, you leave out the most important part. She loves to cook and has become quite proficient at it because she loves to eat!"

"You sound like a bog-house barrister, considering she doesn't pack away that much."

"Oh yes, she does!" Martha and Peggy said simultaneously. They giggled and Martha motioned for Peggy to continue. "Sadie always nibbles when she cooks – not little tidbits, but big spoonfuls – supposedly to test the spices. If any of us did her kind of taste-testing, we'd give the Goodyear Blimp competition in short order. She basically eats two meals each time she cooks."

Martha motioned to Peg that she wanted to speak, serious again. "Jerry said Sadie's down to skin and bones. I believe him. If she hasn't eaten in three days, she must have lost a lot of weight." The room quieted quickly.

"Where is she?" Saul asked.

After a long hesitation, Jerry blurted, "She's in the far corner of the orchard, beyond that old outhouse the historical society asked her not to tear down..."

"Can't be," Saul stated. "My own peepers saw her walk out the gate."

"She returned an hour later. That's when she said she'd fire me if I told you or anyone else where she was." Jerry's volume lowered. He stared at the ceiling. "At first she looked like a goddess, sitting among the fruit trees with her face all aglow. The chipmunks came right up to her and chattered.

"Not now. Even the animals and birds look worried. She just lies there. She doesn't move unless I try to cover her with a blanket or urge her to eat. Then she goes into a rage that I should mind my own business and leave her in peace." Jerry's eyes locked on Saul. "She's never been so nasty to me. I'm worried about her."

"So were we, before you told us she's so close," Jo-Jo proclaimed. "Let's get crackin,' Saul. I'll give you a leg-up getting her back to the house. She can kick and scream at me all she wants." The two went to the door. Peggy followed.

"It won't take two men," Jerry offered quietly. "She must be down to seventy pounds by now."

Jo-Jo returned to his seat. "My stomach's never been strong for this sort of thing, anyways."

Martha stood. "I'll go with Peg and Saul."

Jerry rose to leave too. "When you find her, tell her I'm packing my bags. I'll be gone by noon."

"Piffle!" Saul shot back. "You have a job here as long as you want. For now, take us to her." Jerry smiled in relief.

Despite Jerry's warning, they weren't prepared for what they saw in the orchard. Sadie's once lustrous hair lay dull and tangled. Black eyelids had sunk into their sockets above dry, cracked lips. Her hands rested on her stomach, fingers intertwined, joints twice the size of the rest, with a limp dandelion dangling from them.

Saul fell to his knees beside her. "How could you do a thing like this? Tell me it's not too late."

Silence.

He cradled her in his arms and kissed the top of her head. "Sadie, it's me, Saul. Say something."

Still no response.

Martha walked to the other side of the bony body. As she knelt, she unhooked the fingers and tossed the wilted flower away. She put trained fingers on a shrunken wrist. "She's still alive. Her pulse is weak, but she can make it if she wants to." Martha's voice adopted a nurse's air of authority. "Sadie, I know you can hear me. Open your eyes and look at us."

Nothing.

"I SAID: OPEN YOUR EYES. NOW!"

Sadie complied. Her bloodshot eyes looked like two beets in a freshly-hoed garden plot. She glanced first at Martha, then at Saul, then Peggy. When her gaze moved to Jerry, her mouth opened and she tried to speak. No sound.

A full glass of lemonade sat on the ground near Martha. Jerry had delivered it earlier this morning. Martha picked it up and let a few drops trickle into Sadie's mouth. She swallowed hard and Martha repeated the process.

Sadie slid her tongue slowly around her lips. Then she tried to speak again. This time, her voice squeaked, barely audible. She looked at Jerry again. "You're fired!"

Peggy shook her head, remembering Sadie's fight with Saul. *"Saul, your bullheadedness will be the death of me yet,"* she had said. Now here Sadie was, almost dead from her own stubborn nature, making good on a threat to the man who just saved her life.

"... should call an ambulance," Martha was saying. "She's so dehydrated, her blood must be as thick as her spaghetti sauce. Her heart must be overworked, trying to keep it circulating. She needs fluids fast. The hospital is the quickest way. They can hook up a glucose I.V."

Sadie lifted a hand and squeaked again. "No hospital. I won't let them touch me!" Her eyes closed.

"You're in no condition to mix it with 'em, Luv," Saul said.

Peggy watched Martha, who was deep in thought. Jerry turned to go to his cottage to make the phone call. Peggy grabbed his arm and spoke quietly as she turned back, "Martha, can a patient's negativity affect her recuperation?"

"Most certainly yes. We'll have to direct the ambulance to Strong Hospital in Rochester. They have a psychiatric unit there."

"Will that help?"

"Who knows?"

Sadie opened her eyes. She had an all-to-familiar determined look in her hollow eyes. "I said NO HOSPITALS!"

"Then, will you cooperate here at home?" Peggy asked.

"I'd rather die in peace."

Martha looked at Saul. "Maybe we can do more for her than Strong can. Dr. Gothic will probably make a house call. He can prescribe the medications, IV bags, and equipment, and I can collect them from the hospital. Let's get her to the house."

With Sadie still in his arms, Saul stood and walked with the group to the house, in the front door, and up the stairs. Martha led the way and opened the guest room door.

"No," Saul said. "I want her in my bed."

Peggy scowled. "How can you think of sex at a time like this?"

"I'll kip in the guest room it if makes you feel better," Saul replied, kissing Sadie's forehead. "My Luv gets her own bed."

Martha shook her head. "No Saul. We don't know what's wrong – what's causing her death wish. She needs a neutral setting. But you are very sweet to offer."

Saul studied the woman in his arms. Martha may be right. He carried her into the guest room and tenderly laid her on the bed. He sat in a chair beside her, holding her hand as Martha called Dr. Gothic.

"There's no sense making the doc come here," Sadie said, her eyes still closed. "My body doesn't tolerate many medicines."

"How about the glucose and water?" Martha asked.

Sadie opened her eyes and shrugged. "Dr. Gothic is a busy man. He has more important things to do."

"You're important, too," Saul protested. She closed her eyes without replying.

*

The following few days, Sadie responded when it suited her. She allowed Martha to hook up an I.V., which prevented further weight loss. She also drank the beef or chicken broths Peggy made. That was all. She refused to chew any solid foods Martha prepared. She said she didn't have the energy. Martha liquefied the foods in a blender, but Sadie still refused them. "They taste funny," she would say as she pushed them away.

Dr. Gothic visited several times. He took several blood samples to test. One test reported a healthy patient, the next declared the patient dead already, then the third was back to healthy. To Martha, the doc's normal confidence seemed

265

visibly shattered, as if he felt his training was prehistoric, his forty years of experience with women worthless.

On Saturday morning, Sadie still would not eat and continued to make references to her spot in the far orchard for death. The Spidar family sat around the kitchen table. "Maybe I was wrong to let her stay home," Martha said.

Peggy shrugged. "Why don't we call Gene and explain the problem. She respects him. He may be able to help."

"There's only one problem with that idea," Saul said. "Sadie was serious when she said not to tell any mates about her condition."

"So?" Harry said. "She was also quite serious when she told Jerry not to blab to us. If he hadn't..." Harry shuddered.

Peggy rose and walked to the phone. She explained the situation to Gene, mainly Sadie's unwillingness to accept help. He agreed to come right over. Peggy moved to the cooking area and began to prepare dough.

"What did he say?" Rich asked. "And what are you doing? This is no time to worry about lunch. It's only nine in the morn. We've hardly finished brekker."

Peggy smiled. "Gene suggested a pizza lunch for Sadie. It's her worst weakness. She cannot refuse pizza, no matter how she feels. And a proper dough needs time to rise."

Martha's nose crinkled. "There's a lot of chewing with pizza. She may not have the energy for it."

"Gene knows one more weakness which should give her some quick energy. He said he'd pick up her favorite doughnuts on the way over." Peggy chuckled as she continued. "He thinks we might even get her to drink a glass of milk without complaint as long as it's with the doughnut."

An hour later, Gene carried two dozen chocolate-covered, custard-filled doughnuts into the kitchen. He put the boxes on the table, took out two and placed them on the plate Peg handed him. He accepted a glass of milk from Martha and went upstairs, asking the others to remain in the kitchen. "Enjoy a treat while you wait," he added.

When he walked into Sadie's room, the putrid odor of pre-death assailed his nostrils. He closed his eyes to say a silent prayer for the right words and to gather inner strength, then he slowly crossed the room and set the glass of milk on the nightstand.

He laid one hand on Sadie's head. Her eyes opened. He forced a smile, despite knowing he couldn't hide his thoughts from her if she were in her prime. He wouldn't be able to hide the rising nausea in his stomach either. "I thought you might enjoy a treat," he said quietly.

When she spied the doughnuts in his hand, a faint twinkle appeared in her eyes. Gene set the plate next to the glass of milk and propped some pillows under her back. Then he offered the doughnuts. Sadie slowly raised an arm to take one and nibbled it as she listened to him.

"Starving yourself is suicide," he scolded. "You know suicide is wrong. God has given you life. You have no right to end that life before He is ready for you. You've said for quite some time that you feel God has a special mission for you and your family. You said that's why he allows your different lifestyle. Are you rebelling against Him?"

"No," she whispered. "I feel so miserable. All day long, I cook and clean and take care of the kids and family. Even when I do a good job, the same tasks wait for me within a day or so. Do I really accomplish anything?"

Gene remained silent.

Sadie paused to catch her breath. "I don't know any more. I don't know if I've been blowing things out of proportion. Maybe the men are the ones with a mission. Maybe it's just my ego that makes me think I'll be part of it."

"Why else would you have exceptional powers?"

"I don't know. I don't care. I'm tired, real tired. I can't continue this charade."

Gene smoothed her hair. "What would your family do without you? Have you noticed how haggard they look?" She nodded and Gene continued, "They've been trying to do your work in addition to their own – out of their love for you. You're surrounded by love in this house. It's not like you to feel sorry for yourself, to be so negative." His voice softened. "Before this tired feeling came over you, had you been paying attention to your own body at all?"

A blush rose in her cheeks. "The men were having a rough time. They've gone through a lot the last two weeks. Drug withdrawal should be done in a hospital, but we... no, I should say I wanted to do it at home with love. We set up the men in the den and made sure there was at least one woman in the room at all times."

She lowered her head. "Because of the children, I didn't take care of the men much... just the two hours of the kids' joint naps..."

Gene interrupted. "If I know you, you made up for that in other ways."

Sadie nodded. "I tried to help Carol more with the housework, so the other women could relax whenever they weren't tending to the men, but that shouldn't affect anything. I have more energy than the rest."

"What happened at night?"

"Many nights each man went to his own bedroom."

"Many? What happened on the other nights?"

"Well, there were a few days when the women walked around like zombies. The men couldn't sleep right, and their tossing and turning prevented the women from sleeping too."

Gene nodded. "And Saul was one of those men, so you didn't sleep well in your bedroom, either, when the men were tossing and turning. What happened on those nights?"

"The men were assigned to daybeds moved from the music room to the den. I stayed with them, so the women could get a decent night's rest. That way I could do my share of the tending. I hoped that made up for the lack of time during the day because of the kids."

Gene looked into Sadie's eyes. "Did you get some nights to sleep alone?"

Sadie hesitated. She caught his hint. "No, but I did fine. I'm used to getting up several times during the night with the babies anyway. My body compensates with sound sleep whenever it gets the chance. Even if I lay down for a half-hour at night, I'm refreshed when I get up."

Gene shook his head. "Have you ever gone without full sleep for a prolonged period in the past?"

"This was only two weeks."

"Sounds to me like you expect too much from yourself. Did you lay down every chance you could?"

Sadie's blush deepened. "I couldn't, Gene. By the second day of the men's withdrawal, they were very irritable and shaky and all. Their symptoms reminded me of some patients at Strong."

"What does Strong have to do with this? Did you continue your volunteering at Strong during all this commotion at home?"

"No, I took a month's leave of absence."

"Good. Continue."

"Well, that second night in the den, when I finally had Saul resting in quasi-comfort, I fell asleep in the extra daybed and dreamed that I should compose special music for people who desperately need to relax. So I began the project the next day."

269

She paused to finish the first doughnut and reached for the second one. Her movements had quickened a little. Gene touched her arm and motioned to the milk. She drank some, put the glass back, retrieved the second treat, and her tongue attacked the chocolate on top of it.

Gene smiled. "So you used the music room for that. Was that during the kids' naps?"

"No, the kids' nap time is reserved for the men. When we tended to the men in the den, they would spend some time in the music room themselves if they were up for it. On nights the men were back in their own rooms, I usually tended to Saul's needs. After he fell asleep, I'd sneak down and do what I could between trips to check on him and the babies."

"How many nights before the song was finished?"

"Actually, it's not done yet. If I were a musician, I'd have finished quickly. But, even though I can read music okay, I'm not very good at playing it. An hour flew while I tried to figure out the guitar chords. Then there's all the other stuff."

"Wouldn't the men help? They have the experience."

Sadie stared at the ceiling. "The song was in my head, not theirs."

Gene studied her face for a moment. "I see. Once you wrote the basic melody, you let them help with the various instruments. Right?"

"I didn't need their help. It's MY song."

"Oh, and I'll bet you haven't even told them about it at all."

"Well-l-l... No."

"Didn't you tell me long ago about how these musical geniuses of yours get help from each other regularly?"

"Yeah, so?"

"I see. So when did you first notice your jealousy?"

Sadie hesitated. "I hadn't thought of it as jealousy. They write and perform fantastic songs for the general public. I'm

270

just trying to write something that helps medically. I guess I did become overprotective of the song around the end of the first week, the same time I thought the basic score was close to done."

"Hmm-m-m," Gene said softly. "Your body was already overtired and you pushed it another week." His voice intensified a little. "You said the song isn't finished yet. Since you now recognize the jealousy, will you let the men help?"

She shook her head. "No, there's no instrument that can produce the special sound in my head. Without that, there's really no sense." Her eyes began to lose their sparkle again.

"Perhaps you should check your body for imbalances," Gene suggested. "I called Dr. Gothic before coming over. He thought the problem could be in something called your neurotransmitters, if you know what they are. So far, doctors have no way to test for them except in a hospital. Can you?"

She nodded and put her fingers on her temples. Hmmm. Gene was right. She had overtired her body. Everything was askew. Her hypothalamus lay dormant, her amylase was low, spasms wracked her thyroid. Both serotonin and norepinephrine hid from her search. Not accustomed to the lack of hormones and body chemicals, neurotransmitters shot impulses in random directions and at random times. Sadie made quick adjustments.

When Peggy, Saul, and Martha mentioned pizza, Sadie's eyes glittered for the first time in a week.

Saul ran to her side and hugged her tight. "Welcome back, Luv!" Still holding her, he looked to Gene. "Thanks."

"My pleasure," Gene replied. "You merely have to remind this girl that she's human. Try to keep her resting for a while. She needs to take it easy for the rest of the day." He winked at Saul. "I know it may be difficult."

"Well, maybe for an hour or so," Sadie teased. She turned to Martha. "Do you know how to make eggnog?" Martha nodded, so Sadie continued, "Good. Can you please make me a pitcher of that? I will need plenty today. It has the calories and the protein my body needs to get back on my feet quickly."

When Martha left the room, Sadie crinkled her nose and sniffed the air. "PIZZA!" she squealed like a child. Peggy handed her the plate. She glanced at the generous amounts of mushrooms, peppers, and black olives on top of the red sauce. "Between this pizza and the eggnog, I should be up and around by supper time."

Gene glared at her from the doorway. "I said to rest today – all day."

Sadie raised her hand in a sharp salute. "Yes, Sir!"

He shook his head and left the room. Saul and Peggy remained in the room as she devoured her lunch.

In the kitchen, Martha told the men how good Sadie looked now.

"Boy!" Harry exclaimed. "Peg's pizza works in a spit-spot!"

"No, not the pizza, but that will help now too," Martha replied.

Gene entered from the hallway on his way out the side door. When Martha asked him to explain Sadie's problem, he stopped. "She forgets that she has limitations. If she tries to go beyond them, her body retaliates. We should all remember that. No matter how many things press for our time, we must slow down sometimes."

"We have to stop and smell the roses," Rich quipped.

"Exactly."

That afternoon, Sadie took short naps and drank pitcher after pitcher of eggnog or water. Her face began to fill out, cheeks and eyelids returning to pale pink, eyes sparkling blue like the lake on a summer day. Saul stayed by her side throughout the afternoon. At four o'clock, when she woke from another nap, she blinked her lashes at him. "Can I ask a favor, Hon?"

"Sure, Luv. What?"

"Can you put my things in our bedroom? I'd like to be part of the family again, not just a guest."

Saul raced to his room. He stripped the bed, applied Sadie's favorite mauve sheets, and fluffed the pillows. He shook out the bedspread and applied it, then pulled down all the covers to invite occupancy – the same way Sadie always did. Standing in the doorway, he surveyed his handiwork. No, not right yet. He grabbed a pair of scissors and ran outside. He returned carrying long-stemmed pink buds from Sadie's rose garden. He put them in a slender, crystal vase and set them on Sadie's night stand beside her latest issue of Parents Magazine and The Medical Journal. Then he skipped out of the room.

As he entered the guest room, Sadie walked out from the bathroom. Her skin glowed like a fresh morning glory with a hint of dew. She draped her bathrobe over her shoulders, covering her skinny but already expanding body. They walked arm-in-arm to the master bedroom. At the door, Sadie stopped and raised one eyebrow, a familiar question unspoken.

"I can't in your present lot, Luv," Saul replied.

Wordlessly, she held his hands in hers and slowly backed toward the bed, her eyes twinkling. *How can I say no?* he thought. *I'd have to be a saint.* He kicked the door shut behind him and followed her lead.

Chapter 17

The next morning, as the aroma in the kitchen built to a crescendo like Tchaikovsky's 1812 Overture, Sadie opened the hallway door to let the fragrance burst up the stairs. She assisted by going up herself and opening each bedroom door a tad. Since the children were all fed and playing in the living room downstairs, she woke Saul personally. He was the last one down to Sunday breakfast.

As everyone else ate pecan pancakes, sausage, banana muffins, juice and coffee, Sadie changed whatever diapers needed it again. After dressing the toddling triplets in their best clothes, she returned to the kitchen.

"You're all welcome to come with us if you wish," she said. She had found a comfortable church in Canandaigua. The congregation was both Baptist and Presbyterian, united under one roof. The members compromised differences and worshipped in peace and harmony, which supported Sadie's belief that loving each other was at the top of God's priorities.

The Spidar men declined her offer, but Martha and Peggy joined her. "I'll stay with Jo-Jo," Miki said. "We can watch the infants here."

Sadie's eyes squinted in suspicion. Was Miki concerned about the men's upcoming trip to England? Oh well, the church nursery would be less packed if only the triplets went.

*

As usual, the service began with announcements: events for the week, new births in the church family, and recent hospitalizations and deaths to include in prayer. After that, the whole congregation sauntered from aisle to aisle, shaking hands with others for about three minutes. Dressed incognito, Sadie used this time to meet area residents. Peggy and Martha followed her quietly.

After the sermon, the minister invited the congregation to Talk Back in the fellowship room, combining coffee and tea with a group discussion of the day's message.

"Should we check the triplets first?" Peggy asked.

"No. Karen's working in the nursery today. The kids will be fine." As the oldest of five children, Karen had a lot of experience handling little ones, even as a teenager herself. The Spidar triplets loved her warm, calm demeanor.

In the fellowship room, the three Spidar women sat near Karen's parents, Izzy and Paul. "I have a roast in the oven," Izzy said. "Why don't you bring your families over for a two o'clock luncheon?"

Sadie laughed. "There are sixteen of us, counting the kids!"

Izzy didn't flinch. "The more, the merrier. We have twenty-two people when my sisters come with their children. We all have a great time! How does 1:30 sound for cocktails?"

Sadie hesitated. So much time was spent in hiding nowadays. Izzy and Karen were so nice. But would Karen stay calm if she found out about the men? She is a teenager, after all. She might call a few friends and those teens might call a few friends and those teens would call a few more, etc. By the end of dinner, a crowd would assemble outside the Black's Howell Street house, unlit fuses waiting for a Spidar match. Canandaigua didn't have a police force large enough to handle such an explosion.

Then again, maybe Sadie could test the waters. Izzy always invites her over for tea when they meet at the grocery store. The next time, Sadie could go to tea without the blonde wig, which fell in ringlets around her shoulders. The following visit, she could also drop the daisy earrings and bulky clothes, which widen her dimensions. Eventually, she could visit without makeup instead of the thick layer normally seen by the public on her outings. When the Blacks knew the truth, maybe a serious discussion would help Karen stay sensible. Then the reward for silence could be meeting the men. Yes, that might nip the fuse before it gets lit. It certainly would be nice to be able to be themselves outside the Spidar estate.

"Not today, thanks," Sadie replied. "But I'd love a rain check."

"You're welcome anytime. My daughter loves your children.

Sadie smiled, knowing Izzy meant what it. Previous teas had proven she was the type of woman who treats guests like family.

*

When the Spidar van pulled into the McCarthy estate, Rich stood in the driveway, talking to Jerry at the gate. Sadie stopped. "Would you like a ride, mister?"

"That depends on where you're going," he said with a grin.

"We're headed for a Spidar web."

"Sorry, this chaperone service only goes as far as a bee hive." Rich gave her a lopsided grin this time. "Unles-s-s you're a good tipper."

"Well," Sadie said with a smirk, "the hundred acres on the corner of Routes 96 and 332 appear to hold promise. A housing development could be put in there."

Rich winked at her. "That's not the tip I had in mind."

She shook her head. "Thanks, anyway. We'll go without you then."

"Spoil sport!"

Inside the house, the triplets played while Sadie breastfed two infants, Peggy fed one, and Miki and Martha bottle-fed the other two.

"It's not a fair crack of the whip," Jo-Jo remarked.

"What's not square?" Harry asked.

"The birds get to do all the feeding."

"They have the equipment, Mate"

"Men can use bottles as easily as women."

Martha glanced at Sadie, who shrugged and jerked her head toward Jo-Jo. Martha gave him Dave. Miki and Jo-Jo sat next to each other, looking tenderly at the babies in their arms, and exchanging silent communication. After the feeding, Sadie handed Vera to Saul and Chuck to Rich for burping and entertainment, and she prepared lunch.

During the children's nap time, the adults went out to the pool. Sadie was the last one out. She made sure the intercoms in the children's room were set to transmit only. Then she went to the music room to put some records on and set that intercom to transmit. Leaving the house, she aimed directly for the deep end, climbed the steps to the diving board – one, two, and three – and listened to the music coming from the speakers. A smile appeared as she glided her tongue across her lips. Then she removed her shift and threw it in a heap. One song ended and the next one began.

"It started long ago in the Garden of Eden..."[24] The family nodded. "Alri-i-ight!" Rich exclaimed, taking off his shirt. It was officially play time. "Same rules?" he asked as an afterthought.

"Yes, same rules," Sadie replied, performing a graceful swan dive. Shirts and shifts flew off and the men dove into the water. The three other women walked down the steps in the shallow end, rooting for whichever man they happened to favor this time, as the men tried to corner Sadie.

Each time Sadie surfaced, she giggled and taunted the men. Then she quickly bent at the waist and raised her legs in the air, submerging in slow motion. Once immersed, she clicked into fast forward again. She glided up to each man and then squiggled away. On the few occasions that she tired, she exited the pool via the stairs and climbed onto the diving board to get a small breather.

After ten minutes, Peggy jeered, "What's the matter, boys?"

Harry looked over at her in a mock scowl. "She doesn't play fair!" He made eye contact with the other men. They went into a huddle. Instead of competing against each other, the men would work together.

"Giving up?" Sadie teased with a wiggle of her hips.

"No way!" Rich yelled. The men broke formation and stationed themselves around the pool. Since Jo-Jo had been the least enthusiastic in his attempt to catch anything, he was assigned as guard for the stairs to prevent her from resting.

Sadie just giggled. So, she would back-float around in a circle when she tired. No big deal. A few minutes later, the moment arrived. When Sadie began to float, the three men put all their energies into one last attempt. This time, when she tried to squiggle past Saul, he grabbed an ankle and held tight, only releasing it when she offered her wrist, so she could be upright in the water.

"That's not right, Mate," Rich complained. "You get her from dusk to dawn. You're not supposed to be the one who catches her in the games!"

"In this case, a Sadie in the pool is worth two birds in the bed."

Because of Jo-Jo's low spirits, the men let him get first pick of the remaining women. He surprised the others by picking his own wife for the second half of the game. Rich and Harry switched women.

278

Since the air was cooler than the water, everyone remained in the heated pool instead of wandering into the forest. The arrangement worked out well enough. Each couple was too busy to notice the others.

When all urges had been satiated, Sadie looked around and could tell by Miki and Jo-Jo's long faces that they hadn't played the second half at all. She swam over to where they stared at each other wordlessly. "Can I help?" she asked.

"I bloody hope so," Jo-Jo stated. "I know I can't." One hand rubbed his forehead as Miki announced that she was three months pregnant.

"That's great!" Sadie exclaimed. "So why the long faces?"

Miki stared down at her own trembling hands, pressing against each other. Her voice lowered. "Something's wrong with the baby."

"Why didn't you say something before this?"

"You had your own dilemma," Jo-Jo replied.

"Nonsense," Sadie retorted. She placed her open palm on Miki's abdomen. "We'd better go inside."

Miki didn't move. "The baby's dead. Isn't it?"

"Let's go inside to discuss it."

Jo-Jo shook his head. "It's all my fault."

Miki smoothed his hair. "Jo-Jo thinks he was too exuberant in bed and injured the baby."

"I doubt Jo-Jo's passion caused it. The female reproductive system is quite capable of protecting babies from the bumps we get from time to time."

"If I didn't do it, what did?" Jo-Jo asked, not convinced.

"I don't know yet," Sadie replied. "I'll work inside." Miki followed her into the house. Jo-Jo remained at the pool to explain the situation to the others, who were now relaxing on lounge chairs.

Once Miki was on her own bed, Sadie ran her hands over

Miki's abdomen. She looked up with sadness in her eyes. "We have two choices," Sadie said. "Either we wait until your body rejects the baby or I can do my own form of a D&C now. Would you like to discuss it with Jo-Jo?"

"If the baby's dead, get it out of me!" Miki cried.

"It's not that simple. You should think about your options for a moment. It's usually less of a shock if you let your body do the work itself, less painful too. If I perform a modified D & C, I don't dare use a pain-relieving method, because I want to find out the reason the baby died."

"Won't you have to change things around to do your work anyways?"

"No, I don't use surgical tools. I'll just make your uterine muscles contract hard. I want to get the baby out in one piece – not like a normal D & C, which would chop it to pieces – so you'll feel like two tons have dropped on you."

Miki studied the ceiling swirls for a minute and then looked back at Sadie. "Go ahead and do it – the sooner the better." Sadie left the room to get supplies. She returned a few minutes later with a big bowl, a plastic sheet, and some towels.

After hearing Jo-Jo's explanation, the others didn't want to stay at the pool. As they came into the front hallway headed for a snack in the kitchen, they heard an ear-piercing scream. Peggy ran to the intercom. "What's going on?"

"Sorry," came Sadie's reply, "I forgot to close Miki's door up here. Can you come up and calm the kids. I can hear them crying. They're probably scared to death from her scream."

Jo-Jo ran up the stairs two at a time. He reached his bedroom as Sadie was coming out, carrying a large bowl wrapped in a towel. She reached up and stroked his face gently.

"Miki's okay, just tired. I've increased her endorphin levels now. She'll feel no more pain. See if you can get her to sleep until supper time. She's been through a lot in a short time." He nodded and walked into his bedroom.

*

Saul knocked on the den door. An hour had passed since Sadie secluded herself. "Enter at your own risk," she chirped. Saul opened the door and took an involuntary step backwards.

Sadie sat at a card table draped with a thick plastic sheet. In front of her sat a microscope. Various surgical instruments and bottles of chemicals littered one side of the table. On the opposite side lay a pink doll-like form, three inches long, wrapped in cellophane.

Sadie reached around the microscope and sliced a piece off the pink mound. The mound had surface marbling like the cellulite of a rotund person's buttocks. A pool of blood surrounded the mound. She wiped the scalpel against a slide to deposit her latest fragment.

"Yes?" she asked, turning her head toward the door. A giggle escaped her lips when she saw Saul's green face. "I warned you! Did you want something?"

"Uh, Peg, uh, says, uh supper's, uh ready," he stammered.

"You go ahead without me."

"Uh, I'm not hungry anymore."

*

"Fantastic!" Sadie screamed in the den. The scream made Peggy drop her spoon into her pudding and her head jerked toward the den door. Out of the corner of her eye, she saw a button on the kitchen phone light up. A couple minutes later, Sadie entered the kitchen wearing a big grin. She skipped over to where Jo-Jo continued to push peas and corn around on his plate.

"Is Miki awake?" she asked, kissing the top of his head.

"Yes, she says she can't sleep – too much on her mind – not hungry either."

"Good! Come with me so I can talk to you both at the same time." Sadie bounced out of the room. Jo-Jo ran to catch up.

"I have great news!" Sadie exclaimed as she entered Miki's room. "Jo-Jo didn't cause this problem and it probably won't happen again!"

Jo-Jo settled next to Miki on the bed. "What's that in aid of?" he asked.

"Well, the fertilized egg implanted itself in an area right next to a polyp. The placenta grew over the polyp and a little beyond. The polyp grew too. As the baby needed more nourishment, the polyp blocked the placenta from the source of that nourishment, otherwise known as the uterine wall."

Sadie looked directly at Miki. "One cure for polyps is a D & C to clean you out. Since this totally cleaned you out and I found several different polyps mixed with the blood in my bowl, the problem should be gone."

"We lost a baby," Miki said grimly.

"Yes you did. I'm sorry. However, most women with polyps never get pregnant in the first place. They go a long time thinking they are sterile. Losing this baby is the reason your problem was detected early. I called Dr. Gothic and he agrees. Now, just wait a few months – at least until the men get back from England – then try again, you should have no abnormal risks. Next time, you'll deliver a beautiful full-term baby."

Chapter 18 – October

"You left the blooming lights on, mate," Jo-Jo said to Rich as the Spidars pulled into the driveway of their Chiltern Hills home. Mid-October in England meant overcast skies and lamps on day and night whenever the house was occupied. Each day, one person had to check all the lamps before the group left for the studio.

"It wasn't my turn," Rich protested. "I did it yesterday." Three sets of eyes turned to Saul.

Saul glared at them. "No one frets in the States. Sadie handles the bills." Then he retreated into his mind. *If only she weren't so stubborn. She's most likely enjoying herself right now, playing with the children. I'll be more forceful next trip. We WILL move to England. She's my wife, dammit! Wives, not husbands, are supposed to leave their families and friends when they marry.*

Harry glowered back. "Don't be a bloody bugger to us. We miss the birds and little tikes, too."

Saul nodded. Harry was right. Though the men had only been in England for fourteen days, all of them were restless. They should be done with the short movie they were filming in two more weeks. Several times over the last few days, they had argued like fishwives over the littlest things. Even Rich was affected; he hadn't played any practical jokes in days. As the group entered the house, a familiar aroma met their noses: roast beef, home-baked bread, and cherry pie. Smiling, they quickly headed for the kitchen.

When the excitement died down, and before they actually sat down to dinner, Saul stood at the kitchen window, staring out into the moonless night. The lights from London spread across the horizon, a romantic view if a person had an arm around a loved one. Not him, though.

Martha sensed his spirit. She shed Rich's arms and stepped over to Saul. "Somebody had to stay with the kids," she said in a syrupy voice.

"Why did it have to be her?"

Martha stroked the back of his head. "You know the answer to that. The rest of us weren't going to come, either, but Sadie insisted, as long as we promised to take care of you the way she would. At least now you're not stuck with just the men."

"Thanks a lot, Sugar," Rich said behind her.

"That may not have come out right."

Saul's voice adopted a sarcastic tone. "I married a saint who can't leave her flippin' tots for a few days to make her hubby happy. She used to…"

"That was different, Saul," Peggy interjected. "Gene and Mary were available, but now they have two children of their own. Also, there were only three children to worry about. Now there are eight, seven of which are yours."

"Six are mine," Saul corrected. He remained quiet the rest of the evening. He refused Peggy's and Martha's advances, and Miki didn't even try.

*

The next night, as the others dressed for a party, Saul slumped in front of the television with a glass of scotch and cola in one hand and a bowl of pretzels beside him on the end table. Peggy entered the living room of the Chiltern Hills home, smoothing her skirt. "Saul, if you don't get ready soon, we'll be late," she said. Rich and Martha joined her, as did Jo-Jo, Miki, and Harry.

284

"I'm not going."

"Why not?"

"I'll be the oddball without my bird. It's different when all of us go singular. Now forget it."

The phone rang and Peggy answered it, "Peggy's arachnids. We spin a lace of love." Rich gave her a so-so sign.

"...Okay," she said into the mouthpiece.... "Are you sure? Won't that cause problems later?... If you say so. Bye." She hung up the phone and motioned for Martha and Miki to join her outside. "We'll be back in a short," she said without explanation.

When the women were alone in the car, Peggy chuckled. "That was Sadie on the phone. She didn't want the men to know she called. She also didn't want Saul to know she's read his brain waves occasionally since we came to England. She says she has mainly said goodnight to him and checked to be sure he's okay. She's afraid if he finds out, he'll be mad she's invading his privacy again."

"Ahhh, the reason she made us come here," Miki stated. "Most likely knew the men were lonelier than usual."

"So where are we going?" Martha asked.

"There's an escort service in town. We're supposed to ask for a woman named Michelle. Sadie thinks Michelle can help Saul out of his slump."

*

The Spidar women returned with a lady in her mid-twenties with auburn hair and brown eyes.

"Saul, now you can go to the party," Peggy stated.

"No thanks," he replied without looking up.

"You complained about not having a companion for the evening. Now you do."

"I don't do knock-ups anymore."

285

"She's not what you think. Michelle is an executive secretary with two kids. She's a widow who works for an escort service on weekends."

Saul raised his head and examined Michelle. She wore an A-line dress with a high collar and long sleeves – not the normal apparel of a lady-of-the-evening. With some hesitation, Saul left the room to shower and shave.

The Spidars enjoyed drinks, snacks, and dancing at the party. Saul and Michelle spent a lot of time talking at the table. Everyone wore smiles as they left the party hours later. They dropped Michelle off first and Saul walked her to her door. At the door, he held her hands and kissed her lightly on the forehead. "May I jingle you tomorrow?" he asked.

"I thought you were married."

"I am, but I can't go home for weeks. Since the other wives are here, we'll see more sites with our spare ticks. Can I give a ring?"

"Sure."

For the next two weeks, Saul drove to Michelle's home each night after work and picked her up. The couple spent lively evenings with the other Spidars at theaters, parties, or fancy restaurants. Each night, he drove the others home first, then took her home, and eventually went back to the Spidar's Chiltern Hills home. This routine went on until the night before he was to leave for the States. That night he brought her to the Spidar home for a sleepover.

On the morning of October 31, Halloween, Peggy called Sadie. "Saul has decided to stay here longer with Michelle, and I don't like it."

"He can do whatever he wants," Sadie replied over the phone wires. "Look, Peg. The triplets have been planning a surprise all week, so I'd appreciate someone coming home – anyone – so the kids won't be disappointed."

"What should I do about Saul? You don't want him to stay here, do you?"

Sadie didn't respond right away. When she did, her voice was fainter. "There's nothing I can do. He's still mad about me not coming with you girls. Just tell him the kids miss their daddy and wish he would reconsider."

"Can't you speak to his mind yourself?"

"I won't. I shouldn't have been saying goodnight, either. I stopped interfering on his third night with Michelle."

Peggy thought she heard Sadie's voice crack. Peggy wondered to herself what Saul may have been thinking on that third date night.

"I gotta go," Sadie said suddenly. "I have work to do."

As Peggy hung up the phone, she heard someone clear his throat behind her. She turned and saw Saul and Michelle standing in their bathrobes.

"So what did my saint have to say?" Saul asked.

"She won't hold you against your will," Peggy replied with contempt. "You're free to do as you please, but your kids will miss you terribly." Her voice rose in volume. "If you don't go back to her, you're a fool!"

She looked at Michelle and tried to soften her tone. "I know this isn't your fault, yet if you encourage Saul to stay, you're a fool too. He has a loving and exciting wife at home. If she's not enough for him, how can you ever hope to hold him for long?"

*

In Canandaigua, Sadie spent the day in final preparation for the evening's festivities. Her sister, Carol, kept the children occupied while Sadie finished the costumes and made some alterations to the house.

Carol's husband, Joshua, drove the van to the Rochester

airport while the triplets ate an early supper. Afterward, Carol took them into the living room. Sadie cleaned up the kitchen and looked at her watch. The plane should be landing now, an hour to finish preparations, so she fed the infants.

Carol was helping her dress the children in their costumes when Jerry buzzed to announce the Spidars' arrival. They tied hats on the infants and positioned everyone.

The people in the van were not surprised to be detained at the gate. While they waited, they grabbed candy bars from a large bowl sitting near the road. Rich watched the tree silhouettes dim more and more, meaning the interior room lights were going off. When the woods were almost dark, Jerry opened the gate and Joshua accelerated the van.

"Which door are we supposed to enter this time?" Rich asked. "Both porch lights are on." Joshua feigned ignorance with a shake of his head.

Harry chuckled. "There's a note on the side door. Let's see what it says."

The family stepped robustly to the door. One part of each man hoped there would again be a lavish spread on the kitchen table to fill their hungry stomachs after the seven-hour plane trip, but another part wanted something else. Good eating was an old pair of shoes here. In fact, Rich had teased Sadie before this trip. "We need to get away for a while," he had said. "Too much of this will make us change our name to the brontosauruses, because we'll have such a hard time moving about."

Peggy pulled the note off the kitchen door. "I guess we have to solve some riddles," she said.

The note read:

In the kitchen enjoy the spring
For you will know the reason,
When you find another clue

"What's that in aid of?" Harry asked.

"We'll find out, mate!" Rich exclaimed. "This should be a bit of a giggle."

Perched on the table in their Nip-n-Naps, the infants were dressed in green polka-dot clown suits, gathered at the wrists and ankles. They also wore floppy hats with white yarn balls on top.

The babies cooed as adults lifted them from their plastic bondage. Their delight spread to the adults. Even Saul, who had changed his mind and come home, thought this greeting felt great. Minutes passed blissfully as the group fawned over the infants.

Finally, Rich remembered the reason the room was dark. Turning the lights on, he reread the kitchen door clue. "Humpf!! What in this room is from spring?" The others shrugged and searched the room.

"We'd better find it quick, Chuck," Harry said to the baby in his arms, "before you need fresh nappies."

Peggy's eyes lit up. "That's it! Spring as in the beginning of life. Changing season as in diapers. The next riddle must be attached to a diaper."

"Pretty clever," Rich said with a laugh. "This way she gets five nappies changed in a hurry."

All the babies ended up dry, but Rich found the clue taped to Dave's rubber pants. It read:

> *The Spidar family likes to teasy;*
> *In summertime, this room is easy.*

"This room isn't the only thing easy at the moment," Martha said with a wink at Peggy. Peggy's I-haven't-the-faintest-idea expression made Martha smile.

"Ah-ha, the new bug can contribute, too! The riddle refers to an old folk song." Harry's eyes lit up and he nodded as he walked to the living room, singing along the way, "Summerti-i-ime, and the living is e-easy."

The others followed. Inside, candelabras lit the room, barely. Logs burned in the fireplace, casting yellow onto the dark surroundings. A spotlight centered on a high-backed, intricately carved chair with padded armrests that asserted its regal heritage in the center of the room. Sitting in the chair, Roxanne glowed in a pink taffeta gown, gilded crown, and scepter.

"Daddy!" she squealed, as she squirmed off the chair.

"My little princess," Saul replied. He handed Vera to Jo-Jo and held out his arms to receive her warm hug.

"Why don't you take Roxie and leave the babies with me, while you finish the game?" Carol suggested from a dark corner of the room.

Roxanne handed her father the next clue:

I die if I get cold,
But I never fear cold weather.
I fill a grand estate,
Yet in one room I am better
(According to Sadie).

Jo-Jo laughed as he looked at the puzzled faces around the room. "We'd better plant ourselves for this one." The family agreed. They sat down to collaborate. Soon they merely played with the babies again.

Miki watched the babbling. The one thing missing in England was the warmth of family togetherness. Suddenly, she nodded. "I think I know the answer to this riddle. She said,

'The warmth of love doesn't stop in winter time.' And Sadie would think Saul's bedroom is best."

Peggy shot Saul an I-told-you-so look, but Harry chuckled. "We'll have to speak with her about which room is best." Rich agreed and they all climbed the stairs.

At the top, they found a note on Saul's bedroom door. It read:

> *Sorry, wrong clue, I am so sorry.*
> *I have it straight now, don't you worry.*
> *The room to which you need to go*
> *Is where you work, don't you know?*

This one didn't take any time. They quickly walked back down the long flight of stairs and gathered at the door to the music room. "I can't believe my woman," Saul complained. "She made us climb those bloody stairs for nothing."

"Not exactly nothing," Martha said pensively. "I think she was sending a message with the clue that sent us up there."

"Merely soft-sawder to make up for not coming to England," he replied.

Peggy shook her head. "Saul, she doesn't know you're home yet. That message was for the other men."

Rich laughed. "As Harry said, we'll speak to Sadie about which room is best for love."

Entering the dark music room from the bright hallway, they were unable to distinguish much in the eastern half of the room. As they walked to the middle of the room slowly, someone shut the door, leaving the room lit by a single candle at the far corner.

In a few seconds, their eyes began to adjust. They faintly made out a child crossing the room. Anticipation and suspense filled the air as the group waited to see what would come next.

They saw the child pass by one side of the desk and sit. They could see his arm reaching toward the desk lamp.

A click of the lamp focused a narrow beam of light on a piece of paper. The beam also revealed a mustached and bearded face above a small body, clothed in a dark brown, vested suit. The face studied a contract.

With a jerk, the face turned to the family, which still stood in the shadows. As his hands tore up the contract, the pint-sized person spoke: "There's no resdools in the contract. If flies can enjoy resdools, Spidars should, too." The tiny man laughed at his own joke, with a trace of his elongated dimples showing above the beard. Harry rushed to Jason and threw him into the air, giving him a big hug when he came down.

When Rich turned on the music room lights, Harry inspected the beard Jason wore. It looked real. Then he remembered how Sadie had insisted on giving him a trim job before all the men left for England and put them in a sack instead of the garbage. The clippings of Harry's soft wavy hair were meticulously attached to a closely-woven material and trimmed to shape the beard. The mustache used shorter hair.

The next riddle was taped to the inner surface of the beard:

Little loves,
They can't yet climb a tree;
In this room
The sandman comes to three.

"Not the stairs again!" Jo-Jo complained. He opened the door and walked down the hallway. "I'm famished. I'll raid the larder first." In the kitchen, a pleasant aroma of pizza wafted to his nostrils. He looked around. No one. He side-stepped to the living room.

"Where's Sadie?" he asked Carol.

"You'll find her along the route."

"The pizza smells yummy."

"She timed it to be done when you finish the game. You'd better get going or it will burn."

Jo-Jo rejoined the family at the bottom of the stairs. "Rules state there's no eating until we finish this." They bounced up the stairs to the triplets' room.

Again their eyes had to adjust to dim lights. As they waited for their vision to return, the rocking chair near the window began to move slowly, creaking at each backward swing. Peggy crept toward what appeared to be Carl in the chair, looking out the window. As she poked her head past the chair to say hello, the chair made a quick, long swing toward her, catching her off guard and making her jump. The family laughed. No one would admit their own hearts beat faster too.

Peggy joined in the laughter as she turned the chair around and a dummy flopped sideways. Across its forehead, "Gotcha" was written in fluorescent paint. When the noise died down again, the family could hear a thump ... thump ... thump coming from the closet. Though they thought this must surely be the real Carl, they hesitated before opening the door.

Miki brushed past the men and turned the knob. As they gazed into the closet, a glowing ball bounced on a wooden box on the floor. The ball always went up to the same height and bounced in the same spot on the box. A string was wrapped tightly around the ball. The string led to the ceiling, where it was tied to a control box that pulled it then let it go. Attached to the control box, a timer sent an electric charge and abruptly turned the power off once every five seconds. The ball dropped again.

"Passable," Rich said from the back of the group.

Without warning, a child-sized skeleton fell from the left side of the closet, missing Miki by inches. She shrieked.

"It's okay, Aunt Miki," Carl said, taking his mask off quickly. "It's just me."

Rich laughed with the others, but he stopped abruptly. He felt a tap on his shoulder, even though he was behind everyone else. He turned his head and found nothing.

"Care for a warm roll in the sack with something sweet," came a witch's cackle on his right.

"Surely!" he replied in a lusty tone.

Sadie stepped back to avoid his reaching hand. She pulled a string in her hand and the lights came on, producing laughter from the family. She was dressed from head to foot in black: pointed shoes, calf-length dress, and black tights. She had even blackened a few of her teeth and her long, bumpy, clay nose. She giggled as she held out a small paper bag and handed it to Rich.

He pulled a warm dinner roll with honey in the middle out of the bag. He pointed to Sadie and then to the roll. "Which do I eat first?"

"Guess."

He gave her an I'll-get-even look and ate the roll, as he looked around the room at the strings she used to control the chair movements and the light switch near the door. He nodded his approval.

Sadie giggled again and glanced at the rest of the family. When her eyes locked on Saul, the giggling stopped. A bashful smile emerged. They both stood frozen for a few seconds. Then Saul slowly spread his arms wide. She slid into them without hesitation, resting her head on his shoulder, his arms folding around her.

As the rest of the family headed down the stairs, Saul and Sadie headed in a different direction. "They're going to be a bit tardy with the knife and fork again," Rich said.

Chapter 19 – November

For the next two weeks, the Spidar family followed their normal routine. During the day, the men worked in the music room and the women cared for the children, tidied the house, and worked on their hobbies and skills. After supper, everyone retired to the living room, where they played with the children, reading stories, playing, and listening to child musical performances. Most days, a bracing wind blew outside, but the living room remained toasty warm.

On this particular Friday, Sadie rose before the rest of the family as usual. She was the person who answered Bart's phone call, a call that confirmed a new routine. The Spidars would now be gone for shorter periods, no more than two weeks at a time. These plans were supposed to be a surprise for the women, but Bart didn't realize it, so he told Sadie.

Sadie was in heaven! All day, her soft humming filled the air. She prepared pies and sauces for Thanksgiving and put them in the freezer. All day, her good mood bubbled. All day, the world was beautiful, her premonitions stifled. Supper was put together in a very short, happy time.

Fragrances lingered as the family retired to the living room. Sadie was last to enter, still humming softly. The television began to buzz before the evening news began.

"Oh, my goodness!" Sadie exclaimed. She set Chuck in the playpen and rushed to within inches of the television set.

The family felt an iceberg in the air. The furnace kicked on. Sadie turned white. When CBS finished the story about a Chicago riot, she turned to NBC, then ABC to get their versions. On all three stations, a low-pitched hum accompanied the broadcast. She lowered her head and closed her eyes. All four men stared at her.

"It was only a Chicago bust-up," Rich said, trying to lighten the mood. "Don't they have 'em there often?"

When Sadie looked up again, her eyes betrayed her inner worry. "I need to ask a favor of you all."

Rich raised one eyebrow to suggest some fun. "Our answer will depend on what exactly you desire."

Sadie's grave expression didn't improve. "I know you men plan to concentrate more on writing and recording and less on live performances. I'm totally thrilled with the news, but..." She paused.

"What's the 'but'?" Jo-Jo asked.

"Well, I need you to perform a special concert in the next few days. If you don't, millions of lives will be lost."

Roxanne ran to Sadie. "Mommy, I'm cold."

Sadie hugged her and glanced at the other toddlers. Carl and Jason snuggled with adults, too, their eyes wide with fright. "Oh, Sweethearts! I'm so sorry. You know how some dreams are very scary?" They nodded their heads. "Well, I had a nightmare while I was awake. You don't have to worry. Nothing will hurt you. I promise. You're safe in this house." The iceberg melted. The furnace shut off.

Jo-Jo grimaced. "Did you exaggerate a bit about the millions of lives? Fleet Street said only two people croaked in that rough-and-tumble."

Sadie ignored him. She crossed the room, picked up the phone, pressed the intercom button, and dialed Carol's two-digit number. "Hi, Sis. Sorry to bother you at night, but I need to send the kids up to your place for a while. Is that okay? ... Great! They're on their way."

Sadie turned to the triplets, who were already being herded to the hall by Peggy. "Maybe you can convince Aunt Carol to let you watch the Monkees on her TV. "

"Ya-a-a-ay!" they responded as they ran out the doorway and up the stairs.

Sadie turned to the men with an unusual expression – a mixture of determination and terror. The furnace kicked on again. "It's time," she said. "By Tuesday morning, 25,000 people will die. Most of them will be killed by people they consider their friends. By next Friday, a week from now, the number could reach a million. There's only one way to stop it temporarily. Will you do a concert?"

"How could a concert help?" Harry asked.

Jo-Jo snickered. "Our music is powerful!"

"How did you make the tube buzz?" Rich asked to change the subject.

"Most likely needs fixin'," Jo-Jo stated. He glanced at Harry, whose father was an electrician.

Harry shook his head. "I'm not a fixer-upper. Don't ask me."

"The whole thing is clear as mud," Saul added.

Sadie tapped her fingers on her arm. "Will you do a concert?" The men looked at each other and nodded. "Good," Sadie said, turning back to the phone. She dialed an extra-long number.

"Bart, this is Sadie... I know it's late in England, but I need to talk to you right away. You have to arrange a Spidar concert in Rochester no later than Tuesday. I'd prefer tomorrow night, but there are so many things to do ... Yeah, I know ... No. Cost is not important. This will be a public service concert ... I'll handle the press release. You set up the hall and convince at least one major network to carry two hours of live coverage at prime time, with commercials at the end ... No, no charge.

297

They just have to cover their expenses with the commercials. If possible, I'd like to have final say on which commercials get airtime. They should be positive and healthy ...

"Yes, that would be best. I'll set up the den as your office, and a guest room is available upstairs for your sleep. While you wait for your flight, please start planning ... Yes, this is unusual. These are unusual times. I must know by tomorrow evening if we get voluntary coverage. If not, I'll pull some strings in Washington, which I'd rather not do...."

"That's fine. I'll be up all night, anyway. Whenever you arrive in the States, come right over. I'll tell Jerry to expect you ... Right. Cheerio!" She giggled as she hung up the phone. "I'll never get used to that expression. It makes me think of breakfast."

She dialed another number, a shorter one this time. "Hello, Doc, this is Sadie.... I'm fine.... Yes, the kids are okay, too. Listen, I don't want to waste your time. I need to know if anyone is currently working on air-quality analysis somewhere in the United States by any chance? ... Really? Where? ... Thanks."

She hung up and lifted the receiver again, smiling at the Spidar family as she dialed another. "That was Ivan's father."

"Dr. Boetrich, please ... I know it's after hours. She's working late in her office. Thank you ... Hi, Dr. Boetrich. Can I please speak to your beau? Tell him Sadie's calling ... No that's all he needs. He'll know who I am ... Thanks."

Sadie covered the mouthpiece. "You'll never guess who's back in the U.S." Heads nodded around the room.

"Ivan! How long have you been home? ... Oh really? And you never bothered to call?" She sniffled loudly into the phone. "Does that say something about our friendship? ... I'm kidding. You don't have to explain anything to me... No, really. That's nonsense. Don't ever be afraid to call. No matter how

298

much work there is, I always have time to talk with friends. Anyway, I'm glad you're home."

She giggled into the mouthpiece. "However, your girlfriend might not be so happy when I'm done talking... Yep, you guessed it, another project. If you don't want to do it, just say so. I don't have time to quibble ... Okay, listen carefully. Most of this will seem unbelievable. You'll just have to trust me.

"Somehow, someone is trying to destroy our country by ... what should I call it, not germ warfare, but similar in destructive potential. There's a strong form of phencyclohexylpere piperidine hydrochloride in the air. Since it's a liquid, it's easy to make into a vapor. Someone found a way to stop it from settling to the ground too fast. Instead, the drug clings to human skin and absorbs slowly into the body...

"No, Ivan, this can't wait until Monday. Every day we delay spells disaster for more and more people. Did you see the six o'clock news? ... Well, watch at eleven, then. There will be more riots and killings. I need you and Dr. Boetrich to get the lab people working first thing tomorrow morning to identify the rest of the chemicals. Once they determine what's in the air, it'll take the nation's top chemists at least a week to figure out an antidote.

"Yes, I'm serious. This isn't the kind of thing I'd fool around about ... Please ... Thank you, that's all I can ask. Call me before you pass any information to the government. Maybe I'll be able to help with the solution. Yeah, bye."

"No, wait! Ivan!" she yelled before the connection was broken. "Ivan, none of this can leak to the public. Panic would be worse than the present dangers. Okay? ... Good. Sorry to ruin your date. Bye."

Sadie wouldn't discuss the situation further with her family, instead saying, "Please go to bed. You'll need a good night's rest for tomorrow." Reluctantly, they complied. Many unanswered questions raced through their minds.

The next morning, the family woke to the usual aroma of breakfast cooking. After giving the triplets hugs in the living room, the adults convened in the kitchen. Bart sat at the table discussing something with Sadie, a pile of tapes on the side. She cut the conversation short and served the food.

After everyone finished and the table was cleared, she poured coffee and began her explanation. "I need you men to go through all the songs you've written so far and pick any with love as a theme without heartbreak. For example, the song Saul wrote for Michelle. That one is excellent."

Saul lowered his eyes. "How'd you know I wrote a song for her?"

Sadie smiled. "It's a beautiful song. We need one and a half hours of plain and simple love songs."

Jo-Jo questioned her with his eyes. Sadie could guess what he was thinking, without reading his mind. He was quick to capture odd angles.

"No, Jo-Jo, my tongue didn't get mixed. I only need one and a half hours of your songs. We need to allow fifteen minutes for commercials and another fifteen minutes for a special song to be played several times during the show, at the beginning, middle, and end."

"Which song is so special?" Harry asked.

"Uh, one I wrote."

"You wrote a song?" The men glanced at each other.

"Oops! I forgot to tell you about it." She giggled. "I thought I was writing it for my research into emotional disabilities. I've been testing the song on the worst patients at the state mental hospital. It calms them down for about a week, which enables the psychiatrists to do their work. So far, it's helped some severely disturbed people become productive again..."

"So you were there instead of Strong during the kids' naps," Martha mumbled. "That's why you didn't take me along..."

"I latch on to what you're saying," Harry interrupted. "Yet, I feel a bit slow on the uptake. How can a song help people who are flying high on PCP? That's powerful stuff. We'll all be on the mat before long if it is in the air."

"I know," Sadie nodded. "But you don't..." Screams from the intercom interrupted this time. The babies were awake, with their lungs on full power. Peggy, Miki, and Martha brought all five of them down. They headed for the living room, but Sadie motioned for them to come to the kitchen.

"Put them in these," Sadie instructed, as she pointed to the Nip-N-Naps she had set on the kitchen table. "Now do your best to quiet them without food."

Ten minutes later, Peggy yelled over the noise of five hungry babies. "It's impossible! Their bellies hurt!"

"Do you all concur?" Sadie asked the other adults. They all nodded, ready to give up. She walked to the den and came back carrying a tape player. She took one of the tapes from Bart's pile and inserted it in the player. She turned it on. There were no lyrics, just music. As it played, the cries slowly lowered in volume. By the end of the three-minute song, the babies were cooing to the tune. The adults sat with their eyes wide and their lips parted.

"Impossible," Peggy murmured. "A song can't do this. Music might soothe a savage beast, but not a hungry baby." Sadie grinned, grabbed two of the babies and walked to the living room to feed them on one of the couches. Martha, Miki, and Peggy followed with the other three and two bottles.

The men remained in the kitchen. They listened to the song again, each person concentrating on his own instrument and Saul listening to the keyboard. When the song ended for

301

the third time, they looked at each other with expressions that said, Yes, I can play that. Saul grabbed the tape player and walked into the living room, with the other men following. For a moment, the men simply watched the women, busy with the babies. The room felt warm and cozy.

"Will we get mean to each other?" Martha asked Sadie.

"No," Sadie replied. "Everyone who will be affected is already feeling uneasy. I'm not a chemist, so I can't explain the reasons. Otherwise, I'd be able to come up with the cure myself. However, I researched people in this area. It seems people who feel loved produce a substance in their bodies that counteracts the chemicals, a suppressor of sorts. The substance isn't the reason they feel loved. It's made *because* they feel loved. That could explain why some people are sicker in general. The lack of this substance might affect their body's ability to make other chemicals necessary for good health."

She looked at the men in the doorway. "So you could say love helps people accomplish more with their lives."

"That's all well and good," Saul said, passing off her theory with a wave of his hand, "But, you have us by the short and curlies with this flippin' song. How do we play that peculiar noise in a live gig?"

Sadie blushed. "I thought maybe you might let me play in the show just this once."

"You can play with me anytime," Rich offered.

She giggled, handed her two satisfied babies to Rich and Saul, and left the room. When she returned, she carried an instrument similar to a small harp but with variations. She demonstrated as she spoke, "The hollow strings are made of a variety of materials, made very thin, obviously: nylon, silk, and aluminum. The dove and frame are carved from rock maple."

She blew into the mouthpiece hose. The air went through each plucked string and out the bottom around the inside of the wood frame at the dove's mouth. The dove's mouth was open while air exited but closed when there was no compressed air. It sounded like the coo of a dove, a sound like a flute, but richer. When she pressed the damper, removed her mouth, and plucked the strings, the instrument made a sound that mixed harp and acoustic guitar with greater depth and volume.

"I call this a Cooharp, because the sound is similar in relaxing power to a dove's coo-coos." She held out the tape of the song and hinted for the men to get to work. As they headed for the music room, Bart went to the den to make phone calls.

A couple hours later, Bart emerged with a smile of success. "We're set for Tuesday, Sadie," he said, as she prepared lunch. "All three stations will broadcast from Shriner's Hall. When I told them there was no charge, it was an offer none could refuse. We also have coverage from two of the popular local radio stations. As you requested, your tape will play in the corridors as the TV and radio people set up in front of the stage. With the doors open, the song will seep throughout. And the serenade will continue as the concert goers come into the main venue from the corridors. On TV, the song will air alongside the announcement that regular programming is being pre-empted. With the song in the background, people will be less apt to turn the TV off."

Sadie nodded, set a vegetable tray in the refrigerator, and walked to the phone. She dialed her favorite journalist, Pam Hope, and gave her news about the concert. Then Sadie dialed again. Without giving specifics, she told Mary of the need for churches to be open twenty-four hours a day until Tuesday evening. "...People will need a refuge, where they can feel the love of God. Uh, do you think Gene and Reverend Bee could get the word out to the other churches and temples?... Good. It may get quite dangerous out on the streets. Don't panic, just prepare, and you'll be okay. No, the world isn't going to end now. Not if I can help it."

*

As lunch ended, Sadie casually mentioned that she would go shopping as soon as the children went for their naps.

Bart stared at her. "I thought you told Mary it could get risky out there. "You'd better take one of the men for protection."

"No. The last time I took a man shopping with me, I didn't return for a few days." She giggled. "I'll be okay. All my sensors work. I'm the best one for the job this time. The rest of you will be safer in the house until the concert."

Saul's face turned plum. "If you think I'll stay nicked up in the house for four days, you're daft!" He went to the hall and grabbed his coat. "Where's your list?" he asked as he walked through the kitchen to the back door.

Sadie hesitated, then removed the list from her purse. "Be careful, Hon. You don't know what's happening out there. No matter what happens, don't get into any fights. Just walk away quickly."

"Sure thing, Mum." He left the house in a huff.

The other four men gathered in the living room while the women fed the babies and put all the children in bed for naps. When that was done, Sadie insisted she clean the kitchen alone. Peggy followed anyway, but Sadie shooed her away. "I have excess energy right now," Sadie explained. "I need to use it. Anyone else in the room will be in the way." Peggy shrugged and joined the others in the living room.

Ten minutes later, Sadie entered the living room, looking absent-minded. Peggy shook her head. Even Sadie couldn't clean that fast. Peggy peeked through the door. The kitchen sparkled. Chrome, glass, and enamel, all reflected the sunshine from the window. She shook her head again and turned back to the living room.

"...You know the old proverb, mates," Rich was saying with a gleam in his eyes, "When the cat's away, the mice will play."

Jo-Jo glanced at Bart. "Sorry, Gov'nor," he teased, "The great unwashed might consider you a fifth Spidar, but not us. You can't get into our pact, considering your inclinations."

Peggy motioned for the others to take a gander at Sadie. They all noticed a far-away look in her eyes.

"Find out what she's thinking," Jo-Jo said to Miki. "You should know her channel by now."

Miki tried for a few minutes. "It's no use," she whispered after a while. "Her mind is too powerful compared to mine. She blocks penetration attempts without even trying."

The men looked at Peggy and Martha, who shrugged.

"Well, blimey," Rich said as he crossed the room. "If the bird's fretting about some bloody thing, it's our *duty* to get her mind off it. There's only one way to do that." He put his arms around her and led her to the hallway and up the stairs. Harry picked Miki; Jo-Jo picked Martha and Peggy, but Peggy declined the threesome. The two couples left quietly.

Peggy turned on the television to entertain Bart. When she heard someone run down the stairs and open the hall closet under the stairs, she hurried into the kitchen in time to see Sadie scampering to the garage door. Sadie's worried expression intensified.

"Take care of Rich for me," she said to Peg. That was it. Sadie was outside in the blink of an eye. A car revved its motor and drove away.

A half-hour later, Peggy paced in the kitchen. She had alerted the others to Sadie's bizarre behavior. They all sat around the kitchen table, waiting for news. When Saul entered, his shredded clothes told part of the story.

After doctoring Saul's injuries and adjusting his adrenalin, Sadie sent him upstairs for a warm bath. As he soaked, she put the groceries away and explained what happened:

Sadie picked up Jerry on her way out of the estate, so he could drive the second car home, while she helped Saul escape the mob surrounding him. "Apparently, after Saul put the groceries in the car, he threw half his disguise in the trunk with the bags. Then he winked at a pretty girl walking past his car. The girl recognized him and squealed his name. Other people heard her scream and ran over for an autograph. Saul spent five full minutes signing everything from a matchbook to an arm. The crowd kept getting bigger, instead of smaller, so he tried to leave." Sadie rolled her eyes. "That's when the real trouble began. The crowd decided that if they couldn't get an autograph, they would get his clothes, turning quite violent in the process..."

*

The evening news reported one thousand people died in violence around the country.

As promised, Ivan called at seven o'clock to tell Sadie the contaminants in the air. She told him what she knew about counteracting the substances and made him promise not to reveal her identity when he called Washington. "I think the F.B.I. already has me on file because of my work at the hospitals. I don't want to feed them any more than I have to."

The next morning, Jerry brought the Sunday paper from the gate to the house as usual. This time, though, his eyes were puffy and bloodshot. When pressed, he admitted he had stayed up all night watching the monitors, because Sadie had requested tighter security and he was afraid something might happen while he slept.

"You need help for the next few days," Sadie said. She phoned Jerry's agency, then sent the gateman back to his post.

After putting blueberry muffins and apple quiche into the oven, she looked at her watch. The first interview with prospective security men was scheduled for an hour later. Checking to be sure the toddlers were fine in the living room, she made a cup of tea and sat to read the paper. She laughed at the front page headline: *Sadie McCarthy to Unveil at Benefit Performance.*

The article said the show would pay homage to America's warm welcome toward the Spidars and Sadie had written a special song for the occasion. It also explained the date, time, location, and price of $1 for the tickets to cover the hall's expenses. As Sadie read on, tears formed.

Upon hearing about the national coverage, Shriner's Hall had contacted the big industries in Rochester – Kodak, General Motors, Xerox, Ragu, and Pennwalt. The companies agreed to underwrite ten thousand tickets, and would pass them out to people who didn't have TVs or radios. There would also be free busing for people lacking transportation.

They're helping more than they realize, Sadie thought.

*

The Sunday evening news revealed over 8,500 had died in the last twenty-four hours due to skirmishes around the country. Monday brought over 15,500. On Tuesday, other events for the evening were being postponed, some because of the concert, some because of the unrest. Sadie listened closely to various radio stations during the day. Reporters around the country tallied the numbers of people planning to watch the concert. Most people, it seemed.

Sadie let out several sighs of relief during the day. Usually, when all three stations broadcast similar events, citizens became annoyed. Tonight's concert was the exception. Young, old, rich, poor, none of that seemed to matter. Some people were long-standing fans. Others were simply curious.

The phone rang in the middle of a light, late afternoon supper. Sadie jumped up and her face went white. "No!" she shouted. "They can't do this now!" She rushed to the phone and picked up the receiver. The family stared at her as she spoke into the mouthpiece. "... No, we need it to go on as planned ... Don't worry. There won't be trouble as long as you have the tape playing at the entrance ... Yes, we take all responsibility ... Good. See you later."

As she hung up the phone, she sighed again. "The hall manager wanted to cancel the live audience. Because of the recent rioting, he worried you men might get hurt and Rochester will get a bad name."

She giggled. "I took a tape of my song to the hall yesterday, but I didn't explain the reason. No one suspects a thing." She looked around the table at worried faces. "As long as everyone is subdued by the music, you won't get hurt. Trust me. Remember the babies."

Hours later, dressed incognito as usual for a public show, Sadie drove the van to the gate, with the Spidars and Bart inside. She checked Jerry and his co-worker for imbalances. Jerry was fine, but the other man needed some changes. In a split-second, she adjusted one chemical through his wrist without his knowledge. She had no name for the chemical, but she knew how it felt to her fingertips.

With her children's safety with the other Spidar women assured during her absence, she drove off, keeping her sensors alert. Even under normal circumstances, rush hour could be dangerous. Now there was a possibility someone might use a car as a weapon. She avoided Rochester's "Can of Worms," interweaving expressways, entirely.

Once at Shriner's Hall, she didn't follow the men backstage. Instead, she walked around the bleachers. The auditorium gleamed with a fresh coat of light gray paint on the walls and new wax on the wood floors. "I never thought gray could look so pretty," she mumbled. "It's a nice background to the black seats."

A large area in front was cordoned off for the press. An oval area, large enough for a three-ring circus, presented a wide expanse of nothingness in the center of the hall. There was also a small rectangle in the middle of the oval to be used as a small stage.

During a normal concert, the big oval area filled with a crowd of people, pushing and shoving to get a performer to notice them. Today, because of the general tumult in the country, burly security men stationed themselves at the bottom of the aisles to prevent access from the seats.

Sadie wondered if the Spidars should play in the center, closer to the audience. If they played in the center, though, their backs would face two-fifths of the audience. Also, the television cameras would have to be reset and there wouldn't be any place for Sadie to hide until her part of the show. No, the Spidars would perform on the main stage. Yet, the large oval should be used for something, she thought.

She asked the manager to reassign the guards to the immediate stage area. Folding chairs were set up along the oval's perimeter. To prevent anyone from sitting on the chairs for the entire show, signs were placed on the chairbacks that read:

Temporary Parking Only – One Song Limit.
Violators Will Be Towed To The Dance Floor.
The raised rectangle in the middle was roped off.

Sadie glanced at her watch. She ran to the main entrance to be sure her melody could be heard on the loudspeaker as soon as people entered. Yes, no problem. A crowd milled outside the glass doors. Whole families were out there, even young children.

"They're awfully quiet, aren't they?" the security chief asked.

Sadie nodded, her senses busy. When she turned another switch in her brain, she smiled. "That's why they're subdued. They can hear the song out there."

"Yes, the manager decided to play it outside, too, since you were so sure they could be pacified by the tape. It does seem to work." The security chief smiled. "I hope this continues. I'll get paid for walking around doing nothing." He shook his head as he turned to unlock the doors. Sadie could hear him mumbling to himself. "That'll be the day, when there's no trouble at a rock concert."

Sadie quickly walked to the Spidars' dressing room before the people came through the doors. Her mind replayed thoughts about the 10,000 people set to attend and over 100 million people watching on the television or listening by radio. By the time she joined the Spidars, her face had paled.

"Don't freak on us now," Saul said soberly.

Sadie glanced down at her hands. They shook like leaves in a fall wind. She lowered her adrenalin and felt more relaxed. Now, as long as she could keep her mind off the numbers of people watching, she should be able to have a good time. She busied herself with a game of Pinochle with the others.

An hour later, the Spidars ran on stage to thunderous applause. When the noise died down, Jo-Jo moved to a microphone. The nearest television camera lit up.

"How's tricks, folks? I hope you'll stay for our whole audition." The other men chuckled. *"Our first song will be a tad*

different from the one these live people heard at the entrance. And the next time we play it, our very own Sadie will join us."

In the wings, Sadie checked on her song's effectiveness without the cooharp. Even without the special sound, a noticeable calm settled over everyone.

As the Spidars continued with other selections, Sadie watched the audience. Instead of being a raucous crowd, the norm for a Spidar concert, the fans actually listened. If the fans weren't dancing, they were wiggling in their bleacher seats and clapping or singing along. Others seemed quite pensive.

Sadie felt a compulsion to join the dancing herself. Thinking the compulsion was caused by her anxiety, she shook her head to convince herself to fight it.

Forty-five minutes later, Saul put down his guitar and stepped to the center microphone. *"The next song is the first we played. It has no title yet. We just call it Sadie's Song for the present tick."* He pointed to the wings and motioned for her to come out. She smiled as she walked out in her bright pink turtleneck sweater and emerald green mini-skirt, coordinated with mint green fishnet stockings and silver beaded jewelry. Her make-up made her look about 30 years old.

Applause boomed as Saul went to the keyboard. Sadie curtsied and sat on a thick cushion near her cooharp. As she adjusted the microphone, the applause was replaced by an expectant silence.

"We have a treat for you tonight," she said in a strong voice mixed with a touch of tease. *"We're going to repeat the music you heard at the beginning of the show. As you listen this time, let your mind wander to a peaceful scene where there is no more hate or envy or evil in the world. For you see, this song is special. It's truly YOUR song. You will write the lyrics, so let your imagination flow."*

311

Chatter rose from the audience and Sadie continued, "*At the end of tonight's show, we will play the song again and give you an address of where to send your ideas. The Spidar men will decide which lyrics fit best. The next Spidar album will include the complete song, with the lyricist's name on it. Okay?"*

The live audience applauded. Sadie held up the palm of her hand and the noise died again. Then she motioned for the men to begin. They switched to acoustic guitars and adjusted the microphones to guitar height.

The commencement of the cooharp was barely audible, amplifying slowly until it reached the same volume as the other instruments. Then it changed direction and lazily decreased until the coo-coos returned to an undercurrent. The guitars and keyboard wove in and out of the music with delicate precision. As the keyboard faded, the guitars rose, and vice versa. The brushes on the drums stayed constant throughout the melody.

Releasing the cooharp at the end of the song, Sadie searched the minds of the audience and network crews again. They were at peace with themselves. Her eyes twinkled. *Yes*, she thought, *professional musicians make a difference. This might last longer than a week.*

Silence engulfed the auditorium: no clapping, no talking, and no whispering, not even a cough or sneeze – peculiar for a large crowd at the beginning of flu season. Everyone simply stared at the stage.

As Sadie requested, the Spidars remained motionless until the spell broke of its own accord. Three minutes later, light applause began in the back of the hall and came forward in a wave, increasing in intensity. Jo-Jo motioned for Sadie to move to the front of the stage. A fresh wave of applause swelled and her face turned crimson.

When the Spidars began their next number, the audience resumed swinging and swaying. Sadie felt the urge to dance again. She couldn't blame it on nervousness now, so she walked to the edge of the stage. As she surveyed the crowd, some people were watching her. She motioned for a husky man to come to her. "Can you help me jump down?" she asked him.

With a questioning roll of his eyes toward the stairs on the side of the stage, Al Dukes reached for Sadie's waist, then lifted and turned to deposit her on the floor.

"Thanks," she said with a teasing wink.

Al nodded and walked away quickly, a bounce in his step. When he thought he successfully blended with the crowd, he looked back toward Sadie. A crowd of people had formed around her. He watched as a hand with a pink-sweatered wrist rose above the crowd and waved and he ran to her rescue.

They emerged from the crowd and Sadie led him to the small stage and the Spidars began a slow tune. Sadie moved closer to Al to ask for more help. As Al danced with her, she gave him specifics and a line formed on the stairs with a security guard posted to keep things orderly.

Sadie's plan was for Al to control the line, dispersing one man at a time, three men per song. They each would get a minute to strut their stuff. When Al released another man to go to Sadie, she would kiss the cheek of the man who left.

Having three different men per song meant dancing three different ways. Sadie let the man begin and she adapted to whichever dance he chose. The twist was a favorite, but others chose the Pony, Monster Mash, Locomotion, Jerk, Hanky Panky, Swim, and Mashed Potatoes.

There was only one mishap. When Sadie tried to kiss one departing man on the cheek, he turned his head quickly and kissed her on the mouth, instantly collapsing to the floor. Since another man was already on the small stage, Sadie motioned for him to begin dancing. The one who fainted regained consciousness quickly. By the stairs, Al instructed the rest of the men in line that no kisses on the mouth would be allowed, and the remainder of the concert went without incident.

Towards the end, the Spidars began another slow song. This time, it was "Michelle," the song that told Sadie to head up front at a good clip. As she passed the men waiting in line, she kissed each one on the cheek. Once she was at the end, Al rushed her to the main stage and watched from the wings.

Sadie leaned into her microphone and reminded people to write the lyrics for the next song and she gave them the address to send them to. Then she began to play the Cooharp, with the Spidars joining her.

They arrived back home in Canandaigua without incident that night.

*

On Wednesday evening, the headline in the Canandaigua Daily Messenger read:

NO NEWS IS GOOD NEWS
PEACE COMES IN THE WAKE OF THE STORM
(More information on pages 2-8)

The rest of the front page was blank.

Chapter 20 – Thanksgiving Weekend

A week later, Wednesday morning, Sadie slept longer than usual. The triplets had stayed up an hour past their normal bedtime, so they were sleeping in. As Sadie woke, Saul mumbled something about making love. When she opened her eyes, her smile broadened. Saul was asleep, lying on his back with his closed eyes, flickering. Even with the heavy quilt on top of him, his soldier stood at attention.

Oh what the heck, she thought. She straddled him and lowered into position. As she moved up and down, Saul's lips curled and his hands moved to her tiny waist.

"That's the way, Luv," he mumbled, "O-o-o-o. Here it comes. Ah-h-h-h!" Sadie kissed his chin and lay on top of him for a moment longer, his arms wrapped around her. "Thanks, Peg," he said. "That was top-notch."

Sadie giggled and raised her head to look him in the face. "No, Hon. I'm Sadie, not Peg."

Saul's eyes shot open. "You're right cute," he said, pushing her off his body. "What're you trying to prove with that bloody stunt?"

She sat up, stunned. "What? I gave you a California breakfast. You used to like them."

"That's the wrong end of the stick and you know it. Don't mess with my mind, making dreams of Peg and rape me."

"No one can rape the willing, and I didn't put the thoughts in your mind either. They were there when I woke up."

Saul climbed out his side of the bed and walked to the bathroom. "Rightly so. Peg isn't a she-dragon about moving to

315

England. You are. And that's even with Carol and Josh willing to move with us to support your motherhood."

"S-a-u-l, we talked about that. I still have powers, which means the drug business was just practice. If I'm living in England, I may miss my real mission when it comes."

"Change the bloody record. My ears don't flap for that excuse. Get downstairs and fix a real brekker for a change."

Sadie's face contorted. She wanted to scream: *What have I made for the family every morning? Cold cereal?* Instead, she showered, dressed, and left the room.

Peggy walked into the kitchen as Sadie poured batter into the waffle iron. Though Sadie smiled, the sparkle was missing from her eyes.

"Are you and Saul still fighting?" Peggy asked.

Harry entered and sniffed the air. "What's wrong today, girl? I didn't smell the muffins when I woke. Is the women's lib bilge getting to you, too?"

"Harry!" Peg exclaimed. "It's not Sadie's job to fix breakfast EVERY morning."

"Easy, Pet. I was ribbin' her."

Sadie nodded. "This makes you thankful for the other days when you don't have to wait for breakfast, right?"

"Oh I see," Harry replied, walking to the calendar on one of the cupboard doors. "Must be that time of the month."

The others began to fill the room. "Isn't brekker geared up yet?" Saul asked with malice in his voice.

"Uh-huh. Still spatting, I see," Rich said.

"Yeah, me bird's miffed because I called out Peg's name in a wet dream. Now she has a bee in her bonnet."

Ignoring the comment, Sadie passed around the finished waffles and sausage.

"Are you okay?" Martha whispered.

316

Sadie nodded. "Actually, I thought it was funny at the time."

"Then why do your eyes look so sad?"

Sadie's hands rose to her own temples. The sparkle returned to her eyes. "There. Is that better?

"I guess so."

Sadie continued around the table.

When Peggy saw the sparkle in the eyes again, she glanced at Harry and back at Sadie with a giggle. "With us, it's usually the opposite. The last time I tried to roger Harry without waking him, he thought the hand job was the first in your series. When he said your name, I took it as a compliment."

"You're not getting older, ducky. You're getting better." Rich said with a laugh. Martha shook her head.

"There you have it, Peg," Jo-Jo quipped. "Our sexpert thinks you do a right fine job."

Saul didn't laugh with the others. He studied Peggy. "I have a new wrinkle," he said aloud. "Harry, why don't we swap wives for a week? You take Sadie and I'll take Peg."

Harry's eyes lit up, but he quickly lowered his head to concentrate on his waffles.

Peggy glanced at Sadie, whose eyes still twinkled, then turned to Harry. "You aren't saying anything." He responded with an inaudible mumble. "Don't worry about me," Peggy coaxed. "You warned me before our marriage that you would take care of Sadie if anything ever happened to Saul. Now you get your chance to practice."

Harry raised his head. He watched Sadie at the stove, making more waffles. There had been many times when he wished Sadie was his wife instead of Saul's – when she played with the kids, gave them baths, cooked, swam, cuddled with Saul in the living room, and made sweet love to him. He smiled broadly when she brought two more platters to the table, this time setting them down on either end.

When she was near him, he put an arm around her waist. "Will this include full spousal benefits, like final say on when someone can borrow her?"

"Surely," Saul replied.

"Alri-i-ight!" Harry exclaimed. "Then all of you can serve yourselves. I'm going upstairs with the mother of my seven children." He rose and tugged at Sadie's waist.

"Leave the children out of this," Sadie said quietly. "It will only mix them up."

Harry looked at Saul. They both shrugged.

*

Friday morning, two days later, the triplets played hide and seek in the living room. The adults woke to the smell of sausage, toast, and mushroom quiche. As they entered the kitchen, they chattered greetings to each other, except Harry, whose movements dragged.

Saul laughed. "What's the matter, mate? Is Sadie more than you can handle?"

"Not bloody likely!" Harry said with contempt. "You knew bloody well, when you refused to swap chambers during the bird exchange, that Sadie would worry about the tinies waking me up. With the joint door open between the nursery and your bedroom, their ballyhoo is muffled to us and partly muffled to your room. Yet with the intercom, the noise comes in loud and clear. That's why she always used to shut off the transmitter in the nursery at night, so it didn't wake the rest of us. She can't do that from my room. You also knew Sadie would prop her eyes open to catch their first whimpers."

"What's your pickle, then?"

318

"Guilt. How could I sleep when she didn't? Tonight, you and I will switch beds!"

Saul shook his head. "I don't think so, chap, though my heart bleeds for ya. Peg warmed me all night long... both nights."

"That's because Sadie takes care of Amanda, too," Peggy said. "I haven't gotten up in the middle of the night for many nights now, except when Sadie was sick. Saul, I'm sure your receiver is turned off now and the door between the two rooms is closed." She looked at Sadie, who wore a guilty expression.

*

Sadie hadn't spoken much yesterday, Thanksgiving Day, and not a word to any adults since getting out of bed this morning. She had been silent as she put platters of food on the table. She didn't speak as she nibbled her breakfast. In silence, she cast shy peeks at Saul. Without speaking, Sadie motioned for the women to let her do the dishes alone.

When chores were done, Sadie looked at each woman one by one. Her gaze settled on Peggy. Then she finally spoke. "Can you girls do me a favor this morning and watch the kids for a few hours? I'll feed the babies before I leave."

Peggy nodded and opened her mouth to say something.

Saul interrupted, "No, Ma'am! I may want to do something with my new wife this morning. You won't tie her down with your kids."

"Okay, I'll get Carol to watch them in her apartment."

"Stay home with your family, like a good mother would," Saul ordered. "I pay Carol as a charwoman, not your personal girl-Friday."

Sadie turned away. Peggy opened her mouth to scold Saul, but she stopped before she said a word. Sadie had already

319

turned back, her eyes blazing. The knife had sliced through its sheath.

"Number one," Sadie said razorlike, "YOU don't pay Carol. I haven't touched your money since I borrowed the ten grand – ten grand I paid back with 100% interest a long time ago, I should add. MY money pays Carol and the rest of the household bills. You haven't paid a cent.

"Number two: you are the one who wanted to switch wives. Harry never complained when Peg helped with the kids, neither did Jo-Jo nor Rich.

"And number three: when I get back today, I won't need any more favors from any of you for a long, long, long time. Guaranteed."

"We'll watch the tikes this morning," Peggy offered with a wave toward the other women.

"Thanks, ladies." Sadie marched to the hallway. Her steps could be heard as she climbed the stairs to get the infants.

When Sadie was out of the room, Peggy turned off the transmitter and glared at Saul. "How can you be so nasty? Remember how you felt when she left for one night? Or, when she hid in the forest? Do you want that to happen again?"

"Let her cop. This time it won't hurt a bit... Don't look at me like that. I've treated you right these two days, haven't I?"

"I suppose so."

"Then you can see I would treat her a whole sight better, too, if she would quit putting me last on her priority list."

"Saul, I think you misunderstand her," Martha corrected. "In her heart, you always come first."

"Oh, yeah? Then why won't she move to England?"

"You know that answer. We have to trust her judgement."

"Yeah, sure. Tell me about it. The tikes or the mission, always an excuse."

320

"Her feelings for you are embedded in her ticker," Harry argued. "To pry them loose, we'd need a stick of dynamite. I noticed last year. Do you recall the time we returned to your flat near Rochester after being on the road, the night Peg spent with you and Rich while Sadie entertained Jo-Jo and me?"

"Yeah?"

"I promised not to blow the gaff..." Harry hesitated. "No, you need to know this. She was all a tremble that night, staring at your chamber door, yearning to lie at your side."

"So why didn't she come in?" Saul asked. "Never mind. I know the answer. She knew she was being childish."

"Stop it, Saul," Peggy commanded. "Harry, you didn't even tell me about that."

"I couldn't. The next morn she made me promise to put the mockers on."

"Come off it," Saul said. "You're spinning the whole yarn."

"No, I'm not. Ask Jo-Jo. I chatted with him the night it happened before any oath was taken."

Jo-Jo nodded. "I passed it off as overtiredness with the tikes and all. The next morn she joked as if nothing happened."

"Yeah, she does that," Saul snorted. "She tries to lay on that things don't happen. One of these days, she will grow up."

Peggy's glare renewed. "If Sadie acts childish sometimes, maybe we all should. She's the most sharing person I've ever met. You also seem to forget – she's only 18 years old."

Without waiting for an answer, Peggy left to help with the feeding. The others filed out too.

Saul motioned for Harry to wait. "I still want Peg for a week," he whispered. "I'll swap beds if it'll be easier. At the end, we can decide to extend it longer, if we're both agreeable."

321

"Lengthening the ticks would be quite right with me, mate. You know how I feel about Sadie. With enough opportunity, perhaps I can get her to love me the way she does you."

"Ha! You don't realize the hornet's nest involved with that. Give it a go then."

*

When Sadie returned to the McCarthy estate, lunch was finished and the men sipped second cups of tea at the kitchen table.

"Time and tide wait for no one," Saul scolded her. "Peg's putting the triplets in for a nap and the tots whine for a drink."

Sadie removed her coat and went upstairs. Soon afterwards, the triplets ran down the stairs and into the living room.

"Why shouldn't the kids fall asleep yet?" Peggy asked as she followed Sadie down the stairs.

"You'll find out soon enough."

The four women fed and changed the babies. "Please put them in their Nip-N-Naps for now," Sadie instructed. She walked into the kitchen. "Saul, I need to talk to you privately."

"Speak your peace, Luv. We don't keep secrets in this family, other than you and Harry."

"What?" She looked at Harry and tilted her head, then shrugged. "Saul, I can't continue the way we're going. I know you think I'm too sensitive. I'm sorry about it, but that is just me. The last two years I've done my best to make you happy. I may not have done everything you wanted, but I've done what I could."

She shook her head when Saul opened his mouth. "Don't talk. Just listen. This wife-swapping is beyond me."

"Did I do something wrong?" Harry asked.

"No, Harry. You're sweet and understanding. I love you very much. This has nothing to do with you. Not really."

She turned back to Saul. "For a long time now, you've hinted that you're tired of being tied down to me and seven kids. Well, as of today, you're free of us." She threw a piece of paper at him.

"What's this, cut-off papers?" Saul asked. His voice betrayed a lump in his throat. The other women entered the room.

Sadie shook her head and spoke softly. "I don't believe in divorce, but if you start those proceedings, I won't fight you." Her volume rose. "These are transfer papers, putting the house in your name. If you decide to use the house occasionally, you can. That's why I didn't record the transfer myself. As long as it's in my maiden name, you can enjoy anonymity here. When you want to sell, all you have to do is sign these and have them recorded at the court house. At that time, you should try to get two hundred grand for the house alone... and at least that much for the antique furniture. Four hundred big ones will give you a decent return on our investment, while still being a good buy for the next owners, so you'll be able to sell quickly. At my latest estimation, the house and furnishings are worth at least five hundred thousand."

"You can't go out on the street!" Peggy shouted.

Sadie smiled at her. "Peg, you should know better than anyone else about my financial resources. The kids and I will be okay. I bought a house this morning and I can move in this afternoon."

"Surely, luv," Saul chortled. "No one can go marketing for a house and then move in on the first flippin' day. How about a believable fantasy?"

"Saul, I've bought many houses for my work with the Salvation Army. My Realtor, John Sperano, merely had to make a few phone calls and find a house that fell through at the last minute, with all the paperwork done. The one I bought this morning is the right size and the owners were already loading a truck for a job out of state. They accepted my cash offer on the spot. The lawyers are recording the transfer at this moment."

Saul squinted in doubt. "If you leave now, I won't take you back. You've cried wolf too many times."

A lone tear trickled down her cheek. "This isn't a scare tactic. You know, even without my powers, I'm halfway intelligent. I can't force you to accept me as I am, but you don't want the real me here anymore."

"I'll go with you," Peggy offered. Harry's eyes widened.

"No, I won't be the cause of this family's break-up. Look at it this way, Peg: without my seven kids here, Carol should be able to do all the housework and you girls will have the time to work on your own abilities. You will find the house a lot quieter."

"My 'saint' is at it again," Saul chided.

"I'm not a saint, Saul. I'm me. I try my best." She paused. "While there are no qualms with the way we show our love to each other, sexually and otherwise, I can't continue this charade of swapping wives. If you're that desperate to get rid of me, I'll get out of your life. You can do as you please. You can even move to England. I'll be packed in a short time." At that, Sadie walked out of the kitchen.

Peggy threw her hands in the air. "I thought she was taking this wife-swapping thing as a joke. Her eyes even sparkled about it. Shoot!"

Martha rose, put her hand on Peggy's back, and rubbed softly. "I'll take part of that blame. I should have told you. At

324

breakfast Wednesday, Sadie found out we've been gauging her mood by her eyes' expressiveness. She adjusted them in front of me. Now we can't always tell if she's happy or not. You might say she's growing up, which is what Saul thinks he wants."

"What should we do?" Peggy asked.

"That depends on him," Martha replied. "Saul, do you want Sadie to leave and never come back?"

He hesitated for a moment. "Not forever, but maybe some ticks away will set her straight. She'll return by Monday, I bet." He put his arm around Peggy and squeezed gently.

Peggy pulled away and moved to Harry's side. "Can you forgive me for agreeing to the swap?" Harry asked her.

Peggy smiled. "Of course. You were honest before we married. Considering who Sadie is, and her powers, I can understand your dreams."

*

At dinner that evening, the kitchen seemed quite empty without Sadie and seven of the children. Saul stared at the clock on the wall. "She'll be back by Monday," he repeated many times. "She'll be back by Monday."

Chapter 21 – Christmas

Sadie drove slowly to the McCarthy Estate Christmas morning. Stopping at the gate, she turned the van sideways and pulled up to the pedestrian door. She hesitated before getting out. *I'd rather keep the children with me,* she thought. *If I drive away, Saul might not notice. After all, he has other interests now.*

A week after Sadie's departure, Saul had gone to visit friends in England. While there, he resumed his friendship with Michelle and brought her and her two boys to the States. She was now officially the Spidar's secretary. For the past three weeks, she had taken care of the Spidar mail – and Saul.

Sadie knew Michelle was in the house right now. Saul would have an arm around her shoulder while the couple watched Michelle's two children open their presents. The eight-year-old would pretend to believe in Santa so the gifts kept coming. The six-year-old might be blissfully ignorant.

The house was probably filling with the fragrances of the soon-to-be eaten noon feast. Yes, Peggy would have prepared most of it yesterday. Then she'd only have to bake it or take it out of the refrigerator today. Yes, Peggy would remember Sadie's story about her first Christmas with Saul, how she spent all day preparing the food and by the time she sat down, she was too exhausted to enjoy anything. Ever since, she made at least part of the meal ahead of time. Yes, Peggy, Miki, and Martha would surely follow that example.

A sharp knock at her window broke Sadie's ponderation. She opened her door and jumped out. The triplets screeched with delight in the middle of the van. "There's no going back now," she mumbled.

"I thought you might want help," Jerry greeted her.

"Thanks," she replied. "Where are you going today?"

"Nowhere. No family. They were all killed in the accident."

"What about friends?"

He hesitated. "...None around here."

"You're welcome to come to my mother's place with me."

"No thanks. They might have company here."

"Are you sure? It's hard to be alone on a holiday."

"Don't worry about me." Jerry pointed to the house. "They might want you in there, though."

Sadie ignored the comment and walked to the back of the van, opened the doors, and pulled out four bright red wagons. As Jerry took them through the pedestrian door to the other side of the gate, Sadie grabbed two large bags and carried them to the cottage. Then she returned for the triplets in the center seats and the quads in the rear side seats. The triplets squealed and ran to the wagons. Jerry helped carry well-bundled babies to their waiting vehicles.

As Sadie put bows on top of the infants' heads, kissed them, and turned to the triplets. "A good reindeer goes slow and careful so as not to tip the sleigh. I know you can be good reindeer if you try. Right?"

"Right, Mummy," they replied in unison, calming down. She kissed them and sent them on their way. As the triplets walked along the winding path, Sadie watched. She dabbed her eyes with a handkerchief and turned to Jerry. "Give them a head start before you take the last wagon-child along. They have shorter legs. Oh, and don't forget the bags. There's a gift for you on top of the small one." He nodded. "Did you tell the family we're here?" she asked.

"No. I didn't know if you planned a surprise." He joined the triplets on the walk to the house, while Sadie hurried into the cottage and pressed the blue button on the phone and the number for the living room.

Peggy answered the phone. "Yes, Jerry?"

"Wrong gender," Sadie replied with a false laugh.

"Hi, Sadie!" Others in the living room sat up straight, including Saul, who removed his arm from Michelle's shoulders.

"Peg, the kids are on their way. Jerry is bringing Chuck. He will bring all the gifts after I leave. I weaned the babies a week ago, so you just need to puree whatever you're eating, nothing real spicy, and give them regular milk in the bottles. I guess that's all. Tell everyone Merry Christmas for me."

"Can't you come in, too?" Peggy pleaded. "We're sitting here with gnarled stomachs. It doesn't seem like a holiday without..."

"You'll all be fine," Sadie interrupted. "As soon as the kids get to the house, you'll get plenty of action and noise until nap time... Even then probably. They're really wound up."

"Sadie, it won't bother Saul to have you spend the day with us. Will it, Saul?"

Saul delayed his answer. "...Invite any mates you wish."

"See, Sadie! You're welcome here. You're part of this family. Please call a truce for today."

"I don't think so." Sadie's voice betrayed strain. "If I'm there, everyone will be edgy, especially Saul. Please understand." Her voice trailed to a whisper, "It's no picnic for me either."

"What? I didn't hear that last part."

"You weren't supposed to. I've made other plans for the day. Merry Christmas. I love all of you."

"Wait! You can at least talk to everyone."

"No, Peg, I can't stay on the phone. Bye."

"But, Sadie... Sadie?" Peggy turned to the family. "She hung up! Do Something!"

The room buzzed with activity. Harry went to the hall closet to get his coat. Martha went to the kitchen door to answer the children's knock. Rich went to the front window. Because of the wintertime, he could see Jerry's area, just barely.

"Don't bother, matey," Rich called to Harry a moment later. "She's through the gate and out of eyesight. "

"*We wish you a Merry Christmas*," the triplets sang at the kitchen door.

"Come here, Peg," Martha called out. "You must see this."

"*We wish you a Merry Christmas,* " the triplets sang. Harry met Peggy at the door and held her hand.

"*We wish you a Merry Christmas*." Martha grabbed a camera from the kitchen shelf and snapped a picture of the colorful scene. The rosy-cheeked triplets wore bright yellow coats and green leggings. Behind them, red wagons held royal-blue quilts wrapped around babies, bundles with white bows on top of the headpieces. "*...And a happy new yeah, yeah, yeah, yeah, yeah.*"

As the triplets came into the house, the adults saw hand-lettered signs taped to the front of each wagon: the first read *WITH LOVE*; the second, *FROM ME*; the third, *TO YOU*; the fourth one, which Jerry pulled in the distance, sported a heart.

"What a pity," Martha said. Peggy shook her head, trying to hold back tears so the children wouldn't see them.

With their outer garments removed, the triplets scooted into the living room. "Daddy!" they squealed, each one taking a turn on his lap, with hugs and kisses. Saul beamed. The boys moved from one adult to another with their greetings. Roxanne remained on her father's lap, staring at Michelle.

"Is something the matter?" Michelle asked, self-consciously smoothing her hair.

"No," Roxanne replied. "Mommy says you're a pretty lady. I think so, too."

"Did your mother tell you to say that?"

Roxanne looked at Saul, with a questioning expression as if she may have done something wrong. "Mommy says if I have nice thoughts, I can say them. If I have bad thoughts, I should tell Mommy or you first. I thought it was a nice thought, so I said it."

"It was a nice thought, Roxie," Saul replied, kissing her on the cheek. "Auntie Michelle's a bit touchy today is all."

"I'm not touchy," Michelle snapped. Looking at Roxanne, she continued. "I suppose your mother told you it's wrong to have bad thoughts."

"No, Mummy says everyone thinks bad thoughts sometimes. We just shouldn't say them out loud, because they can hurt people. I don't want to hurt anyone."

"That sounds well-rehearsed."

"I wasn't singing," Roxanne replied with her brows lowered. Saul chuckled.

With the greetings done and the babies lying with Amanda in the playpen, attention focused on the gifts in abundance under the eight-foot tree in the children's play area. Since Michelle's two boys had opened theirs already and the babies were too young to grasp the idea, the bulk of what was left belonged to the triplets.

They attacked the pile with fervor. One by one, though, each found a treasure and lost the desire to open any more: Carl stopped at a set of Lincoln Logs, Roxanne stopped at a striped rubber ball, and Jason stopped at a coloring book and crayons.

"They take after their mother," Harry remarked.

"How's that?" Saul asked.

"They aren't interested in expensive things. They prefer the shilling-a-dozen ones."

"They'll outgrow that," Michelle frothed.

Peggy went to the kitchen and retrieved the oversized construction bags Jerry delivered. She read the note attached to the top of one and laughed.

"What's such a giggle?" Rich asked, as she handed him a large box.

"Sadie is up to something. She wrote instructions. I have to pass out the gifts one at a time and in a certain order. Also, wherever you see a note, you must read it aloud."

"Uh-oh!" Rich exclaimed. "The best is always kept for last with Sadie. Well, at least I'm the first bloke. Who's the last?"

"I'm not allowed to reveal anything ahead of time."

Rich winced at the amount of tape on his package. Minutes passed as he removed it. Then he paused before opening the lid. Slowly, he raised a corner to peek inside. Saucy swine!" he said with a laugh. He threw off the top. Inside was another brightly wrapped box, a little smaller in size. "At least this one doesn't have as much tape." He tore the paper and opened the box, another package and another and another.

Opening the tiniest box, he found a piece of paper that read, *PICK ONE*. Under that piece were three folded pieces taped to the bottom. He read them one by one: "I SPENT ALL MY MONEY ON THE WRAPPING PAPER. THERE WASN'T ANY LEFT FOR A GIFT – OH WELL, NOTHING WOULD FIT IN THIS BOX – OH WELL, and YOU MEAN YOU ACTUALLY FELL FOR THE EMPTY BOX IN A BOX IN A BOX TRICK? GOTCHA!"

"That's for the man who has everything," Harry offered.

Martha's gift was next. Her box was smallish but contained two boxes side-by-side. "Not me! What did I do to her?"

"Open 'em," Rich snickered. "But first you have to read the notes."

Martha nodded. "One says *TO DEFEND YOURSELF,* the other, *TO ATTACK.* A third one is folded. Let's see. The third one says DON'T LET RICH USE EITHER ONE. Which one should I open first?"

Rich tried to look serious. "What's your mood, offensive or defensive?"

"I'd rather pounce," Martha said. Inside she found an embroidered, black negligee. The second package was a book on practical jokes. She smiled at Rich. "This should warn me of your pranks."

"Yeah," Harry agreed. "Perhaps you'll lend it to the rest of us sometime, so we can give Rich and Sadie their comeuppance...." He ended with pursed lips.

Amanda received a purple velveteen dress with white lace around the hem, sleeves, and neckline. Included was a bonnet, also trimmed with lace. The outfit was identical to the ones Vera and Rita wore, the same material as Chuck's and Dave's suits. Peggy dressed Amanda in her new outfit to match the others in the playpen and took a picture of all five of them.

Upon Peggy's return to Sadie's instructions, she looked up and called Michelle's sons over, handing each of them a gift. Their faces shined as only a child's can.

"Why would Sadie give presents to MY children?" Michelle asked with skepticism.

Martha smiled. "Because that's the kind of person she is. She knew your kids would have opened their gifts before these arrived. She wanted to make sure everyone had something to open now."

"A typewriter!" six-year-old Reggie squealed. "Just what I wanted!"

Michelle glared at Peggy.

"It's not what you think," Peggy said softly. "When you first moved in, Sadie called and asked what your kids wanted for Christmas. You were upstairs with Saul, so I asked them myself. Last week, when you explained your superstitions about boys doing girls' work, it was too late. I knew Sadie would have already purchased the gifts. I also knew that if I told her your opinion, she would return the typewriter and buy something else. I didn't want her obligated to make an extra trip to the store."

"Why not?" Michelle snorted. "That's all I've heard since I came here – how much she can do in a day and how special she is and how she makes everyone laugh and how she smiles all the time... Ha! I bet she isn't smiling now!"

Saul slapped her thigh hard. "That's no way to talk. She never did anything to you."

Martha was the only one who didn't smile when Saul put Michelle in her place. "Michelle, I know it's been hard for you," Martha began. "I couldn't live up to Sadie's reputation, either. Yet, the typewriter isn't all that bad. When I went to college, a lot of men studying to be doctors used portable typewriters for their notes. Maybe Reggie will become a doctor."

Michelle's eyes softened. "What about the flute she gave Jimmy? A boy shouldn't play a sissy instrument."

"Musical instruments aren't sexual," Rich replied. "Give a look at Roxie, there. Which cat's paw do you think she plays?"

Michelle studied Roxanne's delicate features, a tiny frame even for a girl. "A violin?" she asked.

"Man are you caught with your knickers down!" Rich chuckled. "Roxie, sweets, can you go to the den for a mo? Michelle wants to hear you play."

Roxanne squealed. "Really, Uncle Rich?!"

"Me, too! Me, too!" Jason and Carl begged. The children's instruments were at Sadie's house. Rich looked at Saul and Harry. Both nodded.

In the den, the children waited at the door as the men adjusted their instruments. Rich changed the spacing on his drums and the height of the stool and made modifications to the foot pedal. Saul and Harry tuned old guitars. Rich led Michelle to a front-row daybed. She sat down, with Jimmy and Reggie at her feet.

Looking at the triplets in the doorway, Saul snickered. They were trying hard to be patient. They were not at a standstill by any means, but they were trying very hard. He warned them to be careful with the instruments and reminded them they were to play only one song. Then he turned them loose. They let out a squeal, ran over, and began. "Merry Christmas to you, ba-a-a-aby," they sang.

"Wait," Harry yelled over the din. "When did you learn a song like that?"

Jason made his fist into a pretend microphone. "Sorry, folks. We forgot where we were for a moment." He turned to his siblings. "It's okay, gang. Mum's not here."

Roxanne began another drum beat, faster and more complex. Before the boys joined in, Saul interrupted. "What did you mean by that, Jason?"

Jason squirmed. The drumbeat stopped. "Come on, boy," Saul insisted. "I asked a question."

Tears came to Jason's eyes. Harry walked to him. "Settle, lad. Whatever the sticky wicket, it can't be that bad."

"Yes, it can," Jason cried. "Mummy will get mad if she finds out I told."

"No, she won't," Roxanne corrected. "We're not supposed to keep secrets from Daddy. Right, Daddy?" She looked at Saul. When he nodded, she continued, "At home, whenever we play

Spidar music, Mummy cries. So, we learned other songs. Doesn't Mummy like your music anymore?"

Rich gave Roxanne a hug. "It's a bit more jumbled than that, honey-pie. You can play anything right now."

Roxanne nodded and began drumming again. "...when I touch you..." 35

Jimmy watched in awe. Michelle did too. The frail-looking girl in front of them could beat the drums like a boy two or three times her size. She was good too.

"All right, Rich," Michelle said at the end of the song. "You've convinced me. I'll let Jimmy have lessons." Jimmy beamed.

"Then let's get on with the presents," Harry said.

They all went back to the living room. The McCarthy children went to their toys. Jimmy went to a corner to try out his flute. Reggie set his typewriter on an end table and pretended to capture the adult conversation on paper.

Miki received a white sweater with delicately embroidered songbirds near the left shoulder. The tag said: MADE WITH LOVE. She slipped it over her head and shoulders. The fit was perfect. Her second gift was a book on telepathy, with a note on top: KEEP PRACTICING.

The next one is for Jo-Jo," Peggy announced. She handed him a box. He opened it to find a green cable-knit sweater with a note and small package pinned inside one sleeve. As he removed them, he saw a songbird matching those on Miki's sweater embroidered on the cuff.

"The note on the wee package says, FOR WHEN YOU ARE AWAY FROM MIKI. Harumph! I don't know if I dare open it. Yet, curiosity has the seat of my pants." Inside the wrapping paper, he found a large pillbox filled with Sweetarts and another note: PRETEND THE YELLOW ONES ARE SLEEPING

PILLS AND THE BLUE ONES ARE SALT-PETER. YOU MAY USE AS MANY AS YOU NEED IN ANY COMBINATION."

Peggy laughed as she checked the sheet for the next gift recipient. She handed Harry a package. When he opened it he found a canary-yellow sweater. He probed inside for the gag gift, but found nothing. He searched his surroundings in case something had dropped. "Is there another one for me?"

"I only received one, an empty one," Rich added.

"Nope, the last one is for me, which means the one in my hand is for..." Peggy paused, knowing Sadie would like the way she added suspense. She walked slowly to where Saul and Michelle sat.

Saul smiled smugly. "Of course it has to be for me."

"Nope, it's for Michelle," Peggy replied.

Saul's face dropped. "She forgot me?"

Peggy scowled. "I wouldn't blame her if she did. No, she gave you the most precious things in her life right now – her children. You have them on a very special day. You should..."

"Alright already," Saul interrupted. "I get your drift." He turned to Michelle. "Open away. It won't be a bomb."

"Wait a tick," Jo-Jo stated. "Didn't I see a note on top? You have to read it aloud."

Michelle nodded. "It says, TELL RICH TO BE PATIENT. HE'LL GET HIS WHEN HE'S LEAST EXPECTING THEM." She looked up with a puzzled expression. "I haven't the foggiest what she means. Perhaps I'm not supposed to."

Everyone looked at Rich, who raised an eyebrow. "Who knows? Not I."

Michelle opened the package quickly, as if to get it over and done. A present from the woman she replaced, weird! When she pulled out red licorice, she stared at it. Yes, very weird!

"Candy pants!" Rich exclaimed. "She never gave me any!"

"Don't fret," Jo-Jo warned. "They must be rubbery by now."

"No," Saul replied, a devil in his eyes. "Sadie found a market here that sells them. She and I relish them often, um, relished, I should say."

Michelle threw the Candy Pants at him. "Then you can have them! They are for you, not me."

"Not true, Michelle," Martha said. "I think Sadie's trying to tell us to accept you."

Harry scowled. "Accept her? You're daft!"

"No, I'm not. Michelle did not make Sadie leave. I think Sadie knows how we're treating her. She's suggesting we knock it off." Martha turned back to Michelle. "We have not acted very neighborly. Try to understand our side of it. Sadie is special to us. Every person she touches… um, anyway, don't expect to replace her in our hearts and we will try to make more room for you."

"I won't be Benedict Arnold," Peggy stated.

Michelle looked at Saul, expecting defense. He was deep in thought, examining the licorice on his lap. She shook her head in disgust.

"Don't forget the last gift," Harry reminded Peg. "It has to be a good one. It's whopping big!"

Peggy's present, inside a chair-size box, towered over the second 30-gallon bag. She took it to the middle of the floor. "The note on top reads: THIS SIDE UP. YOU'LL REGRET A TIP-OVER. TRUST ME. That sounds ominous." She giggled as she tore the wrapping paper off the side and top. Then she gently pulled on the intertwining flaps. Inside, a piece of cardboard covered the contents. "The note on this says: THE TOP GIFT IS YOURS ALONE. YOU DO NOT HAVE TO SHARE IT WITH ANYONE."

Peggy pulled out the cardboard. "Oooo! Thank you, Sadie!"

"So what is it?" Rich asked.

"My favorite: Sadie's homemade, chocolate cream pie!" She lifted it gently out of the box.

"That sounds good for today's dessert," Harry teased.

"No way!" Peggy shot back as she headed for the kitchen refrigerator. "It's mine. That sharing pact is between you men. I didn't sign anything."

Harry smirked. "Quite right. We know you're a beggar for chocolate. You can devour the whole thing."

"Hey!" Jo-Jo said loudly. "Speak for yerself, Matey. I have a yen for chocolate myself."

"So do I, but our yens are not feverish, like Peg's"

When Peggy returned from the kitchen, she dug into the box, removing newspapers and another piece of cardboard. An envelope caught her attention. PEG, THE TIME IS NOW was written on the outside. She pulled out a slip of paper and her eyes moistened as she read it. "That's nice. It's a gift certificate for an accounting course at the community college. It has to be used this spring semester." Peggy closed her eyes and lowered her head.

"What the matter, Pet?" Harry asked, coming to her side.

She shook her head and wiped her cheeks. "This gift reminds me of the first time I met Sadie. I told her someday I'd like to go to college." Her voice broke. When she regained it, she continued, "I haven't mentioned it since then, but she remembered. This is her way to get me started." Peggy's head lowered again as she struggled to stem a flow of tears.

Harry put his arm around her. "We all have fond memories of those days." He moved her head so it rested on his shoulder. "She let us all know she cared."

"Quit blubbering, you two," Saul said. "There has to be more in that big box. Let's put a jerk in it so we can get to the food."

338

Harry scowled at him. Peggy reached into the box. After removing the tissue paper on the next layer, she smiled. "Guess what, Rich!"

"What?"

"One of the gifts on the next layer belongs to you."

Rich straightened. Saul and Harry perked up, too. Perhaps their missing presents would be in this box.

Rich read the note on top out loud: "HOW COULD I GIVE NOTHING TO THE MAN WHO KEEPS ME LAUGHING FOR DAYS AT A TIME?" He opened the box to find another wrapped package. *IT'S EASY,* said another note.

"Not again!" Rich exclaimed. This time, when he opened the second box, he found a red cable-knit sweater. "She must have hit a good pennyworth on these." He opened the neck to examine the tag and chuckled.

"What's so funny?" Martha asked.

"There's a flimsy pinned to the tag. It says: WATCH OUT FOR LOOSE THREADS. THEY'LL GET YOU IN THE END." His laughter faded as he removed the note. He looked up at the other men. "Did you blokes give a look-see at your tags? Sadie made all these herself."

Carl had come over to show his newest creation, a bridge. He heard Rich's comment and nodded. "Mummy had fun sewing and knitting. She says it means more when you give a part of yourself at Christmas."

"My saint's at it again," Saul stated. The room quieted.

Without comment, Peggy reached inside for the next package. It was addressed to Saul. She held it in the air, as if planning to throw it at him, but changed her mind. He opened the package to reveal a cornflower-blue sweater with a note on top. "I CAN'T THINK OF ANYTHING FUNNY FOR YOU. PLEASE ACCEPT MY APOLOGIES..."

"So?" Harry exclaimed. "She didn't give me any refreshing token, either."

Saul didn't hear Harry. He was staring at the last line of the note, which he had not read aloud: I SINCERELY WISH YOU ALL THE HAPPINESS A MAN CAN POSSESS.

Peggy returned to the box. She handed a small gift to Harry. There was no note on the package. Inside, he found a tiny cake in the shape of an oblong pill. In very tiny lettering, the frosting read: USE WISELY.

"I don't get it," he said to Peggy.

She shrugged and opened her own gift. Inside, was a vial of chocolate flavoring from a company in California. The attached note made her blush like a schoolgirl as she read it aloud: "PUT A DAB OF THIS ANYWHERE YOU'D LIKE HARRY TO NIBBLE. BETTER YET, PUT IT ANYWHERE ON HARRY THAT YOU WOULD LIKE TO NIBBLE. PS: IF HARRY EVER USES THE EXCUSE THAT HE HAS A HEADACHE, TELL HIM TO TAKE THE PILL I GAVE HIM. "

Harry winked at the others. "That'll be the day. I'm always ready, willing, and able to serve."

"Like any proper Spidar would be," Rich added.

"The box is empty now," Peggy proclaimed, a tease in her voice. "It's time to eat."

"Alri-i-ight!" Harry ran to the hall door. "Let's go, Pet."

"Wrong way," Peggy laughed, walking toward the kitchen. Harry's chin dropped. Rich roared with laughter.

*

In the cottage, Jerry glanced at the security screens again. In the one that showed the outside of the brick wall, Sadie smiled back at him. She carried bags of groceries in her arms. He went out to help. "I hope you weren't waiting long. Why didn't you buzz?"

"Checking on your efficiency," she replied with another smile. "Actually, I just arrived. Do you feel like company?'

"Yes. And thanks for the gifts." She had given him a bottle of his favorite whiskey, with an envelope taped over the label. Inside the envelope was a certificate for a five-year membership in a singles club as well as a sizable check.

"My pleasure. How will you ever have a family again if you spend all your time working?"

In the cottage, Sadie set the bags on the counter and began to empty them. "I'm not used to cooking for two," she apologized. "So I cheated and bought ready-made from a Jewish deli. It should be okay – with a couple glasses of this." She held up a bottle of J Roget Brut, a champagne made in Canandaigua.

Hours later, Jerry and Sadie were nibbling on chips and watching television specials. A car's horn blared outside the cottage. Jerry jumped up and looked out the window. "It's Michelle," he said. "Her rental car is packed as if she's leaving. For good this time."

"Has she left before?" Sadie asked, walking to the door.

"Yes, she goes out with her kids at least once a week."

"Oh, that. Peg told me during a phone call that Michelle is used to raising her children by herself. Sometimes, she just wants to be alone with them. Don't open the gate yet."

With her purse slung over her shoulder, she walked out of the cottage to the driver's side of the car. She motioned for Michelle to wind down her window. "Hi, I'm Sadie. I've heard so much about you."

"I could say the same. As a matter of fact, that's all I've heard since I arrived: Sadie does this, Sadie does that, Sadie does everything."

"Sorry." Sadie looked in the back seat at the children. "Hi, Jimmy! Hi, Reggie! Did you have a nice day?"

"Thanks for the flute!" Jimmy replied. Reggie didn't answer.

"You're welcome," Sadie said with a smile. She studied Reggie's pout and then looked back at Michelle. "Is something wrong with Reggie?'

"He's upset we had to leave some of his new things here. This car won't fit everything."

"Are you leaving permanently, then?"

"Yes. No one wants me here. Saul is still very much in love with you. I could tell by the look on his face as your gifts were passed out."

Sadie's voice lowered in volume. "I'm sorry. Thanks for taking care of him. I appreciate it. If you give me your new address, I'll make sure Peg sends all the toys to you. No, better yet, I'll send them along myself." She smiled into the back seat. "How does that sound, Reggie?"

The boy's face lit up. "Far out!"

Sadie turned back to Michelle. "So, where are you going?

"Some place along the way."

Along the way to where? Sadie wanted to ask but thought better of it. "If you want to," she said, "You can stay at my house. I could leave the kids here overnight. Saul would love that. And I could sleep at my mother's house. You could start fresh in the morning. It's awfully dark already, hard to find a place to stay on a holiday like this."

Michelle sighed, as if her chest had lightened the slightest bit. "No, thanks," she replied. "I'd rather get as far away tonight as possible."

Sadie took a piece of paper and a pen out of her purse. "Well, here's my number. If you need anything, anything at all, please call. I mean it, really. Do you have any money on you?"

"Enough."

"How much?" Sadie pressed.

342

Michelle shrugged and checked her wallet. She had fifty dollars cash and a checkbook on her. "Fifty."

"That won't get you far," Sadie replied. She reached into her purse, counted out five hundred dollars, and offered it.

"I can't take your money," Michelle protested. "You don't even know me."

Sadie smiled. "I know you were a hard-working single parent before Saul took you away from a job you loved to live in another country with him. I also know you're a good mother. I wouldn't be able to work and care for my kids the way you did and do."

Michelle tilted her head and relaxed a little. "You have a few more children than I do. With seven of them, the babysitter would cost too much, so I couldn't work either." Sadie's hand was still extended. "Put that money away," Michelle commanded. "I can't take it."

"Would you feel better if Saul reimburses me?"

She accepted the money. "Yes. He owes me."

"I'm sorry, really sorry. If you need more for the plane back home, just call me." Sadie opened the car door and hugged Michelle, then motioned to Jerry and backed away. "Merry Christmas!"

As the gates closed behind the car, Sadie rushed to the cottage, chilled from the cool air.

"I wonder why Jerry would do that," Rich said when he glanced out the window toward the security cottage.

"Do what?" Harry asked.

"Have a natter with Michelle. She left ten ticks ago."

Harry grabbed a pair of binoculars Reggie left behind as he joined Rich at the window. "That's not Jerry. It's Sadie!" The rest of the family suddenly listened closer. Peggy and Martha rushed around the room, picking up clutter.

"Oh-oh!" Harry said anxiously. "We're going to have a bust-up. Sadie's opening the car door!"

Rich grabbed the binoculars from him. "Nope, they're not mixing it."

"What's doing, then?" Saul asked from behind the pair.

"They're clinging. Leave it to Sadie. We should've known better with a bird like her."[3]

Saul picked up Vera and cooed to make her smile, as if he no longer cared what was happening outside.

"Michelle's gone," Rich updated. "Sadie's in the bungalow."

An hour later, Peggy paced in the living room. There had been no call from Sadie or Jerry. "Maybe something's wrong." Peggy pressed the blue button on the phone and dialed two digits. "Is Sadie there?" she asked when Jerry answered.

"Yes."

"What the heck is she doing?"

"Watching television. Would you care to speak with her?"

"Surely would!"

"Hi, Peg," Sadie chirped. "Are you ready for me to take the kids?"

"No, we're ready for you to come to the house. Rich and Harry saw your exchange with Michelle and we've been expecting you to buzz."

"I was waiting for my scheduled time."

"You can wait in here. In fact, you can open your presents while we thank you for ours. We had a ball opening them."

"I'm glad they were fun, but I can't come to the house. Try to understand."

"No, I don't understand. Michelle's gone now. Come enjoy the remainder of the day." Jo-Jo and Saul left the room.

Sadie hesitated. "Peggy, if I come in, I might not be able to leave again."

"That would be great!"

"No, it wouldn't, Peg. Look. I'm human. This month has been extremely lonely without all of you, especially Saul. I need to wait until I'm strong enough to leave when a visit is over."

"I still don't understand." A click signaled an extension had been picked up as Peggy continued. "If you've been so lonely, why would you have to leave again?"

"I can't explain."

"I can," Saul said from the kitchen phone. "You're freezing me out to make me pay for bringing Michelle here."

"Michelle has nothing to do with it," Sadie whispered.

"I didn't hear that last remark."

Sadie raised her voice. "Nothing."

"Are you dropping in then?" Saul asked.

"No. When you are ready to send the kids out, give me a call here. I'll wait."

"You'll wait a long tick, woman. I can be snivey, too. If you want the tikes, you'll come and get them."

"That's not fair!" Sadie exclaimed. "You have the rest of the family. Let me have my kids!"

Saul snickered. "I didn't say you couldn't have them. You merely have to come get them. The family wants you back. Perchance then they'll get off my arse."

"I'm not coming back now, Saul."

"That's too flippin' bad, then. I repeat, you pick up your tots inside the house or you don't get them."

No reply came from Sadie's end, just a click. "Sadie?" Peg questioned. "Sadie, are you there?" Peggy looked at Rich, who was at the window again. "Can you see anything?" she asked as she hung up the phone.

"Yup, she's leaving the cottage," Rich replied.

"I knew it," Saul said, returning to the living room. He picked up Rita and rocked her in his arms. "Your Mum can't go home without you tots. You're too precious. She'll enter the kitchen straight away…"

"Not so, mate," Rich interrupted. "She's going to the gate, not the house."

Peggy dialed the gate phone quickly. "Come on, Jerry! Answer before you let Sadie out!… Jerry?… Good! Don't let Sadie leave. Tell her we're getting the kids ready. Give us a few minutes to get their stuff together. I'll call when we're done." There was a pause as Jerry relayed the message.

"I said she doesn't get the tots unless she comes in," Saul huffed. "If she wants to be a mule-head, that's her choice. You've no right to put your boat in the water. They're my tikes, not yours."

"Fine," Peggy shot back. "Then you take care of them with no help." She stomped her feet and ran upstairs.

Saul turned to the other woman in the living room. "I gather you all feel the same."

"Yes," Martha replied. "Sadie's the only one with enough energy to care for the children for any extended period of time. We're exhausted after a while. Besides, you know how she feels about the kids."

Saul thought for a moment and walked upstairs to Peggy's room.

Sadie drove the van through the gate and walked back into the cottage, handing the keys to Jerry, since he would be the one driving it to the house when Peggy called.

"How about one last drink for the road?" he asked.

"No. Driving at night without all my faculties could be dangerous."

Jerry opened the refrigerator and pulled out a soda. "How about this?" She nodded. After filling the glasses, he offered a toast: "To your happiness."

"I can't drink to that. How about to peace on Earth?"

346

"And peace in our hearts," Jerry added. Glasses clinked....

The next time Sadie looked at the kitchen clock, a half hour had passed. "What could they be doing?" She looked out the window toward the house. Something moved in the driveway. "Oh no!" she exclaimed. "They wouldn't!"

She turned to Jerry and spoke rapidly. "I can't meet with them. Listen, I'll be in a spot where I'll see everything, but no one can see me. Warn them not to try anything cute. I won't move until the van is near the road and the gate is closed, with all of them inside the property. I've gotta go. Thanks for a nice afternoon." She pecked his cheek. "And Merry Christmas." She rushed out the door and through the gate. Because of the brick wall surrounding the estate, she quickly disappeared from sight.

When Saul saw Sadie rush through the gate, he ran after her, Vera in his arms. He stopped to deposit the infant in Jerry's arms. Then he ran faster. Too late. By the time he reached the other side of the gate, Sadie was nowhere to be found. He stood with his back toward the rest of the family. "Come on, Sadie," he pleaded loudly. "We really need to talk."

Jerry repeated Sadie's last instructions to the others and they loaded the van inside the gate. "We tried, Saul," Peggy yelled. "For now, let it be. We'll see what we can do another time." Saul shook his head. Jerry drove the van out and accompanied Saul back on foot, closing the gate on the way.

Peggy turned to Martha. "He's been putting up a front this whole time," she whispered. "When he came upstairs, he admitted to me that he had used Michelle to bring Sadie back. He thought she would storm in and fight for him. Obviously, he was wrong."

"I knew he was hurting," Martha stated.

"Yes, he said he feels like a zombie..." Peggy stopped talking as Saul neared. While the others walked back to the

347

house, Peggy and Saul remained.

A car horn beeped from the road. "Okay, party-pooper, move it or lose it." Carol's voice yelled from beyond the van. The van's engine roared. After the van moved to one side, Carol and Joshua pulled into the driveway alongside the van.

"I explained why I was leaving Mom's house," Sadie's voice said above the noise from the two engines. "Was there a problem?"

"Yes, Mom didn't believe you. She was crotchety the rest of the afternoon."

"This hasn't been my day. I'll call her when I get home."

As the van went to the road, Jerry opened the gate for Carol and Joshua. Saul waved for Joshua to stop the car. "What happened at your Mum's?" he asked Carol on the passenger side.

She looked disgusted. "My dear, dear Sis sat like a bump-on-a-log the whole time just staring at your wedding picture on Mom's wall. Then she had the absolute nerve to leave before we sat down to eat. Of course, Mom had some choice words after that."

"Did Sadie say where she was going?"

"Yes. She said something about Jerry being alone. She planned to spend the afternoon with him."

"What time did she leave?"

"Around one, I guess."

Saul's eyes blazed. He motioned for Jerry to come out of the cottage. "Was Sadie here for five friggin' hours?" he snapped at the gatekeeper.

Jerry checked his watch. "It didn't seem that long. I lost track of the time."

Saul grabbed him by the shirt collar. "If you laid one hand on her..."

348

"I didn't! We had the lunch she brought and a few drinks, watched TV, and talked." As Saul's grasp loosened, Jerry pulled free.

"What did Sadie chat about?" Saul asked a little quieter.

Jerry took a moment to reply. "Come to think of it, I did most of the talking – about my family and the accident that killed them. It was nice having someone listen. May I go now?"

Saul waved him away and turned to Peggy, a lone tear running down his cheek. "So near all that time..." Peggy nodded. "So what do we do now?" he asked. She twisted her hands and shrugged.

Saul turned toward the car. "She's your sister, Carol. How can I get her to talk to me face-to-face? Our phone conversations are so stiff."

Carol looked puzzled. "What about Michelle?"

"Michelle was a joke with a waterlogged punch-line. Carol, is there some way I could get to Sadie? Something she can't resist?"

"My sister?... Something she can't resist? Who knows?... Wait a minute. Yeah, that might work."

"What might work?"

"She gets spastic about birthday parties. Since hers isn't until February, I guess that's too far off. You'll have to find someone born earlier in the year."

"Sadie's birthday is in February?" Saul asked.

Peggy glared at him. "You mean that after two and a half years of marriage, you don't know your wife's birthday?"

"You live here, too," he scolded. "Did you know?"

"I never thought about it."

"I did. I asked – several times – but she's strong on hedging the issue." Saul turned back to Carol. "February what?"

"February 25th."

349

"Same as Harry's," Saul mumbled. "That explains why she always changed the subject."

Peggy nodded. "Our Sadie is true to form. She didn't want to take Harry's limelight. And she did always have a party. Harry got all the presents, though, during HIS surprise parties."

Carol smiled. "Yeah, that's my sister. She goes bonkers for surprise parties. She'd have to be dead to miss one."

Peggy and Saul exchanged smiles. They knew what they had to do. The only problem was that February 25th was two months away. A little more thought perhaps....

Chapter 22 – January 1969

One blustery Sunday in mid-January, Sadie arrived at church early. Her children played in the nursery and she enjoyed the solace of the organ solo in the sanctuary. Karen Black was working the nursery and the McCarthy children loved her, so Sadie felt total peace just listening to the music.

A minute prior to the start of the service, Karen's mother, Izzy, walked through the doorway, helping her husband. Paul's gait was slow. His six-foot frame slumped in the shoulders, waist, and knees, slumped so much that he almost looked as short as his 5'1" wife. *Paul's arthritis must be getting worse*, Sadie thought. *I should take care of it before he needs a wheelchair. Forty-three is too young to be crippled.*

The following week, Sadie couldn't get that picture out of her mind. It nagged at her conscience and she argued with herself:

You have the power to stop Paul's decay.

Yes, but I'm too busy already.

Too busy to help a friend? Shame on you!

If I cure him, people will ask questions.

So what?

So I live in a plain house now. I have no security fences or guards. Paul knows who I am, my maiden name anyway. If he tells anyone what I can do, I'll be plagued with reporters who will find out my identity. I'll need to go on the run to keep my kids safe. What kind of life will that be?

If you don't help Paul, what example will you set for your kids? Forget people in need and think only of self, self, self.

Stop already!

351

Call Paul and set a time now.

But....

No buts. You must trust someone sometime. You're building a cocoon around yourself. Expand. Gene, Mary, and Reverend Bee are not the only good people in this world.

I know that.

Explain everything to Paul and Izzy. They will keep quiet, just like Ted White. And, if you cure Paul's arthritis, they will owe you one. Maybe Izzy and her daughter would even babysit occasionally.

I run errands when the kids are with Saul and the Spidars. I don't need a babysitter.

You will.

Sadie's head popped upwards. *I will? Did I just think that?* She shrugged and went to the phone.

*

On Saturday, after dropping the children at Saul's estate, Sadie drove to the Black's house. Izzy led her to the den. The house was silent. "Where are your kids?" Sadie asked.

"They are all with different friends. This is the first time in months Paul and I have been alone."

Sadie snickered. "Maybe I should leave then... and let you two take care of business."

"Not necessary," Izzy said.

Sadie sat on the sofa and asked Paul to get comfortable on the recliner. "Paul, how long have you had arthritis?"

"Since I was a teenager. It's hereditary. Why?"

"What is the prognosis for a permanent cure?"

"Nil. It can't be cured, just controlled with surgery and pain killers. I'd rather not discuss it."

"Would you like to get rid of it once and for all?"

"No, I enjoy the pain," Paul replied in a sarcastic voice. Sadie laughed.

"Tea?" Izzy asked. Sadie nodded. As Izzy poured, Paul and Sadie locked eyes.

"That's right, I am," Sadie finally said.

"Huh?" Paul said.

"You thought my eyes might be boring into your soul to read your mind...I was."

"A lucky guess."

"There's no luck involved. That's part of what I want to show you today. You'll soon laugh again too."

"Now I know you're crazy," Paul said, getting up slowly from his chair.

"Wait!" Sadie said quickly. "Please sit down while I try to explain. You have nothing to lose in the next few moments, do you?" Paul slackened. Izzy stared at both of them. As Sadie explained the history of her powers, the couple sat in silence. "...I'm telling you now, because I have a feeling sometime soon I will need your help with something."

"We may not believe all this," Izzy replied, "but you're certainly earnest in the telling. As for helping, any time you need anything..."

"Please," Sadie interrupted. "Before you agree or disagree to anything, let me convince you my stories are true." She crossed the room to Paul's chair, knelt at his side and laid her hands on his arthritic hands. "Do you believe God can work miracles in our lives?" she asked.

"Of course He can."

"Does He have the power to get rid of your arthritis if He so desires?"

"Why would He?"

"M-m-m-m, I see. You don't think He can do it."

353

Paul's reply was swift. "He could. But why would He want to... at this late date?'

"Maybe He has plans for your family."

Paul looked at Izzy, who tilted her head as if she didn't know either. Sadie's hands moved to Paul's legs and his ankles. "Your joints are bad here too, aren't they?"

"Yes, my ankles and wrists are the worst." As he raised his hands to display his disfigured upper appendages, he stared at them. The swelling was down and the scars from many operations were gone. He felt no pain as he moved his fingers.

As Paul stared at his hands, Sadie stood and walked to the sofa. "How are your feet now?" she asked. He could move his feet painlessly too. Quickly, he bent over to pull up his pant legs. He removed his braces, orthopedic shoes, and socks. His ankles and toes were normal size!

"You won't need special shoes anymore," Sadie stated. "You can wear sandals... or go barefoot, if you wish."

He looked at his hands again then back at his feet and toes. He stood, jumping and hopping like a child who received a new pair of sneakers. "I can't believe it. How long will it last?"

"Forever, I hope. Your form of arthritis is like a cancer. Bone cells in some joints grow into misshaped forms, causing pain with movement. God helped me bomb your joints with an anti-cancer protein manufactured by your own body."

"What protein?"

"I haven't been able to find the name of it anywhere. However, I do know the lumps of bone are gone now, as you can see. I've also adjusted your calcitonin and cortisone levels to keep the lumps away forever, hopefully. Mmm, your urine will look strange for the next couple of days, as your body gets rid of the results of my bombing. Drink plenty of water and the urine should return to normal soon. "

"You have remarkable powers!" Izzy exclaimed.

"No, God has the power," Sadie corrected. "I'm just the instrument He's using at present. I practice on you and others so I can fine tune my mind for a special project in the future."

"What kind of project?" Paul asked.

"I don't know yet," came Sadie's reply.

Chapter 23 – February 1, 1969

"Saul!" "Jo-Jo!" "Rich!" "Harry!"

The audience screamed, each person for their favorite Spidar. Saul, Harry, and Jo-Jo stood in front of Rich, whose drums sat on a raised platform in the back. The band was dressed in denim suits and blue-striped sneakers. Half an hour of the concert remained.

Saul turned to Jo-Jo. "I need a mo."

Jo-Jo nodded and began a short comedy skit.

Saul walked to the wings. "Where is she?" he asked Peggy.

Peggy smiled. "She was out in the audience watching the show. She's in position now, waiting for her cue. I saw her peek a minute ago."

Saul looked at the backdrop behind Rich. Sure enough, there was a tiny opening where Sadie should be. Saul's heart pounded.

*

Behind a thick curtain, Sadie reminisced: "I need to see you," Peggy had said on the phone a few weeks ago. Sadie had been hesitant. *Am I ready for an in-person visit*, she wondered.

"It's important and I promise to come alone," Peggy insisted.

"Okay, I guess."

Later, with tea cup in hand, Peggy explained: "Harry wants a show scheduled on his birthday, so he can spend the day practicing. He hopes the evening will pass faster too."

Sadie giggled. "He should know better than to schedule a concert on his birthday. There's a lot we can do at a show."

356

"So you'll help then."

"Seeing as it's for his birthday, what the heck. Sure!"

"Great! He's been down in the dumps since you left."

"Peg, I'm only agreeing to one evening."

"Fine. We bumped it up to the first of February, to make him less suspicious. Here's what I've planned so far..."

*

It wasn't surprising that tonight, while in the audience, Sadie noticed Harry's lack of enthusiasm. As a great musician, he played well, but his performance lacked his normal radiance.

How will my appearance affect him? Sadie wondered. Will it help? Or will he feel worse after I'm gone again. Will I do more harm than good? For that matter, will I be able to leave? Seeing Saul and the family has stirred up old feelings that will be hard to fight. Should I sneak out now? Should I let tomorrow's clouds ruin tonight's stars?

"Is she suspicious," Saul asked.

Peggy smiled. "No, she's excited."

"Are you sure she hasn't tinkered with our thoughts... to find out the truth?"

"Positive."

"...and now, if we can find our lost sheep," Jo-Jo was saying into a microphone. "We'll sing for our supper. Baa, baa, black sheep..."

Saul skipped onto the stage. "Sorry," he whispered. "Sadie's all set."

Jo-Jo gave Rich a signal and turned back to Saul. "Keep your wits about you when your bird comes out, Mate."

Saul nodded as Rich started a fast beat. Jo-Jo stepped to the microphone again. "We dedicate this next song to Harry."

"...They say it's your birthday..."[36]

357

Harry smiled sideways, an expression that said: This won't work. He winked at Peggy in the wings and she disappeared. With a shrug, he concentrated on his guitar.

A wave of screams came from the audience as Sadie pranced out from behind the curtain in her signature outfit: a bright pink turtleneck sweater zipped up in front and emerald green mini-skirt, with mint green fishnet stockings and silver beaded jewelry. She put a hand in front of her mouth to shush the audience. Behind Harry now, she mimicked Harry's gyrations and threw a kiss towards the others.

Slowly and gently, she put her arms around Harry. Her fingers unbuttoned his suit coat under his guitar. Soon, only a thin shirt separated her hands from his bare chest. She held him tight, her head on the back of his shoulders, her body pressed against his backside.

Excitement rushed to Harry's loins. *Peg's getting good*, Harry thought. His smile was genuine now. He glanced at Saul and Jo-Jo, unsuccessful at hiding their chuckles. Then a movement in the wings caught his attention. Peggy was there, laughing with Miki and Martha.

Wait a tick, he thought. *If all the women are there, including Peg, whose hands are these?* He looked at his chest and stopped playing. He knew only one woman with such a small diamond on her left hand, the woman who preferred all her jewelry to be dainty.

He unfastened his guitar and turned to see an angelic smile directed toward him. "Happy Birthday, Sweet Cheeks," Sadie said. He set his guitar down, pulled her close, and pressed his lips against hers.

Some fans in the audience screamed, some swooned. The flashes from reporters' cameras appeared like Fourth of July fireworks and like the sparks Harry felt inside.

Sadie pulled free and sang with the others. Wiggling her hips, she held Harry's hands and led him forward to dance. Their bodies bounced like waves at the beach. Sadie ended her twirls by bending her knees, as if in a whirlpool, drawn down into the water. Then she bobbed back up and rejoined Harry.

"Go, Sadie, go!" yelled a section of the audience from McQuaid Boys' School. She winked at them. At the end of the song, Harry grabbed her, with urgency in his kiss.

When released, she smirked. "Happy Birthday, old man!"

"Old man? I'll show you who's NOT an old man!" He tried to grab her again, but she eluded him this time.

She giggled. "Yes, twenty-five is old, isn't it?" She avoided another grope. "A quarter of a century. Think about it." He grabbed again, and again she slunk away.

Finally, she pointed to the audience. "We'll discuss this later. These people came to see the group perform, not to watch you chase me around the stage." She took a step toward the wings.

"We also have a surprise for our surprise," Jo-Jo said into the microphone.

Sadie stopped and turned to the other men. Jo-Jo wore a devilish grin. Rich and Saul did too. She felt Harry's arms go around her waist, a kiss planted on top of her head.

"...We need the stage lights dimmed..." Jo-Jo said. Rich dramatized a drumroll. One word at a time, red bulbs on the far wall facing the stage, lit up. Sadie smiled as she read them: HAPPY BIRTHDAY, HARRY! *That's a nice touch*, she thought.

Rich changed the beat. Sadie blushed as three more words lit up: YOU TOO, SADIE! Then the whole row began to flash on and off. HAPPY BIRTHDAY, HARRY! YOU TOO, SADIE!

"It's your birthday, too?" Harry asked. The other Spidars sang the traditional, American birthday song.

"Yes," she admitted with a bashful smile.

359

"Then I'm under obligation." He pulled her closer and their lips met.

When the song ended, Sadie pulled away from Harry and skipped over to Rich. "I owe you one," she said before she kissed his cheek. "You got me good."

Rich shook his head. "Not I. Saul and Peg told the rest of us a few ticks before the gig tonight, while Harry was in the loo."

Sadie's blush deepened. She jumped off Rich's platform, then walked to Jo-Jo and thanked him. Turning to Saul, she hesitated. Her heartbeat quickened as he unhooked his guitar and set it on the floor. When he opened his arms wide, all doubts crumbled.

In a tight embrace, she laid her head on his shoulder. His body heat permeated her clothing. It had been so long. She stood there, her mind reeling, as familiar sensations pulsated through her body. When she raised her head, their lips met.

After a few moments, Jo-Jo spoke into the microphone, trying to silence the screaming fans. Sadie's heart told her to ignore everything, but her mind won this round. She broke away. Saul strapped his guitar onto his shoulder, flipped it onto his back, and then put an arm around Sadie's waist. Her hand lay on top of his, as she listened to Jo-Jo:

"...and you'll enjoy our next staggerer. Fleet Street's been hounding us. We were waiting for the right and proper time. We have a winner in Sadie's lyrics contest." A hush fell over the audience. "Before I tell you who triumphed, here's how we decided..."

As Jo-Jo continued, Saul and Sadie looked deep into each other's eyes. "I'm sorry for not helping on the project," Sadie said softly. Saul replied with a kiss on the tip of her nose.

"To avoid influence by the tricks some writers used, like colored paper or pictures drawn around words, or even by the name of the author, the Spidar women retyped the lyrics on plain white paper. Each entry received a number, no name. The original was filed away. Then the duplicates were distributed. The men graded each one, based on originality, depth of thought, and relevance to the theme. Peggy tallied the scores. Thousands of entries were reduced to the top ten. These were reevaluated and sung to Sadie's tune.... And one delivered the goods best..." Jo-Jo said. "I remind you that we had no names on the entries when we received them."

Sadie grabbed Saul's microphone. "Jo-Jo, you have our attention, for goodness sakes! Who's the winner?"

His smile broadened. "As it happens, the champ is Al Dukes."

"The Al Dukes I know?" Sadie asked Saul. He nodded. She squealed. "Can he sing it with you?"

Saul kissed her forehead. "If you sing too."

Sadie's face contorted. "I don't know the words. How could I possibly..."

"Here's the embryo," Jo-Jo interrupted.

Sadie took the paper and read it. Al's original entry was hand-written on spiral notebook paper. "I like it," she said.

She studied the audience. Al was out there somewhere. She had seen him earlier, during her time in the crowd. She found his seat, still occupied. "Come on up, Winner Al!" she said into the microphone. She watched Al hesitate and then shrug. He walked up the stage steps slowly.

"Will you sing with me?" Sadie whispered as the Spidars began to play.

"I can't sing," he replied.

Sadie smiled and held his hand. "With your beautiful deep bass, you only need to speak the words. Please? The writer can sometimes put more feeling into a song."

Reluctantly, Al agreed. They both stepped to Saul's microphone. Saul moved to share Jo-Jo's mic.

"Love... love... love... lover
Love... love... love... lover
I look high above
On the wings, on a king
Fits like a glove
Your love is all I need."

Sadie nodded. She had been right. Al's voice filled the air with a rich, low tone that made any words sound good.

Peace... please... peace... please
Peace... please... peace... please
Your love gives a new lease
In the home, in the bone
Makes life increase
Your love is all I need.
A friend loves a friend;
A woman loves her man.
Peace comes in the end.

Sadie glanced back at Saul, who winked at her.

Calm... calm... calm... calmer
Calm... calm... calm downer.
When I have qualms
In a crush, in the mush
Your love is like Mom's
Your love is all I need.

Sadie smiled at Al.

Peace comes on the wings of a dove

362

Yeah, peace comes from God's love...
Peace... Love...Peace... Love..."[37]

When the song ended, Sadie curled her finger in a motion which told Al to bend down. She caressed his face with her hands and kissed his forehead. "It's beautiful."

"And now if our sexy sweetheart will return," Jo- Jo said, "We'll close the show."

Sadie walked Al to the stairs and returned to Saul. As the Spidars sang, she stood behind Saul, running her fingers up and down his back.

"...We're going home..."[38]

Saul unhooked his guitar quickly for the final time tonight. He held Sadie for a moment and then escorted her off the stage, with the screaming audience in the background. The other three men joined their women in the wings, and followed the McCarthys.

The hall manager waited for them. "Reporters are going crazy," he said to Saul and Sadie. "You two are the main subject of their questions. Could you give them five minutes before they tear the place apart?"

Sadie looked at Saul, who nodded. They went into the reporter's room and stepped to the podium, inseparable. The other Spidars stood behind the couple. Questions flew immediately: "Sadie, can we presume, from your appearance today, that you and Saul are getting back together?"

Sadie replied with forethought, "Tonight shows that I wish Harry many more happy years."

"And your birthday is in February, too? How old are you?"

"I'm older than my kids," she said with a contented smile. After answering more questions with non-answers, she looked around. "Hey, how about talking to Harry. It's his birthday celebration too."

"Fine," another reporter said. "Harry, tonight you looked quite pleased to see Sadie. On stage you could have been the estranged husband. What kind of relationship do you have with her, and how do you feel about Sadie and Saul getting back together?"

Harry stepped to the podium and flashed a dazzling smile. "We're as close as the hairs on your head. We've all missed Sadie very much. Wouldn't you?"

Sadie stepped up again. "Now it's my turn to ask Harry something," she said loudly. Harry gave her a don't-you-dare look.

She jerked her head and smirked. "You reporters forgot to ask him: How does it feel to be an old man?!" She giggled and dashed out the door. Harry ran after her. The rest of the family followed at a normal pace.

Pam Hope chuckled amidst the babble of excitement. "What was that about?" one reporter yelled. Pam stepped to the podium, waving her arms to quiet everyone. "From my experience with Sadie, that was her way of saying the interview is over. They agreed to five minutes and that's what they gave us." Pam walked away with a gleam in her eyes. There would be a good story for her tomorrow.

In the hallway, Sadie ran fifty feet in front of Harry. She turned down a corridor toward an exit door, which she had closed by the time Harry reached the corner. He darted to catch up. Outside, in a guarded carport, Harry saw a rented limousine waiting with Joshua in the driver's seat. The passenger door was open. Harry advanced slowly, his arms poised in front, ready to grab if she jumped out at him. He moved closer and closer.

When he reached the limo, he stuck his head inside. Nothing. Empty. Behind him, a door squeaked and Sadie giggled. He turned around. "Did you lose something?" she asked with feigned innocence. She slipped inside the building and closed the door. At the first bend, she met the others. As she snuggled into one of Saul's arms, Harry rushed through the door.

"You've got the wrong end of the stick, mate," Rich teased. "The gig's over, so we head out." Martha and Peggy laughed.

Harry glanced at Sadie, then at Saul's enveloping arm. "Let me have her for five minutes," he said to Saul. "I'll show her who's NOT an old man."

"Nope. You had your chance. Now she's mine."

"You'll get yours yet, Pet," Harry said to Sadie. "When you least expect it, you'll get yours."

Rich rubbed his chin. "Seems I've heard that one before."

While the others climbed into the back seat, Peggy sat in the front. Sadie handed a piece of paper through the open inside window. Peggy reached for it. "Give these directions to Joshua, please," Sadie said. "It's the quickest way to my house from here."

Saul shook his head at Peggy. She nodded to say she understood his message and closed the window between the front and back.

With the limousine moving, Sadie rested her head on Saul's shoulder and closed her eyes. The animated voices in the car faded as her mind wandered to earlier days. She rode for a long time in silence. When she opened her eyes again, she glanced out the window. Suddenly, she reached over Saul and picked up the phone. "Josh, you missed the turn."

"Sorry," he replied. "You'll have to speak to Mrs. George. She's directing me." Joshua handed the receiver to Peggy. "Sadie says we missed a turn.

Peggy smiled as she took the phone. "Yes, Sadie? Uh, Sadie... Are you there?" She turned in her seat and nodded. Saul was laying the phone in its cradle, while keeping Sadie's lips busy elsewhere. Peggy faced forward again. "We're right on course."

As the kiss lingered, Saul's arm went under Sadie's knees. Together with the one around her shoulder, he pulled her onto his lap, her back to the others. Their lips parted. "You can't go so soon," he said. "I need you."

"But..." Another kiss, more urgent this time, intruded. Something hard pressed against her thigh. Her body tingled.

His hand began to unbutton her turtleneck sweater. "It's been over two months, Luv. How much longer do I wait?"

Sadie caressed his face. "I'm sure Peg and the others take good care of you."

"It's not the same." He finished her buttons and slid his hand along bare skin. "I'm used to sparks. You've spoiled me for anyone else. Come home. You've punished me enough."

Sadie twirled his hair in her fingers. "I'm not doing this as punishment. I love you."

"If you loved me so much, you'd come home."

You don't realize how much I want to, she thought. "When the time is right," she said aloud. "I'll be home in a flash."

"You're staying with me tonight," he commanded.

Sadie blinked her eyelashes at him and laid her head on his shoulder again. It wouldn't hurt to enjoy the whole evening.

Joshua drove to the kitchen door. Saul and Sadie didn't move, as if neither noticed. Out climbed Rich, Martha, Jo-Jo, Miki, and Peggy.

When it was Harry's turn to exit, he grabbed Sadie's arm and pulled firmly. "Come on, birthday girl. It's time to party."

He had caught her off-guard. As she fell toward the floor, her shirt opened to reveal velvety skin. His hand glided up her side as he caught her. Turning to Saul, he spoke again, "It's my natal day celebration, Matey. Can I borrow Sadie for a while?"

Saul reached over and clasped one of her arms. "Not tonight, chap. I need her myself."

Harry winked at Saul and put Sadie's free hand between his legs. "We could do it the way we did before there were enough birds to go around. I'll take her hands."

Sadie tried to pull her hand away from his growing appendage. Harry held firm and smiled at her. Her eyes misted.

"What's the matter, Pet?" His gaze moved down to the hand he held. Her wrist was red. "Sorry, Pet. I got carried away." He kissed her wrist, but she didn't respond.

When Saul reached over and touched her face, though, Harry felt her hand tremble with excitement, her eyes regaining their twinkling aura. With that, he suggested, "Perhaps you two should pause upstairs before the party."

"Quite right, Mate," Saul replied.

*

Saul had already released his third shot. He fell onto his side next to Sadie. "Ah! You haven't lost your touch," he sighed, as Sadie drew pictures on his chest. After resting a moment, Saul tilted his lips. "Give some more of your magic, Luv. I have a lot of idlety to make up."

Sadie continued drawing on his chest. "I haven't used my powers for sex since the quads were born."

"Gas and gaiters, girl! There's no way I could've knocked off three times in five minutes if you didn't use your powers. And I can already feel my strength loading for another round."

Sadie looked into his eyes seriously. "I have not used any powers tonight."

"Then how would you read between the lines?"

"I don't know. Something like Pavlov's dogs – a conditioned response. Your body is used to responding in a certain way to my touch, so it creates extra hormones on its own." Her hand roamed to his rising soldier.

"Yeah sure," he said. "Roll over. You're getting sloppy. Perhaps this other way, you'll be tight, like when we first met."

"I don't like..." she began. Too late. He had pushed her over and filled her narrow channel. A hushed whimper escaped.

"My little whore," he said. "You enjoy the control you have over the men in this family. You use it every chance you get..." Saul's voice faded as he concentrated his gentle thrusts. When it was over, he lay on the bed, exhausted. "Admit it, Luv," he whispered, "you relish having a bit of an in-and-out with me."

Silence.

"Aye, perchance you didn't delight in the last one. You must admit, though, you use your powers as aphrodisiacs when you're kindled. Luvey?"

She silently pulled away, stood with her back to him, and walked to the bathroom.

"Oh-oh," he said, "My angel's ears don't flap for the truth."

When he rose to clean up, he saw a wet spot on her pillow. He stared at it and strolled to the bathroom. Opening the door, he took a few cautious steps and opened the shower curtain. Sadie was scrubbing vigorously. He reached over and grabbed her hands. "Ease up, Luv. You'll take the skin off."

She looked away as he climbed in and pulled her close. "Sorry," he said, "I know you don't like it in the Khyber pass. Say something, will ya?"

Silence.

"If you're trying to make me feel tatty, it's working. Look here. Don't put the shutters up."

"There's nothing to say," Sadie whispered.

"Wait a tick! It's not all my fault. Your powers drive me mad. Did you transfer too much energy during copulation?"

"I didn't lie," she said, staring at the floor of the tub. "I haven't used those powers in a long time."

Saul lifted her chin. "Then why do you get that twinkle in your eyes a mere moment before I felt the urge rise in me?" Silence. A renewed stream of tears flowed down her cheeks. "What's bloody wrong? Sadie? Damn it, Luv. Perchance, if you'd turn human for a while, things could improve. I get pooped trying to guess what's on your flippin' mind!"

Sadie mumbled something.

"Say what? I didn't latch on." Silence. "Sadie, I said I couldn't understand you. Tell me what's giving you the abdabs."

Silence.

"Like it or not, Luv," Saul yelled, "I'm still your bloody husband and I DEMAND an answer!" Immediately, he regretted his volume. He held her close, her head on his chest. "Please," he added quietly.

"Okay," she said. "I love when you hold me close. And yes, I enjoy your warm juices filling me. Maybe deep inside, I am a whore like you say, but..." Her tears flowed again.

"But what?" Saul asked, as he smoothed her wet hair.

She paused longer. "But it hurts when you don't believe what I say. I've never lied to you. Sometimes I avoid certain subjects, but I've never lied. "

The pulsating spray massaged their bodies. He kissed the top of her head. "Luv, you're not a whore for takin care of your husband's needs."

Minutes later, in the bedroom once more, Saul's hands glided down Sadie's bare neck and shoulder. "How about wearing something quite comfortable?"

Her eyes sparkled. "Not if we're going downstairs."

"This may be appropriate." He handed her a brightly wrapped box. "Happy birthday, a little ahead of time – or a lot late, considering past years."

Sadie sat on the edge of the bed and opened the package. Inside was a pink-lilac silk jumpsuit. It had a dual front neckline, a high collar and a large scooped out semicircle that exposed cleavage. An embroidered belt accented the tailored waistline.

Sadie beamed and slipped into it. "It's beautiful! Thank you." She put her arms around him and kissed his cheek.

"My pleasure," he replied. His hands roved over the slippery-smooth surface. "Now you feel as good with clothes on as you do without them – well, almost."

While Saul dressed in a t-shirt and jeans, Sadie left the room, purse hung from her arm, an envelope in her fingers. "I'll be right back... An errand for a friend." She returned in a minute. Saul was ready. Hand-in-hand, they walked downstairs.

"Oo-la-la!" Rich exclaimed. "We're fit for a night of fun, I see!"

Sadie smirked. "I'm always ready for some fun."

Peggy set a tray of pretzels and chips on the coffee table. "Can I help?" Sadie asked but didn't wait for an answer. She broke away from Saul and trotted to the kitchen. Peggy followed. On the counter sat the preparations for a small party: ice cream, popcorn, assorted candies, carbonated beverages, and scotch. Martha stood at one end of the counter, frowning into a large open box.

Sadie walked over and peeped inside. She laughed out loud when she saw a cake in the shape of a woman's chest. "Harry will love this, but something's missing."

"We know," Martha replied. "We can't seem to get anything the same color as a nipple."

370

Sadie smiled devilishly. "Do you want a virgin or a totty?'

"Let's try the virgin side of the fence for a change of pace," Peggy offered.

"Well, that's easy then." Sadie went to the basement and brought up a jar of light pink, sweet cherries she had canned the previous fall. She opened the jar and took two out, pressing each one into a breast just enough to have the frosting cover the bottom half of the cherry. Then she went to the refrigerator and took out a grape. She used the small brown pit as a birthmark, similar to Peggy's. Then she took a Twizzler out of the candy dish and carved it into a set of lips, before placing it on the side of the other breast. Pleased with her work, she stepped back.

"Why, Sadie!" Peg exclaimed. "You're a dirty old lady!" The women walked the box into the living room.

As Harry opened the box, a broad smile emerged on his face.

"So what is it?" Rich asked impatiently.

"My favorite thing to eat." Harry grabbed a cherry and popped it into his mouth.

"Now it looks lopsided," Peggy scolded. He grabbed the other cherry as she lifted the cake out of the box and put it on the table. "Even Steven now," he replied.

"I get the lips," Rich said quietly, "since I'm the only one who hasn't received my licorice panties yet. Hint. Hint." Sadie pretended not to hear. Or maybe she really didn't hear, since she was cuddled with Saul on one of the sofas.

After cake and ice cream, Jo-Jo suggested they go out dancing. While the others discussed the thought, Sadie looked at Saul wistfully. "Let's simply watch the telly," Saul suggested to the others, and pointed to Sadie. A twinkle in Sadie's eyes said she liked the idea.

Rich turned to a station that carried a Jerry Lewis comedy

movie. Sadie watched with her head on Saul's shoulder and his arm around her. When the movie ended, Sadie was fast asleep, her forehead resting against Saul's neck and her nose under his chin.

"She's the only bird I know who smiles in her sleep," Harry whispered.

"Yeah," Rich added. "She looks a bit like an angel."

"Perhaps she is."

"No, she isn't," Peggy replied, "She just seems like one when compared to other people we know."

"Don't start in tonight, Pet," Harry pleaded.

"I can't help it." She scowled in Saul's direction. "You treat her so rotten sometimes and she always comes back like a loyal puppy. I don't blame her for leaving."

"Never mind that," Harry said, trying to change the subject. "How will we get her upstairs without waking her?"

Saul shrugged. The men watched the late night news as Peggy, Miki, and Martha picked up the dishes. When some glasses clinked, Sadie woke. "Sorry," she said, rubbing her eyes. "I guess I'm not used to late hours anymore."

Martha raised an eyebrow in a knowing expression. The lateness of the hour hadn't caused Sadie to fall asleep, not boredom either. As the family climbed the stairs, Harry and Peggy led the way, with Saul and Sadie next, and the others following. Reaching the top, Harry turned to Sadie. "Thanks for the unexpected good fortune. It meant a lot to me."

Sadie giggled. "The whole thing was Peg's idea, not mine. You should thank her."

Harry squeezed his wife. "I'll thank her in private." The couple continued toward their room, just as Sadie reached Saul's room.

"And Happy Birthday, Old Man!" Sadie called out.

Harry turned quickly. "We're home now. I can show you who's not an old man!" He took a couple of quick steps toward her.

Too late. Sadie had already darted into Saul's room and locked the door. "Chicken!" Harry yelled.

"She gets your goat every time," Saul said with a smirk.

Harry squinted his eyelids. His dimples deepened. He motioned his intentions to the men and then disappeared into the next room, the one that belonged to the quads. The room was vacant at the moment... with an adjoining door, like the ones between some hotel rooms.

Inside Saul's bedroom, Sadie noticed the silence in the hallway and then heard a light knock on the door. "Let me in," Saul said.

"Is Harry gone?"

"I can't see him."

She unlocked the door and slowly opened it. Saul, Jo-Jo, and Rich stood with smirks plastered on their faces. "Hmmm, smells like a double-cross," she said. Arms snuck around her waist from the back, turning her quickly. She squealed.

"You forgot to lock the door to the quads' room," Harry said, "Now you'll get yours!" His lips pressed against hers as he pulled her torso tight to him. He kicked the door closed and walked her over to the bed. He was laying her on the bed gently when Saul opened the door.

"Sorry, mate," Saul said, "She's mine tonight."

Harry looked at Rich and Jo-Jo. "We should put it to a vote. Don't I deserve extra joviality while celebrating the date of my birth?"

Rich crossed his eyes and stuck out his tongue at Sadie. He'd vote for everyone to have a turn.

"Sadie should decide," Jo-Jo declared. "We're celebrating HER date of birth too, the first one we've proclaimed."

"That's not bloody cricket!" Harry exclaimed. "We all know what she'll choose."

"Thanks, Jo-Jo," Sadie said. She pushed Harry away and put her arms out to Saul. The others left the room.

Down the hall, Harry closed his bedroom door. The shower water pattered in the bathroom for a moment then stopped. An envelope lay on his pillow. HARRY – EYES ONLY said the message in Sadie's handwriting. He opened the envelope as Peggy walked into the room. Inside was a picture of Harry as a baby – naked and bending at the waist, with his buttocks in the air and him peeking through his legs. On the back of the photograph Sadie had written: YOU MAY BE AN OLD MAN, BUT YOU STILL HAVE SWEET CHEEKS! HAPPY BIRTHDAY! Peggy laughed behind him.

The next morning, Peggy rose with Amanda and went down to the kitchen. As she opened the door from the hall, she took a deep breath. Ahhhh, the aroma of freshly brewed coffee and strawberry/pineapple muffins! Sadie was sitting at the table, reading the paper and drinking a cup of coffee.

"Hi," Peggy said drowsily. "How long have you been up?"

"Long enough." Sadie rinsed out her cup and set it in the sink. She took the muffins out of the bottom oven and set them on a platter to cool. Then she poured a fresh cup of coffee and set it in front of Peggy. "I thought I'd give you a break from cooking. There's a quiche in the top oven. The timer will buzz when it's done." She grabbed her coat off a chair.

"Can't you stay for a while?" Peggy asked. "The men will expect to see you. I know Saul can be an SOB at times, but can't you stay and work it out? Last night, everyone was so happy."

Sadie studied Peggy's eyes and hesitated. "I have to leave," she finally said, "I know you don't understand. You have to trust me. This is better for all concerned."

"Can't you at least stay for breakfast with us?'

Sadie leaned over and clicked her tongue at Amanda. "It's tempting, Peg. But it's easier to leave before the men get up..." Her voice trailed off.

"Did something happen after we went to bed?"

Sadie came out of her reverie. "Uh, sorry, I was thinking. What did you say?"

"I asked if something happened after we went to bed," Peggy repeated, "and you can't change the subject this time. You looked so content last night. We all thought you'd stay."

"Uh, the night was very pleasant ... very pleasant ... We cuddled and fell asleep."

"Then why do you have to leave?" Peg asked. Martha walked into the kitchen and sat down, unnoticed.

"Peg, Saul has some things to work out. In a way, he has to find himself again." She paused to choose her words. "With me here, he can't do that."

"Why don't you have him move out, then? You need more room than he does, what with your kids and all. The rest of us could help with them as well as with finances."

Sadie put her hand on top of Peggy's. "I'm doing okay financially. My investments still pay off. I am also now a major stockholder in a local wine company. I probably shouldn't keep playing the stock market, out of fairness to others, but it gives me something to do."

"You likely still give at least half the profits to charity too."

Sadie giggled. "You know me too well."

"Yes, and you haven't answered my question. You go off on tangents when you don't want to answer something. How about Saul moving out?"

"No, Peg. Saul needs you. I can't help him, but the rest of you can."

"How would we help, if we even care to?"

Sadie sat on the edge of a chair. "First, you can get off his butt all the time about his relationship with me. I can take care of myself. Saul needs support. How would you feel if all your friends kept telling you you do things wrong with Harry?"

Peggy thought for a moment. "I'd go crazy. How?..."

"I know you, Peg. I'd like to think I know you as well as you know me, and you know me pretty well. Everyone needs acceptance. No one needs their past faults pointed out constantly. They need to have their good points noticed. Saul's no different. Instead of criticizing his errors, help him see his good choices. In fact, for a little while, it might be a good idea to practice what my mother used to tell me and my sister: 'If you can't find something nice to say, don't say anything at all.'"

Sadie looked up and noticed Martha at the other end of the table. "Oh, good morning! What are you doing up so early?"

Martha tried to force her eyes open the rest of the way. "Rich left our door ajar on purpose last night. We both woke to a delicious smell drifting up from here. I came down to help."

Peggy glanced at the hall door. "Oops! I forgot to close the door when I came in. Sorry."

"No problem," Martha replied. "It smells good. Rich is getting dressed. I tapped on Jo-Jo's door, so he and Miki should be down soon too. It's nice not to cook."

Sadie jumped out of the chair. "Peg, remember what I said. Explain it to the others when Saul isn't around. Give him lots of love and you'll help him find his true and better self." She pointed to the clock on the wall. "My babysitters, Karen and Izzy, are probably going crazy by now. I'd better go."

Chapter 24 – June Reunion
Part A

White clouds at sunrise, like puffs of smoke-signals on an orange horizon, and blue sky overhead started this June day with beauty and improved from there. Saul hadn't noticed, though. The family had coaxed him to the pool, where he sat in his chair, staring at everything and nothing. His mind was five miles away.

"This is your birthday, Mate," Rich said from the edge of the pool. "You're supposed to be happy."

Saul replied in a low monotone: "There's only one thing that would make me happy today… and SHE'S not here."

Rich waved his arm toward the pool. "For the present moment, you have your choice of ours, or all of them if you're so inclined."

"No thanks."

Peggy climbed out of the pool and sat next to him. "Saul, it won't do any good to mope around waiting for her. She'll come back when she's ready. Don't fret about it."

Saul shook his head. "She'll never come back. I was a rotter the last year. You never knew the half of it."

Peggy didn't answer. She had taken Sadie's advice and would continue to do so. Only positive thoughts got a voice.

"I was," Saul repeated, expecting a nasty reply.

"She'll be home soon."

"What about today? It's my birthday, and she hasn't even bothered to give a jingle. Perchance…" Saul bowed his head. "Perchance there's another man in her house, giving her other fish to fry. Perhaps she'll never come back. Perhaps... Oh squitters! Peg, you have to help me get her back. I love her!"

"I know, Saul. Sadie knows too. She didn't leave for someone else. Give her time to call. It's not even noon."

"I figured out my perplexity," Saul said, more to himself than to anyone else. "I was flippin' green about the gills. She gave me so much and I felt guilty. Instead of ripening my own contributions, I tried to destroy hers. The harder I tried to break her, the more love she gave and the more frenzied I became. Yet, she was the inspiration for our songs... a necessary weakness in our lives. I thought we couldn't write without her."

One by one the rest of the Spidar family gathered around Saul. "Now I know I don't need her for the work. I want her for me. Peg, I need a chance to show her I can change course. I can give her the love she wants so much. Now that I approve of myself, I can love her."

Peggy pecked a kiss on his forehead. "It sounds like you should talk to Sadie, not us. Why don't you call her?"

"What would we chat about?"

"Tell her what you just said," Rich offered.

Saul stared into the pool. "No. Whenever I hear her voice, I choke. I can't think straight, let alone get my tongue to work. If you think about the bawdy way I treated her, there's no doubt even Sadie would be hard-pressed to forgive all and try again. She'll never retrace her steps."

"I wouldn't bet on that," Martha said with a sly smile. Being the only person facing the open gate had some advantages. "I talked with her last Sunday at church. She admitted she's been planning and hoping to return all along. In fact, in February she was relieved we were all still here. She worried the rest of us would move out because of her departure."

"Why didn't she bop me on the nose back in February then to straighten me out so she could move in again?"

"That's not her style," Miki answered. "She doesn't force her wishes on oth…"

Before Miki could finish, Martha jumped backwards and a ball of ice-blue water descended on Saul. "Ee-e-e-i-i-i-!" Saul screamed as he jumped out of his chair, his eyes wide. A smile emerged quickly as he realized there was only one person known to use this sort of howdy-do. His heart beat wildly as he turned to the open northern gate. "Sadie!" he yelled.

"Nope, just me," answered Carol.

Saul's heart sank. "What the heck did you do that for?"

"Would you believe I tripped?'

"No. Try another one."

A familiar giggle came from behind. "Oh, stop being such a wet blanket – even if you ARE soaked."

Saul turned back to the pool. Sadie was standing on the diving board, removing her jean short-shorts and t-shirt to reveal a low-cut, one-piece bathing suit, with the base of the V at her naval. There was a twinkle in her eyes. "Ready to warm up a little, Sirs?" she asked as she poised to dive.

The men threw off their towels, jumped in, and gave chase. When they surfaced, Saul glared at the rest of the men. "If any of you so much as touch her, you're dog food!"

"All's fair in love and war, Mate," Rich chuckled before going underwater to a better position.

The women on the deck laughed as Sadie evaded the men in her usual style. She swam along the bottom of the pool until she reached one of them. Then she rose, purposely brushed an arm or leg, and swam away with speed and grace.

After ten minutes, the men tired and stood in various places in the shallow end. However, Sadie was still swimming strong and true. She laughed at their huffing and puffing and teased a little more. "It seems to me you men are out of practice." She climbed out of the pool, spoke briefly to Peggy, and ran back to the diving board. "Should we begin again?"

"Start over?" Rich asked. "My energy is a might drained at present."

Saul nodded his head in agreement. He had been chasing her in high gear. Now, he'd be lucky to get out of the pool. He was smiling, though, as his eyes followed the gentle curves of her glistening body. He watched the sunshine reflect off the water droplets that blinked as they slid down tanned hills and valleys, gaining a delicate salty flavor for the tongue, until they landed in a clear puddle at her feet. He could almost taste them already. A quick movement later, Sadie was once again in the pool, swimming toward him. *No*, he decided, *I'll rest up a bit first*. He turned away from the action.

Soon, his peripheral vision caught Peggy handing a cigarette to someone beside him. "Excuse me, kind Sir," said a sweet voice obviously trying to disguise itself with huskiness. "Can you light my fire?"

Saul jerked sideways. Sadie was two feet from him. His heart pounded like tom-toms at a rain dance. He extended one arm. Half-expecting her to dart away, his smile broadened when she didn't. Instead, she allowed him to pull her to him and he enveloped her body with both arms. They stayed there, staring into each other's eyes.

Rich broke the spell with a splash. "You cheated, Honey-pot. You let him win."

She turned to him, eyes sparkling. "That is correct. All's fair in love and war."

"Where are the tots?" Harry asked as he swam up.

"They'll be along," she replied. "My babysitters – you remember Karen and Izzy Black from church – they'll bring the kids and the rest of our personal belongings in an hour. I loaded the van and their station wagon before I left. They let me drive their vehicle and they will drive mine." She turned back to Saul. "The new tenants move into my house tomorrow."

Saul's eyes lit up. "You're coming back to stay?!!"

"If you'll have me."

"The... the..." Saul stammered. She interrupted with a kiss.

"Now we'll return to normal," Harry said.

Rich smiled. "We're back to normal already. They can't hear a word we say – and won't until they've been to their room."

"Who says we need to go to our room?" Saul asked without taking his eyes off Sadie. "This seems as good a place as any."

"Everyone else out of the pool," Jo-Jo called from the deck.

"Sadie," Peggy said as Rich and Harry climbed out, "before you go to never-never land, can you answer a question?"

Sadie smiled, still watching Saul. "I know, Peg, the answer is yes. Saul, last weekend, when I picked up the kids, I could sense you wanted to talk but were afraid of something. So I read your thoughts. I swear that was the first and only time I read your thoughts since Christmas. Really... Truly... First time... Only time... Anyways, I knew then that it would only be a few more days until I could come home again. So, I let Salvation Army know that my house would be available very soon. Saul, I've missed you terribly."

Saul's fingertips outlined her lips. "Why didn't you come home last week, then, if you knew what I was pondering?"

"You still had a few things to work out."

"He told me this morning," Peggy confirmed to the other Spidars. "And I called Sadie to tell her."

Sadie opened her mouth to speak, but Saul shook his head. "There's more," he said to the others, "Besides getting rid of false notions, I've also realized Sadie and I were bound to have more nettles to grasp than hum-drum pairs."

"Yeah," Harry agreed, with a wink toward Sadie, "because of her knee-trembling skills."

"Not only that. We would've had extra vexation even without the sexual adventures. Think about your own hook-ups. You've been able to know each other without tinies involved. Sadie and I haven't. Other than the brief encounter eight months before, she and I were alien to each other when the triplets were born. It would make hard cheddar for any couple when tots come along too quickly, especially three at once."

Sadie nodded. Saul continued, "Whenever Sadie didn't do my every whim, I thought it meant she didn't love me enough. I considered her compromises as assaults on me. I was wrong. Even though she's youthful, she knows the difference between love and worship." He ran his fingers through her hair. "Sadie?"

"Yes, Hon?"

"I love you."

"I love you too."

"Here we go again," Rich said with a chuckle.

After an extended kiss, Saul turned to Peggy. "Peg, I know I told you earlier that I didn't want any fuss for my birthday. However, could you ring up a caterer and have a real blowout today?"

Peggy nodded.

"You don't need a caterer," Sadie said to him.

"Yes, we do. You're not sweating today… unless it's in my arms."

She smiled. "I'm yours forever, but the birthday party's already planned. Joshua will cook lobster and clams on the fire pit. Carol will take care of corn on the cob and salt potatoes. I made salads and other things last night. We'll have an American-style clambake, if you don't mind."

"I won't mind anything, as long as you're now home for good," Saul replied. "How about inviting your mates, the tot-sitters, to stay?"

"I was hoping you wouldn't mind them. Izzy's husband is bringing their children in their second car. We will have plenty of food. I didn't know how many people would be here, so I planned on sixty people when I bought supplies and made the salads and what-nots."

"I didn't want other mates around," Saul said quietly, "I wanted you." He began to stroke her exposed skin, as if to say there had been enough talking. Peggy called Jerry from the pool phone to have him turn off the cameras around the pool. The rest of the family left, some with soldiers at attention.

Saul and Sadie made love in the pool and then moved to the diving board. A short sprint away, they enjoyed it in the middle of the orchard, then back to the children's sand box. They laughed as they stood up from the last one. They both looked like they had been breaded and were now ready for the oven. They brushed each other off as best they could then walked under the outside shower to get rid of the rest before jumping back into the pool for another round.

This time, Saul's heart and mind wanted to do it, but his body lacked the energy. His eyes pleaded with Sadie. She hesitated a few moments. Finally, she put her fingertips on his temples and his body responded accordingly.

Afterwards, they lay together on a single lounge chair in their shorts and t-shirts. Sadie's mind was a million miles away... and as close as her skin. It had been too long. She had been away from the tender touch, warm embrace, and spark-filled kisses far too long.

"The tinies are here," Saul stated suddenly.

Sadie bolted upright and blushed. "Whew! I forgot about them. There's a first for everything, I guess."

*

Picnic tables made a U shape between the house and pool. The sixteen Spidar family members sat along the outside of the U, with Saul and Sadie in the center. The inside area of the tables were filled with the seven members of the Black family, as well as Joshua, Carol, Gene, and Mary. Reverend Bee had been invited but he was indisposed.

At the end of the meal, Saul stood. "I'd like to thank all of you for coming. I'd also like to propose a toast to the one who made this day so enjoyable and special." He kissed Sadie on the forehead.

Peggy took a sip of her champagne and walked to the front porch. She returned carrying a brown bag. She stood beside Sadie, reached into the bag, and pulled out a jeweled, gold crown. "For those of you who don't know what this is," Peggy explained, "this was my first Christmas present from Sadie. She said it was a symbol of my role as the queen of Harry's life. I'm giving it back to her today. She's the queen of the whole Spidar family. No one takes care of us like she does."

The Spidar men chuckled. Peggy positioned the crown on Sadie's head. A glow seemed to appear from both the crown and her head, despite the shade from a large maple tree.

Sadie smiled and hugged Peggy. "You did fine when you were in charge," she whispered in Peg's ear, "You just needed to believe in yourself."

"I still prefer to have you on the job."

Sadie looked around the table. Each Spidar adult had taken charge of one child. *We really are one big, happy family*, she thought, *a perfect picture – except for Jo-Jo and Miki.* Though they were quite busy with Carl and Vera, the couple's faces showed signs of turmoil. Sadie remembered another time she had seen that look. Waiting for them to talk didn't help then, and it probably wouldn't help now either.

"I guess this makes the children princes and princesses..." Sadie said cheerfully, as she sent Miki a mental message. No one suspected. Miki rose from the table and walked over as Sadie continued. "...They will someday grow and begin their own kingdoms. Is that a new frock, Miki?" she asked when Miki stood nearby. "It looks quite soft." Sadie's hands glided over Miki's waist, and then she looked into Miki's eyes and communicated with her mind.

"Thank you," Miki said aloud, a brilliant smile replacing the worried look.

Sadie turned and lifted her glass. "Now it's my turn to make a toast, if it is okay with Miki." Miki nodded. "I'd like to wish Miki an easy labor for the healthy baby inside her belly now." Jo-Jo suddenly beamed as his earlier doubts evaporated.

"What?!!!" came simultaneous exclamations from the others.

"Jo-Jo, you sly devil!"

"Alri-i-ight!"

"Why didn't you tell us?"

Then a quiet voice silenced the group. "Leave it to Sadie."

"What do you mean, Peg" Saul asked.

Peggy shook her head. "Jo-Jo and Miki must have known for some time now. They kept the secret from us. Then, as soon as Sadie gets back, she knows. She knows everything."

"Not exactly," Rich chuckled. "I have a concealment of my own, about which Sadie knows nothing." He glanced at Martha, who nodded.

"Wanna bet?" Sadie asked with a smirk.

Rich shied back. "I guess not. You cheat."

"No, Rich. I don't need to read your minds on this one. I can see the way you tend the kids more than normal. Would you care to make the announcement? Or shall I do it, as the royal buttinski… er, proclaimer."

"Your highness may do it."

"Great! We have more good news today!" Sadie picked up her glass. "Our 'sexpert' is trading in his fast car… trading up for a horse. He's getting hitched so he can sire his own colts. I'd like to toast Rich and Martha's upcoming marriage…"

*

"Mummy, are we done?' Jason said as the meal finished. She nodded and ushered everyone into the den, where the children sang Spidars' lyrics, changed a bit to fit the occasion. "…The kiss our Daddy brings, he brings to me…"[40] The children were energized by their own performance. The adults were too.

Izzy invited the Spidars for her next Sunday dinner. Her sister's family, Annie and Alex Litte and their five children, would be there too. Sadie had already met the Litte family while dressed incognito, since Saul had the children that day. She was sure the Litte family could be trusted with her real identity, too, so she replied in the affirmative.

Part B

The Spidar family was excited as they went into town that Sunday. At the same time, Izzy Black was explaining to her sister's family that there would be additional guests, as well as who they would be.

"Fab!" teenage Sandy Litte exclaimed. "This won't be another boring dinner!"

"Sandy, apologize to your Aunt," Annie said, "That was rude."

Dinner went without a hitch. Afterward, the adults retired to the living room and sent the children to an adjoining den. Though reluctant, the teens went to the den too.

"...Dear Daddy, won't you come out to play...,"[41] The McCarthy children, joined by Amanda George, sang their repertoire acapella in the Black's den. The youngest five danced around and sang whatever they knew, and the older ones danced, bodies twisting, heads jerking, and lashes batting. The teens laughed and danced to the music. With the doors open between the rooms, the adults watched the show and laughed too.

Sadie squirmed in her seat. She motioned for Karen Black to come into the adult's room. "Karen, you don't have to let my kids monopolize everything. The others would probably like records for dancing."

"I have Spidar records I could put on."

Sadie swallowed hard. "Would you mind playing something else? The men, uh, the men get tired of their own songs after a while, though they certainly enjoy your appreciation."

Karen glanced around the room and shrugged, her reddish-brown hair flipping around her pixie face. She returned to the den and put a Monkees record on the stereo.

"Why'd you say that?" Peggy whispered to Sadie. "The men wouldn't complain."

"I know, but the teens seem nervous. Maybe if they can forget who we are, they'll enjoy the afternoon more."

In the den, the triplets began to imitate the way their mother did her exercises in the morning. Soon, the teens imitated the imitators. Sadie prickled to join the fun. When she could stand it no longer, she scratched the itch.

A short time later, Annie commented as Sadie danced in the den, "Sadie seems to really get into the music."

Peggy nodded. "Yes, and when she dances, men have been known to forget all else."

Rich snickered. "Sadie forgets at times too."

"Good idea," Saul mumbled. He walked into the den and spoke to Karen. When he returned, she was rummaging through her stack of records, pulling out a blue album called "British Gold." The other Spidars smiled at Saul. They knew what was coming.

Annie and Alex Litte and Izzy and Paul Black watched with curiosity as Karen left the room and returned with a large soup ladle. She handed the ladle to Sadie, said something, and pointed to Saul in the living room. Sadie giggled.

"Wild thing,..."[42] a song began. Sadie held the ladle near her mouth like a microphone. Her rich alto tone filled the air. "...shake it, wild thing..."[42] The teenagers in the den stood with their eyes open wide and mouths shaped in O formation. Like a night club performer, Sadie glided from male to male in the living room, lightly brushing her hand along a cheek or chin and combing her fingers through their hair. When the song ended, she jumped onto Saul's lap. "Is that what you wanted?" she asked. Saul smiled.

Peggy chuckled, but not at Sadie. The others followed her gaze.

"Alexander Litte!" Annie exclaimed. "Shame on you!"

Alex quickly crossed his legs and held his tea cup over the bulge in his pants, his cheeks a bit pink. The Spidars laughed.

"Don't fret, chap," Rich said. "Sadie does that to all the blokes whenever she sings that song. It's worse with another song, which we won't let her perform in public."

"I doubt it's the singing," Harry quipped.

Saul looked intently at the devilish angel on his lap. "Perchance, she'll turn a willing ear when I ask her to accompany us for a short tour of the Isles. We could make it a working holiday. The fans would love the way she does that song."

"What about the kids?" Sadie asked.

"Martha, Miki, and I can watch them at home," Peggy offered.

"You can't..." Sadie protested.

Saul put a finger on her lips. "Ponder a tick."

*

SPIDAR SPINS RIBBON INTO WEB
By Pam Hope, UPI

Rich Moon was wed in a private church ceremony in New York on Tuesday. Sadie McCarthy was Matron-of-Honor. Peggy George and Miki DeLime were bridesmaids. Moon's co-Spidars were Best Men who ushered guests. Only one reporter was allowed to witness the occasion with no pictures. This reporter almost fainted in her seat after being escorted down the aisle by a smiling Harry George.

The groom and his bride, Martha (maiden name withheld),

389

appeared in the back of the room on opposite sides. The eldest McCarthy children, Carl and Roxanne, handed Rich and Martha the ends of a wide, white ribbon.

As Sadie sang, "If Not For You," written for the occasion by another guest, Bob Dylan, Rich and Martha walked forward, raising the ribbon above the heads of the few seated guests. When they reached the front of the sanctuary, they lowered the ribbon and twirled toward each other, the ribbon winding around their waists.

Sadie McCarthy, spokesperson for the group, explained: "The ribbon signifies a binding love. The normal skirmishes of life may unravel the edges, but it will still hold them together."

The newlyweds plan a two week honeymoon to an undisclosed location. They will return before July 15th, when the Spidars are scheduled to begin a week-long tour of the British Isles. Sadie McCarthy will add her vocals to this tour.

Chapter 25 - England

"I have some errands to run," Sadie announced at the door of the Spidars' Chiltern Hills home. "I'll be back by suppertime."

"Why leave so early?" Saul asked as he checked the clock on the kitchen wall. "You should rest your oars or you'll burn out before tonight's performance." Outside the home, thick dew covered the lawn. Jo-Jo and Rich still slept, but Harry was trying to wake up with a second cup of coffee.

"I'll be okay," Sadie replied. "I just need to go out for a while."

"Don't do it, Luv," Saul warned.

"Do what?" Her face glowed with mock innocence.

Saul let out a sigh. "Don't go playing a stroke or sagging off now. The gig tonight was your whimsy, not ours. You and Mum planned the whole thing. Remember?"

Sadie smiled, adding a lilt to her voice. "I remember perfectly. All I said was I need to go out for a while. Geesh!"

After she left, Harry looked at Saul. "She's most likely a bit fagged. Being on the road's a rock to anyone."

"We're not in a hotel. We're home."

Harry shook his head. "To us, this is a second stall. Sadie's never been here. We bought this place after that skiing holiday years ago. And she didn't come with the other gals on their trip here."

"We don't need her getting antsy before a gig."

"She'll be rum. Ponder back to the first show a week ago. She was all of a tremble then and she soldiered on."

Saul let his mind drift back to London, the first show of this trip...

"If someone put a roof on this place, it could shelter all the poor people in England!" Sadie exclaimed when the Spidars arrived at Wembley Stadium. There was enough room for 90,000 people, nine times the amount of people allowed in Rochester's concert hall. "I think I'll pass on this one, if y'all don't mind."

"We do mind," Jo-Jo replied. "And knock off the southern belle act."

"Then maybe my performance could be first."

Rich shook his head, a smirk on his face. "Nope, yours is part of the encore. We need to build suspense."

By the mid-concert break, Sadie was pacing the floor. Her skin had turned pale. Her hands shook so much that cigarette ashes fell without flicking.

"A strong case of the collywobbles, I'd say," Saul mumbled. He cast suggestive looks around the room. The others nodded. Catching her arm, he squeezed gently. "We'll do your song next, if you'd like Luv." She shrugged.

"Come, Pet," Harry added, "Get yourself glammed up or you'll scare the buffs."

She placed a finger on her temple and her normal color returned, as well as the sparkle in her eyes. "Actually, that's not what I plan to do to the audience," she said.

Rich smirked. "We know."

*

In the week (six performances) that passed since the first show, Sadie became more daring. When Saul's mother suggested a charity concert to end the tour, Sadie agreed immediately and convinced the others to comply. Sadie talked to Ruth on the phone several times, and she always seemed in high spirits afterwards, though she wouldn't tell anyone why.

"I recognize the look of mischief," Harry said, sniffing the steam from his coffee. "We'd be wise to watch our brisket this eve."

The Spidars knew little about the concert, only bits of information. The show would consist of their normal repertoire at the Royal Shakespeare Theater in Stratford-Upon-Avon. The BBC paid to provide live coverage, and ABC would televise it in America next week. The ticket price was set at 250 pounds each. Due to Sadie's business acumen, the British Salvation Army would net over two million pounds – enough to put one extra toy into each poor child's Christmas basket around the country. That was all the men knew.

Sadie returned at suppertime as promised, carrying a bag from a local delicatessen. "You should probably eat light," she said. "You need to be at your peak tonight."

"Is that an excuse for not cooking?" Rich teased.

"That's right." Sadie strutted around the kitchen. "Stars don't have to do chores."

"Whoa!" Jo-Jo exclaimed. "Give the lady a week on tour and she thinks she's heavenly. I think we've created a monster – with wings."

After supper, everyone dressed and left for the theater. When the Spidars jaunted from the dressing room to the stage, Sadie bounced. "Oh, and I've flown Al Dukes from the States to sing his song while you play," she explained.

"What will be will be," Jo-Jo responded to her sly smile.

The men saw Al standing in the wing across the stage, deep in conversation with a stage hand and pointing at a series of ropes and switches. Harry waved to get his attention. "Your Love Is All I Need" was the first song on the schedule. After the song ended, Al lowered his microphone stand to the height of Sadie's instrument mic and put both of them on the side of the stage.

Because of earlier suspicions, the men weren't surprised during the third song when thousands of multi-colored balloons fell from the ceiling into the audience. They smiled, though, when hundreds of white ones toppled onto the stage moments later.

Jo-Jo caught one and studied it. The stage balloons had been imprinted with a Spidar family portrait at the pool in Canandaigua, as if emphasizing a desire to go home. Jo-Jo glanced at Sadie in the wings. She tilted her head and fluttered her eyelashes.

Sadie waited six more songs. She waited for a fast-paced song that included a drum solo in the middle, during which Rich always threw one drumstick in the air for added flair. The stick usually came down in time for him to continue without missing a major beat. This time, Sadie stood directly behind him, hidden by the curtain.

The audience quieted as a butterfly net appeared above Rich's head. Thinking the pranks were done, Rich was immersed in the beat. Drumming wasn't his middle name for nothing. He loved it. With his pride at its peak, he threw the drumstick higher than usual and took a moment to smile at the audience. That moment was all Sadie needed. She scooped the drumstick into the net and pulled it behind the curtain. By the time Rich looked upward, Sadie had closed the curtain.

The audience laughed.

Rich's face colored as he grabbed another stick from his emergency pouch. Attached to the end was a pair of candy pants. He turned plum and shook them off. As he began to play again, he cast furtive glances around the floor to find the stick that had fallen. That one was half of his lucky pair. The song ended and Rich jumped off his stool to look closer.

Unaware of what had happened, Jo-Jo shook his head at the audience and spoke into his microphone. *"Someone should inform Rich that we are Spidars. He looks more like a turtle, with his head bobbin' about and all."*

The audience broke out in fresh laughter as the butterfly net reappeared directly above Rich's head. It tipped upside down and deposited the stick in front of Rich. He poked his head through the curtain. "I owe you one... or more!"

Sadie giggled and ran to the wings again. The other three men chuckled as Saul introduced the next song. No, Sadie wasn't finished yet. When the song began, the instruments didn't transmit. Vocals and a far-away drum beat echoed off the walls. The men checked their lines. Yes, they were still connected.

Rich peeked behind the curtain. "The amps are unplugged." As Rich fixed the problem, Saul sauntered to the right wing, where Sadie and Ruth stood. "Mum, keep an eye on this fasher for me, will you?"

"A fasher?" Sadie asked, fluttering her eyelashes again. "Me?"

"Yes, you, Luv." He kissed her forehead and ambled back to his place on stage. The next few songs went smoothly. As each one passed without incident, the men's confidence grew. "Her trickery's dispatched," Jo-Jo whispered.

The others agreed until they felt a moving sensation at the beginning of a song. When they glanced toward Sadie, she shrugged her shoulders, trying to look innocent but not succeeding. The men continued to play as a large piece of their floor descended, taking them along with it. At the middle point of the song, the floor reversed its movement and had returned to its normal position by the end of the song. Saul again walked to the wings.

"She never left my side," his mother offered.

How can I argue with these two, he wondered. *The audience is eating it up.* He kissed both women on the cheek and retreated.

When the Spidars ran to the dressing room during intermission, Sadie was already there. "This is my bodyguard," she said, pointing to Al Dukes, who puffed out his chest. "Just think of him as a black Mo." Her mouth tipped up at the ends. "But he's here to protect me, not you."

"That's a dare, if my ears flap at all," Rich stated. He grabbed Sadie's arm. Al immediately moved to her aid and pinned Rich in a headlock. "Uncle! Aunt! Cousin!" Rich exclaimed. "I'll be a good boy. I won't tell anyone except my grandtikes. And Sadie can jump my bones as often as she wishes." Al released him when Sadie giggled. "And you are welcome to do so, Sadie," Rich added with a tilt of his eyebrows.

Returning to the stage, Harry accompanied Rich to the drums. "The best is yet to come, I suspect," he suggested.

Rich nodded, glancing toward Sadie. "Quite right."

During each song that followed, both men glanced around for another prank. They watched and waited. They waited and watched. They watched and watched. Soon, the only song left was Sadie's finale. There had been no more pranks, though this was the first time she agreed to have her song last. In the wings, Sadie was now hidden behind a piece of cloth held up by Ruth. The men couldn't see her or what she was doing.

Rich called the men into a fast huddle. "Now's the big one," he stated. "Are you prepared? Or would you like to..."

Sadie peeked out and saw Rich's mischievous grin as he began a strange drumbeat. They were trying to cancel her song! No Way! She hip-hopped onto the stage with a mic in her hand.

Rich stopped in mid-beat with his mouth in a wide Oh!

396

Behind Saul's mother, Sadie had massaged her scalp and now her shiny golden-brown hair fell in lustrous ringlets down the small of her back. She had also taken off her evening gown to reveal shimmering black tights and a glistening, black silk leotard, with a zipper in the back and silver sequins around all seamlines and on the belt.

All the Spidars stared for a moment. The audience silenced.

Sadie began a cappella. "… you make my heart sing…"[42] The Spidars caught up, but the audience remained quiet. She squiggled down the steps and wove her way through the aisles. Her hands caressed one man's face. Her fingers combed through a teenage boy's mop top. She curled the fuzz on a bald man's head. She sat on an older man's lap. She pecked the cheek of a bank clerk. She wiggled her hips at Prince Charles. "… Wild thing! …"[42]

She jumped up the steps and motioned for Al Dukes to join her on stage. Then she sang the last verse again while stroking his face, as she had done for some of the audience. At the end, she kissed his forehead. He walked off the stage as she bowed.

The curtains closed most of the way. The Spidars could only see her and the center of the audience. The men smiled as she continued bowing, her round buttocks held firm by the tights, sticking out at them. She put one hand behind her and wiggled her fingers. Rich did a quick drumroll in response.

Without warning, four muscular hands grabbed at her legs and arms. Her scream, amplified by the loudspeakers, boomed off the walls. Then the curtain slapped completely shut. The Spidars couldn't see anything.

"What the heck?" Saul exclaimed. He quickly unfastened his guitar. Zipper sounds came through the speakers.

Jo-Jo reached over and grabbed his arm. "Security will handle it."

"Stop, ple-e-ease!" Sadie's voice pleaded. Moaning and groaning followed.

"So where are the blue boys?" Saul yelled into his mic. The audience sounded like they were cheering for the strange men. "I don't like this," Saul mumbled. "There's no way a few guards can handle the whole crowd's mix-up."

"Open the bloody curtains!" Harry shouted to a stage hand and motioned for Al to come help.

"I can't," Al yelled back. "I'm under specific orders."

"What's that in aid of?" Saul screamed. "Did Sadie suspect this would happen?"

"I do not get involved." Al stared at his watch, as if timing something.

"If she knew, why would she..." Saul didn't finish. The curtain was opening. Two men stood with contented grins on their faces. Male moans and groans still came over the loud speaker, but Sadie's pleas had stopped. As the four Spidars ran toward the edge of the stage, black tights and a silk leotard flew into the air at them.

"Get away from my wife!" Saul shouted. Two other men stood up, microphones in their hands. Before he could wonder about the additional mics, he felt a tap on his shoulder. He turned quickly.

Fully clothed, Sadie smiled at him. "They're good actors, huh?" she said into her own mic and ran to the rope ladder Al lowered in the middle of the stage. The curtains closed slowly again as the ladder quickly raised Sadie away from the four Spidars rushing toward her. Applause mixed with laughter. The audience could hear Sadie say, "Give us a moment, folks." Then the microphones were turned off.

With the ladder too high to reach, Saul sat on the drum platform. Jo-Jo and Harry stood near him, hands in their hip pockets. Rich disappeared backstage. "You have to admit," Sadie hollered from the ladder, "the scene was convincing."

"It wasn't a bit droll," Saul pouted.

"Come on, Hon," Sadie cooed. "The audience found it funny, because they could see the men and me, as we made the sound effects. Years from now, you will think it was funny, too. I appreciate the fact you were so worried, but did you forget I could floor any of them with one touch?"

"You deserve a good cracking," he replied.

"On her bare arse," Harry added, "and I'm game to aid with it."

Sadie wiggled her index finger at him. "No way! I won't come down until all of you promise to be good."

"Don't promise a thing!" Rich yelled from a narrow walkway above the ladder. "She has to come down to you or up to me. Either way, we have her!"

"Not if I stay where I am," Sadie replied.

"That sounds like a challenge." Rich laughed as he began to climb down the ladder.

"You'll get hurt if we wrestle on this thing," she warned.

"Don't fight me then."

She motioned for Al to lower the ladder slowly. As arranged earlier he also opened the curtains and turned on the microphones. "Time for the second encore, guys," Sadie giggled. "You'll have to wait for my lacing."

"*...if I sing out of tune...*"[22] While the Spidars sang, Sadie set up two extra microphones nearby. One was at normal height and the other was at hip level. "*... with a little help from my friends...*"[22] Near the taller one, she waited for the men to finish.

"*I want to thank all of you for coming tonight,*" she said to the audience. "*You've been great! Many children will benefit from your help. Speaking of help, it's time for the Spidars to find some relief for their vocal chords. I want you to meet...*" She paused and waved her arm toward the left wing. "*...the whole Spidar family!*" Applause sounded.

"Daddy!" the quads and Amanda yelled as they ran out and exchanged hugs with Saul and Harry. Sadie dispersed them to their assigned positions: Amanda in front of Harry, Rita in front of Saul, Dave in front of Jo-Jo, Chuck on Rich's lap, Vera in front of Sadie.

Sadie waved again. The triplets entered, hugged the adults, and stood at the lower microphone. Martha, Miki, and Peggy followed, giving their respective husbands a quick kiss and joining Sadie at the taller mic.

"...Do you want to know a secret?..."[43] The audience laughed as the triplets imitated the men's gyrations, head jerks, and winks. Soon the women moved away from their mic and the young voices sang alone, "...whisper in your ear..."[43]

"So that's why!" Saul murmured as Sadie moved to his side.

"Why what?" she asked, proudly watching her offspring perform.

"Why you were gone the whole flippin' day." He pecked her cheek. "The tots were at my Mum's, weren't they?"

Sadie nodded.

Chapter 26 – Going Home

Sadie skipped up the steps to board the private jet that would take the Spidar family home to Rochester. Since the tour finished, they spent two days vacationing together in England, showing the children their British heritage, which satisfied Saul for the moment. Sadie sat across from the children and smiled at their exuberance. They were happy. The men were happy. The women were happy. She was happy, too.

Or was she? The plane engines came to life with a mighty roar. She sensed a black cloud close in on her. *This is stupid,* she thought as she surveyed the family again. *I'm always apprehensive before a flight. Knock it off, brain. You know perfectly well your childhood fall from that tree caused your fear of heights. You've conquered the stupid thing on the diving board and on the edge of the stage during performances. Now it's time for a conquest on a plane.*

It didn't work; the phobia didn't lessen. Instead, it exploded – literally. She visualized an explosion. She heard the bang and saw a large fireball consume her, its flames leaping high in the air, as if she stood outside her body and observed from a distance.

"What's the fret, Luv?" Saul asked from the next seat. "You're green about the gills. Are you under the weather?"

Sadie shuddered to snap out of it. "No, I just..." She halted when she noticed his worried expression. "Oh, never mind. My imagination goes haywire sometimes, that's all."

I'll be okay once we're in the air, she thought, *as long as we don't hit turbulence. Seven hours of flight. I can control my thoughts for that long. At least we're traveling at night, so I won't see the ground.*

As the plane began to taxi toward the runway, Sadie began a rhyming game with the children to get rid of the burning ball still blazing in one recess of her consciousness. As she played it with the triplets, the other women entertained the toddlers. The men remained silent.

"Fun," Sadie said.

"Done," Carl replied.

"High."

"Fly," Jason replied.

"Plane."

"Fire," Roxanne said with fear in her eyes.

"What?" Saul asked. "Roxie, fire doesn't rhyme with plane." Roxanne stared at her mother, whose eyes had glazed. The seatbelt sign came on, signaling a departure soon.

In her trance, Sadie allowed the scene to go further. An oblong object emerged as the fire smoldered. An ocean rippled in the distance, too far away to help. Over the water, another plane flew west. In front of the flaming inferno, a passenger train whizzed past.

She jumped up from her trance, paler than before. "Oh poop!" She ran to the front of the plane, beyond the curtains, into the cockpit. "Turn off the gas!" she screamed. "Turn off all the motors. NOW!"

The pilot hesitated. Sadie didn't explain. She darted to the instrument panel and flicked every knob. Then she turned to the pilot again. "Is the gas turned off?" she asked.

"I should think so," he huffed. "It was the first switch you touched. Do you realize there will now be a thirty-minute delay? We have to start from scratch."

Whew! That was too close for comfort, she thought. *I should've known by the visions' intensity that a simple phobia wouldn't cause it. A fear of heights doesn't create a monster fireball.* "We see what we want to see," Reverend Bee had once said. How true!

"This plane won't take off for a long time," she said aloud. "Radio for a mechanic to do a thorough inspection of the gas lines and engines right away." She turned to leave, but remembered something else. "Is there a commercial plane going to the States?"

The pilot glared at her in silence.

"Yes," the auburn-haired copilot replied. "In the pilot's lounge, a man said he was headed in the same direction. Flight 909, I think it was."

"Thanks. Can you radio and find out if it has room for us? Also, have someone check all outgoing passenger lists for a C. Train." Sadie returned to her seat and closed her eyes. The pilot huffed as he opened the exterior door and disappeared outside.

Martha unbuckled the children. As they played, the adults talked without disturbing Sadie, who was still quite pale.

"She scared me half to death with that scream," Peggy whispered. The others nodded.

Fifteen minutes later, the pilot returned, looking sheepish. He walked to Sadie and stopped. "How can she find the sandman this quickly?" he asked the others.

Saul answered. "She does this now and again. She goes into what she calls an 'alpha state' to compose herself. Why? What's coming about?"

"We were almost potted off." Jaws dropped. Sadie opened her eyes.

"Thank you," the pilot said to her, "I beg you to excuse my rudeness earlier. I thought you were daft. Instead, you were right on the mark. The gas line to engine three was jerry-rigged so more fumes would enter than gas. The cooling system was also plugged. Someone must have tampered with the cockpit gauges, too, or they would have registered the quick heat build-up in the engine. When the mechanic unhooked the gas lines, he could feel the heat of the fumes. He thinks they were within a few degrees of taking us to our maker. The bobbies have been alerted."

"Any news on the passenger lists of other flights?"

"Alan's checking on it."

As if on cue, the copilot emerged from behind the curtain. "There's no C. Train on the passenger lists. You can board flight 909 to America as long as you're quick about it. They were scheduled to take off before us but were delayed with some minor problems. They can only hold the plane for a few more minutes unless there's a real emergency."

"This is real," Sadie said. "Did you check for different spellings of Train?"

"Yes, there's no listing that even comes close."

"There must be." Sadie studied the pilot's face. "Was there anything suspicious when you inspected the gas lines?"

"As a fact, 'C.L. 909' was written in the dust near the gas tank, but that won't help you. If it had anything to do with that other plane, it would say 'B.A. 909 for British Airways. C.L. means nothing. There's no such airline using this port."

Sadie closed her eyes again. Moments passed.

"C.L... That's it!" She exclaimed as her eyes shot open. "It was locomotive, not train!" She turned to the copilot. "Try C. Loco, or anything similar. He's on flight 909. Don't let it take off."

The copilot hurried to the cockpit. A minute later, he returned. "Yes, there's a Carlisle Lacoma registered on Flight 909 to New York! The take-off has been stopped indefinitely."

404

"Good. Make sure they don't alarm the guy yet, or someone else's life may be endangered. Hopefully, we've been quick enough that he may not be suspicious. He planned to be in the air before the explosion. As long as he doesn't see our plane take off, he may not notice the time. I'll meet the police near his plane."

She turned to the pilot. "Tell the mechanic to get away from the tank. The police will need to test for fingerprints."

The copilot walked to the cockpit and the pilot went outside. Sadie stood. "Peg, can you handle things here? I need to take care of a few things before we can transfer."

"Me?" Peg asked. "My nerves are shot."

"Yes, you. Keep everyone calm. Don't let anyone leave the plane until I make sure the man doesn't have an accomplice with a gun or something."

The police took the suspect into custody without incident. They escorted him off the plane and down the stairs, where Sadie stood. Hatred dripped from Lacoma's shining black eyes.

"Why did you do it?" she asked, as a chill went up her spine.

"Who says I did anything?"

Sadie didn't move. She stared at him without blinking.

"You can't prove a thing," the man yelled, "you nigger-lover!"

"Was that your reason for trying to kill sixteen people... eighteen people counting the pilot and copilot?"

The man slouched as if bored.

How could anyone be filled with that much hatred for a stranger?" Sadie wondered. *How could this happen when "Your Love Is All I Need" had been sung? Is the song losing its calming effect? Are the vocals disturbing it?*

Sadie roamed the man's memory and shook her head. There was nothing she could do to prevent a recurrence of this in the future. Lacoma had turned on his hotel television towards the end of the concert. He missed the calming song, he missed the other songs, and he missed Sadie's trip through the audience. He did see her stroke Al's face and the thank-you peck on his forehead. Upset, the man turned the television off and even missed the children's performance.

"Jesus was not white, you know," she said.

"He most certainly wasn't black," Lacoma spat.

"You're correct. He was more of a dark tan, like a mixed breed..." Sadie stopped short. Arguing would not help. Some people just reject common sense.

As police escorted Lacoma away, Sadie motioned an okay to her family's plane. Then she glanced toward the terminal building. Pam Hope was waving at her. Sadie walked over.

*

COLOR BLINDNESS NEARLY CAUSES DEATH OF SPIDARS
By Pam Hope, UPI

Sadie McCarthy kissed a black man's forehead on stage during the final show of the Spidars' British tour. Someone didn't like it. The jet scheduled to take the Spidar family back to the United States was altered to explode once airborne.

Police have taken a suspect, Carlisle Lacoma, into custody. Until recently, Lacoma was employed at the airport as a mechanic. "We have a tight case already," said Sergeant Pepper, the local constable. He would not comment further.

Although the attempt failed, Lacoma will get a minimum of twenty-five years if found guilty. This is because the case involves a national shrine – the Spidars.

Minutes after the incident, Mrs. McCarthy joked about the irony of Lacoma's methods. "I've always had a fear of heights. If the plane had exploded in the air, whenever the stars twinkled at night like diamonds, they would haunt my mother. She was always scolding me about irrational fears."

When questioned about the color issue, McCarthy was more serious. "Some people can't understand that we need each other in this world. How would Bach sound on a piano with just white keys? How would a fruit salad taste with just green grapes – no bananas, strawberries, or watermelon? Boring!!!"

Chapter 27 – October 1969

October in upstate New York brings cool temperatures, brisk winds, and rain – lots of rain, as if the angels are sad to see the summer go. Then the sun peeks through the clouds, warming the earth and spotlighting the orange, yellow, and red leaves of Indian summer. Another chance.

On this October day, the temperatures climbed to a bright 72 degrees. In sunny spirits, the Spidars rode to a concert to introduce their latest record to American fans. Shriner's Hall was again set up so people could dance. Sadie joined the dancers early in the show. Karen Black was there. Al Dukes was too. The children were at home with Carol and Izzy. As the Spidars rocked and rolled their way deeper into American hearts, young and old alike, an ABC camera crew taped the concert for broadcast at a later date. It would also be sent to England's BBC.

Midway through the concert, Rich jumped down from his platform and meandered to centerstage with a mischievous grin on his face and a briefcase in his hand. *"We're taking a break,"* he said into Saul's microphone as he set the briefcase down. *"Perhaps you can convince our sexy lady to entertain you while we're gone."* The audience applauded.

Still on the dance floor, Sadie shook her head and aimed her feet toward the door. When a group of men blocked that exit, she turned to go out a different way. Another group blocked that passage. One by one, each outlet was blocked. She jumped on the stage, smiled, and walked toward the wings. Boos and catcalls followed her. Al Dukes catapulted himself onto the stage. "You can't ignore them, Ma'am."

"Yes, I can, Al. I hung up my performing hat a month ago. My life belongs to my family now."

"Good. We're all family here, a family of Spidar fans."

Sadie hesitated and then giggled. "Oh, all right, if you put it that way." Her eyes twinkled. "And if you help." She didn't wait for an answer. She grabbed the briefcase near Saul's microphone and waved to quiet the audience. *"Since the TV cameras are off and will stay off during the break, Al and I will sing a few songs that haven't been recorded yet. You can keep the secret, can't you?"* The audience clapped.

A song Saul titled "Black and White" contained two races living together in harmony. Al sang bass and Sadie sang alto a cappella. The next one, written by Harry and still untitled, sang of bright days with persistent love toward others.

After those, Sadie pulled out a poem she had written and spoke into the microphone, *"The first two songs gave possible solutions to some problems we face today. This next one has no answers, just questions to ponder. There's no music yet. I'll read it and Al can add rhythm with his hands.*

"Today, a baby isn't always planned.
Trouble comes, because abortion is banned
But that little baby who wasn't supposed to be
Is saying: Please don't abandon me.
Because parents can give a child away
As if she doesn't have any say
A man can leave his family
As long as he pays the Agency.
   How can that be right?
   Can you give me a clue?
   Isn't there something we can do?

Now if we streak on the beach, we're much too loose
Have kinky sex, we get the noose
Our personal habits keep law makers busy
Mention children's rights, politicians get dizzy.
Because parents can give a child away
As if he doesn't have any say
A man can leave his family
As long as he pays the Agency.
    How can that be right?
     Can you give me a clue?
     Isn't there something we can do?
What will life be like many years from now?
Will private lives still be congressmen's chow?
What will the future hold in store?
Will children still be in a tug-of-war?
Will people still be asking?
    How can that be right?
    Can you give me a clue?
    Isn't there something we can do?
    How can that be right?
    Can you give me a clue?
    Isn't there something... we can do?
    Isn't there something?..." [47]

The audience chanted the last lines with her. Sadie smiled. She was also pleased when the Spidars returned so she could resume her play on the dance floor.

The concert was scheduled to end at ten o'clock, but no one was ready to call it a night. What would normally be a five or ten minute encore extended another hour. The television set in the Spidars' dressing room was broadcasting the eleven o'clock news as they donned street clothes.

Suddenly, the news was interrupted by a low-pitched tone and wavy lines. Saul walked over to shut off the set.

"Not yet, Saul," Peggy said, motioning towards Sadie's strange appearance, similar to a trance but deeper. The others quieted as her eyes reflected the erratic lines on the television.

"Listen," Miki whispered. "Can you hear it? That hum sounds like an alien language." The hum stopped. The lines disappeared. The picture showed an empty desk where the news anchor should sit.

"It's time," Sadie said as she came out of her trance. She marched to a window, opened it, and stretched out her arms, fingers pointed toward the sky. She stared at her hands like a quadriplegic trying to move them. When she extended her arms again, a bolt of lightning flashed, followed by a crash of thunder. Another crash sounded, this time as a brilliant light appeared in the sky.

"*Sorry folks,*" the anchorman said, now back at his desk in front of the camera. "*I was trying to find out what interfered with our transmission. It was not caused by anything here at the station. I repeat: Your reception difficulties were not produced by this station. Other stations had the same problem. We do not know the cause...*"

"If I told them, they wouldn't believe me," Sadie said in a distant voice.

"Why'd you do that?" Saul asked.

"I didn't."

"Yeah, and I didn't sing tonight either," he retorted.

"A better ponderation is how," Jo-Jo stated. "How did you interfere with all the stations at once and how did you make lightning come out of your mitts?"

"I didn't make the TV buzz, believe it or don't. As for the second part of your question, the key was in the power of concentration, Jo-Jo. Technically, you didn't see lightning rise from my hands. Electrical current is a sibling to lightning, not an identical twin."

"A nod is as good as a wink to a blind donkey," Rich said.

"So what made the tube splatter?" Harry asked.

"Please hold on a minute," the anchorman said before Sadie could reply. He had been handed a piece of paper. *"We have received word that a large meteor entered our atmosphere and exploded. The meteor may have caused the interference. According to the National Astrological Foundation in Washington, there is no more danger from meteors tonight. We repeat: The danger has passed."*

Sadie smirked. "No one was in danger. The meteor landed in a deserted spot in the Rocky Mountains. Meteorites have been falling for a long time. That one was just larger, so it didn't burn up when it entered our atmosphere. No big deal. But the meteor didn't cause the disturbance."

Saul strolled over to Sadie and put an arm around her. "Would you care to explain why you popped it, then?"

Sadie's expression adopted a hint of worry. She replied slowly. "Hon, it's time. I know why I have these powers now. I know the upcoming problem I'll have to deal with. I was testing my distance accuracy on that meteor, projecting my power, to help formulate a plan of action."

"So what's the charge?" Rich asked. "Are you going to shoot out the moon?"

"As long as it isn't my favorite Moon," Martha said with a giggle.

Peggy shook her head. "How can you two kid around like that? This sounds serious. Sadie, what's the job?"

"Don't scold, Peg. A sense of humor can help get you through whatever life may throw your way."

Peggy scowled. "Are you going to answer my question? Or are you changing the subject as usual?"

"All I can say right now is that you guys have to do another concert the night of November 22nd." Sadie's face turned so serious that no one spoke as she paused to think. "Let's try Philadelphia this time. No, make it Pittsburgh. Pittsburgh is smaller and less of a target. And if you are in a small venue, that will keep you even safer. You can do any active songs you like, but the children must be present too. They can stay backstage during the show. I'm sure Carol and Joshua will sit with them. I need the family together for my peace of mind."

She paused again. "On second thought, you could have the triplets help with part of the show. They'll increase the viewers."

Harry studied her face. "The way you're talking, Pet, it sounds like you won't grace us with your presence at the time. You would bring in more viewers than the tots."

"I'll be with you in spirit."

"What exactly will you be doing?" Martha asked.

"Right now, I can't say more, but don't worry. I'll tell you what you need to know. Just remember to say your prayers every day beforehand."

"What should we pray about?"

"Pray for peace on earth. That's always a good one."

Chapter 28 – November 1, 1969

"Let's go dancing tonight, Luv, just the two of us." Saul said at the breakfast table. "Today's November first, and you know what that means." Sadie didn't respond.

Martha's blank face showed ignorance of the British tradition.

"Sadie Hawkins Day," Rich whispered. "Ladies get to choose their partners today. Saul wants to get her away from us, to limit choices." Martha smiled.

"Do you have a bug up your butt?" Saul asked. Sadie rose from the table and began to wash the dishes. Martha motioned for Saul to drop the subject. "I won't drop it," Saul said loudly. "We're not blithering idiots. We might be able to help."

Sadie scratched the tip of her nose, then walked to the phone and dialed. "Hi, Mary, this is Sadie. Are you and Gene busy today?… No, I'm okay. It's just, well, I have something to explain to the family and I only want to say it once. Since it involves you and Gene, I'd like you two here. If your kids are a concern, bring them, too. They will be in the next room with Carol and Josh. So, can you come?… Yes, it is very important… Thank you. We'll see you in an hour."

Gene and Mary dropped their children off with family and arrived in less than an hour. The Spidar children were set up with Carol and Josh in the living room. Gene and Mary sat with the adults around the kitchen table.

As Peggy poured tea, Sadie disappeared into the den and brought out a large metal box. The room quieted. She pulled out a pile of papers and handed two of them to Saul.

"What's this?" Saul protested after reading the first one. "What did I do wrong this time?"

"Nothing," she replied softly.

"Then why are you leaving me again? I thought we were getting on quite rightly now."

"Not that again!" Jo-jo said angrily. "All this secrecy because you plan to exit. Change the bloody record, woman!" Miki jabbed him in the ribs.

"I'm not leaving, at least I hope not," Sadie replied.

Saul waved the two papers in the air. "Then why this? These look like you're putting everything you own in my name."

Silence ensued as Sadie groped for the right words. Finally she spoke. "I am just adding your name to everything. I know more about my 'mission' now. I can't tell you much, for reasons you'll understand when it's over." Her voice lowered. "I don't know if I'll survive it."

"Why wouldn't you?" Peggy asked. "Just yesterday morning, you said you have more power stored up than you ever imagined possible."

"That's true, Peg. But this mission will take everything I have now... and more."

Gene opened his mouth to speak, but Sadie shook her head. "No, Gene, when the time comes, every second will be critical. I probably won't notice my energy level going down. My concentration must be absolute, on only one thing."

The air above the table darkened. Sadie looked around the room and smiled sweetly. "Don't be glum. Most people don't get the chance to take care of loose ends before they die. And, if I'm lucky, we'll all have a good laugh about this meeting after the event, that's all. Gene and Mary, I need you to be available that evening. Your faith is strong enough to help the rest of my family."

She turned to Saul. "An hour ago, you said you might be able to help. Now all of you can. I need input. Somehow, I need to talk with the president of the United States. There's one catch, though. If I survive this, I'm quite sure my powers will be completely gone and I can't afford to let the press get suspicious. All the money in the world won't protect us from crackpots. So, how can I speak to the president without attracting attention?"

"I thought you had connections in Washington?" Martha said. "During the germ warfare…"

Sadie interrupted in a teasing voice. "It was more like a PCP attack, not a germ. Yes, I told Bart I'd call Washington if he couldn't help, but that was different. I could have called a few agencies and given them the information without my name. This time, I have to convince the president about events to come, that I can help, and also that he should not retaliate. I realize all this sounds like mumbo-jumbo to you, since you don't know the foundation. Regardless, it is imperative that I deal with the president directly…" The phone interrupted. "Tell whomever is on the other end that we're busy," she instructed Peggy, who headed toward it.

Peggy smiled. "Surely you know who it is already. You always do."

"No games," Sadie replied, "Not now. I don't care who it is. Does anyone have any ideas? I'm serious. I need help."

"You could attend a White House reception," Harry offered. "There's always a celebrity or two there, so no one would suspect. Then you corner the president and tell him you have an urgent matter to discuss… privately."

"Yeah," Jo-Jo quipped. "The Prez won't be able to resist getting you alone in his oval office." Harry and Saul snickered.

416

"No," Sadie protested. "That won't work. The next formal dinner at the White House is a week before Thanksgiving. Not enough time for him to act."

"Sadie," Peggy said, her hand over the phone's mouthpiece. "I think you should take this call. The man says he's J. Edgar Hoover from the F.B.I. You don't want me to hang up on him, do you?"

Sadie shook her head. "Why would Hoover call me?" She rose and went to the phone. "Sadie speaking... Me?... But how did you?... Can you guarantee secrecy?... I'll need to bring my own assistant... Okay, let the ambulance person administer a valium drip to kill pain. And have the person put pressure on the entrance and exit wounds, not too much, or it will cause more bleeding as it squishes the heart. I'll see you shortly."

She hung up the phone and stared at it. "There are forces at work here. My problem is solved. The president has been shot in Buffalo, only 80 miles from here. And he's en route to the Buffalo VA Hospital. I'm supposed to see if I can fix him up." She looked at Martha. "Can you come with me?"

"Me? Get to meet the president? I'd love to!"

"Good. The pilot of a Bell 533 helicopter has been called into service at the Air Force Reserve unit in Chili, just west of Rochester. He's taking off within a few minutes to pick us up and take us to the Buffalo VA hospital, where the president is headed by ambulance. We have fifteen minutes to get to the Canandaigua airfield. A sheriff's deputy will escort us and should be out front momentarily. Get into your nurse's uniform and bring along a wig and hat. We can apply make-up during the flight." Martha hurried to comply.

Sadie scurried to the hall closet, grabbed coats for herself and Martha, as well as a muffler for herself to wind around her head to hide her hair. Then she looked at the others. "I will have to explain more later. Gene and Mary, I'm sorry to bring you all the way here and leave at the drop of a hat. Please keep November 22nd free in the meantime." Martha returned and the two of them left.

*

Hoover personally ushered Sadie and Martha to the operating room. They entered a top security room and ordered all medical personnel to leave. One doctor would stay nearby in case he was needed.

Once in the room, Martha read the president's chart aloud as Sadie worked. "Blood pressure 60 over 30, temperature 95 degrees, breathing labored, heart in spasms…" Hoover studied the movements of both women.

Sadie didn't need the equipment lined up on the tray. Instead, she used one hand like a magnet, pulling the bullet out, while the other repaired the damage the bullet caused. The bullet had nicked the heart. One lung had been punctured and there was extensive internal bleeding.

"If the president had been shot in Washington, our travel time would have been too long," Martha said in a voice that wandered as she took new readings. "Buffalo, on the other hand, is close enough. Blood pressure 70 over 45. When the president reached the operating room, we were in the air, running up the hospital steps by the time his heart went spastic, according to these records. Temperature 97.1."

A drawn-out sigh escaped from Sadie's lips. "Heart and lung done. Now for some specialized touches to prevent scars, so the president won't bore people recounting the story."

Martha took another reading. "His pulse is strong, heartbeat regular, blood pressure 120 over 80, breathing normal, temp 98.4."

Sadie stopped moving. "I've countered the valium. Now we wait for his head to clear." Within a few minutes, the patient looked at her. "Mr. President, first let me say you're all fixed up. In fact, within a few days, you'll feel younger than ever. You had the beginnings of arteriosclerosis, so I adjusted your chemical balance and sparked your liver into action. You now have the wisdom of age in the body of a thirty-year-old man."

The president looked around the room and sat up on the operating table with a smile on his face. "I didn't know there was a fountain of youth in Buffalo."

Sadie giggled and motioned for Martha and Hoover to leave. Martha moved immediately but Hoover hesitated, saying, "The president is not left alone at any time."

"That must be rough on his marriage."

"His wife is, uh, different," Hoover stammered. "She's been cleared."

"And I'm not. Is that what you're saying? What would I do? Kill him after saving his life? Come on. You know my powers, or I wouldn't be here now. I'm sure you realize that if I wanted to hurt him, I could have done it already." She grinned. "Maybe I did. Maybe I changed his chemical balance in a different way. Maybe I don't want him to die too quickly. Maybe I want him to suffer."

"You'll go to jail for life! You'll get the electric chair! You'll...."

'Leave us alone," the president commanded, with a chuckle in his voice. "Haven't you seen this woman on stage? She loves a good tease."

Sadie and the president had their private chat.

*

As Sadie and Martha walked in the kitchen door of the McCarthy estate, Sadie laughed out loud. "No one moved since we left this morning!" Even Gene and Mary were at the table.

Rich, who had risen to greet Martha, looked around and guffawed. "It would appear that way."

"Don't overestimate yourself," Jo-Jo scowled. Miki poked him and added, "The children are asleep for the night."

"Jerry jingled to let us know you were back, so we returned to this room," Saul explained. "I want to know what's coming about, and so does everyone else."

Sadie walked to the stove and poured herself a cup of tea. Her eyes squinted when she returned to the table. "Okay, as I said earlier, I don't know if I'll survive this final mission. You don't need to know what my part is, but you must all be together, so I can make sure you don't get hurt if I end up not being able to do the whole job. Also, the president has agreed that a Spidar concert may help the masses. Maybe what happens that night can be explained as a planned event. Your concert will preempt all other programs, but press won't be notified until a few hours before the event. That way, they don't have time to dig."

"Why can't you tell us what's happening?" Saul asked with an edge in his voice. "You told the president. Why not us?"

"Honey, I'm sorry. Really I am. I know how you'll react. I'm human. You'll have an easy job convincing me to take another route – an easier escape from the problem – which is not the real solution in this case.

"I'm trying to get a few things done ahead of time. All my personal assets – real estate, stocks, and bank accounts – now have your name on them, too. The money from them should help care for the children for a long time." Saul opened his mouth to speak, but Sadie pressed his lips gently. "I know, Saul, you have plenty of money, too. This is my contribution towards my children."

She turned to the others. "I want you to know the rest of my wishes in the event of my death. Most of them will be on a tape in the corner cupboard. I'm not going to bore you with details, but I want all of you to promise not to play the tape unless I don't return."

Sadie glanced around the room. "This is not meant to be morbid, just practical. Even Miki can't read my mind, so I have to tell you what I want." Her gaze fell to her tea cup. "You adults will do okay after a while. I'm more worried about the kids. I've tried to prepare them, but they're too young to understand about death."

She looked up and smiled. "Liven up! Today, I only want to emphasize my wish to have Gene and Mary here to help with the kids for the first month or so. I know how all of you spoil them already. If I don't return from my job, you may let them get away with even more. They can't have that. More than ever, the kids will need routine and discipline. I think Gene and Mary can do that. They helped me in troubled times before, and they should be able to reach the children during the worst part."

Sadie looked at the couple. "Would you be willing to move into this house for a month or so? We have two extra bedrooms, one for you two and one for the boys. Gene, can you take a month's leave of absence from your job? I will pay you double your normal salary for the month, paid in advance."

"Wouldn't we be in the way?" Gene asked.

Sadie turned to the family. "Can Gene and Mary move in for a while after I die?"

Silence.

"Will all of you promise to stay here for a couple of months before you move back to England? The kids will need stability."

Silence.

"I guess I'm presuming too much." She rose from the table and walked to the hall with slouched shoulders. She climbed the stairs when she noticed Saul in the kitchen doorway.

"I can't speak for the rest of 'em," Saul said. "However, I'll remain in this abode for a while to keep routine for the tots. Gene and Mary won't be a bother, either." He moved toward the staircase.

Sadie hesitated, then decided to step down and talk to him face-to-face. "Would you be willing to give Gene and Mary veto power with the children?"

"What? They are my tikes, too. I should have the final say in matters concerning them."

"Yes, but Hon, sometimes you overreact when trouble brews. It would be easier if you didn't have to make decisions the first month."

Saul thought for a moment. "Is that what you really wish, Luv?'

"Yes, that's what I'd like. It would ease my mind a lot ... a little ... Oh Saul, I'm scared!"

He pulled her close and held her tight.

Chapter 29 – November 22, 1969

The next three weeks went fast. The fateful day arrived. At the airport, Sadie jabbered as if she still had a lot to say. "...I'll be in contact with Miki at different times during the show. I may dictate some things that have to go on the air. Please don't question anything..."

"You could come with us," Saul interrupted. "On the blower this morning, didn't the president say he had used a whip hand on everything and no one could possibly cause any problems now?"

"Yes, but he doesn't realize that all the security in the world won't stop this thing from happening."

"What thing?" Jo-Jo asked. "Since we can't back out now, you can give us the fill."

"I wish I could. You're wrong, though. The only thing to suffer if you back out of tonight's concert is your reputation. You will know all by tomorrow."

"Can I go with you then?" Saul asked.

Sadie's stomach tied in knots. She wanted to tell them everything she knew. She wanted to take the family to a remote island. She wanted to let someone else handle the world's problems. In the least, she wanted Saul with her.

"No, Hon," she responded, stroking his temples with her fingertips. Her hands lingered longer than usual. "This mission will require split-second timing. Any interruptions or indecision could cost millions of lives. Whatever happens, remember that I love you. I love you more than I could ever say. If I don't come back, please don't hate me for doing this.

"I admit I could protect you without threat to my own life this time. Yet, if I went that route, the Sadie you know would be lost forever. You called me a saint when you were mad. Actually, I'm very selfish. This course of action is the only way I'll be able to live with myself afterward. I'm doing it this way hoping that God, in his infinite mercy, will let me, the inside me, live and love my family for a while longer."

Peggy had tears in her eyes. "There has to be something we can do."

"You can pray that all goes well," Sadie said, her own eyes wet too. After saying farewell near the plane, she stood at the bottom of the steps and watched them climb, turn to wave at her, and disappear. "Bye, Mummy!"

Sadie wiped her cheeks. She didn't want her children to remember tears. She wanted them to remember happy times. She smiled, love gleaming through her eyes.

"Does anyone know what this is about?" Saul asked the three women in the plane. His voice was quiet but urgent. "I'd like to know if this so-called 'mission' is worth losing her."

Peggy looked at Martha who looked at Miki. All three shook their heads. "I have no idea," Martha replied. "It has to be a tall order. In Sadie's jaunts to the hospital, she has built up tremendous resources of energy. From what Peg tells me, Sadie used to be on the verge of collapse when she came home from her hospital work. I saw the picture of that fireman and..." She paused.

"And what?" Saul asked.

"Sadie didn't want me to tell you, but I think I can now. Do you remember that orphanage fire that was in the papers last week?" Heads nodded. "There were nine children and two adults badly burned in the fire. Five of them as bad as that fireman's picture and the other six not much better. Sadie fixed them all up. That was last Wednesday. Do you recall how she looked when she returned to us?"

Peggy's head tilted. "Yes, she bounced around the house. I thought she had had an easy day at the hospital. How?"

"She found a way to use thousands of times more energy without having to catch her breath, something about imploding the atoms in the air and using that energy." Martha smirked. "She says she kills two flies with one swat. She identifies pollutants in the air and uses those atoms for her energy. She's cleaning the air with every burst she uses."

"Leave it to Sadie not to waste a thing," Peggy said.

The plane engines roared to life. Saul watched out the window as Sadie waved one last time and turned to a helicopter that would fly her to New York City, where she would board Air Force Two. That plane was pre-loaded with juices and carbohydrates. Sadie would speed up her digestive processes and eat and drink most of the way to her destination.

*

"Hi, Pat!" Sadie said, walking into the control room at Cape Kennedy.

"Excuse me, Ma'am," an aide interrupted, "The proper address is Mr. President."

Sadie winked at Pat. "Well, excu-u-use me, Mr. President. I don't want to commit a faux pas on this festive evening."

"You can call me anything you wish, Miss," the president said with a laugh. He waved his aide away and whispered, "A pretty girl like you doesn't need to stand on protocol."

Sadie giggled, combed her fingers through her red wig, and looked around. No one in the control room seemed to notice her. They chit-chatted as if nothing would happen tonight. They haven't been told much, she thought.

Radar monitors filled the room. Each one covered a different section of the country. Sadie walked to monitor 25, the screen that included most of Pennsylvania. Surveying the room, she made sure she could focus on this screen from anywhere.

"Isn't it fantastic?" the operator said to Sadie as she looked at the screen. She glanced up to see a man smiling at her. He had the richest blue eyes she had ever seen and his blond hair was neatly brushed in an early-Spidars style, slightly above the eyebrows in front and below the ears on the side and back. His perky nose and deep round dimples accented his eyes and gave him a young boy's looks.

"What?" Sadie asked, returning his smile.

He winked at her. "We should be arrested for this."

Sadie's interest piqued. "For what?"

"Getting paid to watch a Spidar concert. I hope Sadie's on stage tonight. I saw her on TV a few months ago. She's great!"

"I prefer to watch the men," she sputtered. She looked around again and noticed a large television on the back wall, high enough for everyone to see. "I'm sure we have everything under control," the President had said on the phone this morning. "You are welcome to join me while I watch the Spidar concert."

Regaining her voice, she spoke to the blond man with authority, "You'll earn your pay tonight, believe me. Your screen includes the area where the Spidars are performing, so stay alert." With that, she left the machines and rejoined the president.

The blond man tilted his head toward the man next to him and whispered, "She's wearing a bit too much make-up. Do you think she's hiding something?" The other man shrugged.

"May I have your attention, please," the president said into the microphone. "All of you are familiar with the radar monitors in front of you. I want to emphasize tonight's rules. For security reasons, no one will be allowed off this floor for ANY reason. The press corps is waiting downstairs for any tidbits. It is imperative nothing is said without authorization.

"I would also like to review the procedure for incoming UFOs. If my source is correct, we may be bombarded with them all at once. This means no unnecessary talking. That includes any, A-N-Y, any words that don't give specific information. We also need information in precise order: latitude, longitude, altitude, then direction and speed. Do not interrupt anyone else's figure, but don't take all day giving your information either. Speak fast and distinctly, such as: two-eight-point-seven, eight-one-point-one, fifty thousand, northwest, three-five-one knots..."

The blond at monitor 25 whispered to the man beside him, "They shouldn't need us for that one. If they don't know about it, they need hearing aids and glasses."

Sadie tapped the president's shoulder and pointed upward. "Uh, yes," he stated on the microphone. "That one would be right above us of course. That is all the information we need. No verification will be possible, so make sure you are accurate the first time. The next person should begin immediately. There is no room for error. You are the best air traffic controllers in our armed forces, and we expect perfection tonight.

"All scheduled flights across the US will be grounded within the next thirty minutes. All foreign powers, both friendly and not-so-friendly, have been notified that we will be running a test of our equipment. They know that anything in the air over U.S. territory will be considered part of the test and destroyed. Miss Vosimer, standing beside me, will give further instructions in a minute. Do you have any questions so far?" The president's words echoed off the walls for a moment.

The blond man at monitor 25 raised a hand. "I have two of them, he said. "First, will this testing have the decency to wait until the concert is over?"

The president smiled. "Hopefully. I do enjoy good music, but we need to stay on our toes nevertheless. The simulator is programmed to surprise me. I don't know when it will happen, maybe during one of those blasted commercial breaks." Laughter filled the room.

"My second question is: Has anyone started a pool for what time Sadie will appear on the show?"

Sadie blushed behind her make-up. At least the disguise still works, she thought. Pat winked at her and then answered, "If there is, put me down for never. My source tells me she isn't traveling with the others this time."

"Then again," he whispered to Sadie, "Could the same source be wrong about the UFOs?"

Sadie smiled at the president and stepped to the microphone. "Please remember your job," she commanded. "At the first sign of trouble, the television will be turned off. Make sure you speak loud and clear into the microphone in front of you. Don't panic. As long as everyone remembers the rules, we should have time to react.

"There are two exceptions to the rules. If the object on our screen drops below twenty thousand feet, press the red button on the side of your machine, which sounds an alarm sound for two seconds. Number twenty-five, please demonstrate the alarm for us."

As the buzzer went off, Sadie memorized the sound. "When you hear any buzzers, the person speaking is to finish his information as quickly as possible and no one else is to begin except the one who pressed his button. When that emergency is over, start giving your own information. Don't waste time or we'll get bogged down."

She paused. "Now, there is one more exception to all the rules. Number twenty-five, if it looks like there are any UFOs headed to Pittsburgh, 40.26.23 N by 79.58.35 W, buzz immediately, no matter how high or far away it is or how slow it is traveling."

Sadie shrugged at the controllers watching her as if she should explain that last rule. She smiled. "We wouldn't want anything to happen to our precious Spidars, would we?" A chuckle rose from the group. "Any questions?"

"Yes," a stout man with a receding hairline replied, "What happens if there are several UFOs that go below 20,000 feet? Which one goes first?"

"Excellent question," Sadie said. "The buzzers will tell how many people are waiting to speak. Each one has a different pitch. When you hear another buzzer, immediately punch your altitude, only altitude, into the box in front of your screen. Then watch for the red light to blink, which signals your turn will come next. Recheck the current position quickly and give us the most current information." Sadie looked at her watch. "We have ten minutes before the concert, so let's have a practice session. Watch your screen."

The president looked at Sadie quizzically. No one had arranged a real practice session, yet the men began to give coordinates of fictitious UFOs. He walked around. Sure enough, there were images on the screens, images that disappeared after the figures were given. He listened as three buzzers went off simultaneously. He watched as each man received a blinking light.

"How did you do that?" he whispered upon his return to Sadie's side. "We don't have a simulator attached. That was just a line for the men, as you requested, to ward off panic when the time comes. And what about the red lights? They're hooked up to that machine on the roof as you requested. What is setting them off?"

Sadie smiled. "It was easy," she whispered back. "A simulator is an amoeba when compared to a human brain. I work with people's brains to do my healing. Electronics are much simpler."

*

Throngs of screaming fans met the Spidar jet in Pittsburgh. Police escorted their limousine to its destination. Two hours later, the Spidar family ran on stage for their first song. The applause was deafening. As they waited for the noise to die down, Miki nodded to Jo-Jo, who stood beside her. "Sadie's sending a message. She says Knock 'em out! So far everything's quiet on the southern front."

Jo-Jo took a few steps toward the other men. "Mates, Sadie sends her love." Stepping back, he turned to the microphone. *"We would like to thank you for letting us audition tonight. We hope you like our show. Our first song is dedicated to a very special lady who could not be with us tonight – our own Sexy Sadie!"*

*

"...you talk about destruction..." [50] came from the TV. The blond from monitor 25 walked up to the president and handed him a pile of five dollar bills. Pat told him to put it in the workers' party fund and smiled at Sadie. She didn't notice. *"If you carry pitchers of hate germ around, you ain't gonna make it..."* [50]

As Sadie watched her family perform, her heart swelled with pride. Jason and Carl wiggled their hips and tapped their feet like their fathers and uncles as they sang. The next song was Roxanne's imitation of "Wild Thing." Sadie laughed as she watched Roxanne slink from one Spidar to the next, the way Sadie would do it in the audience, but with variations only a child could do. Roxanne's innocence was plain for all to see.

An hour later, the concert was going well. During the fifteen minute break, Saul asked Miki how Sadie was doing. "The last contact I had, she was watching us," Miki replied.

Saul looked around the room. "Did she tell any of you when the trouble would start?" Heads shook negative.

"Two minutes!" A stagehand yelled through the dressing room door.

Saul mumbled, "I wish tonight was over." The second half of the show would have only the Spidars and the wives in it. Carol and Josh stayed in the break room with all eight children, so they could eat a snack, play, and fall asleep.

The Spidars ran back on stage and the audience screamed again. However, before the show resumed, Peggy noticed Miki's dazed expression.

"Harry, wait!" Peggy said with a jerk toward Miki.

Harry shook his head. "Something better," he said. He gyrated his hips and meandered to the middle of the stage. Rich played a strip-tease beat. Harry began to unbutton his shirt, slowly, very slowly. The audience screamed louder. When his hands were halfway down his chest, Harry's eyes pleaded with Peggy. He had begun something he really didn't wish to finish. Peggy nodded. Miki was coming out of her trance. Harry returned to his designated spot, buttoning his shirt as he went. The audience booed.

Miki stepped up to the center microphone. *"For those of you in our television audience, soon the skies will light up all over the United States. Think of the fireworks as a new age dawning, an age where we make peace, not war, an age where we teach our children by example, instead of empty lip service."*

431

"There must be a meteor shower coming," Peggy whispered to Martha.

*

At the control center, a buzz of activity began. The television seemed to shut off by itself.

"On your toes, men!" Sadie shouted, running to the stairs that led to the roof. She climbed them three at a time and stood at her post with outstretched arms. A specialist had turned on most of the machinery by the time the president and secret service member joined her. They watched as a flash of light left her hands and headed north. Within a split-second, the light disappeared from sight.

"Testing?" Pat asked in a teasing voice. "Looked like a dud to me."

Sadie smiled, the last smile for a while. "It wasn't a dud. The energy was going faster than the speed of light and our eyes aren't accustomed to it."

The president knit his brows. "I'll accept that, but where's the backlash? I don't hear anything."

"No sound yet," Sadie said. A voice from the control room gave a set of coordinates. She sent off another pulse of light. "Sound travels much slower than light. I found a way to make my energy leave in silence. What you'll hear soon is the collision. That wasn't a test shot. The missile was headed for this building. The perpetrator wanted this control tower out of commission, I guess, so there would be no defense." She put on her earphones, flipped a switch to power them, and shot another pulse of light.

A low altitude beep came over the loudspeaker. Sadie stepped to a microphone positioned on the roof. "That last set of coordinates took too long, men," she said as another light spark left her hands. "Get serious. Speak fast with clarity."

The coordinates came faster, several times during the next two minutes beeps sounding a low altitude alert. Then five beeps came at once.

"This isn't going to work," Sadie said to the president. "It's not fast enough. Please tell them just to identify their machines over the microphones. I'll get the rest directly from the machines, but don't tell them that." The president scurried down the steps as the next numbers began. Sadie threw another spark. The sky was bright. Loud booms came every six seconds or less.

As the new procedure took effect, the president rejoined Sadie on the roof. Booms burst every two seconds. She twirled to position herself as each new number came over the headphones. To the president, Sadie looked like a top, spinning and spinning.

The new procedure worked for a while. Then beeps signaled for low altitude objects again. A look of alarm came onto Sadie's face as fifteen buzzers squawked at the same time.

"No time for panic," she mumbled. Identifying each buzzer, she went from one machine to the next, reading it, positioning herself, shooting a spark, and proceeding to the next one. When all fifteen were done, she sent two more, one to the east and one to the west of the U.S.

Ten seconds later, she fell to the floor, exhausted. A secret service man picked her up and put her in a wheelchair.

"It's over," she whispered. "I blew up the two sources of the bombs, the places launching them. I shot them as they reloaded. My explosions were so close to the ones waiting that the whole shebang blew up. Should be quite a noise when it reaches us." The secret serviceman relayed the message to the president, who spoke to someone on his walkie-talkie.

Outside, buildings vibrated with the noise. Inside the control room, silence dripped from the loudspeaker. No one in the control room moved. Their eyes were glued to their screens. This hadn't been a drill, but too many things did not add up. How did the last objects get destroyed so quickly? What caused the thunderous thumps, louder than any weapon they knew, and the last two loud enough to dislodge teeth?

Soon, the blond at monitor 25 walked to the window and pulled open the security curtain. "Will you look at that!" he exclaimed. Because of the sudden blankness of the screens, others joined him. Although the night sky was already as light as daytime, it turned brighter and brighter and in various colors.

"What's causing that?" a muscular man asked.

The blond man pointed to the crowd of reporters gathered on the lawn. "They're probably wondering the same thing."

"Thank you, men," came a voice from the back of the room. The men turned to see the president in front of the central console still talking on his walkie-talkie. The woman with him was half-sitting, half lying on a wheelchair beside him. She wore a neck brace that held her head erect.

The president set the walkie-talkie down and continued, "You should all be proud. You saved our country from destruction. Join me downstairs for the explanation. Stat." Pat turned to Sadie. She shook her head and reached for a phone.

"Isn't that just like a woman," the blond man chortled on his way out. "She couldn't handle the loud noise, but nothing stops her from gabbing on the phone."

*

"... I ain't got nothing but love, Babe..."[17]

The Spidars stopped in the middle of the song as a National Guard officer ran up to them.

434

"*I guess this preempt is being preempted,*" Jo-Jo said into the microphone. "*Folks here, watch the screens. Take it away, Prez.*"

"*Greetings, Fellow Americans,*" the president began. "*I have good news for you tonight! First, I'd like to thank the Spidars for their help in preventing panic across the country...*"

The Spidar family nodded, but they weren't really listening. They were watching the television monitor set up near the left wing. Their eyes sparkled at the sight of Sadie behind the president, still in her disguise.

"She looks quite fagged," Harry mumbled.

"Yeah, but she's alive!" Saul said. "That's all that matters." He motioned for the curtains to close and looked around. Miki was in a trance. He walked to the monitor and shut it off. "So what does my Luvey say?" he asked when Miki's eyes returned to normal.

"Her signal was weak."

"What do you expect? She's in Florida."

"She says she loves us and we should go home without delay."

Saul smiled broadly. "Tell her we love her, too. We'll be home in a tick."

"I can't. She broke the connection."

Rich laughed. "Sadie gets the last word again!"

The Spidars gathered the children and left the concert hall as the rest of the United States listened to the president: "*...There should be no more bombs tonight... and through the aid of a very special person who wishes to remain nameless, we have developed a boron/iodine powder that will absorb the fallout's radioactivity and render it harmless. All over the country, dusting planes have taken off. They should be in your area soon.*

"Stay inside tonight if possible. When you wake in the morning, everything will be coated with a thin layer of a tan powder. Do not, I repeat, DO NOT, wash it off for a week. The boron and iodine should work immediately, but there may be residual radioactivity blowing in the winds. Next Monday, we will give instructions for removal. In the meantime, have a wonderful Thanksgiving!"

The Spidars heard the message repeated and repeated during their air-conditioned limo ride to the airport. An Air Force plane flew them back to Rochester. They rushed to their parked van. As they climbed into it, Joshua found a note taped to the steering wheel.

The note was written in Sadie's handwriting. She had mentioned something about rechecking the parking brake before the family walked through the entrance to the airport this afternoon. It must have been an excuse for this note. It read:

KEEP THE WINDOWS UP.
DON'T WORRY.
I HAD A HEAVY-DUTY AIR FILTER INSTALLED.
THE POWDER WON'T GET THROUGH.
With blue skies of love,
                    Sadie

Chapter 30 – Returning Home

Gene's car was parked in the driveway as Joshua pulled the Spidar van up to the kitchen door. Deciding Gene must have driven Sadie home from the airport, Saul leaped out of the van and ran into the house. Rich, Harry, and Jo-Jo followed.

"Sure," Peggy remarked, "the men run in and leave us out here to get eight sleeping children into the house." She instructed Joshua to move the van to the front door, a shorter and more direct way to the children's rooms.

Joshua, Carol, Peggy, Martha, and Miki each took one toddler up to the nursery. Martha and Carol tucked them in while the other three adults went to get the triplets.

"It's awfully quiet in there," Peggy whispered, pointing to the kitchen during the second trip.

Miki smiled. "The men probably can't pry Saul and Sadie apart."

Peggy smiled too. "Can you blame them? Sadie must have been out of her wits knowing she'd have to fight nuclear bombs. She was right, though. We would have cancelled the show. Personally, I'd have caught the first plane out of the country."

"We all would have," Miki agreed

After the children were tucked in bed, Josh and Carol went to their apartment and the three women went downstairs. In the kitchen, the men sat at the table, and Mary was adding a shot of brandy to the tea cups. Even Gene, who usually didn't imbibe, was having a spiced cup.

"So where's Sadie?" Peggy asked. "Did we beat her here?"

Silence.

"It can't be," Miki whispered.

Peggy turned to her. "What can't be?"

"We saw her alive behind the president!" Saul blurted out.

Gene rose and put a hand on Saul's shoulder. "No, you didn't. That was an illusion. Sadie called me and said she was going to make you think she was fine, so you made it home without incident. She wanted the trip home to be a happy one for the children, and you adults could learn the truth after the kids were in bed. In fact, she didn't even go to the press room. She was in the control room on the phone with me when the president made his announcement to the country."

"Maybe if she had saved the energy she used to call you and for the illusion, she'd still be alive."

"No. She said she used Miki's energy to put the picture in your minds. Even so, she couldn't hold it there long. She was losing her concentration. She seemed relieved when Miki's eyes showed your TV monitor was off."

Gene wiped his eyes. "She said she was calling me with the little energy she had left. She had already tried to recoup her energy with atom bursts, but she didn't have enough power remaining to burst any of them. She could feel power drain without any muscle movement at all. She tried to drink juice and adjust her metabolism, but nothing happened.

"She said to tell you she was sorry. Darn it all! Can you imagine? After all she did, she was sorry for dying on you! Even in her death, she was more worried about all of you than about herself."

Not able to contain himself any longer, Gene broke down and wept. Mary decided this was her signal. "I think we should listen to Sadie's tape."

Sadie's voice came through the tape loud and cheerful. *"Just think, family, I'm only nineteen years old and I saved over 190-million lives directly, a lot more if you consider the people* who would be seriously injured around the world once the winds started to blow. And some people say teenagers don't contribute to society. Ha! Teenagers are people too! I'm nineteen and, with some help from my friends, I saved lives. OUTTA-SIGHT!

"Speaking of out-of-sight, if you are listening to this tape, I must be dead. If not, if you're just killing time because you beat me home, TURN THIS OFF!

"I've heard that only the good die young. I have to disagree. There are a lot of young people, good and bad, who die. We just miss the good ones more. I hope I've been good enough to be remembered fondly."

Sadie's voice turned serious. "*In case you're worried about the future here in the U.S., don't. I convinced the president not to retaliate by unleashing our own weapons. As my mother always said: 'Two wrongs don't make a right.' This attack was planned and carried out by a small group of people. Believe it or not, the people were intent on proving how dangerous an arms build-up is. Well, they proved their point, but I'm glad millions of lives didn't go to waste in the effort. And that small group probably died when I blew up the launching sites.*"

Her voice softened. "*I love you. As I sit here under the oak tree in the backyard, surveying the lake and watching the children play on the grass, I am thankful to all of you for filling my life with a richness I wouldn't have had in ten normal lifetimes.*

"*Don't feel sorry for me, whatever you do. I may only be 19 years old, but the last three years have been so full that I'm not afraid to die. It's the living who may suffer.*

"*As I sit here, I remember how much all of you have done for me. Gene and Mary, you were always there when I needed you, from way before my first pregnancy up to now. No one could ask for better friends. Thank you.*

"Harry, you never knew how many times you helped me cope with changes in my life. I remember the first time you brought Peggy to my apartment. I was so upset and jealous, yes jealous, when she was with Saul that night. However, you were kind and gentle and helped me realize something: inner peace comes when we appreciate the things we have and don't agonize over the things we can't have. You have a warm body – and a warm heart, too.

"Rich, Harry has said he can't compete with you or me for pulling practical jokes. Well, I concede. You are the winner of the competition. You made my life a lot more fun. I have to warn you, though. I may have a few more tricks up my sleeve, so watch out! Also, if there is any way for my ghost to come back to earth, I'll get you yet! Ha! Try getting even with a ghost! On second thought, maybe I'll be the winner after all.

"Now Jo-Jo, dear Jo-Jo. I know my beginnings with Saul angered you. There are times even now that you think back and believe I was lying." Her voice slowed. *"Well, since I'm gone now, there's no point in any more lies. Yes, I was a dirty old lady trying to hook a Spidar. I'm in pretty good shape for a 35-year-old, wouldn't you say?"*

The tape seemed to pause. "She's not thirty-five, is she?" Martha asked. Gene shook his head.

"She wasn't trying to hook a Spidar, either," Jo-Jo added. "In my sane moments, I knew it. She must have read my mind when I was in a wax."

Peggy pondered. "Remember her diary? Some things upset her terribly when she read our minds."

Sadie's voice returned on the tape. *"Is that enough time? I know there will be a discussion after that one. Did anyone pull out my birth certificate? ... No? It's not hidden any more. Well, I'm nineteen years old – no, nineteen and three-quarters. I'll be twenty in a few months. Yes, I will be. Just don't let my soul get*

440

much past twenty-one. At that age, some people begin to settle down. In a way, I'm glad I died at a young age. You can remember me as an active girl, not an old man like Harry. Oo-oo-oo, such sweet cheeks!" Harry and Peggy half-smiled.

"Anyway, I'm not done with Jo-Jo. Jo-Jo, my advice to you is to stop trying to hide your sensitive nature. You try to act so tough, yet inside you're a cuddly little teddy bear. There's nothing wrong with that. We all need love.

"Miki, you're good at giving Jo-Jo what he needs. Keep it up.

"Martha, good luck. With Rich, you'll need it. Your life won't be boring, that's for sure. And he'll treat you right, even if he is a little daft sometimes.

"Peggy, thank you. What more can I say? You were my rock many times. Don't feel like you have to take care of my kids forever, though. Saul can hire a nanny until he remarries. Ha! He'll have fun trying to find a woman who will take on seven kids, even if their father is rich and famous! I wouldn't advise him to bring the woman home on the first date. The kids would likely scare her half to death.

"Peg, you and Harry should consider having another child of your own. No, Harry, you can't have Jason. You know how I feel about separating my kids. Peg, I checked you out. You're in A-1 shape to have another baby without problems.

"Now, Saul... I always save the best for last. Honey, what can I say? Words cannot express my feelings for you. I know I sometimes made you jealous by putting the kids first, but there were only going to be twenty years before they leave for their own life. I hoped to have the rest of my life with you."

She giggled. "Actually, if you think about it, I wasn't wrong. I did spend the rest of my life with you! I love you so much, Saul. I can't repeat it enough. I'm glad you came back for me three years ago. I'm glad you convinced me to marry you. My stubbornness could have caused the triplets a lot of unnecessary *headaches and heartaches."*

The voice paused again, then resumed, *"I was just thinking: Was this whole thing a set-up, as Jo-Jo has thought at times? Many girls gave you anything you wanted. Why did you go to all the trouble to find me... simple lil me?*

"Even before that, though, was the fact that I got the maid's job in the first place. No other hotel believed me and I'm sure that under normal circumstances, I wouldn't have fooled Nolith's manager, either.

"So, yes, it was a set-up. You see, I must have needed all of you in order to develop my powers. I'm convinced that without your love, I wouldn't have gained them at all. You energized me. Your love let me see the invisible and do the impossible. So you could say that all of you were the ones who saved the millions of lives."

There was another pause before Sadie continued, *"Maybe it's a good thing I didn't survive. I'm quite sure that if I did, I wouldn't have any powers. Saul, you fell in love with a special person. Don't be sad that I'm gone, for I wouldn't be all that special any more. I'd just be an ordinary woman with seven active children. I would probably get bitchier. I'd be too tired by the end of the day to care for your needs. You'd end up divorcing me. I couldn't handle that."* In a soft whisper, she added: *"Honey, I love you so much."*

"You fool!" Saul yelled. "I loved you for you, not because of your friggin' powers!" His head fell onto his hand. Peggy turned off the recorder. Saul raised his head with a wide-eyed look. "I thought she knew that!"

Martha nodded. "She did, Saul. She did. She's reacting to her own grief. When a person loses a part of herself, she wonders if she's still lovable. It's a natural reaction. I've seen it many times with amputations and mastectomies."

Peggy turned on the tape again. They heard a click, as if Sadie had turned it off for a moment too. *"I'm sorry that I got maudlin. I don't want to depress you. Saul, I know you love me. I have a favor to ask. When my body returns from the Cape, can you give me one last kiss before my soul leaves my body? If that seems too gross to you, don't worry about it. Just hold my hand for a little while.*

"One of you should let Pam know I'm dead, but be careful what you say. She is a reporter at heart. Still she's been trustworthy in the past and deserves the scoop this time. As for my funeral, I want...."

"Turn that bloody thing off!" Saul exclaimed. "We don't even have her body. A phone call to Gene and a weak message to Miki, what do they prove? Maybe she's not dead. Maybe this is all a prank, a sick one. She's making fools of us again. If that's the case, you can bet she won't sit for a long chalk."

A knock on the side door startled the group. Saul bounded toward the door. "If this is Sadie, you blokes may want to leave the room while I paddle her bare butt."

"No thanks, Mate," Rich chuckled. "I'd rather watch."

The door opened to reveal a man in a three-piece, double-breasted suit. He took a few steps into the kitchen.

"Hello, Mr. President!" Martha exclaimed. The family rose to their feet.

"It's nice to see you again, Martha, dear," the president said. "It's too bad this is under such poor circumstances."

"No!" Saul cried, as he dropped to his knees. "It can't be true! It must be a joke!"

"I'm sorry to be the bearer of bad news," the president said. He put one hand on Saul's slouching shoulder. "I hope it will be some comfort to know that Sadie served her country well tonight. She did get to enjoy most of your concert, too, if that helps." He waited while the words digested.

"Before the action started, she said she expected to die and she wanted no autopsy or embalming solution. She asked to be shipped home as quickly as possible, so she could be with her family one last time before her soul left her body. The Cape's undertaker said any open casket viewing will have to be done within twenty-four hours or the stench will overwhelm. Sadie also asked for anonymity regarding tonight's events, though I can't understand why she wouldn't want her name in history." He paused then continued, "We honored most of her requests, but there was one we couldn't."

"What was that?" Harry asked.

"She wanted a plain wooden box with four holes, one in each side. After what she did for our country tonight, the Secretary of Defense, the only other person who knows everything, agreed with me. She deserves a solid gold casket. Since that would have taken quite a bit of time for delivery, we compromised with her. Here's what the casket looks like, and it has a glass sheet for the viewing." He handed Saul a picture of a casket with gilded trim work. "We did have them drill a hole in each side, so that much she does get."

"Was she alone when she died?" Jo-Jo asked.

"No, when I came back from making the announcement, she had a make-up case open on the desk, and many things strewn around it. I questioned her about it and she said she was the only one who could make herself look alive. The make-up did seem a little thick, though. She was also in the middle of taking off her outer clothing to reveal the outfit she wants to wear for the wake, then cremation later. That's when I realized she hadn't been teasing earlier. She really expected to die." He paused to ponder. His face looked even more somber.

"Actually, she never looked dead. She looked like she was sleeping, except for the smile on her face. When I realized she wasn't just resting, I sent a secret service member to get a sheet to cover her, so the air traffic controllers wouldn't recognize her outfit when they returned from the debriefing to gather their belongings. That bright pink and green is unmistakable."

The president stood by the door and handed Saul two cards. "Her body is being kept in cool storage near here and this is the number to call to have them deliver the body to wherever you wish it to go. Sadie mentioned something about a wake combined with a Spidar show. Remember that must be by tomorrow night. The second card is mine. That's my private number. If I can do anything to help, anything at all, please call me. Again, I'm very, very sorry. Your loss must be great indeed. She was a very special lady."

Chapter 31 – The Wake

CLEAN-UP DISLODGES SPIDARS' WEB
BY Pam Hope, UPI

Sadie McCarthy watched her last Spidar concert from an undisclosed location last night. She died shortly thereafter, according to Peggy George, the new spokeswoman for the Spidars. The cause of death is being withheld, but Mrs. George said, "Sadie was on a cleaning project when she fell ill. Her death was quick and peaceful."

A memorial service and Spidar concert will be held at Rochester's Shriners' Hall tonight at 9:00 PM EST. The service will be televised live on ABC. Sadie will be laid out in her bright pink button-down sweater, bright green mini-skirt, and fishnet stockings, made famous in her appearances at other concerts.

Mrs. George has asked that people celebrate, not mourn, Sadie's passing to an eternal place of peace. In lieu of flowers, the family has requested contributions be made to Sadie's favorite charity, the Salvation Army.

Sadie will be sorely missed by all her friends, including this reporter. Future plans for the Spidars are unknown at this time.

*

Ten thousand people jammed into the Shriners' Hall. Thousands more were turned away at the entrance. Instead of the usual shrieking and clambering for position, the audience stood with heads bowed and hands folded. The song Sadie and Al Dukes wrote played over the intercom speakers inside and outside as people waited for the service. The concert itself went to the outside speakers, so those who couldn't get into the venue could still hear everything.

The squeak of casters echoed off the walls as four Armed Forces men wheeled Sadie's casket on stage, coming to rest at the center front. When they raised the lid, the hall was silent.

"I don't know if I can do this," Saul whispered to Peggy. "How can I lay on to be happy at a time like this?"

"We have to try. Sadie wants this to be a wake, not a funeral."

"Maybe she asked too much."

A Western Union Messenger came out and handed Saul a cable. On the outside envelope, Sadie's handwriting explained the desired delivery date, time, and place. The cable originated at the Cape. Inside, the message was simple: "Remember I don't get mad. I get even. So liven up the party a bit. Please. With Blue skies of love, Sadie.

Rich chuckled as the note was passed to him. "It figures. Sadie's last word is a threat, no less!"

"You'd better be careful, Rich" Martha stated. "Her ghost is watching you."

"Sure, Sugar."

"I'm not kidding," Martha giggled. She pointed to a catwalk above them. The others gawked. It was a cardboard replica of Sadie.

The hall manager saw Martha pointing and ran on stage. "That was delivered today with specific instructions on placement," he said in an apologetic tone. "Since it was signed S. McCarthy, I presumed Saul wanted it there. If not, I'll remove it at once."

"No need," Saul said. "This is Sadie's show. We'll do it her way."

Rich continued to stare at the cardboard ghost. "As long as that thing doesn't fall on us," he added.

The manager shook his head. "It can't move at all. It's nailed securely."

"Was anything else delivered?" Harry asked.

"No, sir."

Peggy stepped up to a microphone as the men prepared their instruments. *"We want to thank all of you for coming tonight. For those watching at home, thanks for being with us in spirit. Sadie picked out the songs for a lively concert. She wants everyone to have a good time. And we will do our best."*

As the music began, people lined up to pay their respects to Sadie. Security guards positioned themselves to manage the stream of people and prevent anyone from reaching the Spidars or the living family members. A glass plate on the coffin allowed viewing without theft.

To prevent lump-in-the-throat disease, the Spidars played as if they were in the music room, with banter back and forth between songs. Within the first fifteen minutes, the floor around the casket filled with an assortment of sweet-smelling bouquets. A stage hand transported them to another large room backstage, which also filled quickly.

Peggy frowned. "Sadie wouldn't like all these flowers wasted. It's a good thing she's not here now. She'd have a fit." Her eyes misted as Sadie's voice on the tape replayed in her mind: *"Don't let people bring flowers. Tell them to spend their money on the living, not the dead."*

Miki left the stage. Upon her return, she informed the group that she had arranged for a truck to deliver the flowers to nursing homes and hospitals in the area. "I think Sadie would approve. They will brighten people's lives – money spent on the living." The others nodded as they continued playing.

*

Forty-five minutes later, Jo-Jo noticed a uniformed man in the wings. He motioned to the other men for a small break and walked over to the man.

During the pause in the music, Saul watched a few people passing by the casket. One woman fainted and her escort was too wobbly to catch her. A security guard helped both of them down the steps. Then something on the near side of the casket caught Saul's attention. He ran over and reached out to a young blond man wearing the dress blues of the Air Force.

The man looked at Saul with sorrowful eyes. "I missed her on your show last night," the blond said. "I watched from the Cape and wondered where she was." Saul put his arm around the man's trembling body and moved him to the foot of the casket so the line could keep moving.

"You know," the man said, as he stared at Sadie, "There was a lady with the president last night who reminded me of Sadie a little. She could have been a cousin."

Saul nodded in silence as the man rambled. "The lady seemed like a right arm to the president, like Sadie must have been to you. I thought about that woman after I went home. She was strong... stronger than many men. I would have needed more than a neck brace if I had been on the roof the whole time as bombs exploded all over the United States."

Saul nodded again. The blond man shrugged and handed Saul a pot of pink hyacinths. "I know you didn't want flowers, but I thought you'd accept these. They'll grow year after year and add beauty to the world like Sadie did. The lady last night wore a perfume that smelled like these, so I thought Sadie might like them too."

"They were her favorites," Saul replied. The man left with the crowd. Saul carried the hyacinths back to the family. "We

449

can plant these near the kitchen door and mulch 'em with Sadie's ashes, so she can say hello every spring." His eyes threatened to flood his cheeks, but he forced them under control.

As minutes passed waiting for Jo-Jo to return, Saul's chest felt heavier and heavier. Soon, he couldn't do it any longer. He sat on the floor and crisscrossed his legs, his head in his hands, which could not contain all the tears that flowed. Peggy tried to comfort him as the others blocked the view from the audience.

"It's no use, Peg," Martha sighed. "We can't continue. Saul needs to rest, and so do all of us. Sadie would understand. We did our best."

"But someone has to at least read her poem," Peggy said with a tear-stained face. They looked at one another. Shoulders shrugged. Heads shook. Finally, Miki volunteered. She walked to the nearest microphone with a paper in her hand and signaled for the security men to stop letting people on the stage.

"We're sorry folks," she said. *"We need to go home. We hope you enjoyed the short informal show. Please remember Sadie in a loving way. Before we go, I'll read a poem Sadie wrote a few days before she died. We like it and we hope you do too.*

> *"I'm not afraid to die, my mates*
> *I'm not afraid to die*
> *For when I die, I'll join my Lord*
> *So high up in the sky*
>
> *My Lord is making room for me*
> *He's making room for me*
> *Please don't cry for me, you see*
> *At peace my soul shall be*

Although I'll miss you all, my dears
Although I'll miss you all
Don't cry for me for I will be
Up answering my call

Come see me when your life is through
And join my happy home
For I'll be with my own dear Lord
In a large honeycomb

I'll have food for you, my friends
I'll have food for you
There's always food for friends, you know,
In the garden that I sow

I'm not afraid to die, my mates
I'm not afraid to die
For when I die, I'll join my Lord
So high up in the sky"[52]

Miki brushed a tear from her cheek. Saul howled and ran to the casket. The television cameras focused on Saul's heaving shoulders as his chest fell on the glass plate. Rich and Harry quickly pulled the casket backwards and asked the stage hands to close the curtains.

After the curtains closed and the microphones turned off, the rest of the adults joined Saul at the casket. Gene and Helen brought the children out from a backstage room.

Jo-Jo returned from the wings. "A Salvation Army man was here, Sauly," Jo-Jo stated. "He said lolly is pouring into local units around the globe."

Silence.

Saul fell to his knees and spoke in a whisper. "Sadie, you've done your job. You did it well. Now come back, please." He lifted the glass template off and set it on the floor. Then he reached out to hold Sadie's hands in his as he looked toward the ceiling. "Lord, she didn't deserve to die. She did what you told her. So, take my energy, Lord, and give it to Sadie. Drain me completely if you must. Exchange my life for hers. The tots need her to teach them right."

Saul lowered his head. "Sadie, if you're still in your body, fight this. You can do it. You're a fighter. Come back." His voice weakened, and tears flowed like a brook down a rocky hill. "I love you."

Suddenly, his hands tingled. He stared at her angelic smile. His tears stopped. "She's not dead!" he exclaimed, kissing the hands he was holding. "I saw her mouth twitch!"

"Don't get your hopes up, Saul," Martha said in a soothing voice. "Your mind is playing tricks. I've seen this happen before. When you stare at something long enough, it seems to move when it really doesn't. You want it so badly that your mind sees something that did not happen."

"B-b-but," he stammered. "Take a look-see. She doesn't look normal anymore."

She never looked normal, Rich mouthed to Harry, who agreed. Neither man spoke.

"Of course she doesn't," Peggy replied. "She's dead."

"No, No," Saul repeated. "Remember when the casket was first opened, how alive she looked with her make-up job?"

Peggy smiled. "Yes, she could create any illusion she wanted with that stuff."

"She should've been in the movies," Rich added before he could stop himself.

Saul glanced at each adult individually. "Don't you see it? Look close. Look at her face. She's changing."

452

"That's decay, Saul," Martha replied without looking. "You knew it would happen."

"Her hands are warm now too!"

"Easily explained. The bright lights pounded through the glass tonight and the heat couldn't escape. You should have also felt a gush of hot air when you lifted the template."

"No, I can't believe it," Saul stated, "God heard my prayer and he's sending her back to me." The Spidar family exchanged worried glances. Sadie's death was making Saul go completely crazy. They all agreed.

"Look at her!" he demanded. "Her make-up looks too thick now. Remember what the president said, that it was too thick while she was alive?"

This time, the others looked into the casket as Saul kissed her forehead and continued, "Come home, Sadie! I know you can hear me. Show me some sparkle and I'll get you to hozzy straight away. You'll have the best doctors and nurses money can buy."

Sadie's eyes slit open. A dry tongue emerged and roved over her lips. She tried to speak, but no words came out.

"Get a meat wagon!" Saul shouted to a stage hand. Sadie's eyes shot open the rest of the way, as if alarmed. She tried to speak again, but no sound came out.

"I'll get you something," Martha offered. She ran to the wings and returned with a glass of ice chips. As Saul lifted Sadie's head and shoulders, Martha tipped the glass. "Not too much. One or two at a time."

Sadie relicked her lips, with a wet tongue this time, and smiled. "I know. I know," she said with mischief. "Too much ice could cause a headache or choking, or when it liquefies, too much cold water will give me a stomachache. That worry is a bit silly at the moment, don't you think?" Martha smiled back.

Sadie's gaze moved to Saul. "Cancel the ambulance. I don't need a hospital. I just need some rest."

"Are you dead sure, Luv?"

"No I'm not dead, but yes I'm sure," she replied, looking past Saul and winking at Rich.

Rich raised an eyebrow. "Were you taking the mickey out of us, Sugar?"

Sadie shook her head. "No. Actually, I was walking along a path toward a bright light when I heard Saul calling me. The light drew me like a magnet, yet I wanted to come back. Then a being, maybe it was God, a being in the light, said I could come back if I wanted, so I did." Saul lifted her gently out of the casket. "Now I know how Lazarus must have felt," she added with a smile.

"There must be more you're not telling us," Jo-Jo stated.

"Do you think she knew this could happen," Harry asked him.

"The bird is a fighter. She must have done something to help this situation." Jo-Jo replied. They both cast suspicious glances at her.

"Well, I did try one little thing," she admitted.

"What was it?" Saul asked.

She looked into Saul's eyes. "Well, I, sort of, kinda, used you in an experiment."

"Me?" Saul asked.

"Yes, you. Just before you climbed the steps to the plane that took you to Pittsburgh, I stored extra energy in you."

"I didn't feel any perkier."

"You wouldn't. I, well, to make it simple, I put the energy in capsules. Your body was supposed to dissolve the capsules in a spurt when you touched my body, if Pavlov was right about his dogs. Yet, I couldn't count on your hormones completely, since the death of a loved one can mess things up a bit. So, I didn't tell you about it ahead of time... although, if I recall talking to the tape machine correctly, I did mention you kissing me one last time or holding hands at least. This time instead of me sending energy to you, you sent it to me."

Sadie smiled at the rest of the family then back at Saul. "You were never in any danger. If you were too squeamish to touch a dead body, the energy would have leaked into your body very slowly."

"I hope Pam will understand," Miki mused.

Sadie twisted her mouth. "This one will be a tough sell."

As Saul carried her to the wings, she raised her eyes to the ceiling above the stage. "Thank you," she whispered.

Seeing Sadie's actions, the rest of the group looked up and then stared at the cardboard ghost. The ghost that was supposedly nailed so securely as to make it immovable was waving, as if saying goodbye to Sadie.

Epilogue – 1975

"KATHY!"

Kathy Voss' mind snapped back. "Yes, Ma'am?" She sat in music theory class at Monroe High. Her friends, Pam, Harvey, Peggy, and Al, looked at her.

Mrs. Lane spoke harsher than usual. "The rest of the class is taking a quiz. You have ten minutes to finish. I suggest you begin writing."

"Yes, Ma'am!" Kathy couldn't complain. Although she had resented having to take a music class when her planned major was science, Mrs. Lane had made the subject interesting, always comparing past greats with current groups. Quiz instructions were written on the blackboard:

1. Pick a popular musical group that no longer exists.
2. Explain why the group was successful.
3. What caused their downfall?
4. Extra credit – Find at least one other group that performs similar music and name a hit song associated with them.

Kathy began writing furiously:

The Spidars

As with all great music, Spidar songs are like drugs. They take you away from your problems and into the world of the imagination. Since most early Spidar songs told of love in one form or another, they made girls dream about being extra special – the perfect lover – so boys would fall madly in love with them. Boys daydreamed about finding the ideal girl, beautiful and fun to have around, and having her love him with all her mind, body, and soul. Some daydreams also incorporate other leanings, like science and fantasy.

The Spidars dared to challenge established thinking. They showed us that we are not supposed to be pall-bearers at a funeral our whole life. It's okay to celebrate life, and we can be ourselves without condemnation for being different. Long hair, which grew longer as time passed, was okay. Men's clothing could be bright and cheery without being considered gauche or feminine.

As Spidar hair and clothing changed, so did their songs. They gained confidence. Their songs matured and began to address the problems of mankind, such as war, prostitution, abuse, and discrimination. The Spidars' songs said what a lot of people were afraid to say out loud. Thus, they became leaders for the younger generation – heroes, so to speak.

Downfall? Did they really fall down the mountain of success? Or did they walk down? Evidence points to the latter. The Spidars recognized that you can't live on a peak. Life is change. You must take those memories back to the valley. Even great things have to grow and develop, or they become obstacles. In this way, the Spidars are still our heroes. They had the courage to break away, to get off the merry-go-round, instead of submitting to the mental, emotional, and spiritual death that was sure to come if they stayed in a group where they lost their individuality. Each member eventually made his own music outside of the group. And they were all quite successful.

Extra credit:
"Game of Love" by Wayne Fontana and the Mindbenders
"Wild Thing" by the Troggs

Respectfully submitted by Kathy Voss, a Spidarmaniac

TO THE READER
Is Sadie real?
Or is she the personification of Spidarmania?
Try reading this novel again with the latter in mind.

NOTES

1. McCartney, Paul and John Lennon. "I Saw Her Standing There." *Meet The Beatles*, Capitol Records, 1964.

2. McCartney, Paul and John Lennon. "Yesterday." *Help*, Capitol Records, 1965.

3. McCartney, Paul and John Lennon. "I Should have known Better." *The Beatles Again*, Apple Records, 1970.

4. McCartney, Paul and John Lennon. "Sexy Sadie." *White Album*, Apple Records, 1968.

5. McCartney, Paul and John Lennon. "Got To Get You Into My Life." *Revolver*, Capitol Records, 1966.

6. McCartney, Paul and John Lennon. "I'm A Loser." *Beatles '65*, Capitol Records, 1964.

7. Johnson, Roy Lee. "Mr. Moonlight." *Beatles '65*, Capitol Records, 1964.

8. McCartney, Paul and John Lennon. "Hey, Jude." *The Beatles Again*, Apple Records, 1970.

9. Yellin, Jack and Milton Ager. "Ain't She Sweet." *British Gold*, Sire Records, 1978.

10. McCartney, Paul and John Lennon. "Can't Buy Me Love." *A Hard Day's Night*, United Artists, 1964.

11. McCartney, Paul and John Lennon. "I Am The Walrus." *Magical Mystery Tour*, Capitol Records, 1967.

12. McCartney, Paul and John Lennon. "Don't Let Me Down." *The Beatles Again*, Apple Records, 1970.

13. Perkins, Carl. "Everybody's Trying To Be My Baby." *Beatles '65*, Capitol Records, 1964.

14. Harrison, George. "Within You, Without You." *Sgt. Pepper's Lonely Hearts Club Band*, UMI, 1967.

15. McCartney, Paul and John Lennon. "From Me To You." *The Beatles / 1962-1966*, Capitol Records, 1973.

16. McCartney, Paul and John Lennon. "And I love Her." *The Beatles / 1962-1966*, Capitol Records, 1973.

17. McCartney, Paul and John Lennon. "Eight Days A Week." *The Beatles / 1962-1966,* Capitol Records, 1973.

18. Harrison, George. "Old Brown Shoe." *The Beatles Again,* Apple Records, 1970.

19. McCartney, Paul and John Lennon. "We Can Work It Out." *The Beatles/ 1962-1966,* Capitol Records, 1973.

20. McCartney, Paul and John Lennon. "Yellow Submarine." *Revolver,* Capitol Records, 1966.

21. Berry, Chuck. "Rock 'N Roll Music." *Beatles '65,* Capitol Records, 1964.

22. McCartney, Paul and John Lennon. "With A Little Help From My Friends." *Sgt. Pepper's Lonely Hearts Club Band,* Capitol Records, 1967.

23. McCartney, Paul and John Lennon. "Martha My Dear." *White Album,* Apple Records, 1968.

24. Harrison, George. "Something." *Abbey Road,* Apple Records, 1969.

25. Ballard. "The Game Of Love." *British Gold*, Sire Records, 1978.

26. McCartney, Paul and John Lennon. "In My Life." *Rubber Soul,* Capitol Records, 1965

27. McCartney, Paul and John Lennon. "You're Going To Lose That Girl." *Help,* Capitol Records, 1965.

28. McCartney, Paul and John Lennon. "Honey Pie." *White Album,* Apple Records, 1968.

29. McCartney, Paul and John Lennon. "Good Day Sunshine." *Revolver,* Capitol Records, 1966.

30. McCartney, Paul and John Lennon. "I Call Your Name." *Rock N Roll Music Vol 1*, Capitol Records, 1976.

31. McCartney, Paul and John Lennon. "Help." *Help,* Capitol Records, 1965.

32. Harrison/Starkey/McCartney/Lennon. *Love Songs (album)*, Capitol Records, 1977.

33. McCartney, Paul and John Lennon. "She Loves You." *The Beatles/1962-1966*, Apple Records, 1973

34. Harrison, George. "I Need You." *Help.* Capitol Records, 1965.

461

35. McCartney, Paul and John Lennon. "I Want To Hold Your Hand." *Meet The Beatles*, Capitol Records, 1964.

36. McCartney, Paul and John Lennon. "Birthday." *White Album*, Apple Records, 1968.

37. Vogt, Sue. "Your Love Is All I need," 1989.

38. McCartney, Paul and John Lennon. "Two of Us." *Let It Be*, Apple Records, 1970.

39. McCartney, Paul and John Lennon. "This Boy." *Meet The Beatles*, Capitol Records, 1964.

40. Paraphrased from McCartney, Paul and John Lennon. "And I Love Her." *A Hard Day's Night,* United Artists, 1964.

41. Paraphrased from McCartney, Paul and John Lennon. "Dear Prudence." *White Album*, Apple Records, 1968.

42. The Troggs. "Wild Thing." *British Gold*, Sire Records, 1978.

43. Lennon, John and Paul McCartney. "Do You Want To Know A Secret?" *Meet The Beatles*, Capitol Records, 1964.

44. McCartney, Paul and John Lennon. "One after 909." *Let It Be*, Apple Records, 1970

45. McCartney, Paul and John Lennon. "Revolution 1." *White Album*, Apple Records, 1968.

46. McCartney, Paul and John Lennon. "Because." *Abbey Road*, Apple Records, 1969.

47. Vogt, Sue. "Isn't There Something We Can Do?" 1988.

48. McCartney, Paul and John Lennon. "Any Time At All." *A Hard Day's Night*, United Artists, 1964.

49. Harrison, George. "Don't Bother Me." *Meet The Beatles*, Capitol Records, 1964.

50. McCartney, Paul and John Lennon. "Revolution 1" paraphrased, *White Album*. Apple Records, 1968.

51. McCartney, Paul and John Lennon. "You've Got To Hide Your Love Away." *Help,* Capitol Records, 1965.

52. Vogt, Sue. "I'm Not Afraid To Die," 1988.

53. Harrison, George. "Here Comes The Sun." *Abbey Road*, Apple Records, 1969.